THE BIG NICKEL

By Calder Willingham

NOVELS:
End as a Man 1947
Geraldine Bradshaw 1950
Reach to the Stars 1951
Natural Child 1952
To Eat a Peach 1955
Eternal Fire 1963
Providence Island 1969
Rambling Rose 1972
The Big Nickel 1975

SHORT STORIES:
The Gates of Hell 1951

SCREENPLAY CREDITS:
The Strange One 1956
Paths of Glory 1957
The Vikings 1958
One-Eyed Jacks 1959
The Graduate 1966
Little Big Man 1969
Thieves Like Us 1972

PLAYS:
End as a Man 1953

THE
BIG NICKEL

CALDER
WILLINGHAM

THE DIAL PRESS / NEW YORK / 1975

Library of Congress Cataloging in Publication Data

Willingham, Calder, 1922–
    The big nickel.

    I. Title.
PZ3.W6783Bi [PS3573.I4565]   813'.5'4   74–20583
ISBN 0–8037–3368–1

THE BIG NICKEL

IT WAS A PECULIARLY AMERICAN THING, THE PARADOX OF
success that destroys. The civilized British, the charming
French, the hardworking Germans were above and beyond
such a barbaric conundrum of victory that contains defeat,
triumph that brings ruination—well, perhaps not wholly so,
but America had certainly made it her own in this atomic day
and age. Richard Davenport smiled in sardonic self-mockery
as his shy and beautiful little wife breathed softly asleep by his
side, unaware of the frightening beast within him.

Succubus and doppleganger demon, Pauline-Polly: a desperate resource and a dazzling stratagem, Pauline her own
sexy self and Polly, an invention invulnerable in his head,
Polly Dawn, Polly alight in the midnight hours of the mind
and soul. Ironically, he had written in a whimsical essay at
college:

"Of all the things that befall men and women in this swamp
of misery called life, failure is the worst. To be exposed as a
total forceless fool before one's neighbors and one's weeping

children, this is bad. The man who tries to kiss a girl and misses her mouth is in trouble. The rule applies in all directions: failure is hell. What can be said of the player of life who drops a perfect pass in the end zone of existence but that he ought to go hang himself, soon?"

How had it all happened, how had he been transformed from a caterpillar into the thing he was, how had he metamorphosed from a bellboy into . . . something like a butterfly? How had he reached this point of lying sleepless in bed dreaming of a big blonde named Polly?

Davenport's history was not very unusual for the youth of his day, laying aside for the moment the winning of what he and his friend St. John called "the big nickel." Exempt from the draft because of chronic sinusitis, he had wandered around the country during the frenzied years of World War II. He had worked as a bellboy in a giant commercial hotel in Chicago. Then he had worked as a bellboy in a luxury hotel on the outskirts of Hollywood. In Miami he washed dishes and was an usher in a movie theater. In New York he washed more dishes and worked as a stockroom clerk at Macy's and as a night elevator boy in a midtown hotel. Finally, he found what his sister Patricia called "a respectable position" writing propaganda for the Office of War Information. It was at the OWI that he met his wife, Naomi.

But the job writing propaganda did not last very long. Davenport at this time was probably unemployable. The work itself was easy, but getting up in the morning at the same hour and sitting at a desk all day long was unbearable to him. After several maddening months at the OWI, he quit and went to live with Naomi in a one-room apartment in Greenwich Village. There, in order to avoid work and because he had been talking about it for months to his sister Patricia and his friend Beau St. John, he began to write what he called in ignorant hope a novel.

Out of necessity Dick lived not only with but on Naomi; she kept her job at OWI and her salary supported them both. It bothered him to be dependent on her, to be taken in like a stray cat, but she assured him it didn't matter, he could pay her back later, and the expense of having him there didn't amount to much anyhow.

One day Naomi said, "Let's get married," and Dick answered, "What?" It was a shock. Marriage? Whatever put such an idea in the girl's head? He explained that he would not get married until he was thirty or thirty-five and at the present time he was only twenty-two; therefore marriage was not a good idea. Naomi in turn explained that her mother would come someday and find him living there and she would have an awful fit. "Jews are puritanical," she said. "You have no idea how puritanical they are. She would fall down on the floor. It's only a formality, why not? You could have a divorce any time you wanted it and any freedom you wanted, too. We're living together and we might as well get married." Dick pondered it. Why not, indeed? Naomi was pleasant, he liked her; the apartment was handy, he had a little table where he could put his typewriter. Thus, they got married. Dick chewed gum during the ceremony at City Hall. "Please stop chewing that gum," said the clerk who tied the knot, "it distracts my mind."

Three years later Davenport lay dreaming of a big blonde from West Virginia. "Jesus Christ," he whispered aloud. "How long?"

Naomi stirred. Her sleep was peaceful but light; a sigh could awaken her. "Dick? You didn't go to sleep yet?"

Naomi was gentle, Naomi was kind, and Naomi above all else was loyal. Davenport clenched his teeth in vexation. There was no getting away from Naomi, her love was all-enveloping. She could hear the faintest snuffle from the baby in the crib in the living room and the faintest snuffle from himself. "I'm sorry," he said. "I didn't mean to wake you up, honey. Go back to sleep."

For a moment Naomi was silent; then she turned on her side toward him. "Have you been awake all this time? It's very late."

"I know, but I'm okay, I'm fine."

"How can you be fine as late as this?"

"Well, I am. Really."

"It must be almost morning. I don't see how you can say you're fine with insomnia like this. It worries me, it really does."

"I'm fine, honey, I'm having a lot of fun with Polly. You wouldn't believe the things that come out of her mouth. What an idiot. But there's a method in her madness, she always gets where she's going."

"I wish you wouldn't dream about her; that fantasy bothers me, I don't understand it. Is the little man still after her?"

"Yeah, with his tongue out."

"He gives me the creeps," said Naomi. "And so does she, even worse."

"I don't see how you can say that about a nice girl from West Virginia who is out to conquer the city," said Dick. "It's traditional to conquer the city. It's traditional and it's nice."

"*Nice?* They are not nice, either one of them. They're horrible."

"They're lovebirds," said Dick with a little smile in the dark. "A pair of cooing and billing lovebirds who want to do it on a limb and bring light to the world."

"Some lovebirds and some light," answered Naomi. "I wish you wouldn't dream about her like this, I really wish you wouldn't. It seems obsessive to me and even if it isn't obsessive it's strange. I don't understand it."

"There's nothing to understand," said Dick with another little sardonic and self-mocking smile in the dark. "In my catatonic state she amuses me. Polly is funny, she's a barrel of laughs. I swear sometimes I almost laugh aloud at the things she says. And do you know it's the honest truth I can't predict her? Of course at times her idiocy becomes a wee mite maddening, but on the whole she's a gorgeous doll. The tits on her would sink a battleship."

"I don't like that word, *tits,*" said Naomi, who herself was very full-breasted.

"What woman does?" asked Davenport.

"Then why do you use it?"

Naomi always slept naked and Dick put his hand on her soft right breast. His palm did not cover it; her breasts were very large and the areolae on them were enormous. Naomi had a great body in a *zaftig* way, very womanly, very beautiful. "I forget," he said. "I realize I shouldn't use the word, but then I forget."

"You don't forget. You use it because you know I don't like it. You do that to everybody. It's a perverse streak in you, like a little boy, a desire to shock and see what you can get away with."

"Is that right?" asked Dick. With a smile, his troubles momentarily forgotten, he moved his hand from her breast over the warm, silklike skin of her back to the plump cleft of her behind. "Words are words, Naomi. Sticks and stones will break your bones, but words are just words. You have a beautiful ass, do you know that?"

"You've told me so many times. Actually that word doesn't bother me, it's more neutral. The other one implies male superiority; it's looking down on women with contempt. But I wish you'd stop that fantasy, I really wish you would; it seems obsessive to me. Do you have any idea why you do it, any idea at all?"

"Sure, Polly puts me to sleep," said Dick, "eventually."

"Well, I'd count sheep if it was me. I'd count from fifty back to zero, then from fifty back to zero again."

"I tried that and all I do is lose count and get mixed up."

"Then you have to try again. Do you want anything now? Milk? A glass of water?"

"No, honey."

Davenport realized in a vague way that however casually he had married Naomi the marriage was casual no more. Her near-pathological shyness often drove him crazy—there were times when the girl wouldn't finish a sentence—but during the three years with Naomi he had grown quite fond of her, surprisingly so. He'd gotten accustomed to her wry, protective nagging and he liked it. And there was another dividend he hadn't expected: he'd become very strongly attracted to her physically. At first, he hadn't found her especially appealing; her breasts were too big and her hips a trifle too broad. But in three years he'd changed his mind. Naomi's body was very womanly, very beautiful.

And there was another thing. Naomi had become a very good lover, especially after the baby was born. In the early days in the Village she'd been virginal and inhibited, but no more. The birth of her son, whom Davenport fathered almost as casually as he'd gotten married, seemed to stir and release fires in her; she became an extremely passionate lover and a very good one. He often said to her, "Naomi, you are *damn* good in bed, just great, beautiful, wonderful."

It was true. She was damn good in bed, just great, beautiful, wonderful. He loved her soft pillowlike breasts, her hourglass waist, her *zaftig* womanly behind, and he loved most of all the marvelous and limitless sensuality that had been revealed in her. She was always responsive and never tired. "I could do it every night all night," she said. "It's the most fun there is in the world, there's nothing like it. I don't know how I got by before, I really don't. When I think back about being a virgin, it horrifies me."

She had that idea now. In the gray beginning of dawn Dick felt her hand on his shoulder and her soft breast against his side. Her breathing was not quite normal; she was awake and interested. All the signs were there: her hand tightening and loosening on his shoulder, her breast swelling and subsiding, her breath against his cheek and neck. In a little while, if he himself did nothing, she would murmur some apology and put her hands on his shoulders and roll on top of him. It often happened in the night or early morning; he looked up half-awake many times at her full breasts and the deep dent of her belly button.

As he had known she would do, Naomi cleared her throat and said, "I'm awake."

"Um-hmm," said Dick.

"I'm wide awake. Are you awake?"

"Of course I'm awake."

"Well, I mean, do you want to?"

"It's late, honey. It's almost daylight."

"Yes, I know, but I'm awake. Are you too tired?"

"I'm a little tired, not too much."

Naomi sighed. "I'm sorry, I don't mean to bother you. It's just that I'm awake. Try to go to sleep."

Davenport smiled in the dark; she'd never let it go at that. Whatever "puritanism" she had inherited from Jewish culture, Naomi had rid herself of. An odd thing, his attraction to Jewish girls. Somehow they appealed to him; he'd known several others before he met and married Naomi. He wondered about it. Why did Jewish girls so strongly attract him? Something exotic, different? His sister Pat, who was a "polite" anti-Semite, had been much against a "mixed marriage" and so was Naomi's family. Her aged grandfather had wept bitterly when she married a gentile and later with trembling hands gave Dick little blue books that contained information about the Jewish faith. The rest of the family was almost equally negative; the marriage was regarded as a probable calamity. As time went by Naomi's mother had grown rather fond of Dick, but even now sometimes at the sight of him she would clasp a hand to her forehead and roll her eyes toward heaven.

"Do you want bicarbonate? Or an aspirin?"

"Honey, I'm fine, I'm okay. I'm sorry I woke you up, go back to sleep . . . unless you really want to make love. I will if you want to."

"Oh, no," she answered, "no, that's all right. I just thought maybe you did, maybe it would help you get to sleep."

Dick took her hand, the fingers of which were very small and feminine. There was something touching about her passion for him and something touching about the small and feminine fingers of her hand. As had begun to happen more and more often in these days of paralyzed trance, a feeling of pain and regret came to him at the thought of the girl he had married in so cavalier a fashion—"the little Jewish girl," as Pat called her with patronizing disdain. He said: "You're a sweet girl, Naomi. I really don't deserve you, and that's the sad truth. I don't deserve you hardly at all."

"Well, well . . . sure you do."

"No, I'm afraid I don't. I often ask myself what a nice girl like you is doing married to a stupid boy like me."

As subsequently he was to hear more than once from his friend Victor Samusson, "Man knows more than he understands." Richard Davenport knew more than he understood. And thereby hangs a tale within a tale.

Sadly, he did not love his wife, or he thought he didn't. He was very fond of her, and during the time of their marriage had become very attracted to her, a reaction that had been a bit of a surprise to him. Often he would say, "I like you," or, "I'm very fond of you." But the word *love* was beyond him. In his vocabulary, this four-letter word was the most gross expletive of them all, more vulgar by far than the language he used to irritate Naomi and others. He would have much preferred being beaten by a cat-o'-nine-tails than to use that cheap and empty term. But he feared more than the rack itself the emotions the word described—that path, he felt, led to the loss of all freedom and identity. In his conscious mind, however, a joke was what it was, an idiocy, a futile escape from mortality to which weak people succumbed. His attitude and that of his friend St. John was mocking and contemptuous, as witnessed by their pet description of any and all works of art: "It is on the eternal theme of love agin greed."

But that was long ago. The old days with Beau seemed to have gone, to have faded away. Beau was not the same and neither was he. "We have lost our innocence," said St. John. The remark itself did not sound like him. Who would have expected platitudes, however true, from the insane St. John?

The baby was named Samuel, and Dick and Naomi moved to a pleasant little apartment on a tree-lined street in Flatbush after he was born. She said: "After all, he is half-Jewish, and even with that goyish hair he ought to have some part of a Jewish name."

"Do you mean," asked Dick, "that his mother's ancestors had a civilization when his father's ancestors were painting themselves blue?"

"Sometimes you're funny," said Naomi with a smile. "I guess I do mean something like that."

Dawn was coming through the window. He felt a soft glow from his wife's breast against his side and saw in the gray light an even more beautiful love and warmth in her eyes. Naomi was wonderful, Naomi was lovely; the beast within him was not. What gave the beast such a terrible and paralyzing might? What greater power could conquer her and lay her low?

ON AND ON HE CAME, FOLLOWING. SOMEHOW, THE FEL-
low reminded Polly of Dr. R. Wherry Murger, although he
was skinny and Dr. Murger was fat. But there was a similarity,
the intense ratlike look in the eyes was the same. And Polly
knew the ratlike look very well; she'd seen it many times. It
didn't scare her, but it put her on guard, that was for sure.
Well, she'd come out of the Murger thing with sixty-seven
dollars and two dresses; that fellow had better watch out or
he'd lose his wristwatch and more besides.

But his motives were unclear and his approach was strange.
Why was the little man slinking and slinking along and what
was his name? Joe? Bob? Henry? Why didn't he introduce
himself, say, "Hi, I'm Andy," or some other name? Polly was
confused. Despite her best analysis of the situation, she
couldn't figure out what the bird wanted. As always, life
flowed by her like the time stream around an object lodged
out of phase in the fourth dimension, not really touching her,
just brushing her now and then.

However, Polly never got upset. Not Polly Dawn. Never. An insane billy goat could trot up and eat her shoe and it wouldn't have upset her. She was practically imperturbable.

But Polly was nonetheless a bit baffled, surrounded as she was by an inexplicable swirl of happenstance like a chicken scratching intently for worms in the eye of a hurricane and now and then tilting her head sidewise with chicky solemnity and semi-reptile-orbed obtusity at all the disturbance, perhaps with the not at all coy but rather flutter-and-fly and squawk-and-cackle thought that a large rooster was behind it.

Yes, baffled. The problem remained: this fellow—what did he want, anyhow? Was he lost? Did he have hank-panky in mind, and if so, why didn't he say something? With a switch of the hips that she knew would congeal his blood, Polly turned the corner. Her confusion was strictly metaphysical; in other forms of expression she was as articulate as a silver dollar. "Try that on for size," she thought. Polly wasn't six foot three for nothing. On she strolled, purse in hand, cool as spinach and twice as popular. A hundred feet down the block she glanced over her shoulder, and there he was, a little slinking man with red rat eyes and ears like a shrunken monkey.

What a crumb. Was he a purse snatcher? Some type of private eye on the prowl? A white slaver? A mad rapist or a trunk murderer or something even more outlandish? It was odd. Very peculiar. Weird. Tagging along like that and not only tagging along but tagging along like a fox almost panting. Look at him, mopping his forehead with a handkerchief, patting his eyes, all winced down and shrunk—hmm, there he stands, peeking over the handkerchief, little close-set dark eyes bugged out something awful, face gray and sweaty, mouth a long thin slit and Adam's apple bobbing up and down like a prune seed in his throat. And what a throat, what a neck. You call that thing a neck? Polly could have encircled it with her middle finger and thumb, easily! What was the cause of this bird's condition? Was it an emotional urge of some type, otherwise known as hank-panky?

Hmm-mm, probably a little hank-pank there somewhere. But if the man was thinking along those lines, why didn't he come up and make an introductory remark instead of slinking along in the background block after block? Couldn't he job up and say something on the order of, "Hello, my dear, I am Bob Watson. Who are you?"

Polly shrugged her big shoulders and walked on. Men were so unpredictable. It was hard to tell what they were up to, and he really did remind her of Dr. Murger when she was fourteen. Three different things had come up before squat Dr. Murger got down to what was actually on his mind, and even then he reversed himself. A rather interesting incident, that private conference with Dr. Murger. Predictable and totally inane and banal to the blood core though it was, the Murger affair was not wholly dissimilar in many respects to the sort of adventures that befell Poll in this early period of her life, which foretold her later growth and laid the groundwork for the art that made her Chinatown's favorite Manhattan sweetheart.

Briefly, the private conference with Dr. R. Wherry Murger, Ph.D. and principal of Dotesville High, consisted of four stages, each of them equally confusing. It was even more confusing to her than her adventure with Max Race, otherwise known as Arnold "Archie" Schnerd, the forehead-mopping, rat-eyed, monkey-eared slinking shadow six years later on her first day in New York.

"Now, Polly," said Dr. Murger, "what's this I hear about you having intimate relations with the Jones twins and that Whofford boy down in the girls' john at recess yesterday? Is that true, Polly? Now don't be afraid, my dear, look right up at me and answer. No one knows you are here, this little talk is private."

"Thank you," said Polly.

That was the first stage. Was it true, really true? The Jones twins and that horrible Whofford boy, all three of them in half an hour while the other girls came in and stood around tittering and giggling and watched with wide, innocent eyes and no doubt got ideas? Hmmm? Was it true? Did an awful thing like that happen?

It was obvious that this question of fact was all Dr. Murger had on his mind, or so it seemed; but then he became worried about other matters. The dress she had on did not suit her. Her mother should, by all means, try to get her more attractive attire to aid her in adjusting herself on a healthy, natural, girl-like basis to the life of Dotesville High.

"Uh, muh, huh huh huh," said Dr. Murger confusingly, then with a loud gnash of the teeth he snapped back into half-focus with a series of murky thoughts. *What, no bra? Ah, careless youth. Was it possible, no bra at all? Mmm, the dress wouldn't do, a shapeless tent, hardly becoming in the least, for example here, too loose, much too loose, altogether too loose, yes, ah-h . . . too . . . in the . . . down here, yes.* Such were Dr. Murger's murky thoughts, but then he broke into speech and came truly into focus. "Puh-puh-polly," he said, "just slip this over your sh-sh-shoulder. Uh. Ulp. Yes, that's right, my child. Don't fear, the door is bolted. Goodness, God help me. Dear child, don't be nervous, my goodness how mature you are, let's sit on the couch a moment, I want to talk seriously to you, but first God help me let's get off this unbecoming dress and perhaps your panties too, yes let's do that, dear, let's be completely frank and honest with each other. . . ."

Polly would have been flabbergasted if she were capable of it. Of all things, a sex urge had come over Dr. Murger. What an incredible turn of events, short little balding Dr. Murger with his battle-ax wife and seven children! She could hardly believe it, was it a sex urge, really, an old goot like him? Was

that why he had called her into his office after sending away
the janitor in a subtle manner? Was that why he bolted the
door as sweat ran down his face and his eyes bulged out like
blue balls? Was that why his tongue was hanging out down on
his necktie? It sure seemed so on the couch when he took off
all her clothes and half his own as well, a very suspicious thing.

"Umm-mm, uh. You *are* mature, what large breasts you
have, my dear." A lewd laugh came from him. "Heh-heh-heh-
heh-heh, what love jugs, and only thirteen."

"Fourteen," said Polly.

"Fourteen. Gulp, what love jugs, heh-heh-heh. More like a
grown woman than a child, hee-hee-hee-hee-hee. Oh, God
help me, this is wonderful, oh, oh, oh-h-h . . ."

"I was fourteen last week," said Polly, "but I do have a
lovely bust, you are right about that. 'Nother Daddy said I had
the best pair of bubs in Dotesville when I was twelve; now he
says I got the best in West Virginia. He just loves 'em, 'Nother
Daddy, plays with 'em day and night, I can't hardly get no rest
or do my homework."

"Mmm, yes, yes. Um, um."

Shuffle off John is right, get lost, John, a disciplinary problem. Vanish, go wash the blackboards, flush the toilets, catch
mice, make yourself useful around here. A true sex urge had
come upon Dr. Murger. It sure seemed so on the couch, but
for a moment he changed his mind, confusingly. No sooner
had he gently helped her out of her dress and assisted her from
her panties and socks and shoes, no sooner had he done that
than the lewd squat Murger collapsed in a heap, asking, "What
have I done?" It was very confusing! So far he had done
nothing, though Polly expected he would, and then sure
enough he did, groaning and whimpering and ever so often
saying, "Forgive me," but in such a tone it sounded like,
"Gimme." Luckily it didn't last but about a minute. Polly
stared up at the ceiling and thought of paper dolls and other
pleasant things.

But then it really got confusing; the carrying on of Dr. Murger was fantastic. The pacing back and forth, the right hand scrubbing the left and the left the right, the rolled eyes like a terrified horse, the moans and groans and blubbering whimpers as Polly sat there in wonder, her clothes in a pile on the creosote-scented floor and a daisy still stuck in her hair. But after a while she turned her thoughts elsewhere to a robin outside the window. Dr. Murger was having a fit, that was all, and it was boring. To amuse herself Polly sang softly a favorite little song of 'Nother Daddy's as she stared at the robin: *Something's runnnning down my leg, something's runnnning down my leg! It's just a shot that missed your twat, said Barnacle Bill the sailor. . . .*

"Out! Out!" screamed Dr. Murger. "Go home to your mother and stepfather, you wicked girl! Go home, you little slut, go home!"

"Yes, sir," said Polly.

In the doorway he grabbed her by the arm, eyes popping madly. Suddenly he fell to his knees and clutched her legs. "Don't tell them! They'll put me in jail, behind bars! Oh dear God, they'll put me in jail, they will, they will, and you don't want that, do you, dear? They'll put me in jail and then when I get out my wife will kill me, she'll cut me up into little pieces and grind me into hamburger! Don't tell them, dear, I'll give you money, do you want some money? I didn't hurt you, it isn't news to you, you're all right, there's no reason for you to tell! Don't tell them, dear!"

"Oh, I wouldn't say a word," said Polly. "Don't worry, Dr. Murger, I wouldn't tell a soul."

And then to her surprise he jumped to his feet and grabbed her by the arms, his eyes still popping madly. Gruesomely he smiled and said in a low whisper: "Tell them and I'll deny it! I'll deny it! It never happened! Nothing happened, do you understand? Do you get that, you little bitch? You were here for a talk in my office and stayed no more than five minutes.

See? I asked you about the story of your being with those boys down there at recess, and you said it wasn't true, you denied it, and that's all that happened."

"But sir," said Polly, "it isn't. I didn't deny it because to tell a lie would be worse, that's what 'Nother Daddy says all the time and he's *smart*. They gave me money to take off my pants and do it with them. Billy Jones gave me fifteen cents, his brother Willy gave me twenty and Hog Whofford gave me a quarter."

"Oh, no!" said Dr. Murger with a sly grin. "Oh, no! You denied it and I accepted your denial and that's that. Get me? You tell on me and I'll tell on you, and what's more I'll deny it to the skies. Yes, yes, I'll deny it. Yes. Now let's be friendly, dear, there's no need for conflict. Here. Here. I have a nice half-dollar for you. Here you are, dear, a half-dollar all for yourself, isn't that nice?"

"Is it a gift?" asked Polly.

"Yes, yes, it's a gift."

"Dr. Murger, aren't you sweet!" said Polly. "Why, that's more than Hog Whofford gave me!"

"Yes, yes, well take it, dear, in good health. And remember we have a secret. Don't tell anyone, not a soul."

"Oh, I wouldn't breathe a word of it, not a word."

"All right, now run along, dear."

"Thank you for the half-dollar!"

"Don't mention it, now run along, dear, you'd better go."

Polly smiled happily. "You've been so kind," she said. "Before I go, Dr. Murger, will you do me a special favor?"

"What is that?"

"Well, next week it's 'Nother Daddy's birthday. . . ."

Predictable and inane and banal to the blood core though it was, the affair of Dr. Murger was a noteworthy incident in the early beginning of a great career. Dr. Murger was kind enough to give Polly two dresses and lend her sixty-seven dollars before he had a nervous breakdown and fled from Dotesville forever. At fourteen, the great whore bitch was on her way and nothing could stop her, no man born of woman could tame her.

3

PATRICIA HAD SAID: "I COULD CRY WHEN I LISTEN TO YOU and the saddest thing is that you yourself know it's all an act. You're not even kidding *yourself*. And yet you have the nerve to threaten to marry this little Jewish girl if I don't lend you money to write a novel you'll never write. How can you even dream of exploiting her so heartlessly? Shame, Dickie, shame!"

And Davenport had replied, with a folly beyond egotism and a confidence based on absolutely nothing: "You will eat those words. I can do it and I will. As for Naomi, that's her business and mine, not yours."

What had transformed him from a caterpillar into something like a butterfly? No informed person could reasonably have expected such a metamorphosis. Everything Pat, Beau, Dan Hennessey, and Isidore Esserman said made perfect sense. Pat was dead right; Dick himself did not believe it. The whole thing was fun and games, a gag that had started in the most idle manner imaginable back at the University, where he and his friend St. John were the stars of a class in English composition. A class in composition was a long way from a serious career as a writer, but that fact didn't bother them. One night they were both half-drunk on beer, and suddenly for no reason St. John narrowed his eyes in an evil manner, blew cigarette smoke in Dick's face and asked:

"Are you going to be a purposeless slob all your life? What are you going to do when you finish school? Be a fireman? A policeman? Work in a bank? Have you given this some thought, honey? What are you going to do in the world out there?"

Dick replied, "God, I don't know. Something, I suppose. I try not to think about it."

"Are you serious?"

"Sure I'm serious."

"You don't think about it?"

"Well, no. Once I thought about being a doctor, but I can't stand blood."

"You don't think about it. Well, I think about it. And I know exactly what I'm going to do, and that's write."

"Write?" asked Dick. "You mean journalism, being a reporter?"

"I don't exclude journalism as a means to an end," replied Beau. "But what I have in mind is books. Novels."

The idea was amusing. St. John had a million erratic notions. "Books, novels? You think you can do that?"

"Sure, why not? It's just telling a story by means of the written word, that's all it is. And I can do that. I don't want to go from the sublime to the ridiculous, but I get an 'A' practically every week in English C-10."

"Well, so do I."

"Richard, let me tell you this. It is one of those things that nobody does because they think they *can't*. But that isn't reality, that's illusion. The fact is, granted a little verbal ability, *any*body can write a novel. It's just storytelling in the form of writing, that's all. There's nothing to it."

"Hmmph," said Dick. Somehow, the way Beau put it, the idea sounded plausible.

"What's more, it's the only kind of writing to do," declared St. John. "Being a reporter is *work,* you have to go around and interview people and confine yourself pretty much to facts. But writing a novel is *fun,* it's all a pack of lies out of your head. And look at the rewards. If you have a knack for it and come up with something real wild and startling, what happens? You become famous, make piles of money and get all kinds of tail. As Wolfe said so aptly, 'Fame, fortune and the love of beautiful women.' Think about it, just think about it. Scotch whisky, a library of leatherbound books, pretty girls sitting on your lap. It's waiting out there, all you have got to do is do it. See this nickel? It's a mere nickel, but that nickel out there isn't a mere nickel. And it's waiting for the grabbing, it's there waiting for the grabbing."

When Richard Davenport later was asked the inevitable question, "How did you first decide to be a writer?" he could not answer because the truth was so silly. He could hardly reply: "Well, I was drinking beer one night with this friend and he thought of it and I decided I wanted scotch whisky, leatherbound books and pretty girls on my lap. I also liked the idea because I've always been very lazy and it struck me as a way of getting through life without working. And I figured I could do it because I got a lot of 'A's' in composition at school." It was ridiculous, but true; it was exactly in such a way that Davenport decided to be a writer.

His ambition not only appeared frivolous but in fact *was* frivolous. Naturally enough, it was highly disturbing to his older sister, who had been something like a mother to him for many years. Both their parents had been killed in an accident in Dick's early childhood and Pat had practically raised him.

She called his announced plans "silly pretense" and secretly he agreed with her. The idea of his writing a novel that a publisher would actually publish was ridiculous. He had no notion on earth how to do such a thing. And Pat, he knew, was quite right about the stories and sketches he had written thus far—they were, as she said, "a handful of inept, incoherent, cuckoo little things no magazine would dream of printing."

Beau St. John, Dick's best friend, was equally discouraging. He said: "I feel guilty for having put the thought in your mind. You could no more do it than a chicken can swim. I'm sorry but I've read all your things and nothing could be more obvious than one plain and simple fact—you are not a novelist."

Another discouraging voice was that of Daniel J. Hennessey, a renowned novelist of the realistic school with whom Dick had become acquainted through correspondence. He had written the protean Hennessey a fan letter while at the University and to his surprise—he had not thought the great man would even answer a mere student—a voluminous correspondence had ensued. It was voluminous indeed—a fourteen-page single-spaced typewritten letter from Dan Hennessey was not unusual at all.

And as Dick learned in New York, the man talked the way he wrote, at length. But the most striking thing about Daniel Hennessey was not his prolixity, overwhelming though that was, but his honesty and goodwill. The man loved writers and writing; he was dedicated and consecrated in every bone of his body to what he called with a solemn reverence "serious literature." Hennessey's selfless generosity was beyond question; he had promised in letters several times to meet with Dick and give him advice about writing. Therefore, after getting nowhere with Patricia and Beau, both of whom refused to lend him money to write a novel, Davenport called on this famous author for counsel. Hennessey greeted him at the door of his book-lined apartment with a deceptively tongue-tied diffidence, sat him down to a cup of coffee, and said:

"Call me Dan. I found your letters interesting, germane, lively, energetic, irreverent, curious, intelligent, a bit immature at times but that's to be expected, occasionally overwhimsical, arch, erring toward the trivial, excessively cute and often viciously and even brilliantly derisive; that is a dark gift there and I wouldn't want you for an enemy. I notice now and then a kind of human humor rather unusual in one so young, and I would go with this, encourage it, nurse it. Humor is not taken seriously by the critics but it is very rare in writing and a great gift to the reader; I would go with it rather than with the fury and the rage and the cruel derision, although those things are needed too at times, they add power and shock and force, they are the balls of writing and above all things else a writer needs balls; but he needs more than balls and more than sympathy; he needs *seriousness* and those sketches you sent, well, well, let me say this——"

There was nothing Davenport could do but let him say it. Open-mouthed, he listened:

"——when I was a student at the University of Illinois, I wrote constant stories, letters, essays, articles, reviews, everything you can think of. I was writing day and night, all the time, I wrote and wrote and wrote, and that is my advice to you, Dick, write and write and write. And read. I also read, I read constantly, omnivorously, incessantly; I was at the University of Illinois library day and night, there was nothing I wouldn't read. I read everything I could put my hands on, it didn't matter, nonfiction, novels, abstruse scientific journals, medical publications, law reviews, magazines and of course Marx and Freud and all the philosophers, all of them, I read indefatigably. And that is my advice to you. Read. Read, read, read, and write, write, write. Because you see when I wrote

Buster I was ready, I was prepared, I was primed, I was saturated in writing and reading, totally saturated, because you see *Buster* didn't come from nowhere; *Buster* came out of preparation; *Buster* was the product and result of endless preparation, tireless preparation, remorseless preparation. . . ."

At the end of the interview Hennessey said: "As for your own writing. I myself am perhaps not too good a judge, but it seems to me those were just sketches you sent me, not real writing. However, I won't say you have no writing gift, I can't make such a statement as that. We are dealing with a mysterious phenomenon when we talk of a writing gift, a very mysterious phenomenon that no one understands, with the possible exception of one person I know, a scholar and an intellectual I want you to see, a man who is one of the few authentic geniuses I have known in my life—undoubtedly you've heard of him, Isidore Esserman; he might understand the mystery of creativity, but no one else does. I'll ask him to read your things and speak with you—maybe he will, he is eccentric, he might not. But meanwhile I've got to say I don't think you're being very realistic in your approach, I honestly don't believe you are; I'm saying your plans and expectations are a little naive. The odds are at least a hundred thousand to one against you. If you think you can come to New York out of the provinces and in your early twenties knock off a novel and that it will be published and get rave reviews and be a bestseller and you'll be famous and rich, then you are dreaming. It doesn't happen that way. As I told you, the first volume of the *Buster O'Brien* trilogy sold five hundred copies. It was only later that *Buster* was recognized as a classic. I want to be helpful, I want to do everything I can to encourage young talent, but, let me tell you, the life of a novelist is not easy."

Davenport went back to the little apartment in Greenwich Village and said to Naomi: "Dan Hennessey wouldn't help me get any money from foundations because I haven't published anything. And worse than that, he thinks I'm not serious enough, I'm just playing around. He didn't say it exactly but that's what he meant. And worst of all, he thinks the things I have written are trivial and show no real talent."

Dan Hennessey's ego was perhaps larger-than-life-sized and his garrulity was perhaps larger-than-life-sized too, but there was much intelligence and perception in the midst of it all and the man's honesty and goodwill were beyond doubt. He was absolutely right about what he said, and Dick knew it.

But the most disheartening voice of all was that of the fabled Isidore Esserman, Professor of Fine Arts at New York University, dazzling lecturer on a host of subjects and frequent contributor to the most prestigious literary quarterlies, a scholar of staggering erudition and an intellectual of penetrating insight regarded as an authentic genius not only by Hennessey but by the entire New York highbrow world as well. Dick said of his interview with Esserman: "The man is monstrous. Naomi, I have never been so intimidated in my life and the only question is should I cut my throat now or later. Let's take a look at the want-ad section and see if I can get a job cleaning toilets."

The incredible Isidore Esserman not only was formidable, he *looked* formidable. Dick walked over to the musty apartment on Bleeker Street without too many trepidations despite all he'd heard about this legendary man, but he soon was awed. The apartment, which was very dark and gloomy, contained shelves to the ceiling filled with unbound books in French, Spanish, Italian, German, Greek, Russian and Chinese, plus of course many regularly bound volumes in English. In addition to his other accomplishments, the fantastic Esserman was a great linguist. Each year in his spare time he learned another language. The knowledge in the man's head was beyond belief. His specialty was art, but he had a vast storehouse of knowledge of Marxism and radical politics, of philosophy, economics, history, psychology, architecture, archaeology, literature, games and many other subjects.

"Come in, come in," he said. "We will have tea. My son is here, I hope you don't mind."

Professor Esserman was about forty years old, but he seemed to have no age. He was very Jewish looking and very beautiful; it was the word that came at once into Dick's head and there was no other word to describe him. The man was beautiful, with a great shock of iron-gray hair, a chiseled classic profile, and deep brown eyes that often flashed with fire and pure intellect. To call him handsome was inadequate; he was beautiful.

But the son wasn't. He was a peaky, pimpled, extremely skinny and furious-looking boy of about seventeen who, when introduced to Davenport, did not say a word, or at least not a comprehensible word.

"This is Dedalus."

"Muh," said Dedalus.

"He is home from school today. He didn't feel like attending."

"Muh," said Dedalus again, with a grimace of pure rage.

Mrs. Esserman wasn't beautiful either, and she was as silent as the boy. At first Dick didn't know who she was; he thought she was a housekeeper or something. Soon after he was settled in a dusty sofa, a white-haired and somber-faced woman came into the room with a tray bearing tea and cookies.

"This is Mrs. Esserman, my wife."

"How do you do?" said Dick, with a smile that faded as the white-haired Mrs. Esserman stared broodingly at him without a word. In silence she turned and left the room. Was she upset because the boy had stayed home from school? Was there tension in the house? Evidently not, because the professor said:

"Mrs. Esserman is a woman of few words, she doesn't mean

to be rude." And then he added: "Dedalus often doesn't attend school. Of course he works at home. Lately he's been annotating Gibbon's *Decline and Fall of the Roman Empire.*"

To Davenport's shock, the boy glared at his father with utter hatred and said, "Oh, go fuck yourself."

"Now, now," said Professor Esserman. "Ha, ha, ha, ha."

"What a shitass," said the boy to Davenport. "Did you ever see such a tiresome shitass in your life?"

"Ha, ha, ha, ha. Now, now. Now, now, Dedalus. Would you like a cookie?"

It was an incredible scene. To Davenport's even greater shock, the boy suddenly leaned forward, hunched down over the coffee table, put his face down into the tea tray, and bit fiercely at the cookies. In fascination, Dick watched him snapping and muzzling at the cookies, in the process knocking half of them off the plate with his chin and nose. The boy was something else. Mouth filled and cheeks pouchy, crumbs in his eyebrows, he stared with a glowering anger at his father, who finally smiled and said:

"I should think if one does that one would say, 'Bow-wow!'"

"Phlluuhh!" said the boy, as he spat out a cloud of crumbled cookie on the coffee table. The sight of his father was too much to bear. He turned to Dick and said: "Do you hear his shit? You can stand it, not me! I'm going to my room!"

Professor Esserman sat bowed in silence for quite a while after the boy had gone, then he shrugged wearily and said: "Well, Jews spoil their children, everybody knows that. Actually he's a nice boy and very brilliant. You're seeing him at his worst. Dedalus is very worried about sex and girls. He masturbates all the time. I tell him it's all right but it worries him. And the activity is a little excessive; his anxiety is great. He has a blister, that's why he's upset today."

"Mmm, well, uh," said Dick.

"Now about your work, I am afraid I can't give you very much time. I find it interesting but unformed. I will speak to you frankly because I am confident anything I might say is unlikely to crush your spirit; the one thing implicit in your writing is audacity and independence and that is about all it has got at this point and all it might ever have; it is possible you are no writer of any kind. I am sure that thought has occurred to you, I sense a tentativeness. But artists do sometimes make quantum leaps, not every day but occasionally, it is a remarkable thing, a sudden and amazing leap to a new level of performance and achievement. It is rare, strange, incomprehensible, like lightning gathering and suddenly striking out of a blue sky. This happened to Gauguin, to van Gogh, it happens to all artists really, but about your pieces——"

Davenport blinked in a daze as he listened. The garrulity of Dan Hennessey was nothing in comparison to that of Isidore Esserman, and yet the things he was saying no doubt were true.

"——in all candor whimsical, amusing at times, facile, yes very facile and at points imaginative, and the writing itself is clear, very clear; I liked that, most beginning writers adorn and elaborate to excess, and you seldom make that mistake and this is a good indication. And I find also a certain vitality, a certain energy, a certain love of life as hateful as a lot of it is, and very possibly you have some of the gifts of a writer; that is, you have got some gifts or might develop some gifts; but the all-important thing I missed in your work was reality. Let us never forget that art is the imposition of order upon chaos, the mere reflection of chaos is not art. Perhaps it would be useful to you if I attempt to cite a few of the gifts and qualities of a great writer. Do you feel this would be suggestive and helpful?"

"Well, sure," said Dick in a stricken voice. There was pity, real pity, in Isidore Esserman's eyes.

At home that night in the little apartment with Naomi, Dick sat at the rickety table he used for a desk and stared at the feeble beginnings of what he hopefully called a novel. It was pathetic, really. "This is hopeless," he said. "I don't have *any* of the qualities he mentioned! Naomi, you should have heard him. *Power to convey an unlimited range of emotion by the written word, hidden mastery of language, near-schizophrenic ability to invent lifelike character, narrative genius, moral wisdom, originality, determination, independence.* Good God! And those are *some* of the gifts and qualities required, he says, not all."

"I don't see what point there was in his discouraging you," said Naomi. "He can't be very nice. I don't wonder that his son puts his face in a plate of cookies. And I must say I'm sick and tired of Jews themselves making flip little anti-Semitic remarks. All Jews don't spoil their children and if he spoils his then that's *his* problem. He can't be nice."

"He's nice," said Dick. "He's nice, nice, nice. And what he said to me was the truth."

"I don't believe it," answered Naomi. "He's an academic, a scholar, an intellectual, what does he know? Did he actually read your stories?"

"Of course he read them. And he's right about them, they're trivial."

"I don't think so," said Naomi.

"Well, you're all alone. Pat, Beau, Dan Hennessey and Isidore Esserman disagree with you."

"They're wrong," said Naomi.

"No, they're right," said Dick.

He hadn't a doubt of it, but for want of something better to do he kept pecking on the typewriter at his so-called novel. And then it happened. To Davenport's surprise, a publisher read the first hundred and twenty-five pages of the manuscript and gave him two hundred and fifty dollars and an option contract for the book's possible publication when finished. It was amazing. A real publisher had given him money for a thing he had written. Not much money, true, but money, real dollars, he could spend them. But the most incredible fact was that if the publisher liked the completed manuscript he would print the book. He, Richard Davenport, dishwasher and elevator boy, would be a published author.

Except for one sad truth. He couldn't finish the book, so it all would come to nothing. In mortal fright he said to Naomi: "I can't do this. To tell the honest truth, I don't know how. I've written it so far but I don't know what comes next, I haven't the vaguest idea. How can I write a book when I don't know how and I don't even know what it's about?" And Naomi answered: "Just keep on writing it the way you are. Don't worry, you'll think of what to write next. It's good, Dick, it's very good."

For Davenport himself, the experience was frightening. Naomi was right; the book was good, and from where had it come? The story was altogether different from anything he'd done before and it came from him with a rush as if it were writing itself. As work progressed, he submitted the parts of the manuscript to the publisher, who wrote to him: "I am impressed. I am more than impressed, I am astonished. I can only quote the boast of the Austrian Corporal: 'I will move with the precision of a sleepwalker.'"

In due course, Davenport's novel was finished and published. It was one of the successes of the year in which it appeared. The book received very favorable reviews, including a rave by Daniel J. Hennessey in the *New York Times Book Review*. Surprisingly, since the novel told a grim story, the fastidious regular reviewer of the daily *New York Times* gave it another rave. It was the same everywhere. The *New Yorker*, the *Saturday Review of Literature*, the *Philadelphia Inquirer*, the *San Francisco Chronicle*, the *St. Louis Post-Dispatch*, the *Washington Post* all gave it favorable comment. The book was described as "brilliant," "overwhelming," "a work of art." It was said to have "enormous power," "born storytelling genius," "masterly dialogue" and a lot of other such things. Davenport was interviewed on the radio and by the press; he had his picture published in *Life* magazine; he got fan letters from many readers. At twenty-three, to the surprise of everyone who knew him—and most of all to himself—he had written a novel that had proved to be a triumph.

And so begins the prisoner's song. The words haunted him as he lay there in the dark. "If I had the wings of an angel, over these prison walls I would fly. . . ." He heard a sigh from Naomi in the darkness and said to her:

"Naomi, *help* me. Where do I go from here? I don't know how I wrote that book!"

"Dick, listen," she answered. "I know how you feel, I understand it."

The big nickel had been won, true enough, but the only value such a coin possesses lies in the spending.

FREEDOM. THE DOOR OF THE CAGE HAD OPENED AND THE
bird had fluttered out into the sunshine. Polly was exuberant.

"Do you have any further urge?"

"Nawr."

"Thank you."

"Mmm, mmm-mm."

"Sleep tight, 'Nother Daddy, dear."

"Mmm, your big laig's in m'back. Hist over, yuh crowdin'
muh."

"Sorry, 'Nother Daddy, dear. Forgive me."

"Mmm, mmm-mm, bugs bitin' muh. Got to get some
screens in the winduh. Cats hollerin' on the fence. Roof a'lea-
kin', termites is chompin', can't sleep nohow. Hist over, gal."

"You have a further urge, after all?"

"Mawg's in the way, shove 'er off."

"Gawr! Gawr! Wha'?"

"Shet up, Mawg. Spraddle, gal."

"Yes, 'Nother Daddy, dear."

Freedom! It was Polly's first day in New York City. She had the clothes on her back, four dollars cash and a black patent leather hatbox that contained undies, slips, stockings, several blouses and skirts and a nightgown. It was all she owned in the world except for the natural gifts fate had bestowed upon her. She had no job and little idea of a job other than a dim notion to sell perfume at a department store and thus meet the interesting men who would come to buy the perfume for other girls and ladies. She did have the plan to enter a few bathing beauty contests in case there were any around. She knew she had a stunning figure and thought she might win a contest and thereby get a job in the spanking new medium, television. A great thing. There were funny little aerials cropping up all over on rooftops, and she'd seen a set in the Dotesville Bar and Grill and Gorgeous George was a scream.

It didn't last long because other things occupied her, but television at that time was Polly's dream. It was her ambition to become a famous TV hostess and interview celebrities at breakfast or lunch. This was what she foresaw for herself. It would be the most exciting of all possible careers to smile and talk before the television camera to one famous person after the other, to chat with them on an intimate basis and call them by their first names, such as: "Harry, isn't it thrilling beyond words to conduct such a great work of art as 'The One O'Clock Jump?' Oh, I should think it would be! Tell me, what is it like and how is Betty?"

However, in those first confused days of her arrival in the city, she realized she was far removed from such glamorous possibilities as interviewing Harry James. She knew she could not expect to achieve such a success without hard work and struggle. In the meantime, she was prepared to enjoy life come what may and devil take the hindmost.

Polly saw a wealth of clothes, suitcases, jewelry, antiques and all manner of interesting and wonderful things in the windows. She saw interesting things in the gutters, too, and there were all varieties of fascinating people on the streets, well-dressed men striding along with newspapers under their arms, stylish-looking women leading dogs with weird, amazing haircuts. It was even more marvelous than the Port of New York Authority Bus Terminal, a streamlined dream of white tile and catvus light.

Naturally she was excited, so excited she hardly thought much about the man who was still following her, the man who had just followed her from the drugstore at Times Square all the way across Forty-second Street past the lions of the library then up the strange gutters of Fifth Avenue to Forty-seventh Street and across to Madison and up Madison to Fifty-third. There he was, following along, sometimes twenty feet behind, sometimes forty, sometimes fifty. He was back there all right, slinking like a polecat. But it didn't bother her.

It didn't bother her in the least. She had other things on her mind. Aside from the fact that it was her first exciting look at the greatest city in the world, this was also the day after her twenty-first birthday. She was grown. No one could tell her what to do or what not to do. There would be no more scenes in the juvenile court.

However, she really had to agree with her stepfather, Another Daddy. He had said that all things considered it would be best for her to wait until she was twenty-one and a fullblown woman before leaving his bed and board. And that had indeed been best, Another Daddy had been so right about that. Mawg, too, had been right about it, but the true credit had to go to 'Nother Dad. Mawg was wishy-washy and would have let Polly go when she was nineteen, but not Another Daddy, he had insisted she wait before launching forth on her career. "That can wait, Poll," he said. "Your Ma and me don't want you to leave here till you're a broke-in gal and a votin'."

"Yes, sir," said Polly.

"No-how," added Another Daddy for emphasis.

And that settled it. Oh, it had been hard to wait, the two years seemed endless. But it was best she hadn't come all alone to a vice-filled place like New York when she was so young, so inexperienced, so unaccustomed to the hustle and bustle of a big city. Oh, she'd been only too ready to do it, but no doubt that was because she hadn't grasped the pitfalls. At that earlier age she was quite naive. Who knows what might have happened to her if she'd come to New York at nineteen? The place was loaded with vice, and Polly had a horror of vice. Of course much of the public greed for vice, which approached wholesale slobbering, originated as a result of flames fanned by the press. She could not help associating love with all the brutelike cruelties she had known as a child. May Lou Gundy had gone into prostitution and she had a mole the size of a frog's eye on her chin. What kind of a life was that, three licks of an ice cream cone? Besides that, she stammered and was cross-eyed and didn't remember what street she lived on. But the obscene and sleazy "Pudgie" Hyden (it was in all the papers, the press inflamed it) had gotten fees of *two hundred dollars* and, in the face of all that halitosis, this was amazing; who would ever dream mere nasty flesh could bring such a price? All the same, one had to grasp and not fall into pitfalls.

On the bus there had been another man, also a New York man. As a matter of fact, the one on the bus had looked something like this one following her right now. Perhaps all New York men looked like that? Polly could see him reflected in the plate glass windows, this man who was tagging along after her like a breathless fox. The one on the bus had been a little taller, but like this foxy one he had a dark complexion and was red-faced and sweaty. They looked quite similar except that the one following now was dressed better and wore a gray hat on the back of his head. What a life, what an interesting world, it was one thing after the other!

Idly, Polly strolled along to the next window, her patent leather hatbox in her hand and her flowery hat perched on the side of her blonde hair. It was held with a pink hatpin; she always had a hatpin, it could be a weapon. Her purse was over her shoulder and locked under her arm against one of her huge breasts in case he was a purse snatcher. The man was now not too far away at all and he was getting closer. What was he up to? Either he should say something or go away. The manner in which he was behaving was distracting her from looking in the windows.

"Excuse-meh," said a hoarse, croupy voice behind her. Polly's eyes brightened but she refrained from turning around. Not at once, that would be too eager. Play hard to get. Coy. She kept her gaze focused ahead through the window on a display of glasslike purple jewels and samples of the rough stone from which the jewels had been cut.

"Excuse-meh," said the man again, mumblelike, and now Polly turned and looked at him full in the face, her blue eyes friendly and clean as the autumn sky and a smile on her red lips.

"Yes?" she said.

"Uh," said the man. He was a little purple around the eyes now, and sweat was dripping in paths down his forehead; even his hair seemed wet. The man wore a tie of bright, unmistakable red. He had on a green shirt, a kind of silky green shirt which made the bright scarlet tie stand out all the more. He looked, she thought, like a bookie or a gangster, with a heavy, dark beard that was close shaven, a long thin nose, sunken ascetic cheeks and small gray teeth stained with tobacco tar. The hat the man had been wearing was now politely in his hand.

"Excuse-meh," he said once more, croupily, and Polly watched with her usual expression of friendly interest as the tip of the man's tongue nervously darted out and then suddenly zipped in anxiety from side to side, then in the flash of an eye withdrew into the thin slit from which it had appeared. All at once the man gave a kind of grimace, a wince like a pin had been stuck into him, and his eyebrows leaped up and his eyes bulged forth and his nose and one side of his mouth twisted horribly. A purse snatcher for sure, thought Polly. But then he said:

"I notice you back in the pharmacy, uh, in the pharmacy with the hatbox, see, and I was thinkin' allatime you got lost, y'unnerstand, lookin' for an address or maybe someplace, see? A hotel or somewheres. And could I be of any assistants?" Again the man grimaced, his eyelids quivering half-shut as his mouth and nose twisted to the side.

But it was with hard, sarcastic eyes that he stared at Polly as she herself gazed calmly back at him. The iron stare had drained his every last ounce of will power and left him shrunken there, a mere chitinous remnant of the departed cicada or a bare carapace after the naked, screaming turtle has fled it; but his gaze was hard and ironic and determined, even as the frenzied shark snaps at its own entrails with hunger: in him, thus, logically were combined singing cicada, shrieking turtle and gnashing shark. His name was Archie and he didn't have very much manhood.

"Gu-lup," he said.

It was funny to Poll the way the peach seed in his throat slid up and down. He probably didn't have much manhood, somehow she felt that, but even if he did it wouldn't matter. Men were so filthy with their whiskers and everything. She stared in fascination. The man talked strangely, as if chewing up his words or trying to, almost as if each word were a piece of gum over on the far side of his mouth and he couldn't quite get at it.

Mmm, thought Polly, he did look like the other man on the bus. He too had a long, sharp nose and close-set dark eyes, but he was older and shorter. The man on the bus was the one who said for her to go with him to the Astor and take a room so she could rest after the bus trip, but then his wife and little fat daughter were at the terminal to meet him, so he had said good-bye and rushed off after telling her to take a cab herself to the Astor if she wanted to go there. As if she could afford to take cabs in her present financial situation! With four dollars and nine cents to her name! Or stay at the Astor either! What a kettle of fish!

"I'm sorry, talkin' to you like this," said the man, but he didn't look sorry, though he did look sick. "I thought you might be lost, that is. Lookin' for some address, see?"

"That's very considerate of you," answered Polly. She smiled. Her voice, as always, was pleasant, natural and friendly. "I was just trying to think if I had ever met you before. . . ."

"Met me before?"

"Yes!"

"Uh, uh," said the man. "I don't think so."

"But you do look terribly familiar," said Polly. "Mr. . . .?"

"Er, Schn——," said the man. "I mean, Race. Max Race, professional name." He then swallowed and added incomprehensibly: "Use it cut some sides back in the thirties. Use it professionally. Call me Max Race. Old professional name used to have, still use it."

"Oh, I see," smiled Polly. "Well, Mr. Race, it's a lovely day, isn't it?"

"Ah, yeh, yeh. Sure."

"My name is Polly Dawn and I'm delighted to meet you." Gray and shrunken, the man peered at her from beneath lowered brows, his mouth no bigger than a comma.

"Uh, the pleasure's mutual."

Polly smiled pleasantly and looked again at the display of purple stones in the window. It didn't hurt to make conversation and have good manners. Why, certainly not. Max Race. He was a gangster, she felt it in her bones. This man was a white slaver and wanted to get her in his meshes. Never!

"You just in the city?" asked the man. He seemed more nervous than before and was staring at her in a funny way.

"Why, yes," said Polly. "I sure am. How did you know it, Mr. Race? Or may I call you Max?"

"Uh-h," said the man, as he grimaced nervously again. "I had a idear you were, one way or another."

"Why, how extremely perceptive of you!" exclaimed Polly. "That's extraordinary deduction on your part, Mr. Race! I mean, Max!"

"Yeah," said the man, his voice almost inaudible. "I guess you figure I'm tryin' to pick you up or somethin'. It's the least of my thoughts. I figured you was new in town from the way you was talkin' to that soda jerk back in the pharmacy and . . . er . . . I . . . ah . . . New York is a little town at heart." The man grinned. He had very dirty teeth and his grin was rather like that of a weasel, but he seemed good-natured and of course he couldn't help his appearance. He probably didn't have very much manhood, somehow she sensed that, but actually the man wasn't really so bad looking. He vaguely resembled some movie actor, sort of a small Edward G. Robinson, but with sunken cheeks and a long nose and a much smaller, commalike mouth, more like George Raft. And after all, he was trying to be friendly. He reminded her of a wizened Robert Montgomery.

"Oh!" exclaimed Polly. "You don't know what it means to me to hear you say that! The tales I've heard of the hard-heartedness of New York . . . but I never believed them! I knew, I just knew New York had a heart of gold! Everybody said it was filled with vice, but it isn't!"

"No, no," said the man, shrinking back a bit from Polly. "You think I'm kiddin', but . . . but New York is a little town at heart."

"How lovely!" said Polly. She clapped her hands.

"Well, okay, maybe it isn't all that warm-hearted," said the man. "But it's got its points compared to the sticks."

"I was just admiring those rings and bracelets in the window display there," said Polly. "Aren't they divine?"

"Yeah," said the man. He looked as if he were about to slink away. A puzzled, beaten expression was in his eyes, a whipped look that seemed to express a lifetime of kicks and abuse and a deficient manhood as well, but there also resided in his gaze a sneaky, ferretlike gleam of the urge for retaliation.

"I love jade," said Polly. "Jade is beautiful, don't you think?"

The man stared at her for several seconds, eyes narrowed to slits as he rubbed thoughtfully at his almost nonexistent chin. He wasn't licked yet. Finally he said, "Yeah, but that ain't jade. Jade's green."

"How right you are!" said Polly.

Freedom! Of course in Dotesville she had lived on the outskirts of town and had stayed at home pretty much and she hadn't had really attractive clothes. Also, Another Daddy was intensely possessive; he hardly trusted her to go down to the A&P for butter. "Let Mawg do it," he'd say. "Poke her and wake her up." But those days were gone forever!

"Look at him, notice that expression. He wants me to grab his foot."

"He's just smiling, that's all," said Naomi.

"No, he's willing me mentally to grab his foot."

Certain parts of Flatbush can be very agreeable to concrete-bound New Yorkers in late springtime, and the day after Davenport's confession that he was having a little trouble getting to work was a beautiful and cloudless day in May. On that morning he sat at a dinette table in the kitchen of his and Naomi's apartment and smiled at her in a manner that was boyish and amiable. He felt much better. He felt a million times better, until he picked up the *Times* and learned that James Meaghan, a brilliantly successful young American novelist, had drowned himself in a bathtub at the tender age of twenty-six.

"This waffle is very good, Naomi," he said. "Sometimes I think you're a born cook. Cooks are born, you know, not found in stumps."

"Are they?" she asked with a smile. "Well, that's nice." Her attention was half on the baby. As she talked she spooned baby food into Sam's pink little prune-smeared mouth. "But I'm afraid a waffle isn't very complicated."

"A waffle is very complex," said Dick. "I couldn't make a fucking waffle. I wouldn't know how to begin."

"Umm, well, I wouldn't know how to write a screwing book. I can't do what you do, Dick. I could never do it."

"I can't either," said Dick with a grin. "But I guess I'll have to try. God knows what will come out. I might vomit. Not only have I got no ideas, I've forgotten how to type."

"Well, I know it's bothered you more than you've let on," said Naomi as she opened another jar of baby food. It was a task she very much enjoyed. The baby to her was literally a miracle. At the hospital when Dick went in her room she was drunk on ether and not her usual reserved self. Tears were in her eyes and she threw her arms around him and said: "They took him away, but I saw him and he's beautiful! He has tiny fingernails and they're like paper and they need cutting! He's beautiful! He's a miracle!"

"A great day outside," said Davenport. "Too bad I have to go into Manhattan, we could have a nice walk in Prospect Park with Sam."

"Yes, we could. But I'm very much worried about your insomnia. I think it's serious and I think you ought to do something about it."

"Got your foot," said Dick. "I've got it, Sam!" It was a game of which the baby never tired. He always laughed in delight when Dick suddenly grabbed one of his fat little feet. Young as he was, it seemed he wiggled his legs to provoke it, intent baby eyes on his father. Could a child of that age know enough to play a game? It seemed so.

"Sam, Sam, the beggar's man. Sam, Sam, stick-stack Sam, I've got your foot, your pedal extremity, I might even eat it and spit out the bones!"

"You shouldn't talk to him like that, someday he'll understand you."

"He only knows the tone, Naomi. And that's all that counts even if he knew the words. You can't fool a baby. I wouldn't eat his foot and he knows it. He knows it with a knowledge beyond knowledge, because he has radar, baby radar."

Davenport felt much, much better. The sun was warm, the sky was blue, the day in May and the baby both were beautiful. The idea of fatherhood still was a little startling, but Sam really was a lovely child, almost the miracle Naomi believed him to be. And Naomi herself was not only very sweet but a very intelligent girl, too. Talking to her the night before—or rather in the early dawn—had been a big help and making love with her afterward had been great. A very sexy girl, Naomi. Just beautiful. Most men would thank their lucky stars to have the love of such a woman. Why had he even dreamed of philandering around with little Mrs. Riccobono?

Pauline Weisenschaft Riccobono was her name, and in the endless hours of the night he stared at the dark bedroom ceiling and invented a bigger if not a better world for her. Poor little thing, pathetic little creature. At the lunch when she had baldly propositioned him she'd said: "If you think that fat little Natalie is imaginative, you should of seen me at her age. Boy, the dreams I had when I was little. I used to imagine I was a big beautiful blonde with fabulous boobs and all the guys were dying to screw me, I had to fight 'em off. God, the dreams I had, crazy, huh? A beautiful blonde with a fantastic figure from West Virginia or someplace, instead of a little dark-complexioned, flat-chested Jewish nothin' from Brooklyn. What a dream! I was a real imaginative child, more'n Natalie, a lot more. It was Polly not Pauline, that was what I called her, and God the adventures she had, the good-lookin' guys she screwed, the money she got, the jewels and clothes and things! She had a fabulous life! But . . . well . . . I don't dream about her no more, or I haven't for a long time. I dunno. I kind of gave up. I mean I accepted it I'm myself and that is all I ever will be, just a plain little nothin' who married an Italian boy and lives on no dollars a week. The worst thing about Nicky is he's got no ambition, he don't want to do any better. On Saturday night for fun I squeeze the pimples on his back, that's a thrill. It beats makin' love to him, and I'm not kiddin'. The way that guy makes love you wouldn't believe. A pig could do better, show more interest. . . ."

A bigger if not a better world, that was what Pauline Weisenschaft Riccobono wanted and needed. And so he conjured it for her night after night with a racing brain as Naomi slept peacefully by his side, unaware of his acquaintance with Mrs. Riccobono, if not unaware of the trouble on his mind. Dick was seriously considering accepting little Pauline's frank proposition. Why not? Hadn't Naomi said he could have any freedom he wanted? Sure she had. And Pauline was attractive, much more so than she herself realized. It was true she was nearly as flat-chested as a boy, but she had nice legs, a pretty face and a very sweet smile. "Come any afternoon when Nicky isn't there," she said. It would be fun, why not? A small, slender girl like that would be delightful.

"I'm not joking myself, though," said Naomi. "I think it's serious, the insomnia. I think you ought to talk to Samusson about it, Dick, I really do."

"Samusson?"

"Yes, I think you ought to talk to him. Both about the insomnia and that fantasy."

Victor Samusson and his wife Clea were social acquaintances of Dick and Naomi. The Samussons were clinical psychologists of the Adlerian school; their practice was limited to disturbed children—and, they always added ironically, disturbed parents. But Victor himself had a few adult patients as well, people who for one reason or another particularly interested him.

Dick had gotten to know the man through Naomi's

younger brother Allen. It was the custom of the Samussons to hold open-house soirees on Wednesday evenings at their large Brooklyn apartment, the purpose of which was to advocate and advance the teachings of Alfred Adler. Dick and Naomi had gone to one of these affairs and to their surprise had found it interesting. They'd gone back on the following week, and thereafter Wednesday evenings at the Samussons had become a kind of habit.

"I talk to Samusson every Wednesday night," said Dick.

"I mean talk to him alone."

"I did. I talked to him the other night after the others were gone for a good half-hour. In fact, I told him about Polly and he found her amusing."

"Well, I mean talk to him professionally."

"Professionally. You mean as a patient?"

"Well, yes, I think so. Why not? It couldn't hurt anything?"

"Is that a statement or a question?"

"What?"

"I said, is that a statement or a question? It couldn't hurt anything."

"Well, could it?"

Dick tapped his fingers in a soft drumming manner on the kitchen table, his mouth pursed as he resisted an impulse to grab Sam by the foot again. It was fun the way the baby was always delighted, and "Got your foot!" would be an answer of sorts to Naomi's suggestion. In a gentle tone, as if speaking to a slightly retarded child, he said: "I'm *not* crazy. I know sometimes you *think* I am, but I'm *not*. Perhaps it's to be regretted, perhaps I'd do a little better in some ways if I were crazy, but I'm not, I'm sane."

"No one said you aren't sane. Of course you are. But I don't see why it would hurt to talk to Samusson about this insomnia. It's very bad."

"It isn't bad, you're exaggerating. Insomnia is the most

common thing in the world, everyone has it once in a while."

"Well, I just hate to see you go through this."

"Go through what? Actually I'm having a lot of fun with Polly, as I told you. And it isn't pointless, it's a kind of experiment."

"Oh, now, come on, Dick. In what sense could it possibly be an experiment?"

"Well, now," said Dick in a grave manner, "well, now, now let me see. In what sense an experiment? Okay, you know the gags and talk that go around in advertising, those guys with their martinis at lunch on Madison Avenue, the ones who tell us Coca-Cola refreshes and all of that. Well, the thing is an experiment in this sense. I'm running it up a flagpole to see if anybody salutes it."

"Now that is hardly a serious answer. You just don't want to talk about seeing Samusson."

"Polly *is* an experiment. I'm writing a book in my head. It's antistyle, antinarrative, antimind, yet it makes sense. It has an iron inner logic."

"Well, maybe you do know what you're doing," said Naomi with a pensive stare at him. "Antistyle, antinarrative, antimind. Some of your stories are like that, and the weird thing is they do work, they are still stories and in a way even more effective because they're not sensible. But you aren't writing a book in your head, Dick, you haven't put a word on paper, and a book only exists when it's on paper. I wish you'd talk to Samusson, I really do."

At this gruesomely appropriate moment, Davenport picked up the *Times*. "What's in the paper?" he said, and then as he glanced at the front page a shock hit him. For a moment he could not speak, then he said, "Good God. Good God Almighty."

"What is it?" asked Naomi. "Dick, what is it, what's happened?"

Again, briefly, Dick could not speak. Then in a voice that sounded odd in his own ears, he said: "Jim Meaghan committed suicide."

"Jim Meaghan?"

"Yes, it's here on page one. He killed himself. Sleeping pills, drowned in a bathtub. No accident, they found a razor blade in the water. . . ."

"That's terrible, dreadful. Dick, it's awful, just awful. Why did he do it?"

Davenport shrugged helplessly, stunned and speechless with shock. James Meaghan, whom he had met several times and knew on a casual basis, was one of the most enormously successful young American writers to have appeared since World War II. His first novel had not perhaps achieved the same critical success as Davenport's own first novel, but it had been far more popular and had been the basis for a gigantically successful Broadway play.

It was horrifying. Why should such a man kill himself? Meaghan was young, attractive, talented and rich besides. He was making thousands and thousands of dollars every week from the royalties of his play and more thousands from the worldwide sale of his novel.

"Why did he kill himself? Why did he do it?"

"God knows," said Dick. "I can hardly believe it but here it is: JAMES MEAGHAN, NOVELIST AND PLAYWRIGHT, DEAD. It doesn't make any sense. I hate to use such a cliché, but he had everything in the world to live for. Maybe he went insane. . . ."

"In a way I guess he did," said Naomi in a shaken voice. "You knew him, didn't you?"

"Yes, slightly. I met him a couple of times and he sure didn't seem like a suicidal type, whatever that is. And frankly I've never understood it. Why would anyone want to kill himself? It's a damn fool idea. Kill yourself and you're dead forever. What does that prove or accomplish, not a damn thing, nothing. . . ."

"Well, it isn't exactly a rational idea," said Naomi with another pale smile.

"I mean, maybe if you're sick or something," said Dick, who was half reading the paper while he talked, "vomiting up feces or something horrible, I could understand it under conditions like that, maybe. But Meaghan was young and healthy as far as I know."

"What was he like?" asked Naomi softly.

Dick frowned at her. He didn't much like the tone of her voice or the way she was looking at him. "Well," he said, "a little shy, maybe. But perfectly normal, average. A nice guy, I'd say, modest, unassuming, kind of witty in an understated way, like his book. I'd never have figured him for such a thing as this."

"Was it some girl or woman, a problem like that? Or could he maybe have been sick even as young as he was?"

"Well, no, I don't think so. It says here, they quote a friend as saying Meaghan was his . . . what? . . . his . . . he was worried about his second novel. *Holy shit.* Now this is ridiculous. He was worried about his second novel. He couldn't write it. He had tried and he couldn't. He felt that he had no real talent, that his first book was a lucky accident. Then they quote some doctor as saying he was suffering from 'acute anxiety' and was under psychiatric treatment since the condition is recognized as dangerous. Very dangerous, acute anxiety the most unbearable of human ills, if it continues for long the victim often suicides. And it goes on . . . he had severe insomnia." Dick put down the paper and looked up and stared across the dinette table into Naomi's soft hazel eyes. To his exasperation and dismay, he thought he could detect a faint hint of tears. "Holy shit again," he said. "That's the craziest thing I ever heard of in my life, killing yourself because of a goddamn second novel. What could happen? The critics say it's lousy, so what?"

"Well, I don't see how they could stand by and let it happen," replied Naomi. "You'd think the psychiatrist would put him in a hospital where he couldn't do such a thing."

"The guy sort of answers that. He's quoted as saying it's impossible to predict the reactions of patients to acute anxiety; they can seem to be bearing it very well and then suddenly go to pieces. And he says you can't put everyone who has it in a padded cell because it's a common human experience."

"I can't believe it's common," answered Naomi. "Not that kind of thing."

"All right," said Dick, "okay, *I* myself have got insomnia, and I've got to write a second novel and I've been putting off getting to work on it. But I haven't got any anxiety, acute or otherwise, and I'll tell you this, I'll never do what Meaghan did, never. It's tragic and pitiful, he was crazy. So calm down, relax."

"I didn't say anything like that," answered Naomi. "I didn't say a word."

"No, but your eyes looked worlds."

"Well, I didn't mean them to. I'm sorry."

"Naomi, I'm lazy, that's all."

"Are you?"

"Yes, I am. I'm bone lazy. If I had my way I'd never do any work at all. One of the reasons I got into this damned thing is because I thought there wasn't any work to it."

"Dick, you aren't lazy. I've seen you work twelve hours a day seven days a week for weeks on end."

"Naomi, how can you be so stupid? That is just *exactly* my point! This whole thing is crude disillusionment. I thought there'd be less work to it, and there's more. And being bone lazy at heart, I don't want to do it."

"Don't you?"

"Holy shit *again!*" cried Dick. "Do you expect me to go in the bathroom and fill up the tub?" He flinched as the baby in the highchair let out a sudden wail of fear. "All right, Sam, don't cry. It's all right, don't cry. Daddy's not in the bathtub, Daddy's in the kitchen."

"You scared the baby," said Naomi.

"Oh, Christ, I know I scared the baby and I'm sorry. But for God's sake quit looking at me like that. I'm *fine.* I don't have any damn anxiety and my insomnia is not all that bad, either. And I'll tell you this if it'll cheer you up. I decided even before I read the paper to start that book tomorrow. I swear to God I was thinking about it with the paper right there on the table. I've stalled long enough getting down to that book. It's ridiculous the way I've put it off and this sad, pitiful, tragic thing about Meaghan is just the shock I've needed. I'm starting that novel tomorrow morning at eight sharp and I'm not kidding."

"Well, that's wonderful," said Naomi.

"Cheer up, Sam! Smile, Sam! We can write that book, can't we? Daddy's not in the bathtub, he hates bathtubs. There's nothing to worry about, Sam, there are bluebirds in Brooklyn and crocodiles, too. Hell, I'd start the damn thing today if I didn't have to go teach creative writing to those brats at the Educational Union and see Beau and Pat this afternoon. I really would, I'd start it right now."

Naomi smiled. "Wonderful," she said.

Davenport meant it. On the following morning he would start that book come hell or high water. However, if the truth be known, the sad demise of James Meaghan at twenty-six shriveled him more than slightly. It was very frightening. Why should a man who had won such a beautiful success destroy himself? Why?

ARNOLD "ARCHIE" SCHNERD DIDN'T KNOW WHAT HE'D
run up against. His inadequate whork was stirring already,
practically rampant, all three and five-eighths inches of it.
Little did he know the grisly fate ahead of him. He had a few
doubts and reservations, sure, but he had once heard somewhere a manhood-bolstering aphorism and he'd foolishly believed it: "It is not the size of the weapon that matters, but the
fury of the attack that counts."

The lady who loomed over him had no such uncertainties.
As any young girl might, Polly had wondered back in Dotesville how it would be when she got out into the world on her
own. The question occurred to her as it occurs to practically
every normal girl: "Am I attractive? Am I cute? Am I appealing? Will anybody ever *want* me?"

Polly knew that sensitive young girls undergo torments for
fear the answer is, "No, you're not cute and you're not appealing, you're awful." What is worse than to be . . . unwanted?
The tears that are shed because of this dread fear would fill the
salty sea.

Polly herself shed no tears; her interest was purely pragmatic. The important thing, of course, was that she appealed to *herself*. The question of whether or not others also were drawn to her was not vital in any personal sense, though naturally she had some curiosity on this score for *practical* reasons. In this respect she was a mite nervous.

"Sure," said Archie, who finally had confessed that his real name was Arnold "Archie" Schnerd and not Max Race. "I figured you was new in town from what you was saying to that soda jerk. That's all. Asking him which way Madison Avenue ran and what become of Park Avenue."

"But how amazing," said Polly. "How astonishing that you would have heard, Mr. Schnerd."

"Oh, it was nothing."

"You must be very observant."

"Oh, I dunno," said the foxlike Archie. His forehead was still covered with sweat and he remained a bit purplish around the eyes. Also from time to time he continued wincing in his strange manner, his entire face suddenly skewering over to one side as an eye bulged out and his tongue stuck forth. Not one of the most attractive men in the world, Archie, what with his inadequate whork and his other defects.

"Why, I think it's marvelous," declared Polly. "You must be a fascinating man."

"Uh, well," said Archie. "If you're looking for a hotel I can recommend one. I happen to know a nice place not far from here."

"You're so kind," said Polly. "What sort of location is it? A pleasant atmosphere and all of that? Adequate service and whatnot?"

"Ah, yeah," replied Archie, his eyes bulging forth even a bit more as he stared in consternation at Polly. "Sure, sure, it's okay. But say, I got a idear. You can stay with my aunt, she's a nice old lady."

"Oh, I couldn't," said Polly. "Such an imposition!"

"That won't matter. See, she's about eighty."

"But . . . but . . ."

"Yeah, about eighty. She won't even know you're there. She's deaf, can't hear so good. Don't see so good, either."

"But are you sure?" asked Polly. "I mean certain? Positive beyond any question?"

"Ah-h, yeah. Yeah, I'm sure. It's okay, don't worry, she sleeps a lot. She's half-blind."

"Well, even so, I really couldn't," answered Polly thoughtfully. "It would be entirely too much of an imposition."

"Yeah, but I wouldn't be there myself," said Archie. "You'd just be there alone with the aunt."

"Mmmm," said Polly. "Alone with the aunt . . ."

"Yeah."

"Mmmm, your aunt, well . . ."

"She won't mind," said Archie. "She and me are real good friends. I mean, I'm her favored nephew."

"That's wonderful," said Polly. "And you live with her?"

"Yeah, where else?"

"Mmm-mmm," said Polly.

"She'll be right there to watch after you. So don't worry about it. The aunt is right there all the time."

Polly stared at this man, Archie. He was the first man she had talked to in New York, really, not counting the soda jerk. He didn't look like much, this man. It was doubtful if he had any money, but on the other hand there were tiny diamonds on his wristwatch and his clothes weren't bad. He probably had *some* money, anyhow, if not much. Of course, as an escort he wouldn't be so good. He was skinny, had a long thin nose like a mouse, dark squinty eyes, a blue shadow beard of the patchy type, a slitlike, lipless mouth with stained and crowded and carious teeth and he was only five foot one, a good fifteen inches shorter than Polly herself. A shrimp, really. If he tilted his long thin nose upward at a forty-five-degree angle, it pointed directly at the center of the great valley between her giant honeydew melon breasts. What's more, there was something nasty and evil about him. He probably was a bookmaker or some sort of gangster type, perhaps a white slaver.

Polly had gotten no farther than Diketown before she began to think about the question of what she was going to do to support herself in New York. She had no money, except a few dollars for departure thanks to Aunt Gomorrah, and she knew she'd have to find something to do to make a living. That's why she'd thought of Gimbel's as a temporary stopgap measure. Of course she hated the idea of getting the usual, ordinary type of dull job. The regular hours, the grilling monotony, the tediousness of typing up bills or letters in an office or the hard labor of carrying dishes back and forth in a restaurant or standing on her feet all day selling perfume in Gimbel's—it didn't appeal to her at all, the average sorts of jobs she might get.

Besides, she wanted to try to find a career for herself on the stage or in television, and she'd have to have time to make the rounds. Therefore, she had decided secretly without even telling herself that the best way to arrange things in New York would be by locating patrons of the arts, men who wanted to see a mature culture develop in America so that it could catch up with France, men with faith in the nation and interest in the arts who could contribute to her career in the form of loans.

"I'd be very happy to stay with your aunt," said Polly, "and thank you so much for inviting me. You've been so kind I want to ask you for another favor. May I?"

"Sure," said Archie.

"That's wonderful," said Polly. "The favor's a little different, though. Fair warning! Prepare yourself!"

"Shoot," said Archie.

"All right. You see, I'm here to make a career for myself in the theater or in television, and I need help in getting started. So I'm just going to be point blank about it and ask! That's what I'm going to do, Archie, ask my friends to chip in with loans to help me get started; then when I'm a success I'll pay them back and remember them affectionately always. So. What do you think? Is it a good idea?"

"Well, yeah," said Archie. "I guess so."

"You're very nice. Can you lend me twenty dollars? I need it to start out with."

Archie stared, his thin lips slightly apart, a dim look in his eyes. "Twenty dollars," he said.

"Oh, you're so kind," answered Polly. "To think, just meeting me like this and being willing to invite me to come and stay tonight with your aunt, and also being willing to lend me twenty dollars! Human nature isn't really so bad! People are good in their hearts, they're nice!"

"Yeah, well," said Archie. He looked uncomfortable and gleeful at the same time. "I can slip you twenty if you need it. On a kind of loan. Your career like you say. But when we get up to the room. I mean, I'll give you the twenty when we get up to the room."

Twenty dollars and a place to stay if she wanted it. Well, it was a beginning, and in the nick, too. Polly stared happily in the window of the shop, her gaze fixed on the display of purple jewelry. "I do hate to impose on your aunt, though," she said. "It's quite an imposition bringing in a strange person that way. Why don't you . . . do something for your aunt to make up for it, buy her a present or something? Did you buy your aunt a present lately?"

"What?" asked Archie.

"I said, did you buy——"

"No," said Archie, "not lately."

"Then why don't you buy her a nice present?" Polly smiled and looked into the window. As she turned she took a deep breath and thrust back her big shoulders, moving a bit sidewise as she stared through the plate glass. The profile of her body stood forth like the prow of a clipper ship, awesome. Archie seemed blinded and almost fell backward. An obscene thought ran through his mind: "Those knockers, those boobs!" His teeth chattered despite himself—click-click-click-click. No wonder she didn't wear a bra, they didn't make 'em big enough for her. What a sight. Each great melon mound was crested by a huge acorn nipple that showed pinkly through the thin material of the blouse, merciless man-maddening protrusions each surrounded by a cup-sized paler rose. "What a pair of honeydew melons!" was his lewd thought, a man could lose himself in those globes. He saw himself spread on her like a fly and it *maddened* him. "For instance," said Polly, "one of those lovely bracelets in there. Aren't they beautiful?"

"Yeah," said Archie.

"I think the one right there is divine. How much do you suppose a bracelet like that costs? Isn't that the tag, that little thing on it there—what does it say? Can you read it?"

"Thirty dollars, I think," said Archie. "Thirty or fifty. I can't make it out."

"Do you like it?"

"It's okay."

"It's beautiful. Don't you think so?"

"Yeah, it's fine."

"Why don't you buy it for your aunt? Right now, just go right in and buy that bracelet for your poor old blind aunt."

"Buy the bracelet?"

"Yes, for your aunt."

"What aunt?" asked Archie, his eyes narrowing. "You mean my aunt?"

"Why, Archie," declared Polly in a stern tone, "don't you try to deny it now, don't attempt to avoid it with a fib! You just go right in there and buy that old aunt of yours a gift to show her how much you love her. It's only thirty dollars and I'm sure she'll simply adore it."

"Naw, naw," said Archie, "not her. She wouldn't like it, she wouldn't be able to see it. I tell you, she's practically blind."

"Well, she could *feel* it," said Polly. "She'd know it was there."

"She couldn't feel it. Her rheumatism's so bad she can't feel hardly anything. Her hands are like curled up, you know?"

"Well, you could *tell* her she has it."

"Naw, naw, she couldn't hear me. I tell you, she's deaf."

"Well, then," said Polly brightly, *"you'd* know she has it! And it's the *idea* that counts! Now go right in there and buy that bracelet for your poor old aunt!"

Archie hesitated, looking first at the bracelet and then at Polly. "Well," he said, "twenty bucks and a thirty-dollar bracelet. That's fifty bucks. Fifty bucks don't grow on no trees. What makes you think I got fifty bucks to spare?"

"Are you financially stricken?" asked Polly. "Oh, well, in that case, I wouldn't want you to go around buying your aunt nice presents, not if you can't afford it. I always say live within your means. If you can't afford that nice bracelet, then just don't get it, let it pass."

A sly, shrewd look was on Archie's face. Again he seemed both uncomfortable and gleeful at the same time. "Well, all I said was fifty bucks is pretty steep, doll."

"But it's only thirty," said Polly.

"I know, thirty plus that twenty you want makes fifty."

"The tag says thirty, I think."

"Okay, okay, okay. I got the money, that ain't the point. It's just that it's a lot."

"For a bracelet like that?" asked Polly. She touched at her blonde hair, idly.

"Okay, sister," said Archie. "I'm not Rockefeller, I'm just a hard-working musician on a salary, that's all. Now I think the original twenty is pretty good and you don't need to go raising the ante with any bracelets. I mean, my aunt don't need that bracelet."

"But I'm sure she'd love it."

"Oh, hell," groaned Archie slyly. "All right, I'll get it for you then. You win. But no more, that's tops."

"For me?" asked Polly, alarm showing in her face. "Archie —listen. The bracelet isn't for me, the bracelet is for your aunt. You understand that, don't you?"

"Oh, hell, yes," said Archie.

The bracelet was fifty dollars, not thirty. Archie bought it nevertheless. As they left the jewelry store, Polly took him by the arm and led him down the sidewalk a short distance under the green-striped canopy of a small luggage shop. For a moment he thought she was going to ask him to buy her a suitcase, but then she said solemnly: "Listen, there's one thing I must ask of you. Please forgive me if I do you an injustice, but . . . you *will* treat me like a sister, won't you, Archie? I mean . . . you won't . . . you won't *take advantage* of me, will you? I . . . I . . . you see, I'm very young and inexperienced and being in the city alone and everything . . . *promise* me you won't treat me in any different way than you would if I was your younger sister."

What kind of a game was this, thought Archie, was this doll nuts? "Well, ah-h," he said. "Well, I . . . ah-h . . ."

"Promise! Promise or I won't go!"

"Well, ah-h, yeah, sure . . ."

"Thank you," said Polly. She took Archie's thin arm and off they went down the sidewalk toward the Caravan Hotel and what plainly promised to be the greatest experience of Archie Schnerd's life. He could barely restrain himself his glee was so great. With slyness and shrewdness and superb foxiness, he had gotten himself a thousand-dollar broad for a mere seventy bucks! His less than mighty manhood was stirring already. In a little while, she would be all his.

"I HAVE A DISTURBING BUT PROFOUND THOUGHT FOR you," said Richard Davenport. "Life goes on——"

"Of course it does," answered Naomi.

"——unless you're dead. Now take Jim Meaghan, life doesn't go on for him because he's dead. He's dead as a dodo, his lungs are full of water and he's lying in a pool of formaldehyde on a cold marble slab with wads of cotton on his eyes and his palms pointing upward while medical students cut out his liver and his guts and his heart. Do you know sometimes those guys eat sandwiches while they're doing an autopsy?"

"Now *that* is gruesome. I don't know what you think you're accomplishing by being gruesome, and you do it all the time."

"Wrong," said Dick. "I only do it when my back is to the goddamn wall. That's the reality, Naomi. Jim Meaghan committed suicide, he's dead and medical students are cutting out his liver while they eat sandwiches and talk about balling nurses. That's the truth, and there's no romance to it of any kind, it's a grim and sordid and stinking thing and nothing more."

The day, which had begun so well, had acquired a fair-weather gloom, a mockery of blue skies and gold spring sunshine, an April-is-the-cruelest-month quality. Of course it was not April but the merry month of May; perhaps a few encouraging and fun events would change the cast of things, such as coffee with the old Beau St. John and an amiable drink with Patricia and her new boyfriend, or maybe he would give a real reply at last to poor little love-starved Pauline Riccobono. Life did go on and that last was a good possibility. It was cruel and ungentlemanly to say no to a lady, and what better thing than dalliance to cheer a man up on a gloomy, beautiful day?

"Of course it's a terrible thing. But brooding about it isn't going to help."

"True, I will grant you that. But ignoring it won't help, either. I'm not gruesome, the thing Meaghan did is gruesome."

"Well, you put it gruesomely. Do you want more coffee?"

"No, thanks. I've had too much as it is."

"A little, half a cup?"

"No, thanks, honey."

"Well, there's more in the pot."

"Thanks, I've had three cups already."

"There's no point in wasting it. You don't want it, half a cup?"

At times the *Yiddishe Momma* in Naomi was maddening. She got it straight from her own mother. Eat a little potatoes. Have more pot roast, it wouldn't hurt you. Do me a favor, take another piece cake. It was the chicken soup syndrome, this nagging mania to make any child or male eat, eat, eat. But it was hardly a Jewish phenomenon; his Aunt Mae had done the exact same thing. Pat did it, too. All women did it. Something in the double XX chromosome gave them an insane urge to see food going down the gullets of the child of God.

"Naomi, if I was your brother I'd call you a *yenta*. I said three times I don't want another cup of coffee and now I will say it four times. I don't want another cup of coffee."

"Well, you don't have to snap my head off or make anti-Semitic remarks. I only want you to be satisfied."

"What's anti-Semitic about a good solid word like *yenta?* Your brother calls your mother a *yenta* all the time."

"I know he does and he's a rude boy with no manners. Instead of laughing at him she ought to wash his mouth out with soap."

"Is it that bad? I don't even know what *yenta* means, except a female who asks you three times to have coffee when you don't want it. My Aunt Mae was a *yenta.* So is Pat. Terrible *yentas,* both of them."

"It's a very vulgar word. I ask you to have coffee only because I want you to be well and happy. I don't have any motives, I don't have any motives at all, I just want you to be satisfied."

"I know. I know, honey." Dick put a hand on the blondish hair of his son Sam, gave Naomi a smile as if to say, "Don't be mad," then walked from the kitchen into the small but pleasant living room of the Flatbush apartment. As he got a pack of cigarettes from the desk he glanced at his new portable typewriter, which so far had not seen very much use. Dick shrugged. It was just a machine, neutral and innocent, the keys did not really resemble the teeth of a shark, that was an illusion.

"You're leaving?"

"Yeah. The kids at the EU are waiting breathlessly for me and I'm waiting breathlessly for them."

"Well, I guess it's a good thing but I wonder if it isn't a waste of time. I don't see how you can teach writing to children that age."

"Neither do I. But we've got a writer in the class. Natalie, she writes up a storm."

"You're seeing your friend later, that towheaded boy?"

For some reason, Naomi refused to call Beau St. John by his name. On the few occasions she'd seen him, Beau had behaved very badly and she disliked and feared him. "Yeah, I'm seeing Beau after the class. He sounded like his old self on the phone. He has a story he wants me to read and he says it's a breakthrough at last."

"I doubt it, he has no talent at all, not even a trace. I'd feel sorry for him if he wasn't so revolting and egotistical. The one thing I can't understand is why girls seem to like him. I know he's your friend, but to me he's totally repulsive."

"Beau is very clever. You don't understand him."

"Maybe he is clever verbally sometimes, but he's no writer. That thing he wrote last year was absolutely horrible. Anyhow, you're seeing him and then you're seeing your sister?"

"Yeah, then I'm seeing Pat. Drinks with her new fellow if he shows up, she's been having trouble with him. He is bald-headed but very good in bed, she told me all about it; she told me more about it than I want to know. Just like when I was a child she told me all about her menstrual cramps. Any other questions, honey?"

"Oh, no. No more questions. I was just asking."

"Okay. I'll be home around seven. You and Sam have a nice day."

"You have a nice day, too." Dick turned and walked down the hall toward the front door of the apartment before she could ask him anything else. It was a little irritating at times. Naomi had to know where he was at all hours. She was insecure in her relationship with him and it made her possessive; she herself admitted it. If he even looked at a girl on the street she got upset. And she'd said he could have "any freedom" he wanted in the marriage. As it happened, however, he had never been unfaithful to her, and he wondered how she would react now if she knew he was thinking seriously of philandery.

In fact, he was thinking very seriously about it; he had just about decided to accept little Mrs. Riccobono's invitation and visit her sometime soon at her apartment when Nicky wasn't home. But somehow the idea gave him butterflies in his stomach, awful butterflies—was he dependent on Naomi in some way he didn't understand? Very possibly, and if that was so, wouldn't it be a good idea for him to break out of it?

Maybe so, thought Dick as he walked up a Brooklyn sidewalk toward Church Avenue. It was a pleasant, tree-lined, residential street of fairly modern apartment buildings. In the other direction the street had houses with lawns and flowers, and a big Catholic church was not far away, although the neighborhood was mostly middle-class Jewish. Living conditions were much better in this area of Flatbush than in areas of Manhattan with comparably priced apartments, and that was why they'd moved after the baby was born. Finding the apartment had been very difficult and Dick himself hadn't thought it would be worth it. The image he had of Brooklyn, and of Flatbush in particular, was that of a concrete jungle; but it wasn't so at all. The street could have been in Atlanta or Boston or St. Louis or any large city in America. As Naomi said, the neighborhood was "nice." And it was, it was nice. Mothers and children were on the broad sidewalk in the May sunshine, the mothers chatting with each other and the children throwing balls or riding tricycles. It was a downright idyllic scene for a city street. Numerous baby carriages could be seen; the neighborhood had many young marrieds and a lot of the mothers were attractive.

Well, rough, thought Dick as he strolled along with his walking stick toward the subway and the distant towers of Manhattan. It was rough, there was no denying it. The sad and pitiful suicide of Jim Meaghan while trying to write a second novel would upset anyone who happened to be in an identical position. But there was a solution: *get to work.* "Pock," went his walking stick. For some reason, Dick had recently begun affecting a walking stick, a heavy, gnarled Irish cane that was practically a cudgel, and now he tapped it on the sidewalk as he walked along. "Pock," page one, "pock," page two, "pock," page three—that was the way to do it, just sit down and write it. The day was looking better already, much better. But then an unfortunate thing happened.

"Yeee-ow!" cried Dick as a stab of pain hit his right foot in the Achilles area and he almost pitched forward on the sidewalk. Gasping with shock, he turned and saw a fat little boy of about ten staring up at him with brooding, resentful eyes. The little beast had deliberately run a large tricycle into him from behind. In pain Dick stared at his torn sock and the blood on his heel, then he looked up at the child and asked: "Now what did you do that for?"

"You were in the way, you were blocking traffic," said the child.

"I was blocking traffic?"

"Yeah. You were in the middle of the sidewalk."

"Oh, now is that so?"

"Hoibie!" cried a voice. "Get away from that man!"

Twenty feet away Dick saw an angry-eyed woman sitting on a canvas folding chair by a baby carriage in the entrance of an apartment building. The woman was good-looking; she had even, perfect features and a very good figure. Dick had noticed her before. She had a vague resemblance to the movie actress Paulette Goddard and she was one of the sexiest mothers on the block. She was in a furious mood and for a moment he considered saying nothing to her at all. "Now look, lady," he said. "I don't want to cause any trouble, but your little boy ran into me on purpose; my foot is bleeding. The little brat did it deliberately."

"Oh, shut up," said the woman. "Hoibie, get away from that man!"

Dick couldn't believe his ears. How could the woman tell him to shut up when the little beast had run into him like that? And he wasn't even obeying, Herbie wasn't moving. He was right there on his oversized tricycle staring up at the enemy with sullen angry eyes. "Jesus H. Christ," said Dick in a hollow voice as a frightening impulse came to him to lift the heavy walking stick high and crack the nasty brat's head. There wasn't a chance he would do such a thing, but the very idea was scary, unnerving.

"Hoibie, I said get away from that damn man!"

"Damn man?" asked Dick. "Well, he had better get away, the little brat! I never heard of such a thing, telling me I'm 'blocking traffic,' what kind——"

"Hey, you! Don't you talk to my child in such a tone!"

"Don't talk to him in such a tone? Now what kind of tone have *you* got?"

"Just get off of the street! Get off of the street!"

"Oh, go to hell, you . . ."—what could he say to her that would really *get* her?—"'. . . you . . . you *yenta!*"

"Why, you, you . . ." A grimace of fury came to the woman's face, a teeth-gnashed distortion of rage. At the moment she didn't resemble Paulette Goddard hardly at all. "An anti-Semite, huh, a cutie! Bullying children and insulting mothers! I'll call the police! I'll get the cops on you, we don't have that kind of stuff in this neighborhood! I'll call the police!"

A supercilious mood came upon Dick. "I'm half-Jewish myself," he said. "Well, practically. My son is half-Jewish and that's the truth. We had a bris for him and his grandfather cried. It was a great little ceremony, ouch!"

"You, you . . . get off of the street! I'll call the police!"

The woman was impossible. What would *really* get her? Dick narrowed his eyes and said in a polite Dracula voice: "Oh, you vill, hah? Wal, if you do I'll cut oudt Hoibie's heardt with a dull spunn and drink his bloodt, every last red drrrop. Then I'll drink yourrr bloodt, too." *That* would get her.

And it did. Except to his surprise, Bela Lugosi didn't make the woman angrier. She didn't splutter, she stared in horror at Dick for about five seconds, then suddenly jumped up, grabbed the baby carriage and pulled it rapidly toward the entrance of the apartment house. "C'mere!" she cried, but the little boy didn't have to be told. Shoulders hunched and his eyes bugging with fright, he pedaled the tricycle into the building after his mother.

"Oh, Christ," said Dick. He stood there on the sidewalk feeling foolish. How had he gotten into this damn thing, anyhow? He gave a little helpless shrug. Now probably the woman *would* call the police—after all, with a vampire loose in the neighborhood, what else? The woman was hysterical, she had seemed really afraid. How could she take seriously such a ridiculous threat? Surely she knew Bela Lugosi, the Hungarian actor who had played Count Dracula? In the seventh grade everyone had gone around saying: "Kees me. I vant to drink your bloodt."

Of course he wasn't exactly being nice, but he *was* joking. Did the woman actually believe he was an insane Nazi who might murder her and the child? Impossible, no sensible person could think such a thing. But maybe she did, maybe she wasn't sensible, her fear had seemed real enough. Dick shook his head and scratched his shock of thick Indian hair in dismay. His trace of Chickasaw blood had betrayed him, or his Scotch-Irish blood or something; he'd overreacted and he'd better get out of there before the cops came and drove a stake through his heart. With another embarrassed shrug, he turned and walked on toward the Church Avenue subway stop. From now on he'd have to go all the way around the block to avoid Herbie and his mother.

Of course it was annoying, even infuriating. The little boy

was impossible and the mother was worse. As Dick walked on he gritted his teeth and muttered to himself, "Damn little Jewish brat," and at once felt a twinge of liberal shame. Now *that* was no kind of thing to say or think. What did the child's being Jewish have to do with it? A brat was a brat. The correct formula was, "Damn little *human* brat."

Certainly. A little human brat was what he was. The brilliant Isidore Esserman had said Jews spoil their children, but Naomi had shot down that generalization.

Dick thought about it as he crossed Church Avenue and walked past Ebinger's toward the subway entrance. The generalization "Jews spoil their children" was empty, like all such generalizations. Some did, some didn't.

The episode was unfortunate. He should have followed his first thought and said nothing at all to the woman. So what if a child hit him with a tricycle?

On the platform of the Church Avenue stop, Dick had an impulse to throw himself under an approaching subway train. It was just an impulse, no more, but he stood behind a steel column as the train roared by. The Meaghan tragedy had put such ideas in his head of course, that was all it was and nothing to be afraid of. But he shouldn't have used the Bela Lugosi accent to the woman, that was an error; she thought he was stupidly and crudely mocking her people.

Archie's name, in his own opinion, was one of his larger misfortunes, perhaps the primary misfortune of them all. How could anyone possibly respect a man named Arnold Schnerd? It was a perfectly good German name—his grandfather had been next door neighbor to Hitler's grandfather, it was the single claim to fame his family had—but it sounded funny in English. Schnerd, an awful name, horrible, the cause of all his woe, it ruined him in the first grade then and there.

"Arnold Schnerd?"

"Here."

"Tee-hee-hee-hee-hee!"

And his nickname Archie was even worse. As for example:

"Sue, I'd like you to meet Archie. Archie Schnerd."

"Are you kidding?"

And yet strangely enough, he had never changed the name, not really; he couldn't get away from it somehow or other, it was *him*. That was the essence of it, he *was* Archie Schnerd. And not Arnold but Archie, as his friends called him—or

rather, his acquaintances, since it would be inaccurate to say
he had any friends. Archie Schnerd, it was *him*.

Briefly he had used the pseudonym "Max Race" back during the early 1930s when he had made the error of trying to
form a small Dixieland band. He had wanted to sell himself
to this big blonde doll as Max Race, but the truth would out,
that lie had no more chance than the musical organization
known as "Max Race and His Orchesnorter." It was an interesting but common psychological phenomenon. Archie was
thoroughly dissatisfied with himself but he couldn't get away
from himself because he *was* himself. Archie Schnerd, that was
him.

The so-called Dixieland band had failed because Archie and
the boys he got together unfortunately possessed no knowledge whatever of Dixieland music in any of its various forms.
New Orleans, Chicago, Kansas City—they'd never heard of
any of it and didn't even know who Louis Armstrong was,
much less King Oliver. The band had performed in black face
and old plantation-type pink zoot suits à la Broadway 1937.

The true zoot suit had not been evolved of course in that
dim and distant period, but this was only a minor inauthentic
aspect of Max Race and His Orchesnorter. The musicians in
the band often jumped up and waved paper hats and said,
"Hotcha!" Fundamentally what the band tried to do was
render more smooth and pleasing to the ear a crude nigger-
type music that in Archie's opinion had no art to it. What came
out was a sort of small Guy Lombardo band that seemed to
have gone insane in a pathetic, droopy, hooty manner. Audi-
ences used to shout and throw things.

The sad truth was that Archie was not even a swing musician, much less a jazz player. He played a straight dance band
saxophone, colorless and accurate in a technical sense, and that
was all. But it was something at least; it was better than nothing. The alto saxophone was in fact his only triumph in life

excepting the time he hit his father over the head with a shovel. He'd been taught the violin as a child and was extremely bad on it, but one day he heard his mother observe that thank God at least he didn't play one of those awful saxophones.

So, in order to get back at his mother, whom he loathed, he learned the saxophone and, inspired by hate, he did much better than he had done with the violin. It was his ambition to achieve such a mastery of the instrument he would be able to perform on it "The Flight of the Bumblebee." He did finally learn this masterpiece of musical expression, and he sounded very much like a bee—a large, honking bee, but a bee nonetheless. He executed the composition often while playing in the high school band, usually three times during each dance. People would say: "Listen to Archie Schnerd play that saxophone!"

Archie was forty-four years old and currently occupied the second alto sax chair in the regular orchestra at Café Milano, a large East Side supper club that boasted pseudo-Continental food, an expensive show (usually a name girl singer of the more sophisticated type), and two dance bands, a large regular orchestra and a small rhumba band. Archie worked in the big band and also did many of its routine arrangements.

Marijuana was not generally known to the public in those days, but it was commonly used by musicians and many of the members of the band smoked it, but not Archie. He didn't use the stuff because it made his eyes water painfully, burned his nose and throat, had a stink and made him throw up. And besides he didn't enjoy the supposed effects of it. It scared him, really. Most things did, even coffee; he was an extreme hypochondriac. And as for all that passing around of spitty roaches, ugh.

The so-called palship of blowing a stick was beyond him. What was palship, anyhow, or friendship either? Horseshit, that's all. The fact is, he was just not a sociable person, he didn't like the human race, people disgusted him and he stayed away from them as much as possible. He had no friends among men and none among women either. He had nothing remotely like a steady girlfriend. Every month or so he picked up a down-and-out prostitute in the Broadway area and made as cheap a deal with her as possible.

Thus Archie. Nervous as a cat, terrified, isolated, under-sized (he was only four feet eleven without his elevator shoes and he weighed a scrawny ninety-seven pounds), timid, sickly, unsure of himself to the point of hysteria and with hair grow-ing from his cavernous nostrils, he went through life a whin-ing, nasty mess, a repulsive petty scoundrel, mean-natured and small in heart, mind and soul, with no taste, no sensitivity, no sympathy, and except for the alto sax and "The Flight of the Bumblebee," no cultivation in any respect whatever.

It was regrettable but true. Whatever imagination Arnold "Archie" Schnerd ever possessed had long ago withered away through total lack of use. No doubt as a five-year-old child he had had daydreams of some complexity, an awareness of pos-sibilities of life deeper than ten two-dollar tickets on a daily double or a wretched twelve minutes with a down-and-out whore, but such capabilities had long ago perished in Archie.

One might conclude that Arnold Schnerd was hardly alive, but such a conclusion was not quite true. Angels came some-times and sang in his ear. A great gold, or possibly green, angel all spangled with the light of life stood by as he snatched up the phone and breathlessly dialed a number. "Joe, it's Archie." A gray croak. "Put down ten for me on Whattababy in the third."

Another angel, dark and wild and bat-winged, hovered overhead as he gobbled pills and gulped powders, clammy with desperation as he realized that cancer, tuberculosis, jaun-dice, heart disease and billions of little sucker-mouthed, hairy-legged germs were after him.

There was also the greatest angel of them all, the angel of the basic frustration: the thousand-dollar broad, free. He always visualized her as big, practically a giantess, with pink skin, blonde hair and blue eyes, with a great behind like a horse's ass and huge breasts like honeydew melons. And he had seen this angel perched on a barstool in a drugstore. There she was, with a figure that would stop the hands of a clock and make them go backward, a thousand-dollar broad dumb from the sticks! His dream come true! A tremendous piece of tail that could be had for nothing, free! There it sat on a drugstore stool just waiting for a smooth talker to come along.

But there was a problem. Violently, murderously, chokingly, hideously horny though he was (the basic frustration), the body of a woman was scientifically repellent to Archie, on the grounds that the female, even more than the male, was chock full of germs. Women to him were walking reservoirs of virulent bacteria even though he lusted after them horrendously. They made him tremble all over with a mixture of fear, nausea and desire. He never got in bed with one of the creatures without being convinced he was exposing himself to trillions of nasty germs, which he pictured as ghastly little hairy-legged bugs and horrible tiny fishlike things that squirmed through the blood and all over everywhere. The smell of an armpit would practically make him faint. And a crotch . . .? Yuh-ugh-gh-GH!

All of this, naturally, hampered his marital technique, which was not too good in the first place. Once a girl (one of the few nonprostitutes he had ever known) had peevishly accused him of being a poor lover. He answered that he couldn't help it, he was decent. "I am decent," he said, "and I am clean, which is more'n I can say for *you,* doll." It was true that he was clean, or at least it was true once a month. It was Archie's custom on completing an act of intimate relations to suppress a shriek of horror, jump up, rush into the bathroom and scrub his entire

body from head to toe with a strong disinfectant soap, meanwhile hoping and praying that the lady was not ill, or "boint."

Since occasionally Archie did manage (if that is the word)
to sleep with, or half sleep with, or one-tenth sleep with (or
whatever chilling fraction), a woman who was not a prostitute
(the last such incident had been three years before), it could
not be maintained that he was utterly lacking in *all* initiative
insofar as the opposite sex is concerned. But the women he got
were crazy or drunk. The truth is, no girl or woman in her
right mind could possibly want Archie in any way, shape or
form. He was, and he knew it, the very personification of
worthlessness, misery, ugliness and impotent hate.

Yes, he knew it and often the thought occurred to him: why
live? He had cancer anyhow, probably, and would suffer un-
told agonies unless he was lucky enough to fall down against
a curb and knock out his brains. The trouble with his stomach
must surely come from cancer, what else? Why continue to
endure those terrifying pains, why let that pulpy mass grow
and grow and grow, and at the same time live an awful and
empty and loveless life blowing "The Flight of the Bumblebee" on a small horn? Cut your throat, Archie, and do yourself
a favor, throw yourself before a Mack truck and let it grind
you into a bundle of blood and bones, hurl yourself from a
high window and go down, down, down and smack on merciful concrete in a splatter.

Polly, when he saw her perched on the stool at the soda
fountain, restored him to life, or to a semblance of it. The
dumb thousand-dollar broad who could be had for nothing,
free!

As he beheld the round, soft, twin flare of her beauteous
behind, a baleful ache struck him in his vitals. There she sat
trying to drive him wacky as if he wasn't already, her magnificent dimensions perched up and poked out in the seersucker
skirt so as to be all the more maddening. She knew it, the

whore bitch, she knew what a soul-shattering behind she had! She knew, all right! And he knew, too, that he had to possess it, he had to get that thousand-dollar piece of tail no matter what! A wave of semi-insane, ravenous determination went through Archie Schnerd, a wave that left him shaken and white and trembling but still on his feet. Not too long thereafter, he stood by in the jewelry store as Polly said to a bald clerk:

"Thank you so very much. Gift-wrap it."

Archie lived at the Caravan, a rather frumpy residential hotel in the upper midtown Broadway area not too far from the Pepsi-Cola sign at the peak of the pudendum of Times Square. It had a tiny green lobby in which were placed here and there drab articles of furniture covered in yellow plastic. Two small potted plants already in decline stood by a plate glass window overlooking a tense, nervous Broadway side-street.

The Caravan, by and large, was patronized by occasional stray visitors to New York, by petty salesmen and buyers, and by a regular clientele of hack musicians, small-time press agents, gambler pimps, common-grade dope peddlers, and waiters, actors, floozies, chorines and whatnot. At this hour in early evening, the green lobby was deserted except for Pop, the dyspeptic-looking, sour-eyed old day clerk and elevator boy, a cynical type disliked by all.

"Hello, there, Pop," said Archie. "My key, please."

"Yehhh-hh," snarled Pop. He was staring under his gray brows surreptitiously and in considerable awe at Polly, a doll stacked from here to the Poconos if he ever saw one. Good God, the knockers on her, where had that pissant Schnerd found her? As he squinted at her, Polly looked around idly at the green lobby, a pleasant expression on her face, her red lips apart and a half-smile in her wide-open blue eyes. Archie leaned toward her coral ear.

"Just took this place for the time being," he said. "I was staying at the Waldorf, see, but a fellow was lookin' for me I din wanna see, so I come over here temporary. Wasn't nowhere else I could get in. Room shortage in town."

"A convention, I suppose?" asked Polly.

"Shortage all around," said Archie. "I'm only here temporary."

"Well," answered Polly, "it's luxuriously furnished."

"Only temporary," said Archie.

"But such luxury," replied Polly, opening her eyes very wide. She tilted her head back and her eyebrows went up even more. "What extreme luxury!"

Archie swallowed miserably. The sarcasm of this dame or whatever it was, was getting him dragged. "Yeah," he said. "Well, I just come over here like I said, to get off from that guy I din wanna see." Sweat ran down his forehead and dripped in his eyes, salty and blinding. He gestured to the small elevator where a sullen, brooding Pop stood waiting. "I don't care so much about my surroundings. Never notice much where I am. But they . . . they ought to have air conditioning here. That I miss, air conditioning. I miss that a lot. Step down, doll."

With a slow paranoid clatter the elevator door rolled across the track as the obtuse, brooding Pop shut it. "What a nice elevator!" exclaimed Polly.

"Is that so?" said Pop. "Well, it runs."

"Heh-heh-heh," said Archie. "It's a little old. Just a little old."

"Yeh-h?" asked Pop. "Want to walk up, wise guy?"

"Come on, come on, cut out the comedy," said Archie, with a frantic, fearful glance at Polly. "Take us up. You ain't Bing Crosby."

Angrily, the gray-haired Pop slammed down the tarnished lever to the brass letters that spelled U-P. With a shudder and with weary *folie à deux* creaks and groans, the ancient elevator slowly, reluctantly ascended as chains rattled somewhere.

"Why, it certainly does run!" said Polly brightly.

"Yeh-h?" replied Pop. "Heh!" He glowered sullenly at Polly. This dumb broad coming in here and being sarcastic first about the lobby, then about the furniture in the lobby, and then about the elevator—who the hell was she? And where did a pissant like Archie get hold of her, anyhow? Schnerd couldn't afford no such broad as this. Well, to hell with her, thought Pop.

A schizophrenic trembling came over the elevator and suddenly it stopped, shuddering at a floor uncertainly, as if it might fall. *"Five,"* said Pop defiantly. He unlatched the metal door and pulled it back.

Polly walked out upon a faded blue carpet the threads of which were worn bare near the elevator entrance. A large crockery urn full of sand and cigarette butts and shredded cigars stood against the opposite wall beneath a streaked mirror. The corridors led off glumly to right and left, small, dim, whorey globes spaced periodically overhead and brindle numbered doorways on either side. It had the smell of spaghetti sauce, gym socks and unwashed toilet seats with a trace of Lysol.

"I love it!" said Polly.

"Uh-h, down this way," said Archie, who was uncomfortably aware of Pop's eyes boring into his back. He was also aware of several other things besides the obtuse, leering Pop. Archie was worried. The girl had kept talking on and on about his aunt as if there really *was* an aunt. Back in the cab she had asked:

"What's your aunt's name?"

"Mathilda," said Archie.

"Oh, really! How nice! How genuinely and truly nice! Mathilda!"

The lurking suspicion would not go away that *somehow* she meant everything she said. Could that be possible?

Another question worried Archie even more: the fact that he had only eight dollars left and the price was twenty. What would he say when she got in the room and asked him for it? "Okay, mister. Twenty bucks, please." He would have to tell her the bracelet would have to be enough.

Archie's room was small and the window overlooked a court, but it seemed not too badly furnished. Polly was puzzled, though, by the fact there was no bed. It looked like a living room. "Where's the bed?" she asked.

"In such a rush?" asked Archie. He had turned deathly white. "Let's have a drink."

"Is there another room?" asked Polly. "Where's your aunt? This is a sitting room, isn't it?" Bewildered, she gazed around, then opened a door. It led to the bathroom.

"The next one," said Archie.

Polly opened another door and saw inside the tuxedo Archie used in playing with the Café Milano orchestra. It was an ordinary black dinner jacket but a pleasant tingle went through her. His stock rose greatly. She hadn't known for sure he was a musician in a band; she'd thought that was probably a lie and that he was a gangster or a white slaver. But seeing the tuxedo convinced her he was something, anyhow, a waiter at least if not in the rackets.

"The other one, doll, the other one."

"This one here, possibly?"

"Yeah," replied Archie, who stood disconsolately by the window, an apprehensive, sneaky gleam in his eyes and his hand on a bottle of whisky that rested on the sill. "But watch out, it'll fall on you."

"Fall on me?" asked Polly. She tugged at the door. "Auntie? Are you theah? Surprise, surprise! Where are you, Aunt Mathilda?" Suddenly, an entire unmade bed came tumbling from the wall. "Oh! It's a bed! It looks like a bed in the very wall!"

"It *is* a bed," said Archie.

"We live in an age of scientific wonders!" said Polly.

"Yeh-h," said Archie. "Excuse-meh. Got to go in the bathroom and take a pill."

"Have fun," called Polly.

"Ulg," answered Archie. "Ullgh, gluh." White as flour, tongue and throat all constricted, he half-collapsed through the bathroom door, a film over his eyes. He was not entirely conscious due to the intense nervous strain that always afflicted him before the moment of lovemaking, a strain which on this occasion was multiplied many times. Could he live through it if he actually got this thousand-dollar broad, and what would happen if he didn't?

PAULINE RICCOBONO WAS A RATHER PRETTY LITTLE BRU-
nette of twenty-two or twenty-three who was an elementary-
grade teacher at the Educational Union, a grim and depressing
settlement house on New York's Lower East Side. She had
thick, curly black hair, a sexy petite figure, a shy expression
and a smile of even white teeth with a small gap between the
upper incisors. Her maiden name was Weisenschaft and she
looked like a typical "nice Jewish girl," a neat and proper
young lady solidly grounded in the Judaeo-Christian ethic.

Why he did it he did not know, but Dick went after little
Mrs. Riccobono in a manner most people would consider
definitely outrageous. It was a type of behavior he had not
been guilty of since he'd married. He thought he had out-
grown such immature frolic, which he described as the com-
pulsive chase. Often, in the midst of his hammer-and-tongs
pursuit of Pauline, he asked himself, "What are you trying to
prove?"

But something about her appealed to him. He saw her in

the halls, he saw her at staff meetings, he saw her in the coffee room, and a little game developed between them. It was a very simple game. He would stare solemnly at her and she would stare back solemnly at him. Of course at first she wouldn't do that; she would avert her eyes, blink nervously, look else-, where; but then she began to return his gaze and it was highly titillating. In his belief, the flat stares exchanged between them were far sexier than coy flirtation. He felt that her eyes said plainer than words: "I know what you have in mind. You want to take off my clothes and screw me. Okay, I'm interested. Do something about it."

Until he married Naomi, Richard Davenport for a long time had had a weakness insofar as girls and women are concerned, a weakness that he liked to regard as an overall plus rather than an obvious minus, as an amiable trait rather than a sinister failing, as a kind of nice thing rather than a bad thing despite his conviction that there was something wrong with it somewhere.

But good or bad, he couldn't help it; the weakness—if weakness it was—was indelibly imprinted upon the circuits of his brain. At the age of fifteen on a local town bus, he had suddenly, to his horror and surprise, put his elbow against the soft breast of a young married woman who was sitting beside him. To his even greater surprise if not horror, the young married woman, who was very pretty and only about eighteen or nineteen, did not slap his face or bawl him out; on the contrary, she cooperated with his sly move, subtly lifting her arm and turning imperceptibly to the side so he could get at her better. Innocently, she stared ahead as if nothing was going on. Wild! Heart-pounding! Maddening! Delightful! There his elbow was right on her soft titty and she was cooperating. It gave him the Great Insight that *they*—those hitherto mysterious and remote creatures known as girls and women —had the same desires as himself no matter how much they protested, the same awful trouble down below the navel and the same terrible urge to do something about it. Logically it followed as day follows night that they would cooperate even more if given the opportunity. He had never gotten over this Great Insight; it was stamped forever on his brain and it was wild, heart-pounding, maddening, delightful.

One day in the hall he said to Pauline:

"Where did you get that gap between your teeth?"

"I don't know," she answered. "I just have it."

"Is that so, hmm. You've always had it?"

"Yeah, always."

"Well, you'd better watch out. Chaucer says gap-toothed women are very sexy, they have raging fires in them. You look so sweet and innocent I can hardly believe it, but that's what Chaucer says and he's very wise."

"Uh-huh, I see. Chaucer says that."

"Yeah, he says that. I can quote him exactly. It's from the Tale of the Wife of Bath. He says, 'Beware of a gat-tothed woman, she hath in her innards raging fyres'—and that's spelled *ef, wye, ar, ee, ess, fyres*. It's Middle English, of course."

"Well, you're pretty flirty."

"That's what Chaucer says. Is he wrong?"

"Well, I don't know and you shouldn't ask. I'm married. My name is *Mrs. Riccobono*, not *Miss.*"

"Another bad sign is curly hair," said Dick, "or a good sign depending on your point of view. I never saw a curly-headed girl yet who didn't have a problem like that. You really are very cute, Pauline, and if your husband ever gets tired of you, let me know."

"What gall," she answered. "You really are a terrible flirt. I'm half a mind to tell Mr. Hines how you talk to the teachers here. For your information, I'm happily married and I have no problems."

"None at all?"

"No, none."

"I can't believe it," said Dick. "Not with that sexy little gap between your teeth and that pretty curly hair. If your husband ever does get tired of you, let me know, because I really would appreciate you."

"What a nerve," she said. "You're impossible."

On another occasion when he was alone with her in the coffee room, Dick smiled in his most amiable manner and asked her: "What's your husband's name?"

"Nicky," she said.

"Riccobono, he must be Italian, huh?"

"Yes, he's Italian."

"Are you Italian yourself?"

"No, I am Jewish."

"Really?"

"Yes, my maiden name was Weisenschaft. It was the name of the people who adopted me, but my mother was Jewish, too."

"I see. But you're Catholic now?"

"No, I'm not anything."

"You don't believe in God?"

"No."

"Neither do I. But I don't know, there might be a power out there. Pauline, tell me something personal and confidential. Is Nicky a good lover?"

"Is Nicky . . . wha-at? You're an *awful* flirt! How can you talk to me like that? What business is it of yours?"

On still another occasion Dick walked up behind her in an upstairs corridor and audaciously put his hand on her bottom. He'd touched her before but not in such a way as this. Slowly, she turned and looked at him over her shoulder in empty-eyed shock as if she couldn't believe it. It was a sexy moment. Very sexy. Pauline's breasts were small, but she had a comely girlish behind that fit plumply beneath his palm, and she made no move to step away from him, her protest was only verbal. "What are you *doing?*" she asked in a slightly breathless voice. "Get your hand off me."

"I like having it here. Don't you like it?"

"No, I don't!"

"Pauline, I don't know how you do it but you've gotten under my skin. It must be your sweet smile and that cute little gap between your teeth. What's more, you have a very sexy behind. Is Nicky tired of you yet?"

"Look, quit it, someone will see you. Take your hand off me!"

"Or more to the point, are you tired of Nicky?"

And on still another occasion he said to her: "Pauline, let me ask you something serious. If I invited you to come to Nassau with me for the weekend, would you?"

"What, Nassau?" she asked, flustered. "Now . . . what would I do in Nassau with you?"

"What do you think?"

"I can't imagine!"

"Well, we'd spend the whole time in bed, what else? It would be *terribly* sexy, Pauline. Just imagine it, hours and hours in that bed making beautiful sweaty love under a tropical moon. Every now and then we'd have a cigarette and exchange little kisses and whisper sweet things and passion would come over us again. It would be *fantastically* sexy, Pauline. Will you come with me to Nassau sometime?"

"Of course I won't! Are you crazy?"

And on still another occasion he put his hands on her shoulders, stared into her eyes and said: "If you won't go to Nassau, then how about meeting me in a hotel here in town? Will you do that, and if so when?"

"Never," she replied.

"Why not? It would be fun, Pauline, great fun."

"Oh, it would be fun, huh? Is that what you think, it would be fun?"

"Sure it would be fun. Tell me something. Do you like to do it on top or do you always like to be on the bottom?"

"Now really, that's insulting. Let me go, I've got to go to class."

"I'm sorry, Pauline. I was just wondering if you are liberal or conservative. I'll bet you're liberal. And what's more, I'll bet that your husband is conservative. Me, I'm downright *radical.*"

"It's no business of yours what Nicky is. Now let me go!"

"I'm sorry, Pauline, forgive me for prying."

After about a week of such damn-the-torpedoes flirtation, Davenport felt that little Mrs. Riccobono was ready if she ever would be and he invited her to lunch. It was his belief that an outrageous approach was the best and beyond doubt the quickest to a certain kind of passive, insecure and shy girl, which this one seemed to be. In view of her marriage and her niceness, it was probably impossible to get her no matter what approach was used. But there was something attractive about her aside from her prettiness; the hesitancy in her eyes and the uncertainty in her voice gave her an appealing vulnerability. Very likely, though, nothing would come of it.

Ironically enough, Dick had been cruelly hoist with his own petard in the case of Pauline Riccobono. He had been crudely disillusioned about both her character and her outlook. The disillusionment was not that she was unavailable, but that she was *too* available. Until the lunch at Hamburger Heaven she had played the part of a nice Jewish girl, and she was no such thing. When she finally opened her mouth, the impression she made was of a crass, mindless, self-pitying creature loaded and drenched with hostility. It was sad, it was shocking. She was a nasty and heartless little bitch, that was what Mrs. Riccobono was, but strangely enough he still found her attractive. In fact, he found her far more attractive and interesting than before. Pauline had become a real problem. Until the horrible luncheon the whole thing had been a kind of harmless dirty joke, or so he believed; but since then the very thought of her made him dizzy with desire. Her slender body and her small cone breasts and the little gap between her teeth obsessed him, and most of all when his conscious mind had no control. Awake he dreamed of Polly, asleep he dreamed of Pauline. Something was going to happen between himself and this girl, there was no doubt of it at all, it was inevitable. Twice while he was in Naomi's arms he had dreamed he was making passionate love to her and his disappointment upon awakening was unbearable.

What to do about Pauline? Nothing. There was nothing to do. But surely there was a better way to put it than "hoist cruelly with his own petard." If there was still an adult writing class, he'd put an X in the margin for that and make some such comment as: "A very tired cliché. The adjective 'cruelly' helps but doesn't redeem it." How about instead: "Living flypaper catches a tarantula!"—? Horrible. Terrible. Living flypaper, good God.

What to do about her? Or maybe the question was, *when?* The girl was demanding an answer and she'd been waiting for him that morning on the stone steps below the huge oak doors. It was grim. He couldn't get away. Before he could even speak to her she said, "Hi, I gotta talk to you," and pulled him by the hand down the dark front hallway and into an empty classroom. She was in a state, her knees were trembling and her voice was unnatural. "Listen," she said. "Tomorrow is Thursday; it's a half holiday for me but not for Nicky. Do you want to come out to the apartment? We'd have all afternoon with nobody there. He has to be at the hardware store, it would be completely safe. Do you want to come?"

Christ Almighty, thought Davenport. Of course he wanted to come, she was a pretty little girl with a sexy smile and other charms; what man wouldn't want her or at least flirt with her? But grim frank adultery in her own apartment in Nicky's bed with Nicky himself lurking in the background scratching his pimples and sharpening an Italian knife on his shoe? Maybe that was what would happen, the husband would stick a dirk in him. But even if he didn't, the whole thing was so naked, raw, nervy and downright squalid—how had he gotten involved with the goddamn girl in the first place? Well, silly question, he knew how he'd gotten involved with her, he'd been hoist on his own living flypaper, worse luck. And little Natalie, damn her, was listening at the door.

It was a grim scene and the Educational Union itself was grim. The big brick building on Delancey Street was grim and the neighborhood in which it stood was grim. Derelicts from the nearby Bowery wandered hither and yon blinking in the May sunshine; stooped peddlers with pushcarts sold iron-hard pretzels and secondhand clothes; children ran and screamed on dirty sidewalks. What a world and what a life.

The Educational Union was an old-time Lower East Side settlement house, and the people who benefited from its charity were bitterly poor, with few advantages, few opportunities and few hopes. It was a world and a life Dick had never seen before, although he knew in the abstract that it existed. The reality of the Lower East Side made his academic knowledge pale into nothing. How could various of Naomi's relatives be sentimental about it, talk of it nostalgically? The place was horrible. After his first day there Dick said to her:

"The clothes the children wear are practically rags. Most of them wash their faces and hands, but they don't bathe, I don't think so, not very often. You can smell them and it's awful, a mixture of stale piss and sweat and cooking fat; that's what the whole Lower East Side smells like. The stink of poverty, that's what it is, and it's worse than I'm describing it. It's a sweetish smell like a corpse under candles, a sick sweet smell that clings to everything. Why are your relatives sentimental about it? It's the most godawful mess I ever saw, and if Harlem is half as bad I don't know why the Negroes don't cut every white throat in this country."

And Naomi answered: "You'd be sentimental about it, too, if you'd gotten out of there. The truth is a lot of people didn't. And Harlem isn't half as bad, it's worse. I was up there. I did a laundry piece on it last year for OWI and had to throw it away. They haven't made soap yet that can wash Harlem. Rats the size of cats run all over the place. Of course they're all over New York, rats. Exterminators can't do anything about it, they have an almost uncanny intelligence, they recognize traps and poison. They're everywhere, but in Harlem they come out and bite babies, eat their noses and ears off."

Pauline Riccobono to one side, the Educational Union had proved to be an interesting and revealing experience. Dick had volunteered to work there on a part-time basis as a result of a peculiar malaise that had come upon him after publication of his first novel. On a Wednesday evening at the Samussons he had complained to his friend Victor about it. "I have a peculiar malaise," he said. "I don't feel like working, but I don't feel like doing anything else either. Nothing interests me, no prospect pleases, I am totally and abysmally bored." And Samusson said: "I have a perfect antidote. Go down to a settlement house on the Lower East Side and see life in the raw and your boredom will be cured. I know the director of the Educational Union and I'm sure he'd be delighted to have you teach writing to the children. But I guess that's a little beneath the author of a celebrated bestsmeller." It was typical of Samusson, bad, needling jokes like bestsmeller. To prove him wrong, Dick said he would do it.

The job, however, had another purpose besides merely proving Victor Samusson wrong. Richard Davenport knew more than he understood. The instinct of survival was not dead in him, it was only stunned. He sensed danger. "Here dragons reside." He had known long before he read about the suicide of James Meaghan that monsters were around. The idea of the job at the Educational Union was to avoid a deadening isolation, a removal from common human strivings, an illusion of being above and beyond it all because of a talent he'd done nothing to earn or deserve. As pointless as the work seemed, the Educational Union was no ivory tower, it was life.

And actually the work was not pointless; it was more than an effort to benefit his own soul. Of course it was ridiculous to teach writing to children, it was ridiculous to teach writing to anyone. By its nature such a thing could not be taught. But he could help them express themselves so others could comprehend them. Communication was the fundamental human faculty, the thing that made men and women human beings, nothing was more important.

Furthermore, he could encourage rare cases such as Natalie. Little fat Natalie, who looked like a sensitive pig but who had in her something beautiful. He couldn't tell her how to do it, but he could tell her when she'd done it, he could encourage her and maybe even inspire her to lift herself out of the miserable life in which she was caught. Yes, Natalie. When he read her first story he'd gone to the director and said: "There's a remarkable little girl in the class. Her name is Natalie Greenbaum. Considering her age, this story of hers is very unusual. I think she's got something. . . ."

Of course Natalie was gifted, said the director, but it would be very difficult to do anything for her. The child was hysterical and often could not control her natural functions. Bright as she was, she was paranoid and extremely hostile and on numerous occasions had attacked other children. Her home situation was very negative. She was the third of seven children and lived in an unheated, filthy railroad flat. Her father was a drunken sadistic ragpicker who twice had been jailed for incest with an older sister, a rare thing among Jews but it happened. Her mother had multiple sclerosis and could not remember to feed the children even when food was available. The wonder about Natalie was not that she had an IQ of 180 but that she was fat. Often, she had nothing to eat.

"Well, class, here we are again and a beautiful day it is, too. I hope you have some beautiful things to show me. Or at least some things. Who'll be first?"

"I got a question first," said fat little Natalie with a sly smile. "Are you Mrs. Riccobono's sweetheart?"

It was a good question, God knows. In his vulgar way he'd asked it of himself many times: "What to do about Pauline? To fuck her or not to fuck her, that is the question." He couldn't make up his mind and despite all the evidence to the contrary life somehow seemed to beckon in Pauline. The girl was not madly in love with him as Natalie kept insisting, but she was very interested. That morning when she waylaid him on the stone steps her knees were trembling and her voice was shaky; he had thought she would cry. Maybe the mutilation of Shakespeare had more meaning than appeared at first glance. "To be or not to be, to live or not to live . . ." Although what connection grimy adultery could have with survival was a mystery to ponder.

"No, Natalie, I'm not Mrs. Riccobono's sweetheart," said Dick. "Why do you ask such a silly question?"

"Well, you're with her all the time."

"Now that is an exaggeration. I'm not with her all the time."

"You were with her this morning in room five. I saw you in there talking real low. Your heads were together; it was real intimate; she had a look in her eyes. She's madly in love with you."

"Natalie, I have a wife and a little dear baby at home. Mrs. Riccobono has Mr. Riccobono. Do you get the picture?"

"Yeah, I get it. But you could still be her sweetheart on the side."

"You are shrewd beyond your years," said Dick with a pained smile. It was practically impossible to shut the little pig up once she got started. The only thing that worked consistently was to get her off on her own writing. "I really love you a lot, dear. But to answer your question in a serious way, I am sorry and I know it disappoints you, but I'm not Mrs. Riccobono's sweetheart, we're just good friends. Now class, I realize Natalie is hilarious, but cease the mad tittering and come to order. Let's see what works of the literary art we have today. How about you, Natalie, do you have anything?"

"Don't get me wrong, I don't mind. You and Mrs. Riccobono are a cute couple, everybody says so."

"You're cute yourself. But let's get off the subject of Mrs. Riccobono."

"Okay, but she really is madly in love with you. Her husband doesn't understand her, he has no ambition. That's what she tells us in history class. Nicky doesn't understand her and he has no ambition. She teaches us her own history. I bet she'd run away with you if you asked her. Too bad you have a wife already. Tch, tch, tch, tch."

"All right, Natalie, that's enough of that; you're getting annoying now. Do you have a story today?"

"Well, yeah, I do."

"Splendid, that's wonderful. What's the title and what's it about?"

"Well, it's called, 'Once a Tree, Now a Paper,' and it's about death in the North Woods."

"A great title, Natalie, and it sounds like a great theme, too. Death in the North Woods. The class and I can't wait. Will you read it, please?"

Natalie was about thirteen, fat and wore glasses. She had buckteeth, freckles, an un-Jewish uptilted nose and stringy hair that was never combed. She considered herself a woman, and there was some reason for her to do so, since already she had breasts considerably larger than those of her rival Mrs. Riccobono. Once she had bragged in class of having "a lot" of pubic hair, which naturally had created an uproar among the boys. But she was a child; her breasts were squashy and sexless. It was impossible to think of her as a sexual object.

My two girlfriends, thought Dick, Natalie and Pauline. He had a love-hate relationship with them both. But Pauline was no child and the conflict remained: what to do about her? It had all begun at the lunch, that was when he'd gotten obsessed with her. About halfway through the lunch, after aimless chitchat about the settlement house, the children, the meager pay, the depressing neighborhood, she had begun to complain about her husband and his lack of ambition, his pimples and his bad lovemaking; then she fell suddenly silent and stared motionless out of the plate-glass window of Hamburger Heaven, her long lashes lowered and her mouth pursed angrily together. Dick thought she was angry at him, that in some unknown way he had offended her; but finally she looked up directly into his eyes, took a large bite of her hamburger, chewed it carefully, swallowed, sipped her coffee in a ladylike manner and said in an unpleasant whining voice:

"Well, I've always been a lonely person because I was an orphan. I was an unhappy child and I wasn't very happy as a young girl either. And because of that sometimes I'm attracted to people. Honestly, I like my husband Nicky, he's okay, I've got nothing against him at all. But I don't see any reason to be faithful for a whole lifetime under all conditions. I mean, it's ridiculous. There's a lot of hypocrisy on this; people lie about it all the time because they think they have to. But I believe in facing the truth and who knows what problems and attractions might come up? And why is physical fidelity such a good thing? It might be a very bad thing sometimes. Of course I'm just talking theoretically, but can you imagine never screwing anybody except the person you're married to for the rest of your life? Well, maybe you can, but I can't. To me it's all a pile of crap. To me it's ridiculous. And to tell the truth I'm sexier than Nicky and that can be a headache, believe me. Maybe it's my fault, is that what you're thinking, maybe I'm too sexy? Well, I don't know about that, I don't know how other girls feel. But don't let them kid you; they want to as much as men, and some of them more. It's no secret what they want, they want to get laid, that's what they want. Of course they won't admit it, they call it love and romance and all that crap, but what they really want is to get screwed. Why not? It's only natural, it's a natural thing. And that's what it is, there's nothing else to call it. You look funny. Does the way I'm talking shock you? Well, this is the real me, the way I talk back at the Union, that isn't me, this is me. Were you fooled by my act? You have to act like that, hypocrisy is what it is. Of course you don't want to hurt anybody, that would be immoral. But Nicky and your wife wouldn't have to know if you came out to the apartment sometime when he wasn't there."

Dick couldn't have been more startled if toads and spiders had come out of her mouth. And it wasn't true she had nothing against her husband. She had plenty against him. Later she said: "Nicky's a slob, he's got no ambition at all. He don't make hardly enough wages for us to live, I've got to work, too. And I've never been strong, you got no idea how tired I get. Of course I wouldn't mind working around a home, that would be different, although I admit I'm not the best housekeeper in the world, washing dishes and making beds and all of that crap. But there's another thing. I don't want a baby right now; the idea scares me. I'm very sensitive to pain. But I couldn't have a baby if I wanted to, we couldn't afford it, and is it right for a woman to be denied having children? How can a person respect a guy like that? And he's so goddamn dumb, all he likes is drinking beer, just sitting there like a fool and drinking beer, he don't even talk to me, he's got nothing to say. And Jesus Christ, the way he makes love you wouldn't believe it, I wasn't kidding about that, he rolls on and three minutes later he rolls off and a minute after that he's snoring and spit is hanging offa his lip on the pillow. Now what kind of lover is that? Isn't a girl entitled to more than that? Like I said, a pig would be more interested. He's disgusting and he really does make me squeeze the pimples on his back, I wasn't just saying that, it's what I've got to do. He makes me do it, he lies down on his stomach on the floor and I've got to get the rubbing alcohol and kneel down and squeeze his damn pimples, and let me tell you they're nauseous. But what I've really got against him is that he's a dumb ignorant guinea who won't ever amount to a thing in this world. Nothing. And he was telling me he had a cousin in the rackets, trying to impress me. The lying fool hasn't got any cousin in the rackets, all he's got is pimples on his back and a job as a clerk in a hardware store and that's all he'll ever have. The truth is Nicky is a goddamn slob. I don't hate him or anything, but that's what he is, a slob, and I've got no respect for him. Of course he means well, and he is kind of sweet, and generous in his way. . . ."

That was when the obsession began. Awake he dreamed of Polly, asleep he dreamed of Pauline. Something was going to happen between himself and this girl, there was no doubt of it, it was inevitable. But why? Why did he want her? Why did he want the nasty and heartless little bitch?

"We are waiting breathlessly, Natalie," said Dick. "Please, favor us with your art."

"Okay," said Natalie. "Once I was a tree growing happy and minding my own business in the deep Far North Woods of Canada. Birds nested in me but I didn't mind. I held them in my tree arms of love and protected them from snakes and things. It rained on me sometimes but I liked it. I liked the snow, too. My tree arms made like a house for little animals in the winter. And then one day some cruel lumberjacks came and chopped me down. Oh, it hurt, it hurt! My bark was everywhere, my chips was all over. I lay there all cut down, my tree arms of love chopped off, I was a log. They floated me down a river and grinded me all up in a kind of soup and now I am a paper. Yes, it hurt when they grinded me up and boiled me until I died, it was terrible. But now I am a paper and people can read the news off of me. It is a good thing to do being a paper so people can read the news off of my dead body. The end."

"Natalie, you are a thundering explosion," said Dick. "Love you a lot."

WHILE ARCHIE GAGGED AND RETCHED IN THE BATH-
room, Polly stood before a cigarette-burned bureau and stared
at herself in an oval mirror that just showed the top of her light
blonde hair, she was almost too tall for it. As always, on
beholding her reflection, Polly smiled.

"Hello, beautiful," she said.

With a devil-take-the-hindmost look of snapping eyes, Polly
inhaled deeply and turned sideways the better to see the scen-
ery. A hot little thrill went through her as she responded to
the pneumatic miracle before her eyes. What a view, wow,
what terrain. She breathed even more deeply; her face was
getting slightly red from all the oxygen. But look at that, wow,
what topography. The challenge had been cast and it was not
refused. Sensual surrender glowed in her eyes, transforming
cool blue into dark velvet. A delicious evil electricity pulsed
through her, causing her behind to squeeze shut tight and her
belly button to protrude. Ooo-oo-ooh, melting, melting, her
bones themselves were melting, her belly button was going in

and out, her behind was quivering so hard that if she'd been naked the outline of it would have been a blur, ooo-oo-ooh, melting, melting, melting.

These somewhat narcissistic moods came over her. Polly's love affair with herself had been going on for years. When she played with herself it was mutual masturbation. She and herself were made for each other. The sight of herself excited her like Niagara Falls and the Grand Canyon combined, all that water pouring down and what a hole in the ground. She was sexy as an anthill, no doubt about it. However, from time to time she wondered if she would ever meet *the* man who would break through the shell she had built around herself as a result of her terrible experiences as a young child at the hands of that demanding fiend, Another Daddy. Could it be this man who seemed at the moment to be throwing up in the bathroom? Hmm-m?

Not tired of admiring herself (that was impossible) but satisfied for the moment, Polly left the mirror and sat on the edge of the bed as the bathroom door finally opened. A green-looking Archie came out, stared at her in terror, then slunk by her to the window and picked up the half-empty pint of Four Roses. Biting his almost nonexistent lower lip, he poured whisky into a jelly glass then sat in a chair by the bureau.

"Want a drink, babe?" he asked.

"No, thank you, Archie," said Polly. She stared thoughtfully at him. "Where is your aunt?"

"My aunt?"

"Yes, your aunt."

"My aunt?"

"Yes, Archie. Your aunt. Where is she, may I ask?"

"Oh, well," said Archie. He held onto the bureau so as not to fall off the chair. "Well, ah-h, the aunt's out right now."

"I see," answered Polly. She gazed solemnly at him. "Out. She does live here, however?"

"Oh, sure. Sure she lives here. She's out right now."

"Where does she sleep?" asked Polly.

"Where does she sleep? Well, where do you think she sleeps?" Archie frowned with what seemed to be a kind of irritation. At the same time, his complexion turned an even deeper shade of suet green. It was hard to believe he was wholly in his senses, the expression in his dark ratlike eyes was clouded, unsure. He had, apparently, stuck his entire head under the faucet. His hair was still wet, though it remained parted in the center and kept its smooth regular waves because of the heavy amounts of grease in it.

Polly studied him with interest. He had taken off his coat, unloosened his shirt collar and removed the red tie. He had also unbuttoned his shirtsleeves and rolled them up five or six inches above his thin hairy wrists. The undersides of his arms looked like the long slim bellies of strange fish. He wore leather suspenders.

Pretty scrawny, thought Polly. With his coat removed and the padding in the shoulders gone, he looked much more gaunt and exhausted, and his boniness too was more evident. The gray material of his trousers was shaking in the area of his knees. It seemed that at any moment he might collapse from the chair. Nevertheless, Archie's voice was ironic, confident and even a bit peevish when he finally spoke again.

"In the bed, of course," he said. "Where you think she sleeps, on the floor? Whatsamatter with you, doll, where you think she sleeps?"

"In *this* bed?" asked Polly.

"Sure," said Archie.

"And where do *you* sleep?"

"Where you think I sleep?" asked Archie. "On the floor?" He tossed up the glass of whisky and swallowed a few mouthfuls in a confident manner, a bit of brown fluid nevertheless escaping to run in a trickle down his chin. "I sleep in the bed. Where else?"

"I see," said Polly. She stared long and hard at Archie. "You and your aunt sleep there in the bed?"

"Sure. Why not?"

"No reason," said Polly. "Both of you sleep there on the bed."

"That's right. See, she don't take up much room. She's kind of old and thin like."

"I see," said Polly.

"Besides, she's a quiet sleeper." Archie cleared his throat casually. "I don't even notice she's there. She just lies there like a log on the other side. It don't bother me."

"Hmm-mm," said Polly. "And she's out now?"

"Yeh. You don't see her, do you?"

"Where did she go?"

"Where did she go," repeated Archie. It was difficult for him to think. He hardly knew what he was saying. The entire room threatened at any moment to turn upside down and capsize him onto the ceiling. It was all he could do to hold it down to normal.

"Yes, where did she go?" asked Polly quietly. She would get to the bottom of this. Firmly she stared at Archie.

"Oh, I remember," said Archie. "She went to the zoo. That's right, the zoo, sure."

"The *zoo?*" asked Polly, dignified.

"Yeah. She likes the monkeys. She goes up there all the time. They sort of know her around there. The keepers, I mean, not the monkeys. But you see it's not only the monkeys. She plays chess up there. They have those chess tables and every afternoon she goes up there to play chess and see the monkeys."

"Every afternoon, she does this?"

"Yeah."

"Every afternoon. Not in the mornings?"

"Oh, well . . . both," said Archie. "Mornings and after-

noons. Monkeys in the mornings, chess in the afternoons
. . . like that."

Polly stared. Her red lips were set in a firm line. Slowly she
walked across the faded flowery rug toward Archie, who
shrank back from her, head twisted a bit to the side and eyes
looking up imploringly. Gently, Polly laid a hand on his arm.
"Tell the truth," she said. "Has your aunt died and you just
pretend she's still here?"

"Uh," said Archie.

"Are you just carrying on a sort of *make-believe?*"

"Oh, no," said Archie. "The aunt's here. The aunt's here,
don't worry about that!" Suddenly he reached out for Polly
and she moved back a step, gracefully avoiding his clutching
hand.

"But where are her clothes?" asked Polly.

"Uh-h, I feel sick," said Archie. "Excuse-meh." Weakly he
sat in the chair by the window, a hand on his stomach. "You
get the bracelet. If that's what you're talking about, you get
it. You get the bracelet. It's on the bed and it's yours. Fifty
bucks, it's yours."

"You look really sick," said Polly.

"Well, my stomach has been bothering me," he answered
with a quaver. "It's my guts, they can't take it, they're nervous. But mainly it's my liver. That's what it is mainly, my
liver. It's four times the size of a regular liver and . . . well,
and . . . and when you get a reaction to food like I got it's
awful. Between my guts and my liver it's godawful. It's some
sort of ulcerous condition, like. Probably something malignant from the signs of it, an ulcer condition that might turn
out malignant. It's probably farther along than that and no
wonder, the kinda life I lead." Archie drank from his glass
of whisky, still holding his thin stomach. His face was a contorted mass of wrinkles as though he were in severe pain,
which at the moment he was—his stomach felt as if it were

filled with a huge basketball that somehow had worked its way up very high, so high it was about to choke him senseless.

"You really and truly do look sick," said Polly. "Maybe you ought to lie down and rest a while."

"Yeah, I ought to rest." Frowning, Archie reached into his pocket and took out a cigarette and lit it without looking up at her.

"Why don't you do that then?" asked Polly. "You look bad."

"I know. But the pill will fix me up. This is nothing worse than an ulcerous condition coming on with a swollen liver. The pills are for that. It'll be all right in about ten minutes, maybe five."

"Well, I'm sorry you're feeling poorly," said Polly. "I hope it's nothing permanent. Incidentally, were you just joking about giving me the bracelet?"

"No," said Archie. "It's yours."

"Really?" Polly walked to the bed, reached down and took the package and tore it open. As she put on the bracelet she said: "You're sweet. You really are. Giving me a bracelet and lending me twenty dollars." A bright smile came on her face. "And I'm going to hold you to that! You committed yourself and I'm not going to let you out of it!"

"Uh-h," groaned Archie. "You're not?"

"No! I'm not going to be modest even though I want to—twenty dollars, please!"

Archie groaned again. "I only got eight." His voice was an almost incomprehensible croak. "That bracelet cost fifty, not thirty. So I only got eight bucks left. I'll give you that. It's the best I can do. It's all I got."

"Eight?" said Polly, her smile fading. "Eight's all you've got? But you were going to lend me twenty. Now that isn't *fair.*" Peeved, her red lips fixed in a pout, Polly stared down at him. If there was one thing she couldn't stand, it was a man who didn't keep his word.

"I know, but the bracelet," said Archie weakly. "It cost fifty bucks, and we thought it was thirty."

"*You* thought it was thirty," said Polly. "*I* couldn't read the tag."

"Well, eight's all I got," declared Archie. Nervously he jumped up from the chair and pulled forth a thin little roll of dollar bills. "Here. Take it. Eight bucks. It's all I got and it's yours."

Polly took the money. "Thank you," she said coolly.

"Now don't be like that," said Archie. "It's all I got. I can get you the other twelve later. Tonight. I'll get it for you tonight. When I go to work. So help me, I'll get it for you. Okay?" Unsteadily, he got to his feet and half lurched, half fell toward Polly, managing somehow to grab her on the shoulder. "Now, now . . . let's go to bed. Take your clothes off, doll."

"Take my clothes off?" asked Polly. "What are you talking about? Don't you remember, you promised to treat me like a sister."

Archie felt like crying. In a feeble voice he asked: "Ain't you gonna ball me?"

"Really now, Mr. Schnerd! What a way to talk!"

Polly was not an average type because of her unusual background. She had had the unfortunate experience of falling into the power of the morally corrupt fiend, Another Daddy, and naturally had then become the prey of all the little boys in the neighborhood, her defenses having been sapped by Another Daddy and the useless Mawg, and undermined later by the young fellows around grammar school and after that the young studs of Dotesville High, it all being a bad experience for her and not healthy. But as the years passed she had learned the hard way having no other resources and not being

educated, it happening to be a coal-mining town and Another
Daddy a slight fiend, while Mawg held her; an awful experience, it was a backward area.

"You said you were going to lend me twenty dollars,"
declared Polly, "and now you hand me eight. Well, I may be
old-fashioned but I think a man should keep his word. That's
what I think, so you just keep your word and give me that
other twelve dollars."

Archie sat hunched on the edge of the bed. "I'll get it," he
said.

"Oh, sure. Next week."

"No, tonight when I go to work."

"Eh-heh, well, promises are one thing and keeping them is
something else," said Polly. She stared angrily at Archie.
"Here you come around pawing at me. Well, you want me to
be nice, sure, when you don't even love me, and you'll lend
me the money tonight or next week sometime. Oh, no. You
lend it to me right now and keep your word."

"I'll keep my word. I swear to God I'll get it for you
tonight."

"How do I know you're a musician?" asked Polly. "Just
because you say you are doesn't mean anything. No, siree!"

"What about my watch? Look, take the watch as security.
It cost two hundred and fifty bucks. See?" He held up a thin
trembling wrist to show her the watch. "You can keep this for
security. Then tonight I'll give you the twelve bucks and you
give me back the watch."

"Oh, is that so?" asked Polly. "Is that how cheap you are?
The watch is worth two fifty, but you want me to give it back
to you for nothing more than twelve? Well, I like that!" Eyes
flashing, Polly stood up. Hands on her hips, she loomed over
Archie. Her giant breasts hung over him, but they were tilted
upward and the nipple dents in her dress were aimed at a
thirty-degree angle over his shoulders. "So that's the kind of

man you are! What a nerve! You have really got a nerve, Mr. Schnerd!" Pouting, she stared down at the stricken Archie. "What has the watch got to do with the loan for my career? At least you might give it to me to keep for a while. You don't need to know what time it is and besides there are clocks all over. Give me the watch for a while, that's the least you can do."

"Okay!" said Archie "Take it!" Frenziedly, he dragged the wristwatch from his arm and handed it to her. Polly took it and studiously examined it, then held it to her ear to listen for a tick. Her expression was sullen. Archie leaned toward her and in an uncertain manner put an arm across her big shoulder.

"Stop that," said Polly. "Don't be so intimate." She got up, went to her purse on the bureau and put the watch inside. "Well, it doesn't look like much of a watch to me, but it does tick."

"It's a Longines!" screamed Archie. "That's platinum! Them's diamond chips for the hours! What are you talkin' about, that watch's worth four hundred bucks, I got it cheap for two fifty!"

Mollified slightly, Polly looked back over her shoulder at him. "Well, I just don't think you love me," she said.

"Okay, but what's that got to do with it?"

Polly blushed and hung her head. "But you said," she answered. "Before, you said . . ."

"What?" asked Archie. "What did I say?"

"Oh . . . you know."

He stared in puzzlement. "Said? When?"

"A little before, on the bed. About . . . you know."

"What? What are you talkin' about?"

Polly blushed all the more. "About . . . about," she said, then wet her lips and swallowed. "You know, about wanting me to . . . you know."

"No, I don't know. What do you mean?"

"It begins with a *b*," said Polly shyly.

"Begins with a *b?* You mean ball me, is that what you mean?"

"Yes," answered Polly, *"that."*

"Well, what the hell am I paying for?"

"Not for *that*," replied Polly in horror. "Why, I would *never*, not in a million years. You've got the wrong girl, I don't do such things. I'm sorry, but you have definitely got the wrong girl."

"We'll worry about it later. Right now, just take off your clothes."

"Take off my clothes? I couldn't do that, I'd be naked!"

"Look," said Archie in a low voice, "cut it out now. I'm warnin' you, just cut that out. I had enough. Now take off your clothes and lie down on that bed and open your legs, this is it!"

"The only way such a thing would ever be possible," said Polly calmly, "would be if a man *loved* me. If a man loved me I'd do anything for him, anything under the moon. But you don't love me, you just want me. You don't love me at all."

Archie gritted his teeth, fury shining in his eyes. His voice dropped as a barracuda-like smile came on his face. "Yes, I do," he said. "I love you, dear."

"Do you really?" asked Polly hopefully.

"Yes, I do. Sincerely."

Polly pouted. "Well, I don't see why you don't let me have that other money, then."

"Because I haven't got it!" yelled Archie.

"Ohh-hh," cried Polly, her face becoming contorted with tears. "How can you shout at me like that if you love me?"

"All right," said Archie in a hoarse half-whisper. "All right, doll, all right." Decision came into his eyes. Purposefully, he stood up and took off his leather suspenders. With a sly furious glance at Polly, he strode across the room toward the bathroom, holding his trousers with one hand. A moment later he returned, his face gray beneath the suet green. In his hand now he held a razor blade. Bitterly but with a subtle foxiness he stared at Polly, then he held up the suspenders, twisted them around and located a particular point bulging the least little bit in the leather. Carefully, foxily, he cut with the razor blade, ripping the sewed leather seam. And then hoarse with emotion he said: "I paid a shoe man a buck to fix this, aside from what it's costin' me otherwise."

Polly looked on with interest, curious to see what he was doing. As she watched, he tore apart the suspenders even more, until she could see folded and refolded a thin crisp bill.

"This is a C-note," said Archie coldly. "It's my bank account. It's more'n that, more'n a bank account. I put it here when I had some dough last year I won on a long shot, for the time when Caruso fires me outa the band, which he's gonna do sometime since he don't like me. This dough I absolutely never touch. It's for when I lose my job and it's goin' back in here, too. Y'understand?"

Polly nodded and held out her pink palm. "Let me see it," she said.

"Now I owe you twelve bucks," replied Archie, withholding the bill. "So the deal is, I give you this hundred bucks as security since you don't trust me. You already got a bracelet, eight bucks and my watch outa me, and I tell you right now I got to be crazy. But this C-note you don't get to keep. You give me this C-note back when I give you the twelve bucks, which I am gonna do tonight. Y'understand?"

"Yes," said Polly. She reached out for the green bill but it was again withdrawn.

"You agree to that?"

"All right," said Polly.

"And no more arguments, either?"

"Oh, no," said Polly. "That'll be fine."

Reluctantly Archie let her reach forward and take the money. With bitter but crafty eyes he watched her put it away in her purse—what the dumb doll didn't realize was that she was a thousand-dollar broad, he was still ahead of her. Way ahead, hundreds ahead. But would she come through? He clenched his jaw as she said:

"Well, you could let *me* keep it for you till you lose your job, then you wouldn't be tempted to spend it."

"Oh, no. Not in a million years, baby. Enough is enough, you'll give me that C-note back tonight. I ain't lettin' you outa my sight till that C-note is back where it belongs."

"All right," she answered, "though I could give you back this eight dollars you just gave me and we could let it be a loan for a hundred, then you wouldn't have to give me anymore and you'd save twelve dollars. Do you want the eight——"

"Oh, no! Nothin' doin', baby! Forget it!"

"All right. All right, that's okay. Don't worry."

"I ain't worryin'," said Archie. "We made a deal and that's it. Now. Now there's been enough talk. Let's sit down on the bed and . . . well, no more arguments. You hear me, doll, no more arguments."

"Who's arguing?" asked Polly. She sat beside him on the bed, crossed her legs, put a hand on her hip and then shrank back as he tried to embrace her. "What are you *doing?* Really, is this your idea of honor? Please, Mr. Schnerd, I don't want to slap the wine out of you, but——"

"Cut out the comedy!" yelled Archie, beside himself. "You ain't slappin' the wine outa nobody! Get your clothes off and lie down on this bed and cut out the comedy! I haddanuffa that!"

"But you don't love me," said Polly. "I couldn't do such a thing as . . . *that* . . . unless you really loved me. It . . . it wouldn't be right."

"I love you," said Archie between his teeth. "Now get off

the clothes, peel off your duds, get 'em off."

"Say that you love me again," answered Polly, "and say it *nice,* with real feeling."

"Uhh-hh-hh," said Archie. With great effort assisted by an awareness that this melon-breasted giantess could probably throttle him as easily as blowing her nose, Archie held himself in check. He took three deep breaths then smiled a sickly smile, his eyes shiny as a corpse and his gray teeth gleaming in the light of the ceiling's catvus globe. In the most sugary tone of which he was capable he said: "I . . . love . . . you."

"Well, good," said Polly. "But I don't know whether *I* love *you.* And it would be wrong for me to do *that* with a man if I didn't love him."

"I got nothin' else!" cried Archie in desperation. "You can't get nothin' more'n you got already!"

"You don't understand me. A girl has feelings. I can't do . . . *that* . . . without having feelings, Mr. Schnerd. It's very *intimate.* And it's also very *personal.* It's one of the most intimate and personal things in the world, think about that."

"I *am* thinkin' about it," said Archie. "Now take off your clothes!"

"But I'm embarrassed to be naked. I . . . I don't want you to *see* me, to look at me, to see my body all *nude. . . .*"

A whimper came from Archie as sweat ran down his nose. What to do? By degrees, that was the answer. "Okay," he said. "Okay, you're modest. Then lift up your skirt and pull down your pants."

"Oh, no," said Polly. "I might as well take off all of my clothes if I'm going to do that."

"Then take 'em off!"

"I would, except for my feelings. If my emotions were just touched, if I could feel some love for you, then I would take off . . . everything."

"All right!" said Archie. He jumped up and stumbled across

the room and yanked open a bureau drawer. His hand plunged into the drawer and drew forth a small tinted photograph in an oval frame. "This picture means more to me than anything I got! It is a picture of . . . *my mother!* Now that has gotta touch your feelings, doll, a picture of *my own mother!*"

"Well, I don't know her," said Polly.

"You couldn't, she's dead. And this is the only picture I've got of her. How about that?"

"Hmm, well," said Polly thoughtfully. Her gaze was fixed on his shirtsleeve. "Your mother, mmm. But I didn't know her."

"All the same she was my mother. She brought me into the world, doll."

"Mmm," said Polly as she stared at the tinted photograph. "Quite a family resemblance there, she has your same nose."

"And that's a solid gold frame. It's worth at least forty bucks. It's solid gold, feel how heavy it is."

"Mmm, well why don't I just keep the frame," said Polly, her eyes still fixed on his shirtsleeve, "and you keep your mother. Those are beautiful cufflinks in your shirt, just lovely. What stone is that in them?"

Archie shuddered. "Cat's-eyes," he said. A mist was before his eyes. "Cost me seventy-five dollars."

"Hmm," said Polly.

A grating sound came from Archie as he gritted his teeth. "Okay, solid gold frame of my mother's picture and the cufflinks. But that's it! Nothin' else!"

"Well, thank you, you're very sweet and generous and you mean well," said Polly, as she removed the tinted photo and put the gold frame and the cufflinks in her purse. "And it does give me a different feeling toward you, but I'm still not sure I love you . . . enough. It's so . . . intimate and personal. And I . . . I . . . well . . ."

Stir her up, thought Archie. *Arouse her, get her hot!* Quickly,

he whipped off his shirt and then his undershirt, exposing his
scrawny black-haired arms, thin sloping shoulders and sunken
rib cage. She stared blankly at him; his body seemed to have
no effect on her. Blind with desperation, he tried to put his
hairy broomstick arms around her waist. "You'll learn to love
me!" he cried. "You'll learn, doll!"

"I doubt it," said Polly, shoving him away with her right
hand and almost knocking him off the bed. "I don't think so."

"Then give me back my eight dollars, give me back the
bracelet, give me back my watch, give me back the C-note,
give me back my cat's-eye cufflinks, give me back the solid
gold frame of my mother's picture—either that or ball me!"

"You mean . . . make *love* to you," said Polly primly.

"Yeah!"

"A girl gets so tired resisting," said Polly wearily, as she
lifted her hands to the buttons of her blouse. "It's easier just
to give in rather than go through all the argument."

"Then don't argue, go on, take it off!"

"Oh, all *right*," said Polly in a sad little voice, "if *that's* what
you want. You men are all the same, it's the only thing you
can think about. Love, friendship, nice conversation mean
nothing to you, you just want to do *it*. That's all you think
about, doing *it*. Oh-h, sometimes I get disgusted."

"So do I," said Archie.

"Hmmph," said Polly with dignity, as slowly she unbuttoned and took off the white blouse. Archie's eyes bulged in
his head. She had on no bra and there they were, great
white cream mountains with bull's-eye cherries on the top.
Thousand-dollar knockers and more to come! Archie was as
paralyzed as a crab and breathless as a gargoyle; his eyes
bulged even more as she stood up and calmly unzipped her
seersucker skirt, pulled it down and off, then stepped with
slow dignity out of her white panties and there she was—stark
raw naked, all six foot three and five-eighths of her, belly

button and wheat and cherry-topped mountains and everything, a staggering and incredible one grand broad! "Go ahead and have your way with me if you must," she said, as with calm precision she planted her round plump behind on the bed, opened her legs and made a saddle. "But don't bite me."

Archie tore off the rest of his own clothes then got on the foot of the bed and crept cautiously toward her. Anxiety flowed through the core of his bones like lava. The whork wasn't up, not quite, not yet. His blood pressure, he was sure, was four hundred or more. How could flesh endure such a strain?

11

AFTER WALKING WITH PAULINE TO THE SUBWAY AND
promising to come to her apartment on the following afternoon, Dick put her out of his mind insofar as possible and took
a train uptown and met his old friend Beau St. John for coffee
at the Astoria Cafeteria in Greenwich Village.

St. John sounded like himself but he did not look like himself in the least. In the old days at the university and in Chicago
he sometimes wore outlandish things and on occasion bragged
of never bathing, but on the whole he had been rather fastidious about his dress and his person. At times, although he
wouldn't have liked the idea, he could even have been mis-
taken for a Virginia gentleman. No more. That was gone,
finished, tossed into the dustbin of history along with the
Mensheviks.

He was already in the crowded cafeteria when Dick arrived,
but for a moment Dick did not recognize him. His glance
passed over a creep in a motorman's cap and a torn English
raincoat, a vaguely familiar Village type hunched over coffee

alone at a table back by the steam trays. That silly idiot with the lace-up basketball shoes and three days' growth of blond stubble and yellow hair half to his shoulders couldn't be Beau, such conformity was beneath St. John.

"I can't believe it," said Dick. "You've gone Village."

St. John stared up at him from beneath near-albino eyebrows, his pale blue hyperthyroid eyes giving him, as always, the look of a slightly mad rooster. "My appearance is a matter of sublime indifference to me," he said. "Go get coffee. I take extra cream but leave room for sugar."

Dick resisted an impulse to say, "Go get it yourself." Years ago St. John had gotten in the habit of ordering him around. He would put a cigarette in his mouth and say, "Light me," or point to a pile of books and say, "Check those in at the library for me, you're going by there." Originally, when their friendship began, St. John had dominated Dick intellectually. He was a class ahead of him at school and he was cleverer, more articulate, he knew more. Dick considered himself lucky to have such a brilliant friend. The relationship had turned around completely since publication of Davenport's novel, but Beau persisted in giving Dick petty orders.

"You didn't leave room for sugar."

"Well, I'm sorry about that. How much goddamn sugar do you want?"

"Sit down," said Beau. "I have an idea for a movie and I'd like you to put it on your head and see if your ears stop it. Straight out of Kafka, but thrown by Louis B. Mayer. A fantastic idea, legs on it like Man O'War. It's whinnying and breaking wind already. And remember, a farting horse never tires." Dick grinned wryly. That sounded a little like the old Beau. Maybe a bit strained, but pretty much the way he used to talk before his nervous breakdown—extravagant, fanciful and deliberately gross, that was the old Beau. And a trifle crazy. Dick watched as St. John casually put not three and not four but five heaping teaspoons of sugar into his coffee. "Of course first it would be a play or possibly a novel. I think a play. It's straight out of Kafka, but, unlike the arid and sere Czech, it is wet with sentiment and that suggests a dramatic rather than a contemplative medium. Don't collapse, Richard. There is nothing wrong with sentiment. As we know from Louis B. Mayer and Walt Disney, sentiment keeps the world spinning in space. What are you looking at while I speak?"

Suddenly bored by St. John's stylized prattle, Dick was idly glancing around the crowded cafeteria, which even in midafternoon was filled with coffee drinkers and talkers. Greenwich Villagers. When Dick had first come to New York he'd been impressed by them; he had believed the romantic myth that the "bohemians" of the Village were intellectuals, artists, writers, poets, a group of brave souls defiant of convention and deaf to the siren call of materialism. He had lived down there a couple of years and he'd learned that nothing could be farther from the truth. It was a cruel thing but nearly all of them were tame and talentless nitwits playing a part. Few intellectuals, artists, writers and poets were among them, or at least few of any real ability and independence. They talked and smoked a lot and herded together in unpleasant places to sustain an illusion of superiority, that was about the gist of it. The Astoria Cafeteria was certainly unpleasant; clouds of cigarette smoke hung in the air and mingled with the smell of the steam trays as a drone of talk rose from the people at the tables like an endless melancholy grumble. Dick was as disillusioned about Greenwich Village as a betrayed lover. A girl he had known down there, a painter who did not paint, had once complained to him: "The word *bohemian* is ridiculous even though no one uses it except uptown. We have to get a better word or term, we are not bohemians, that's mid-European and nineteenth century. What we are is 'the Aware.' That is better, 'the Aware,' don't you think?" And Dick had said: "Aware of *what?* I don't think you're aware of a goddamn thing except that you've got a pussy." The girl, who did not know him very well, had been extremely insulted; and no doubt the remark was rude, but it was, Dick felt, true—all she did was get in bed with everyone in sight, except him of course, because he was such an insulting and deep-down-inside conventional bastard. "As if," she said, "there is anything wrong with being aware of my pussy! It is only a part of the human female body!" Too bad about that girl, thought Dick, as he stared through the Astoria murk and dimly heard St. John complaining about something. Too bad. She had sexy little cone-shaped breasts like Pauline, very sexy, much nicer than the girl in the sweat-shirt at the next table, who had boobs almost as big as Polly's. Too bad, too bad about that girl; he was just joking with her and she hated him a lot. Sadly, some people had no sense of humor; but life went on; the girl at the next table was pulling back her shoulders and eying him sidewise. One thing was beyond doubt, there was a lot of tail in the Village, that much could be said for it if not much more.

"Hey! Hey, you! Come out of it!"

"What?" asked Dick. "I'm sorry. I'm sorry, excuse me."

"May I ask again, what are you looking at while I speak?"

"The tits on that girl," said Dick. "But I am listening, I was following you. You were saying there's nothing wrong with sentiment, that Louis B. Mayer and Walt Disney keep the world spinning in space."

"The *sentiment* of which they are *masters* is what keeps it spinning," said Beau, as he casually put a sixth spoon of sugar into his cup. The coffee had long since slurped over into the saucer. Archimedes' principle, the eureka phenomenon. How could he drink practically pure sugar? This was a desperate wrinkle even for Beau. Maybe he was worse, not better. He supposedly had recovered from his nervous breakdown. "L.B. and Walt are merely *tools* of this force. Can you grasp that?"

"Yeah," said Dick. "What you're saying is there's no getting away from the eternal theme of love agin greed."

"Precisely. There is no other theme. Oh, it has guises. War, power, family life, that type of thing. But love agin greed underlies it all. The human heart in agonized conflict with itself, that is the universal theme of all art, and this idea of mine strikes it on the button. We should do it as a play, and I'm serious. I really am. I can't afford persiflage and flummery anymore, not since I saw those rats coming after me last year. An army of insane rats, I saw them coming after me to get my ers, a whole pack of crazed rats like a wave. A gutter had broken and they had gotten out of the sewers and they were coming after me."

"Yeah, I know," said Dick, "down Broadway."

"They covered it like you couldn't even see the curb. The little bastards wanted my ers in the worst way, that was why I climbed that telephone pole or lamppost or whatever it was they pulled me off of when they took me to Bellevue. I know it was crazy, but you'd scream too if an army of insane rats was after you. It was a rational act considering the situation. Christ, they were about to gnaw my ers to shreds. I don't mind admitting I went up that thing like a fucking monkey."

"I don't blame you," said Dick with grave seriousness. It was the least he could do, play straight for a little while anyhow. But it wasn't funny. The magic, if it had ever existed, was gone. Maybe something could be done with an army of rats but Beau wasn't doing it. The only good part was them coming out of a "broken" gutter from the sewers—had they been perhaps trapped down there so as to infuriate them? Maybe, that was interesting, but on the whole, if it was the old Beau, it wasn't much. St. John of course had never imagined that an army of rats was after his ers and he had never climbed a telephone pole or a lamppost. The drab and pathetic thing he'd done was expose himself to a young girl in the New York

Public Library. When arrested, he burst into tears and said he loved the girl and wanted to marry her. Since the girl was a total stranger, the police took him to the psychiatric ward at Bellevue and he didn't get out of the place for eight horrible days.

As if in response to the faint smile Dick could not quite suppress, Beau said: "Well, a breakdown is no joke. Maybe I didn't see rats literally, but I saw them. And I did wind up in Bellevue for seventeen horrible days."

"I thought it was eight."

"It seemed like seventeen. The first night they actually had me in a restraining sheet. And do you know there's a true story about a horrendous thing that happened to a guy in a strait-jacket in the Bellevue psychiatric ward? This is *not* bullshit, it's the truth. It *really* happened. There was this accountant as normal as you or me, as normal and healthy as anybody, except he had diabetes without knowing it. The disease didn't show but one day all of a sudden on the street he had an attack and went into diabetic coma, or half into it; he was out of his head, delirious, raving. Later he got better and came to his senses, but by then he was in a straitjacket in Bellevue in a ward full of restrained maniacs. One of the maniacs got loose and came to him in the dark. The man screamed for help at the top of his lungs, he screamed as loud as he could what was happening and begged for someone to come help him, but they ignored him of course. What happened was that the maniac bit off his penis and his balls."

"Oh, now, Beau, come on, for Christ's sake!"

"It's true! I swear to God it's true! He sued the city for a pile of money and won! It's true, Richard, I swear it. Now you'll have to admit even *I* couldn't make up a thing like that. It's true."

"I don't care if it's true or not," said Dick, as pain throbbed in his temple and the murky room blurred. He had an urge to throw his cup of coffee into St. John's smiling face. "I didn't come all the way into Manhattan to this filthy Village to watch you wallow like a hog in horror in this goddamn phony cafeteria with a motorman's cap on your head. I don't want to hear such things, I don't want to hear them."

"Listen to him," said Beau, "listen to him rave. You silly hypocrite, you yourself have written *worse* things."

"That's a lie. That's a flat, absolute lie."

"The hell it is. The only difference is that I joke about it. You write about horrible things with the solemnity of a morbid fucking owl. I myself meet horror with a smile, I toss it aside and dissipate the tension of it, whereas you lie down in it like a grave and push daisies up through it."

"Oh, go fuck off, Beau, you're an idiot. How did I ever respect you?"

"A brilliant retort. There speaks one of this country's most promising young writers. What was it *Life* magazine said about you beneath that cross-eyed picture? A startling maturity in one so young? Oh, brother, they don't know what being really startled is yet. Wait'll they read your *second* book if you ever write one. And how are you coming with it, by the way?"

All right, said Dick to himself, now just be calm, be cool, relax, that is what he wants, to provoke a reaction, and he's already succeeded. "Fine," said Dick. "It's coming great."

"Really? You've started work?"

Dick nodded; he did not quite trust himself to speak. The lie bothered him; not the lie itself but the fact of his telling it. Why did he have to lie to Beau? But it wasn't a total lie. After all, he was starting the book in the morning, that was a firm and irrevocable decision.

"Well, I just hope you don't imitate yourself," said Beau. "That's what usually happens, you know, when success comes too soon as it did in your case. Self-imitation. They liked your act so why change it? Do it all over again. Of course that's fatal, but it happens every day. The old insecurity, dank fear. Is your new book different?"

"Totally," said Dick.

"Well, good. A whole new approach, huh? Different subject matter, different theme?"

"Yes," said Dick.

"Different feeling, mood, attitude? Different technique, method, style?"

"Yes, all of those things are different. I wouldn't want to write the first book again, I really wouldn't."

"What about the philosophical attitude of it, is that different? You reacted like Aunt Tildy to my story about the maniac in Bellevue, is that an indication of a different philosophical attitude? Are you through with stark reality now? Are you going to write something sweet and nice and pretty?"

Dick felt paralyzed. It was as if he were back at the university. "Well, it's a new approach," he said.

"Okay, I'll tell you a more cheerful story about Bellevue, then. Maybe you can use it. I'll give it to you free. And this also by the way is a true story. They have a medical museum there and one of their prize exhibits is an infernal machine like you never heard of, and I do mean infernal and I do mean like you never heard of. But this is not a grim story in its overall implications. It has a sad ending but it is saturated with life force. Do you want to hear it?"

Dick clenched his teeth. It had been an error to meet with Beau. The truth was that St. John would never forgive him for writing a successful novel. "Sure," he said. "I'd love to."

"All right, in this medical museum at Bellevue, which by the way is closed to the general public, they have a fascinating infernal machine. It was invented and built by a Brooklyn Jewish lawyer aged thirty-seven, I think his name was Schwartz or something like that; let's call him Bernie Schwartz, although that isn't right. Well, Bernie Schwartz invented and

built this ingenious machine because he was what you might
call an oddball. He was not the run-of-the-mill Jewish lawyer
from Brooklyn, although he seemed to be that; he had a wife
and a couple of kids and the neighbors all liked him, they said
he was a nice quiet man. But he was creative, inventive. He
had a workshop that he kept all locked up and in that workshop he built his infernal machine. He took a Morris chair and
tore the seat out of it and made a plywood platform with an
ample hole in it; then he constructed cams and levers and that
sort of thing. Finally, with his own two hands, he lovingly
carved an enormous wooden phallus, a gigantic eighteen-inch
dong with a head on it like a tangerine. He affixed this great
dong to the cams and levers in such a way that if a large handle
like a railroad switch were pulled, it would thrust up mightily
through the hole in the seat of the Morris chair. Took a lot of
time to make, a lot of patience and fortitude, to say nothing
of creativity; but one day it was done. He sent the family to
Miami and repaired himself to the workshop and the infernal
machine. They found him a week later sitting on it, dead."

Davenport took out a cigarette and lit it. He blew smoke
into the murky air then asked: "Did the skeleton have a smile
of pleasure?"

Beau grinned. "You are down but not out, Richard," he
said. "I knew you'd dig that story. There's life in you yet and
I'm sure your next book will be just as bloodcurdling and
revolting as the first one. I was kidding you, of course, just as
you were kidding me. But what do you think about that nice
Jewish lawyer doing such a thing, what do you make of it? It
really happened. They have the infernal machine at Bellevue.
What do you think of such a thing philosophically?"

Dick hesitated. To give Beau a serious answer would only
set him off again. There was no point in saying: "There is
nothing to think of it philosophically. Some people become ill,
some people go crazy, some people destroy themselves in one

way or another." He shrugged and said: "The man was very creative. He was too creative. His creativity got out of hand and destroyed him. Creativity and madness are intimately related of course; genius is only a stone's throw from mania." An idiot answer.

"That is my very own thought and it is profound," said Beau pensively. "I was right, there *is* life in the old boy yet. Frankly I thought success was going to ruin you, Richard, but I don't think so. Creativity and madness, you surprise me a little, I didn't know you understood that. It is very, very true. Creativity can get out of hand and destroy you, that is exactly what happened to me. I had a real breakdown and it's no joke. It did something to me, I've never been the same since. It's like when the block of a car cracks and that vital fluid runs out. Oh sure, you can patch it up, weld it, stick it together with spit and a prayer and chewing gum, but it's never the same again. I was serious before about that idea for a play and a movie. I can't afford to kid around anymore. Time has run out on me, those days are gone."

"You've lost your innocence," said Dick. "The days of wine and roses are no more."

Beau frowned. "I'm serious. This is no gag. I'm broke, you know. The inheritance such as it was is gone."

"Really? You're broke?"

"I sure am. I should have loaned you money to write that book, I should have bought a share in it like a prize fighter, then I'd have the money now to write a book myself."

"What are you living on?"

Beau shrugged indifferently. "On nothing," he said. "I get reviews once in a while, this girl I know let's me sleep at her place. And frankly I'm tired of it; I'm stone broke and I need money. I can do real work later, right now I want to do something commercial. I'm really serious about this idea for a play. If you like it I want to do it with you. There are a lot of practical advantages. You have a knack for dialogue and I can construct a play. Plot is damned important in the dramatic media. It might not be so crucial in a novel, but it makes all the difference in a movie or a play. I'm good at structure and you do have an ear for dialogue, and what's more you have a little bit of a name for yourself now and that would be a big help from a practical standpoint."

Dick stared down into his empty coffee cup. A play with Beau was the last thing in the world he wanted to do. Was he serious or was this a joke? In the old days it was impossible to tell if St. John were serious or joking, he had a kind of genius for making unbelievable things sound plausible and it was a gift he had not wholly lost. "Well, I am busy on the book," he said.

"There's no rush, we could do it later, next year. I could block it out then you could do the dialogue."

"Well, I'm not sure the dialogue I write is *theatrical* dialogue," said Dick. "There's a difference."

"Not really," said Beau. "Let me tell you this idea, I think you'll go for it. You ought to, it's a very commercial idea and you didn't make any money on that book. Not real money. What'd you make, thirty-five, forty thousand dollars?"

Dick's headache was worse. "Something like that," he said.

"And you pissed away your royalties of course. Europe, Mexico, a hi-fi and some furniture, a pile of books, some clothes for Naomi, the expenses of the baby. That wasn't real money, not to any serious extent. What's forty thousand dollars, or fifty? Your success was a lot bigger than the money you made and you ought to exploit it. This is a viable idea. You'd be good for the dialogue and my main job would be structure and concept. Especially concept, and the concept of this thing is fantastic."

Maybe Beau was joking. "There's this Jewish lawyer in Brooklyn and he's very creative . . ." said Dick.

"I am *serious*, Richard. This is a very commercial idea, it would make more money than a dog could piss on. The American public would eat it up, the sentiment of it would get them. That is what is wanted in the world today: sentiment, feeling, emotion, an honest tear."

Dick suddenly saw a bleak vista of dirty snow on the sidewalks of West Chicago. Relieved, he said, "Sounds good, tell me about it." There would be no play with Beau, or rather no need to wriggle out of a play with Beau. Incredibly enough, it was the Judge Hardy idea.

"An honest tear," said Beau, "shed in the darkness of what we blindly in our ignorance call life. This thing is a natural, it can't miss. The public would stand in line in a blizzard to see it, they'd plow through snowdrifts up to their arses to get to the theater, and when they got there they'd slobber in their handkerchiefs because this story has got what they are hungry for: sentiment."

"Heart, you mean," said Dick. It had to be the Judge Hardy idea, and he'd heard it all before. Dick listened with a grave attention.

"Yes, heart. I wouldn't actually call it a tearjerker, but it will certainly tug at an audience's heartstrings, you can bet on that. Aye, you'll be hearing sniffles in the theater, me boy, that you will, begorrah, when this story gets all mellow and golden and tender and sad. And it has a great title. I call it *Three Babes on a Toot*."

A weariness came upon Davenport. *Three Babes on a Toot.* What was it before, *Three Girls Have a Ball?* No, *Three Girls on a Lark,* that was it, and somehow it wasn't very funny the second time around. Maybe it never was very funny. Dick resisted the impulse to say, "Sounds familiar."

"Now, there's this old man. Only one actor could play him, and that's that fellow that plays Judge Hardy. He's the only one who could give the role the correct interpretation. In the play he's called Grandpa Sweetheart. His name is Jasper L. Sweetheart, but they always call him Grandpa Sweetheart. Now he has these three young granddaughters, real beautiful girls, Shirley Temple would be perfect for one of them, and the story is about how they try to murder the old barstard. You see, these granddaughters are insane homicidal whoors. . . ."

It was long, long ago. Could it be Beau already had the beginning of a widower's peak? Yes, his forehead was higher, not much but a little; it was perceptibly higher on either side of the shock in the middle. He also had an unmistakable commencement of crow's-feet at the outer corners of his even more hyperthyroid pale blue eyes. The skin of his face was not the same, an unhealthy sallowness had begun to replace the fearless flush of youth. Did Beau suffer from a chronic form of the rare disease that caused children to age superswiftly and die of senility at nine?

No, his ailment was both more profound and more common than that. It was no disorder of the pituitary that afflicted him. Worse by far than any sign of departing youth was the look of fear and uncertainty in his eyes. He had the expression of a man who expected a hand to clamp without pity on his shoulder from behind. Judge Hardy being murdered, what a hollow laugh. That time was gone, gone and forgotten as the cinder-stained snow in the streets of West Chicago, gone and forgotten and never to return, as remote and distant as the little lying girl they'd been enchanted by and had fought over, the girl who'd made fools of them both and walked on to happiness ever after with a serviceman who looked like a monkey. And if romance was dead, then where was glamour, where was adventure, into what warp of time and space had they fallen? They were gone, gone and dead as the hermit in the cave with the bones of his goats and his dogs, gone as the Wisconsin playboy wasting his seed in a Hollywood whoor, gone as the beautiful Gloria with finger bruises and a bite on her perfect ass. The dream itself was dead and gone, the dream that had supported it all from Chicago to California to New York. Like a broken projector, it would flicker on for a while, soundless and blurred. The dream was gone. In his early youth, Beau St. John was all washed up. He was finished at twenty-six. No wonder he brooded about horror stories. What could be more horrible than his own situation?

What, indeed? What pit was deeper and more deadly, what fate a greater strain upon the heart and mind and soul?

A GOOD PHILOSOPHICAL QUESTION. IT GOES WITHOUT
saying that the measure of a man is the ordeal to which the
gods and his own nature subject him, but are there not limits
to the strain mere flesh can endure? Confronted by the great
whore bitch in person, what man would not feel a certain
hesitation, a certain pusillanimous limpness in the whork?
Who would not flag and falter, who would not quail and
quake, what hero ever so intrepid would not suffer a certain
shrinkage confronted by the great mother cunt of them all?

The question cannot be sensibly answered in a vacuum, and
we have a mordant history to consider here, if only briefly.
The truth must be faced that the life of Archie Schnerd was
a strain on him from the start. He was a wretched child, sickly
and irritable and repulsive, a gray little monkey-eared brat
who whined and whimpered constantly.

To be sure, he whined and whimpered because of the hate
within him. Pure, undiluted hate. His earliest memory was of
hate. He hated everyone and everything in sight, there were

no known limits to his hate. If he saw a postman, he hated letters. If he saw a taxi, he hated transportation. If he saw a loaf of bread, he hated wheat and had an urge to throw the loaf on the floor and stomp it and spit on it.

But most of all he hated people. He especially hated his father; he hated him even more than he hated his sister and almost as much as he hated his mother. And with reason. His father, or Poppa as he called him, was a choleric, nasty little man, a bully and a cheat and foul-minded as well. There were no redeeming qualities to Poppa, none.

Poppa was a louse. He tormented Archie's mother, he pinched her viciously on the arms, breasts, legs and buttocks, leaving blue and yellow marks which he called "love hickies" because mostly they occurred during lovemaking, if his obscene mounting of Momma could be called such. "I pinch Fat Pig," he said, "and give her love hickies, heh heh heh." That was the worst part, the verbal abuse. He insulted Momma constantly, calling her Fat Pig as if it were her name. He'd come home at night, hang up his hat and say: "What slop have you got to eat tonight, Fat Pig?" Or: "Hello, Fat Pig, is the garbage on the dinner table yet?"

And that was the truth, the unrepentant swine really talked that way, and he did it in a loud, strident voice so the neighbors would hear. He wanted the neighbors to hear; he liked it when they threatened to call the police. He hit one of the neighbors with a hammer and two of the other neighbors beat him up. Furthermore, he tried to rape the lame niece who lived in the house with them. The urge wasn't even wholly sincere; he wanted to seduce her mostly in order to pollute and get the best of her and make her cry and screech. "Want a love hicky?" he would say to her.

The girl was his wife's niece, Christine. If Momma didn't watch him closely, he would attack Christine. He almost got her several times before she died of meningitis at the age of seventeen, and at the funeral he scowled bitterly because (Archie was sure) she had died before he could give her some love hickies.

On the last occasion that Poppa tried to attack Christine, a few months before she became sick, Archie's mother had to hit him over the head with an electric iron to get him off her. Her panties lay in torn pieces all over everywhere and he had her pinned down on the living room couch, his bald head red as a neon sign with lewd desire. Her withered, stunted leg was hanging off to one side and her good leg was off to the side too, as if she wanted him to succeed in his goat lust. She probably did, but that didn't prevent her from complaining vociferously about it; even as she opened her legs and lifted her body up toward him, she was shrieking and weeping and flailing her arms and trying to bite his ears.

Archie and his tubercular sister witnessed this scene after Momma burst the latch on the living room door. They saw him rooting like a boar at Christine, and young and innocent as they were, they thought he was not only trying to rape her, but also attempting to break off her good leg and make her a total cripple.

Archie and his consumptive sister hoped their father would break Christine's other leg and twist it off and throw it out of the window as he had threatened to do many times. They hoped it because Christine herself was such a hateful, ill-natured and spiteful girl. She often stuck pins in little Arnold and the rail-thin Mergin when Momma was out shopping.

"Get offa-meh!" yelled Poppa.

Crunch came the iron on his bald head, and again, and again. It was wonderful. Poppa's head was all covered with blood, which showed it really *hurt* him. He fell off Christine on the floor all tangled in his trousers. Archie saw Christine without her panties. It was sickening, she had hair down there. He thought she would be like Mergin but she wasn't. Poppa didn't see her; he was crawling on the floor in a blind manner, grunting and groaning as Momma hit him with the iron. And then Christine jumped up, pulled down her dress and hit him on the head and shoulders with her high-heel shoe, her little chinless jaw gritted and her blue eyes bulging like china balls, one of them, as usual, pointing off to the side but the other focused right on him. Archie never forgot seeing Christine without her panties; that horrible sight left a mark on him for life. How could women act normal and smile and make light conversation when they were so horrible? Of course Poppa was horrible, too, so horrible Archie couldn't even think about it.

The next morning Poppa pinched both Momma and Christine, poured a pot of hot coffee on Christine's head and kicked Momma in the belly. He was very angry; he had scabs all over his bald head. Momma finally got a butcher knife and chased him out of the apartment. "I'll kill you," she said. He was a total louse.

Archie's mother, however, was worse than his father. She talked from very early morning until very late at night. She talked in a continuous, monotonous, nasal whine about how bad her husband was, how bad Christine was, how bad her children were, how bad the neighbors and the neighborhood were, how bad everything was—the city, the country, the government, foreign countries, the world itself, the hot sun in the day and the cold moon at night, the snow, the rain, the ice, the sleet, the wind, it was all bad and pain was everywhere, pain and misery; she talked on and on endlessly with rage and hysteria about her own aches and pains and torments, which were terrible and often would render her momentarily speechless, at which point she would scream, pull her hair, fall over in a heap on the floor and moan and sob with great expiring gasps, rolling her eyes and tossing her arms and legs around wildly so as to show her unwashed underwear to everyone, and then she would stagger to her feet, screech with fury and grab any handy object and throw it at whoever was in range.

Archie's sister was just as miserable and mistreated as he was and hadn't turned out much better. Unfortunately, she got over the TB and married a moronic shoe salesman, and the last Archie had heard of her she was in Boston and had had a Mongolian idiot. Thus Momma's work lived after her. She died, poor soul, of cancer. It took her two years to do so, and when she passed on she weighed forty-seven pounds. She screamed continuously for the last year and a half. Even when she was shot with five different kinds of needles, her cupid's-bow lips still formed a silent scream. It would be hard to say she enjoyed the cancer, but if anyone ever enjoyed it she was that one. Undoubtedly, in a way, it was the climax of her spiritual development, those silent cupid's-bow shrieks. As for Poppa, two months after Momma had at last passed on, he dropped dead of a heart attack and was run over by a truck.

Such was Arnold Schnerd's family background. Was it any wonder, then, that Archie's knees trembled as he crept toward Polly? True, the measure of a man is the ordeal to which fate and his own nature subject him, but there are limits. A convulsive shudder ran through Archie as he stared into the great pelvic basin and caught scent of the overpowering liquors, waxes, drippings, droppings and other nameless debris located there. From it rose a primordial miasma that hung in the air like swamp gas, coffee fumes, burned rubber, blinding ammonia, electrocuted cockroaches, pole cat juice, boiled henbane, chitterlings, octopus ink, shark fins and other odors.

"Ohhh-hh-hh," he groaned feebly, as he stared hunched and paralyzed on all fours at the great twat of twats with its valentine foundation and giant rising column thighs. The cleft was nine inches long and there was a pound of wool on it; bees, wasps and fruitflies hovered and droned angrily over it, or so it seemed in his terrified imagining. How could any mere mortal cope with such a thing? She was beyond the animal kingdom. A horse wouldn't do, a bull would be inadequate, an elephant couldn't fill her up, a whale would get lost in there. Well, as he had once heard somewhere: "It is not the size of the weapon that matters, it is the fury of the attack that counts." Archie glanced down between his spindly legs at his less-than-whalelike endowment and groaned again—far from rising to the occasion, the damnable whork had shrunk almost to nothing; the cowardly thing was shriveled practically to the size of a twenty-two short; he could barely see it.

"Ohhh-hhh-hh," groaned Archie. It was a desperate situation. How could he make a furious attack with a twenty-two short? "Ohhhh-hh-hhh!"

"In all my life I have never been treated so *cruelly* and *brutally*," said Polly. "But . . . so be it. Don't worry about my feelings, my emotions. This is what you wanted. Well, go ahead, it doesn't matter about me, my feelings don't make any difference. You men are all the same, you can only think of one thing. Go ahead, have your way with me. I don't have the strength to resist any longer, I get tired of arguing, tired of conflict. Well, that is how it is . . . tragically, that is how it is . . . I am yours."

"Ohhhh-hh-hh," groaned Archie. A blind dizziness had come upon him, his eyes were watering from the miasma. But maybe . . . maybe if he crept forward and clambered upon her, the whork would awaken? Considering the pusillanimous way it was acting, it probably wouldn't, but maybe in real proximity its manhood would awaken. The trouble was he had a long, long way to go. His head wasn't even past her tilted knees—did he have the strength?

Maybe, maybe not, but it was worth a try. Trembling like a thin rat, his scrawny buttocks clamped tight and his eyes squinched shut, Archie crept slowly forward. Don't weaken now, he said to himself, stay there in the groove Archie boy, keep pedaling, you're getting closer, stay in there boy, it's . . . it's . . . "Ohhh-hh-hh!" groaned Archie. His eyes were shut tight and his teeth were gritted so hard he could hear the roots make a cracking noise. The miasma was overwhelming, the fruitflies seemed to be droning around his face, he had to be right over it. A lewd, mad thought came to him: why not take a look? It was costing him plenty, he might as well get a good close look at what he was paying for. Yeah, yeah, a good close look, he thought madly, why not? Throwing caution to the winds, Archie opened his eyes and sure enough, there it was, inches from his nose. "Uh-h-yak!" cried Archie, as he shuddered violently from head to toe and then for a few merciful moments knew no more. Unfortunately, however, he soon revived. The drone was louder but the miasma was gone. In a dim dream he wondered where he was and why he couldn't breathe.

"Mr. Schnerd! Mr. Schnerd, now that's not normal! That's not nice! Get your nose out of me and do it normally! Do you hear me, Mr. Schnerd? Take your nose out of me. What are you, a pervert or something?"

"Ohhh-hh-hh!" groaned Archie. His head snapped back and in a reflex of terror and horror he lunged forward like a leaping frog. It was one way to get aboard but there was no strength in him. He was in the saddle but totally collapsed. And he was in it only technically, because the whork was gone, vanished. It had withdrawn into his body, and so had everything else.

"That's better, more normal," said Polly. "But I don't feel anything, not even the least bit. Where *are* you?"

Archie weakly lifted his head from between the giant cherry-topped mounds; it was hard to get his breath down there in the valley between them. "I . . . I don't feel so good," he said.

"Maybe you need stirring up," said Polly, as she put large hands on his scrawny behind and banged him against her several times. "Do you want me to stir you up?"

"Uh!" cried Archie. Suddenly he saw stars as a large, soft but massive object struck him across the side of the face and head. Before he could fully recover from the blow, he was struck on the other side of his face. It was the cherry-topped mounds, she was tilting her big shoulders from side to side and slapping him across the face and head with them. At the same time, she had a grip on his rump and was lifting him up and banging him down on her. Archie couldn't take it, he had had enough, she was rattling his brains.

"That's it!" he cried. "Th-th-that's it!"

"Already?" asked Polly. "So soon?"

"Lemme up! Lemme up!"

"I still don't feel anything. It's strange. Have you got one? Were you wounded in a war or something? Or is it just that your approach is very *subtle* . . .?"

"I said lemme up!" With a strength born of desperation, Archie crept backward off her like a crab. Thank God he hadn't actually done anything; thank God in heaven the whork had prudently shrunk back in on itself. But even so he was horribly contaminated; such a woman as this must have quadrillions of germs of all varieties. It took stern self-control for him to avoid leaping at once from the bed and rushing into the bathroom and jumping all the way from the doorway into the bathtub, clutching out at the disinfectant soap on his way down. "You're a sweet doll," he said.

"You're sweet yourself," sighed Polly. Her lashes fluttered demurely. "You made love to me so tenderly I hardly even knew you did it."

"I . . . ah-h . . . done it internal," said Archie, "like mental."

"Umm-m," said Polly. "How nice, how original." She was holding onto one of his hairy little skinny legs. Intuitively, like a woman, she sensed that he was dying to go in the bathroom and take a bath in soap and rubbing alcohol, but she wanted to delay awhile so he would stay all the longer once he finally got in there; thus she held on firmly to the leg. "Do you love me a little bit?" she asked. "A teenie-weenie little?"

"Doll," said Archie, "you're sweet."

Tears welled in Polly's eyes. "I don't know how to say it . . . but that . . . that was the . . . it was my . . . it was the first time ever. . . ."

"Uh, ah-h," said Archie. "Well, ah-h . . ." Gently, he wiggled his leg, trying to work it free, but Polly tightened her grip. Not yet.

"As far as I'm concerned, it was love at first sight," said Polly. "You have such a way about you, so experienced and everything, your charm just swept me off my feet. I thought you really did love me. It seemed so real. You said you did . . . and I . . . I believed you."

"Oh, yeah?" said Archie. Again he tried to wriggle free his leg.

Polly stared down, ashamed, at her huge naked breasts and her big naked belly. Briefly, she put her hands on the thin blondish fleece between her thighs and winced as if in pain, then lifted teary eyes to Archie, who in his own turn blinked with surprise. Was it that he was calmer now? The area down below her navel looked ordinary now, just like any doll; what had he been thinking? The hair there was skimpy, as usual with blondes. True, she was a big girl, but in that area she was more virginal-looking than most. Could it be that . . . oh, no, good God! As if reading his thought, she said in a low tone: "That really was my first time. I know you don't believe me, but I never . . . did it before. And I feel so guilty, so ashamed. You *are* going to marry me, though, aren't you?"

"What?" asked Archie. He shrank back on the bed, his mouth open. "Are you kidding? Marry you?"

"Say that you will. Say you will even if you don't mean it —just say it so I'll feel better. Say it so my conscience won't bother me so."

"Well, gee, doll," whined Archie.

"Just say it, the words, the words! As a favor to me, say it! Say you'll marry me, Archie!"

"Well, yeah, doll, sure but——"

"Oh, darling!" exclaimed Polly. "Now I feel so much better. We'll set a date soon." With a sigh she released his leg and propped on her elbow, a dreamy smile in her eyes. "I love you," she said softly, and then she lay back on the pillow. "Now, I'll sleep." With another sigh, she stretched her big legs, stretched out her big arms, took a deep breath, and as the cherry-topped mounds swelled high she shut her eyes.

"Excuse-meh," said Archie. Eyes narrowed with concentration and care, lips set tight together, he crawled over to the side of the bed, moving as gradually and carefully as one cat surveying another in an alley. But he was not moving toward romance; he was moving away from it as far as he could get. Stealthily, his big toe came out like the head of a cobra and touched down on the rug. He half-lifted a shoulder at the reclining, pleasure-satiated Polly and said, "Going in the bathroom a minute."

"Mmmmmm," said Polly dreamily, her eyes closed and a little smile playing on her red lips.

Archie tiptoed across the room, entered the bathroom, shut the door, locked it and crept up to the tub and turned on the hot and cold faucets full force; then he steadied himself, a hand over his eyes. A low keening moan came from him. Usually at moments such as this he said such things as, "Ugh, yuck, no more dames for me!" But now he was beyond words because he hadn't *had* any dame, internal-like or mental-like or any other way; the cowardly whork had haired over, and it was still somewhere deep inside his abdomen, hiding.

Archie staggered toward the medicine chest. The bathroom was turning around and around; his mouth and throat were dry as leather, his belly was a core of pain and the entire length of his nose was hot and tingling as if it had been dipped in brimstone. Holding the nose in the fingers of one hand like an ocarina, he somehow got to the medicine chest and splashed alcohol and athlete's foot liniment all over it; then he swallowed four sleeping pills and another of the large horse capsules for his stomach. On top of it all, he gulped down a small bottle of milk of magnesia to coat and calm the stomach, then he licked his lips and tried to concentrate on the disinfectant soap.

Not that any of it would do any good, because this was too much, it was just too much. There he had her, a thousand-dollar broad at a bargain, and the whork had haired over. Enough, more than enough! Archie had determined that he would drown himself in the tub, just hold his head under and drown, drown, drown. Panting, he stuck his hand in the water and adjusted the knobs to make it a bit cooler; he might as well be comfortable as he drowned.

Out of this world, gone! Tub brimful, he shut it off and stepped into the water, wincing because it was still very hot. But he sank down with a grateful groan. The end would come soon now. Knocked back and forth by the sleeping pills and the horse capsule, Archie stared dull-eyed into space and then with a resigned sigh shut his eyes and slid down, down, down till the hot water flowed over his head—and thus, tragically, Arnold "Archie" Schnerd went to a better world. So he thought and believed.

Peace at last! There he was, head under the water and knobby knees sticking up in the cold air. Gone from this ghastly world. He had been beaten and betrayed once too often. Lights inspired by the pills danced in his dying brain.

When he got out to the bedroom half an hour later, pink

from the hot water and in a drugged haze but fully alive despite repeated efforts to duck his head back under the water each time he came up for air, Archie felt much better. In fact, he not only felt better, he felt strangely optimistic. He felt even better and even more optimistic when he saw that Polly and her clothes, her hatbox and her purse, all were gone.

Archie felt definitely better. The whork had returned; the wise little fellow had survived to fight again another day. All two and a quarter inches of it dangled there. Of course it measured more, rampant. And fight again it would! The whore bitch had won a skirmish, not a war. True, on this occasion the whork, in nervous overcaution, had fled the field; but there was always tomorrow, and unto tomorrow the day thereof was sufficient.

A skirmish, not a war, thought Archie as he hunched beneath the catvus light on the ceiling and poured himself a slug of the remnants of the pint of Four Roses, which was about all the whore bitch had left him. But it was not a total rout. After all, he'd fucked her with his nose, there was that; he'd had her proboscis-wise. And next time, up and at her with the whork! "I'll get her yet," said Archie with a thin smile of maniacal ambition undiminished.

13

ST. JOHN'S HEART WAS NOT IN IT, HIS VOICE TRAILED
off and his lips bit together in a line. Dick knew the look well.
Beau had been impossible as a small child, and a black nurse
in Louisiana had called him "Bait Mouth" because of it. The
bitten look was an expression of anger at rejection, and in the
old days was an invariable portent of vulgarity and grossness
to come, a sign of an emotional shunt from whatever the
subject might be to a particular kind of male talk that Dick
didn't like but felt he couldn't object to without being a pan-
tywaist.

Dick himself sometimes talked like that; a little vulgarity
was good for the soul and gave a sharper appreciation of
butterflies and daffodils. But Beau carried it to an intolerable
extreme, the son of a bitch did it not out of a philosophical
regard for candor or a dislike for euphemism but just to be
annoying, a pest, a schlub. Soon now old "Bait Mouth" would
start talking about buggering chickens "to get that dying shudder," or how in the Dark Ages people believed that cords

filled with female ejaculate ran from a woman's breasts so she could "fire her gun" when screwed, or how it was a scientific fact that young girls farted more than women and women farted more than men, or some such damn thing no one wanted to know about or listen to. The explanation was simple. It had pissed him off because Dick hadn't liked the Judge Hardy gag. His act had fallen flat and he couldn't stand it.

". . . well, to hell with it. I thought that dab of floating shite from the past would amuse you, but you look like you've got a pickle up your ass. Do you know that's what they do in Corsica, the bandits, if you don't pay the ransom right away? They don't want to kill you but they want to discourage you, so they stick an enormous pickle up your ass. Too bad that Brooklyn lawyer wasn't captured by them, he would have liked it. But let's get down to the purpose of this meeting. How about reading a story I've written?"

"Okay," said Dick. Eyes shut, he rubbed his aching forehead; the smoke and noise in the Astoria seemed worse. "But can't we get out of this crummy joint? The place gives me a headache. Let's go sit on a bench in Washington Square and I'll read your story."

"Well, it's a fragment more than it is a story. It isn't important, it's just a thing I wrote. But what I do with language in it seems to me kind of interesting. Washington Square? It's a little cold, it's a little windy."

"It isn't cold and it isn't windy, it's a perfect day."

"Well, all right, all right, we'll go to Washington Square. But this isn't all that much of an effort, this story, I want you to realize that ahead of time. But frankly I think it is a kind of a breakthrough. What I want to do with prose is give it a physical reality, to give words themselves a concrete existence, to flesh them like life itself. When I write 'table' I want the surrounding context to be such that the word *is a table*. When I describe an arch I want the words themselves *to form an arch*.

When I refer to an orange I want the reader practically to be able *to eat the orange.* Do you understand what I mean?"

"Well, not exactly. Let's go over to the park and I'll read the story."

"It's a fragment, not a story. You look peaked; is anything bothering you? What's eating on you? Do you have any problems?"

"Me, problems?"

"Yeah, you hardly even look at me, your mind is somewhere else."

"Well, I was looking at that girl at the next table with the sweatshirt."

"No, no, you're not looking at that girl, she doesn't interest you at all. What's bothering you, Richard?"

Dick sighed in gloom. "I didn't know it showed," he said. "To tell the truth, I have a headache not just from the Astoria. I've been trying not to think about it, but to tell the truth I do have a problem and it's driving me slightly crazy. There's this girl down at the Educational Union, a very sexy little thing, and I said I would meet her at her apartment tomorrow when her husband isn't home. I told her I'd come, I said I'd meet her there at two o'clock. And I don't think I can get out of it. If I go there I'll be unfaithful to Naomi."

"Sometimes your naïveté astonishes me. So go ahead and be unfaithful to Naomi. What is so horrible about that? That's not the end of the world."

"Of course it's not the end of the world, but . . . well, I don't especially want to be unfaithful to Naomi, she doesn't deserve it. Besides, I don't really want this girl. She's attractive enough; in fact she's pretty—slender, curly black hair, a sexy little figure, very nice legs, a sweet smile. And from what she says she's a very sexy girl; she likes nothing better than bed play. You'd go for her, any man would, but unfortunately she's a vulgar little bitch."

"The very thought of her stirs me up," said Beau. "If you don't want her, give her to me. For some reason I've been feeling very horny lately. I've been screwing the ears off of Lois, this girl I'm staying with; she can hardly walk. And you say this girl is a vulgar little bitch, huh? Sometimes that's the sexiest kind. What's her name?"

"Pauline, and you don't realize what a little bitch she is. She's a brainless, heartless, cold-blooded little slut. She's loaded with nasty hostility and all kinds of unpleasant things. I can't get over the crass way she talked to me. Maybe I shouldn't be shocked, maybe it's the kettle calling the pot black. I was pretty flirty myself and said some raunchy thing to her, but I was appalled listening to that girl. And the strange thing is that the way she talked made me want her all the more. I don't understand it. The girl kind of obsesses me, and so does her dreamself Polly. . . ."

"Let's go to the park and you can read the fragment," said Beau. "You might as well, but bear in mind that it is a fragment. . . ."

St. John wasn't interested in Pauline or Polly. He'd gotten onto the subject only out of anxiety at the prospect of having his story read. For once he hadn't gotten off on buggering chickens or being whipped with a dried rhinoceros penis; he had more pressing things on his mind. As annoying and even revolting as Beau could be, Dick couldn't help but feel sorry for him. His face was sallow with anxiety and his hands were trembling. St. John's cocky egotism was a transparent pose; he had no confidence in himself at all. The hunger in him was transparent, too, and it was pitiful.

"Aha, now I've got you," said Beau. "This monster here, queen to queen four. Watch out for that long diagonal."

And for *what*, what in the hell was the point? What did it amount to, what did it matter, who cared? It was an illusion of significance, that was all. "Published novelist." So what?

Only a handful of people read the silly books, anyhow. And suppose more people did read them, suppose by some fluke this or that damn fool could tell a story, what then? So what? None of it made any sense; bullfighting is horseshit.

"I have the power and the glory," said Beau. "You are mine, you belong to me. There's no play in your position, Archie. If you don't give up your queen you're in a mating net."

On the way to Washington Square, St. John insisted on buying a cheap little dollar ninety-eight chess set on Eighth Street. He and Dick sat hunched over the pieces, which were tiny and made of badly cast plastic. The day still was beautiful, and quite a few people were in the park enjoying the rare perfect weather. Beau was very good at chess. Dick could never come even close to beating him.

"Hmm, how about knight checks?"

"You *potzer!* Are you blind? Bishop takes."

A dumb idea, the bishop was indeed pointing that way. "Mmm," said Dick, "yeah, that's pointless. How about queen takes pawn?"

"Make a move, Archie. Don't ask me."

"Seriously, what's wrong with queen takes pawn?"

"Go ahead, make the move."

"I don't see anything wrong with it. I just get your pawn, then you can't capture the queen."

"Make the move."

"All right. All right, I'll make it."

"Potzer! You really are that guy Archie. What was it you said he could do? Play 'The Flight of the Bumblebee'?"

"You're all wet about that. There's another guy, he isn't even the hero."

"If there's another guy, he isn't you. Let's exercise this monster. Rook to king eight."

"Hmmp," said Dick.

"Didn't I tell you I have the power and the glory? You are mine."

"Hmmp. King up, bishop checks, pawn interposes and then queen mates next. You were right. I'm no better at this game than Naomi—omigod, that reminds me, I've got to call her. Get us a seat on a bench, I'll be right back."

"Hey, where are you going?"

"I've got to phone Naomi. Get us a bench."

Exasperated with himself, Dick hurried to the building in which Eleanor Roosevelt was rumored to have an apartment. No phone booth there, and none in the next apartment building either. He finally found a phone a block away in the Café Granados, which was owned and managed by a man named Larry whom he knew. A good place to eat, the Granados, and it had a phone.

"I'm sorry," said Dick, when Naomi answered. "Hines told me you wanted me to call, but I got distracted, I forgot. What's wrong?"

"Nothing's wrong. I just wanted you to bring some wine for dinner tonight, something nice."

Dick pursed his lips. He and Naomi practically never drank; he didn't like the effect of it. "Why wine for dinner?" he asked.

"I was afraid you forgot, I meant to remind you. They're coming to dinner, Nathan Hammerfield and his wife."

"Oh, shit," said Davenport. "That's all I need, another goddamned writer. I'm having enough trouble with Beau."

"Well, we can't disinvite them. Will you get the wine?"

"Are you sure it's tonight? I thought it was tomorrow."

"No, it's Wednesday. Don't you remember? We were going to take them to the Samussons' afterwards."

"Oh, Christ. I don't want to talk to that guy, he's too doctrinaire. Old-hat Stalinism and of all things Henry Wallace. Jesus Christ, I don't want to talk to him."

"You wanted him to come, it was your idea, you invited him."

"I know, but I'm having a bad day. Beau is driving me crazy; he's worse, not better. I've got to read his story and I don't know what in hell I'm going to say about it if it's bad. But all right, I'll bring wine. What are you having to eat?"

"I told you, we agreed, fresh roast ham. That'll be all right, I'm sure; he couldn't be religious. I'm sure he isn't religious. Get a red wine."

As he walked back to the chess tables, Dick's headache returned. Nathan Hammerfield was a young novelist like himself and he had had a very big success with a war book. Dick had met him at a party given by *Life* magazine and he had liked him. Hammerfield seemed less pretentious than most of the writers at the *Life* party; he was a serious, quiet young man with a dry sense of humor and a self-deprecating manner that took the edge off his apparent ambition. Dick also had liked the war book, a very readable and inventive story that had kept him up till late at night. The only thing he hadn't liked about the book was its implied Marxist politics. But it was a first novel; that didn't matter; the important thing was that Hammerfield had great narrative ability and enormous verbal powers. He really could write like a streak. It would be very interesting to see how he was reacting to his great success.

It was a good idea to know the writers of one's generation. It would be interesting to talk to Hammerfield, and his coming to dinner wasn't the real reason for Dick's headache. On the way to Washington Square he had told Beau at some length about Pauline and his fantasy of her dreamself Polly. Beau had listened with a knowing smile and then had said: "Very amusing. Obviously you are Archie. Are you *sure* you've started that new novel, Richard? When are you going to stop kidding yourself and realize you need psychiatric help?" And then during the chess game he'd kept calling him Archie. Samusson had said the same damn thing a week ago at the end of one of the Wednesday nights. Could it be true? Was Archie Schnerd some kind of ridiculous subconscious projection of himself? Impossible. Archie was not even the hero and was never meant to be; the hero was waiting in the wings, darkly, with stainless steel teeth filed to points.

"Well, you took long enough," said Beau. "I thought you had headed for the hills; I thought you'd gone; I thought you'd taken a powder to China rather than read this story. Really, it *isn't* that bad, Richard. You are going to be surprised. I'm not the total idiot you believe me to be. I wasn't going to tell you this, but I will. No. No . . . I won't. You just read it, form your opinion, let's see what kind of judgment you've got."

Beau was depressing, very depressing, but fortunately Dick had an excuse to get away. "I really don't have much time, Beau. Naomi called to remind me people are coming to dinner tonight. I've got to go get wine, and before that have drinks with Pat and her new boyfriend."

"No one is coming to dinner; you just don't want to read the story."

"That isn't true; people are really coming. Nathan Hammerfield and his wife, Leah."

For a moment Beau stared emptily at him, then a small shock came in his eyes. "Nathan Hammerfield?" he asked. "The writer? You know him?"

"Yes, I know him. Why's that such a surprise to you? It would figure that I would know him, wouldn't it?"

Beau bit his lips together in a line. "Who's surprised? I don't care who you know, and if you ask me the guy's a bum. I'm not impressed with a bestseller like that; he's a commercial hack. If I couldn't do any better I'd cut my throat. What interests me is an altogether different thing, a thing that has nothing at all to do with the likes of Nathan Hammerfield. He can kiss my ass and so can you if you value what he stands for. I am not impressed, Richard."

Beau was very, *very* depressing. The only way to get out of it was to read the story and make some polite, encouraging comment—if, that is, St. John would ever let him see it. "I really have to go soon, Beau, you'd better let me have the story if you want me to read it. Pat expects me. I've got to meet her new boyfriend Charles; he's proved to be an important lover and might even be *the answer.* I can't be late. Pat's been looking for *the answer* for years and Charles is very promising even though he's bald and shy."

St. John had the "Bait Mouth" expression and his eyes were narrowed. "I once screwed a bald girl," he said. "She was completely bald, wore a wig; in fact, didn't have a single hair on her entire body. Her name was Anne; she'd had tetanus or scarlet fever or something as a child and it killed every last follicle on her. There wasn't even a trace of a hair on that girl *any*where. It was very interesting, made her seem very *naked.*"

"Yeah, I guess it would. Anyhow this guy Charles is bald and I've got to meet him. Patricia even hinted she might marry him."

"God help him, then; that sister of yours is a castrating harpy if I ever saw one. With an upbringing like she gave you, no wonder you're having trouble writing your second book. But let's don't get off on your sister. I was telling you about Anne. You know it was sexy, that girl, the nakedness of her hairlessness. I had an awful time luring her into bed and when I did it was all hell getting off her panties. She held onto them for dear life. She thought it was unattractive, the bald twat. Do you know how I convinced her it wasn't?"

"No," said Dick.

"Well, I told her that in ancient Rome they used to pluck it. And that's a fact, they did. They used to pluck it and then fuck it. When I told her that she took her panties off, it reassured her."

Dick glanced at his wristwatch. "Good God," he said. "It's almost five, what happened to the afternoon?"

"Those Romans knew a thing or two. A bare twat *is* very sexy. Of course they're sexy with hair on them, too. This girl I'm staying with now is just the opposite of Anne; she's got a bush on her you wouldn't believe. Do you know how to tell when a girl has a big bush? There's a scientific way; do you know what it is?"

"Take her pants off," said Dick.

"No, I mean without taking her pants off. There's a way to tell, a scientific way, do you know what it is?"

"No," said Dick.

"Her eyebrows. If she has thick eyebrows, she's got a big bush. It never fails. Remember that. If you see a girl or a woman with thick eyebrows, you can be sure she's got pubic hair galore."

"Well, that's good to know. I don't know what point there is in knowing it, but it's good to know."

"Don't you ever undress women mentally?" asked Beau. "What are you, an unnatural creep? It's good to know so you can form a picture of what they look like naked. And I'm telling you, thick eyebrows mean a hairy twat. Now take Lois for instance, this girl I'm with, she has real dense, thick eyebrows and more pubic hair than you can shake a stick at; it grows all the way up to her navel. I swear to God the hairs on her are four and five inches long and thick as a mat. You can hardly get in her. You have to comb it to fuck her. And it's all because of her eyebrows."

Dick sighed. The conversation was not helping his headache. He glanced again at his watch and said: "I'm going to be late at Pat's if I don't leave."

"I'll say this for Lois, though, she's a good piece of ass once you get past the bush. Just takes a little persistence, that's all, and a comb. You have to part it in the middle, you know, make an entry. Would you like to meet her? I'll call her, she'll come over. I'm sure she'll be thrilled; she's read your damned book."

"Beau," said Dick, "making this girl look silly is not going to make your story any better. It's not going to make it any better and it's not going to make it any worse. Now do you want me to read it or not?"

"I'm not going to show you the story," said Beau. "I'm going to show you something else, something that in a way is more important than the story. It's only a fragment, true, but it's what I'm talking about when I speak of giving words a physical reality. It goes beyond the story. And I'll tell you this, I'll tell you this much. Gil read it and said it was very interesting. And Flight read it; I showed it to him yesterday evening. He's printing a long essay of mine you know, on Kafka."

Dick suppressed another weary sigh. There *was* no story. St. John had written a page or two of something, that was all. It wasn't surprising; for a long time Beau had suffered from a terrific writing block. He would sit at the typewriter for hours on end and stare emptily at it, unable to write a word. "Well, okay," said Dick. "Let me see it and I'll read it, then I've really got to go."

"It's only a fragment," said Beau as he pulled a sheet of paper from his raincoat. "But I think it does something with language. Not much, but a little. It's more the principle than anything."

"Okay," said Dick. He took the sheet of typewriter paper, glanced at it and looked back at Beau. "But there's almost nothing here. Is this the complete thing?"

"You son of a bitch, I said it was a fragment. The point is, it's compressed. There's more in that paragraph than in twenty pages of ordinary writing; every word is physical, material, concrete. But I don't attach too much importance to it, it's just a fragment, no more. However, do me a favor. Before you comment, read it *twice.*"

Dick hardly expected miracles; he had a feeling disaster was at hand. Slightly ill, he said, "All right," then looked again at the sheet of paper and saw a title at the top of the page: "The Howl of the Asphalt." Hmp, a pretty foolish title. How could asphalt howl and what possible significance could such a thought have? Well, maybe in the sense of the teeming city or something, a little poetic license. Dick nodded to himself and then read the text of Beau's fragment:

"The asphalt howls. It is a reechoing charlatan (buffoon) closed of the Street Road with no fourteen tasty pleasing, truly, tear gas, then perhaps fishery, *there,* it is a repulsive piece of merchandise and the sequined harlequin is rancid, a foul breath and no fair flower and this is how the soil sears but a cat can look at a king, doubt it not, doubt it never, the street reeks and the asphalt roars, it reeks and it roars, it reeks and it roars, the asphalt of the street reeks and it roars, etc., etc."

Incredible. Was St. John joking, was it a gag? No, he was serious. Dick kept his head down over the page as he pretended to read the fragment twice. He had no idea on earth how to reply. Beau had not gotten over his nervous breakdown; he was right in the middle of it, and he was worse. What could he say to him, what polite and evasive remarks could he make about such a piece of writing as that? As he stared down at the page in his hand, he remembered the comment he had made earlier in the day on another writing effort:

"That is very good, Natalie. Very, very good. 'Once a Tree, Now a Paper' is a damn good story. Notice, class, how simply and clearly Natalie tells this tale of woe, self-sacrifice and spiritual triumph in the Far North Woods. That is the secret of writing, make it simple, make it clear and make it true. Write what you mean and no more and write it from the heart. Of course you've got to have a heart to write from it, but our authoress here has got one. 'Once a Tree, Now a Paper' is a classic of its type. Natalie, you are beautiful."

Dick kept his gaze down on the sheet of paper. It wouldn't hurt to pretend to read it three times and he didn't want to look up, he couldn't, it was impossible to face what he knew he would see in Beau's eyes. Of course he'd seen it already. The basketball shoes, torn raincoat and motorman's cap made perfect sense. And Beau knew himself. Fluid running out of a cracked block was not a bad comparison at all, except maybe there was no fluid there to begin with. Something vital had been taken away from Beau, something he thought he owned but perhaps had never had in the first place.

"Well, of course as you say it's a fragment. And . . . and it's more poetry than prose. The language is very vivid. I like that part, 'this is how the soil sears,' it's . . . evocative. And the 'sequined harlequin.' But actually poetry is not my forte, Beau, I'm kind of a philistine about it."

"Don't give me that shit!" said Beau. "All your stuff is poetry; it's the only thing you know how to do!"

"No, no, that isn't true. I have no poetic gift at all. I don't understand poetry, I never did."

"Look, you bastard, either you smell and hear the asphalt or you *don't!*"

"Well . . . well, I . . . yes, yes, I think I see what you mean. The incongruities, the harsh contradictions . . ."

"Oh, fuck off," said Beau. "I'd rather hear you talk about that goddamn little girl you want to screw if that's all you can say. Go see your castrating sister, go have dinner with Nathan Hammerfield, but first tell me more about that damned little girl you've been talking about all afternoon, that goddamned little insignificant *cunt* who is more important than something serious I've written. That's all you can tell me, okay, you are some friend, you are sure some friend. . . ."

What to say? Beau was right, polite words about poetry wouldn't help. The truth was obvious and there was no justice in it, no mercy, no pity. It was not by chance he'd thought of

Natalie Greenbaum. She was a child; Natalie was a fat and ugly little girl and lived in a slum; but she was a writer. To her it was given and to Beau it was given not. The prophet had said it all in the Bible: "For to him who has will more be given; and from him who has not, even what he has will be taken away."

Cruel words, cruel truth, a fate to be dreaded, a fate the fear of which had put James Meaghan dead on a cold marble slab. Who was he himself to tell St. John his effort was a senseless and meaningless word salad, a sample of hebephrenic gibberish that would never bring sunrise to the world? Fearful liar and philandering procrastinator, who was he to talk? The prophet Mark had said it all: "*. . . and from him who has not, even what he has will be taken away.*"

To express the essence in gridiron terminology,
it was a desperate situation. The team was backed up all the
way to the one-inch line and it was fourth down and thirty-two
to go. The highly touted Arch Schnerd had fumbled the ball
three times in succession and was out there sobbing in his
hands and jumping up and down on his helmet. It didn't seem
that he could go on, the kid had lost his nerve, he was cracking
up.

Was it too late, was the game down the drain? The coach
chewed his cigar and paced slowly back and forth, head bowed
and hands clasped behind him as the stands screamed for
blood. Finally, the decision was made. He lifted his arm and
pointed a rigid digit. Quietly, he said: "Get in there, Nick."

Intoxicated by the ease of her triumph over Arnold
Schnerd, who in a larger sense was for her merely an obscure
cipher, Polly made haste to depart from the frumpy Caravan
Hotel with her hundred and eight dollars, her cat's-eye cufflinks, her platinum diamond-studded wristwatch, her bracelet

of filled gold and semiprecious amethyst, and the solid gold frame of Momma Schnerd's picture. She dressed in efficient silence, her ear tuned to the music of running water in the bathroom. Then she gathered up her spoils, tiptoed across the sleazy room and, with a blue-eyed stare at the catvus globe o'erhead, she traipsed into the glum corridor and walked away unworried on her high-heel pumps to the elevator, rang the bell and waited for sour old Pop to come up. As she waited she smiled. Before her stretched a vista of conquest all easy and simple and profitable.

Little did the whore bitch know, however. The months that followed were neither easy, simple nor profitable. The best that can be said for those terrible months was that they were broadening.

For then began her ordeal.

One of the unlikely places to which Polly wandered during her first week in New York was the Hotel Seamus. She went there initially simply because she happened to see the hotel while out for a walk. The idea occurred to her to stroll inside and see what the place was like. She did so. She sat on a sofa in the lobby, put a cigarette into her long black holder, smoked it with quiet dignity, then got up and left.

Her recollection of the Hotel Seamus subsequently was rather vague and dim. She remembered a large and old-fashioned lobby with ancient stuffed furniture and oil paintings on the walls. She also remembered a number of old ladies dressed in out-of-date clothes and a few elderly gentlemen. The clientele of the Seamus seemed largely limited to guests of an older generation and they seemed to live at the hotel on a regular basis.

The Seamus had an established, quiet, ultrarespectable atmosphere, a Boston mood, though at the same time it was a bit musty, a trifle frayed at the cuffs and seedy despite the ballroom lobby and the sweeping marble staircases that ascended to the mezzanine floor in twin curves around the open gilded grillwork of the four aged hydraulic elevators. Cupids adorned the ceiling, floating there in bas-relief in the company of painted sexless angels on a blue sky now cracked and long since faded to gray. The huge rug on the marble floor was worn thin in numerous places; large, urnlike polished brass spittoons stood here and there on rubber mats. It was a somnolent environment.

Deep within the ancient bowels of this old hotel, hidden far from the eyes of the elderly ladies and gentlemen who lived there so quietly, and concealed even from other employees of the hotel as well as the management, Nicholas Lordgod Sampson had his domain. It was here, hidden with the greatest skill and ingenuity, that the Unknown King of Harlem reigned with brutal ruthlessness over his three slave subjects —the bright and cheerful Suzette, the submissive meek Wan Lo, and the tormented Vasentesenka.

Black, yellow and brown. Nick had recently cut the throat of Running Moose, his other subject. That had occurred in a moment of fury. He had such moments. The beautiful red-skinned Running Moose had crossed him, a crime he could not forget or forgive, so he had seized his razor and backed her in a corner and neatly lopped off her head with one powerful stroke of his arm as Suzette, Wan Lo and Vasentesenka stood by and watched half-fainting with horror.

The story of this huge jet monster and his crimes, however, would fill many volumes in itself. It is his effect and influence on the life and career of Polly Dawn that is of primary concern. The career of the unknown King of Harlem with its incredible ups and downs might someday, however, merit a page or two in a sociological history of mid-twentieth-century America, and a condensed résumé of his hair-raising exploits will be provided. There certainly have been few careers more horrifying or anthropologically significant than that of this

Destroyer of the White Race, the Unknown King of Harlem, "Black Nick" Sampson, the notorious monster wanted for murder in many different states, for white slavery on numerous counts by both the federal government and by local governments—and these were only his more *obvious* crimes. A dark type both spiritually and physically. More about this fiend later for scholars.

Polly fell into his meshes by accident. It was really a matter of the spider and the fly, except that this time Polly was the fly and not the spider. Well, she was a fly until, thanks to Mr. Gaylord and the false Whork, she got him with her hatpin and lobotomized him. But that is getting ahead of events. It was pure chance (seemingly) that she happened to wander into the Seamus lobby that afternoon on a warm and beautiful day in May. She'd been out for a stroll in her midtown habitat. At this time, she was living in a rather hoity-toity furnished suite in a rooming house in the Murray Hill district not far below Forty-second Street, the street of dreams and song.

First she had strolled over to Fifth Avenue and window-shopped a bit. This remained a favorite pastime of hers, although in the last week she had been to buy, or to arrange to have bought for her, quite a few clothes and trinkets of her own. She had made an exuberant beginning in New York, no doubt about it. But she still enjoyed looking in the windows and imagining that she owned all the things therein. It gave her the thrill of ownership to do this.

So, on this afternoon she wandered along, not particularly looking for business though not averse to it if it should come up. She strolled to Fortieth Street and turned across Fifth Avenue toward the New York Public Library. Several times previously she had gone into the library but had found poor pickings there, so this time she did not stop; she wandered on, strolling slowly past the park toward Sixth Avenue, on past the pigeon feeders and the young hand-holding couples, the newspaper readers and those occupants of the big city park benches who sit blank-faced and motionless in an obtuse, semi-paralyzed stupor.

A few of the people in the park glanced up at her as she went by. She had on a new outfit, a summery silk dress and a small white hat with a tiny matching white cloth purse. Her shoes also were white. The dress fit her tightly about the midsection and it had a low-cut bosom, but from the waist down it was full and graceful. The silk had a green and black willow pattern with red buttercups. Her blonde hair was set high on her head, braided in behind and combed back from her forehead in fluffs so that the hat seemed to be resting on soft goldilock waves. All in all Polly looked very fetching and quite dignified. It was true that anyone approaching her from the front would have perceived the large soft V of her bosom, due to the low-cut dress and the almost British cleavage that resulted —but of itself this was not too extraordinary in modern times, although of course it was sexy and some people would have found the effect lascivious.

In her innocence, Polly thought that all of Broadway was like the Broadway-type Broadway. She was naively unaware that Broadway was also a street and that the famous Broadway part of it extended only from Forty-second to Fifty-ninth. Above this area, unbeknownst to her, it became something quite different. Central Park was up there—no, it wasn't, that was Sixth Avenue, and Seventh, or rather Seventh including Fifth, which ran along it—and that wasn't Broadway, not really, and below those bounds it was also different, with no theater flavor.

However, the area between Forty-second and Thirty-ninth was not entirely different from that above it, not entirely. A theater or two, an opera house thrown in there somewhere, a number of bars and tinkly honky-tonks, it had the same mood, same thing, no difference. And so she didn't notice the change as she strolled not to the right but to the left—*down-town.* This accidental turn to the left led her to a fate that befalls few women, fortunately for the sanity of the human race. That one little error, that slight thing, put Polly within reach of the grasp of a large black monster.

Unknowingly, she strolled on down Broadway to her rendezvous with destiny in the form of Nicholas Lordgod Sampson. On she went, on down to Herald Square past the great squat, mad glory of Macy's and nearby lewd Gimbel's —and she didn't stop, she continued onward, on down into a region of the city unlike any she had ever seen before. On she went, beyond the last mark of uptown Broadway, the very last outpost, a great glittering and shining delicatessen, "the largest deli in the world," run by a berserk restaurateur devoted to the names of cities—in this instance, Minneapolis, thus, "The Minneapolitan." By the gaudy Minneapolitan strolled Polly, swinging her white cloth pocketbook and dreaming idly of nothing, indifferent to the hot pastrami and chopped liver inside the Minneapolitan. She had entered the *downtown mid-town* area. And she *did not know it!*

This area has certain ethnographic, cultural, commercial and anthropological peculiarities. In olden times it did comprise within its bounds the "old Broadway." Long ago, Twenty-third Street, now a rather dismal and rundown thing useful mainly in getting across the island, was the theatrical core of New York. In those days, "Broadway" ran from Twenty-third Street to Herald Square at Thirty-fourth—*this* was Broadway two or three generations ago, or whenever it was. In the days of Diamond Jim Brady and Lillian Russell, this was Broadway. But time changed all of that. Did away with it. Vamoosed it.

The movement, first gradual and then rapid, was *up*town. Mercilessly, irresistibly, like a great measuring caterpillar folding over upon itself, the famous street of sin, frolic and electricity folded over and forward, becoming alive to the north as it left behind it an area dead and consumed. The old theaters were torn down, the old restaurants, with very few exceptions, either died or moved uptown. The gaiety, the vivacity perished.

It was into a *dead swathe* that Polly walked. She thought it was getting a bit "odd-looking," but that was all she noticed. She walked on out of inertia, simply because that happened to be the direction in which she was headed.

However, the area did have many fascinating aspects. It naturally divided on either side of Broadway into different commercial zones or commercial accumulations. To the left, heading downtown, one could discover many dozens of rug or linoleum establishments, most of them wholesale but a few retail, and many furniture dealers of both sexes, as well as a veritable slew of traders in office equipment new and secondhand. All for business, that was their attitude. This is true. Farther east an Armenian settlement appeared, with a sprinkling here and there of Syrians, Iranians and other representatives of the Middle East, now Americanized. Or more or less Americanized. Still eating shish kebab and bread that opens up with a hairy interior. It was a district devoted mostly to big business.

However, mixed in this area one could find countless random businesses of a petty type, a few elaborate tiled old-fashioned Turkish baths now the precinct of uptown elves on the hunt, and of course a brief dignified stretch represented by Fifth Avenue. Also intermingled in the district were a number of quaint old churches stuck down amongst high buildings—among them probably but not certainly "the Little Church Around the Corner," a charming spot that got its original reputation as a theater church by marrying many actors, actresses and producers in the days when nearby Broadway was really Broadway and not just a dead cobbled pavement.

In this area one could still find a number of aged moth-eaten hotels. Ancient, old-style hostelries stuck here and there amongst the side streets, left over from the days of yore, faded but still respectable. The Seamus was one such. It was recently demolished to make way for a housing development for the Chinese, but in the era of this history it still stood intact, its gruesome secret hidden deep in its clogged and long-forgotten bowels.

The anthropological explanation isn't finished, however. The right, or western, side of Broadway, the area stretching across to the Jersey vistas beyond the Hudson River, can be dismissed with a less scrupulous description. It contained the wholesale mannikin district, the wholesale florist district and a large part of the fur district and the glove district and not much else.

However, a certain amount of job printing occurred down there, especially farther to the west, and there were numerous binderies, small-time calendar and desk set manufacturers, Christmas card makers, flockers and hard-rubber turners and whatnot. But from a sociological standpoint, several blocks to the west one met first the old established downtown area of the Greeks. There were a great many Greeks in this district out walking on the sidewalks and standing around.

However, even more importantly, surging up against the Greeks, was a tide of Chinese from the docks. The cribs of Chinatown were saturated. It was a womanless situation for these Orientals, which made them, in Sampson's opinion, great for business because they come quick, a big turnover. Like a tide. This same condition of waxing Yellow Perilism prevailed on the other side of the area, although practically nobody knew about it—the East Side beyond Lexington, they were all over there, thick. You never saw them, they were so silent about it, so Far Eastern and furtive, but they were there, the tide surged up against the Armenians and the Syrians and the Iranians. The whole district was surrounded, packed in and crushed inward by these largely unobserved Chinese so as to create a vast area of hidden but real social pressure.

However, fortunately the area was bounded on the north by Thirty-fourth Street, which acted as a natural barrier with its rushing cabs and heavy trucking. It was bounded on the south by Twenty-third Street, also a natural barrier because of its convenience in getting across the island. At the far eastern edge one found heavy industry along the East River, great cranes and power stacks. And at the far west the docks of the Hudson, with dock workers and foreign sailors and swarms of boat-jumping Chinese.

Thus, lower midtown Broadway as Polly walked into it *without knowing where she was going!* So are the mighty fallen, such is the hand of time. Once a street of song, now an area of population pressures. Such an area was, of course, a natural haunt of a fiend of the type of Nick Sampson; he fit in there perfectly.

"Hmm, I wonder what that old place is like inside," thought Polly, as she caught sight of the crenelated front of the Seamus, with its stonework and massive elaborateness. This sidestreet was quiet and dark, but busy too. Furtive little Chinese slipped by and drunken Pelasgian delivery boys well in middle age stumbled past carrying roses and chrysanthemums, weaving along the street past the busy Armenians. It was a colorful atmosphere and the hotel was cute. "Hmm, think I'll go in, "thought Polly. She strolled up to the ancient white-haired doorman in a gold-braided red uniform with silver epaulets.

"Pardon me, sir," she said. "What is the name of this hotel?"

"Begorrrah," said the doorman, who was Irish, "I'll declare upon me name—Rogerrr Whorrrk at ye service!—and upon the name of me old mither that gave me birrrth, if 'tisn't one of the auldest establishments of its koy-ind in the entire worrrld! By me auld grandmither on me fither's side, I'll swear it for sartin!" The old doorman cleared his throat. "Mmm, begorrrah," he added subtly. "Me throat is awful dry. 'Tis all parrrched-like, I declare it by the dead boones of me great grandmither. Would ye be havin' any, shall we say, liquid refrashment on ye, laaass-ss?"

"No," said Polly.

"Bless ye, then," said this colorful old Irish type. He struck out blindly at a passing tiny little dark-eyed Chinese, who jumped to one side in a puzzled manner. "Blahsted furriners," said the old doorman. "As me name is Rogerrr Whorrrk I'd like to lay a shillelagh acrrross the arse of 'em all. Lil Russell would've made shorrrt hash of 'em, and so would Doymin Jim Brady, begorrrah!"

"Yes, but what's the name of this fine old mansion-type hotel?" asked Polly with a pleasant smile.

"Why, 'tis the Saymus," answered the old Irishman, who had served in wind and snow so long and faithfully. He was a bit addled, it was clear. The years had left their mark on the poor fellow. And now, his personal tragedy, the baffling numbers of Chinese, had overwhelmed him. He stared after the scuttling little Chinese with bleared rheumy eyes, cap hanging askance over his snow-white pate and his jaw slack, a bit of senile spittle shining on his tired old lip. (Hint: he could play "The Flight of the Bumblebee" on the alto saxophone.) Haunted by memories. Bewildered by the modern scene, he could only turn back to the old days and assume in his inferiority-superiority complex an even greater Hibernian accent. (Hint: it wasn't an *authentic* accent, he *wasn't* Irish.) In the gaulden days of auld lang syne, the accent had been appreciated. (Hint: who says so?) Thus, despite the fact that in modern times the accent was not received well, he clung to it blindly with the stubbornness of decrepit old age, his bleary rheumy eyes barely able to focus of all the passing Asian riffraff. (Hint: as the result of *a terrible, traumatic experience* at the hands of a *certain person* not far away at *that moment,* he had compensated *fantastically* and become *a master of disguise.*) Yes, sadly, the main thing about him now was his personal tragedy in connection with the Yellow Peril situation. (Hint: he was not the *true* Roger Whork, who had gone back to Ireland to die, he was *someone else.*) Those furtive varmints!—now the old doorman swatted out at one, as Polly stepped carefully to one side, thinking that perhaps the innocent Chinese who had done nothing might retaliate. But the passing Oriental merely dodged, his almond eyes becoming puzzled at the sight of the creaky, rheumatic old doorman's rage. (Hint: he wasn't a real doorman at all, he was *the false Whork.*) "Hong tong won ton no tickee?" asked the Chinese politely, with dry, almost crumbling, irony.

"And be runnin' along about ye biznis if ye got any!" exclaimed the old doorman with racist narrow-mindedness.

"It was awfully nice meeting you," said Polly. "Good-bye, Mr. Whork."

"Ah, begoorrrah," said the old doorman slyly. And to himself, as she walked up the short flight of worn marble steps to the lobby of the hotel, he added: "Heh, heh, heh, heh, heh! Didn't know-meh!"

As Polly went up the steps she almost bumped into an old lady who was carrying a wolfhound under her arm. "Oh, pardon my audacity!" she said. "How crude of me. Is the wolfhound injured?"

"Oi veh, begorrah," said the old lady, "thot's all right, me choyild. Caun't hurt a wolfhound, ye know."

"What a cute dog!" said Polly. "Hey, poochie! Hey, poochie! What's his name?"

"Tolstoy," said the old lady.

"Oh, he's such a cute dog and such a tiny little thing. Does he chase rabbits, maybe?"

"Oi, thot he does, dearie, two at a toyme and cotches 'em, too!"

"How exciting," said Polly. "But he's so *small.* I never saw a six-inch wolfhound named Tolstoy before."

"Oi, but the robbits he's chasin', them is small, too, dearie."

"How interesting," said Polly. "Think of it, running into a lady with a remarkable wolfhound like that. And you are Mrs. . . . ?"

"Brrrigit McGillicuddy, the mither of Flight hisself, member o' the team of McGillicuddy and Schav."

"Who?" asked Polly.

"Surely you've heard of me boy Flight and his friend Gil? Where have you been all your life, dearie? You never heard of McGillicuddy and Schav and their famous dog and monkey act?"

"Mmm, Flight McGillicuddy and Gil Schav. They sound familiar but I can't place them."

"Why, they invented this breed o' dog," said the old lady. "Begorrah, they're the toast of the town!"

"Well, I just got in from West Virginia," said Polly. "I'm not up on the New York situation. Anyhow it was so nice meeting you. Good-bye, Mrs. McGillicuddy."

"Tara lara loo, dearie," said the old lady. She was authentic Irish, unlike the false Whork. "Oi, 'tis off to the auld sod with me, Oi'm embarkin' for the Emerald Isle this blessed day. God rest ye and keep ye, dearie."

"God rest you, too, you poor old thing," said Polly. "Love your wolfhound."

Hmm, thought Polly, as she entered the hotel lobby. She had her doubts about that doorman out there. Didn't seem very authentic, somehow, that doorman. Could he be someone else brilliantly disguised?

She also had momentary doubts about the elderly desk clerk. There was something *evil* about that gentlemanly-looking old man, a touch of concealed mayhem and slaughter, maybe. A *very* old clerk looked over his spectacles at Polly when she walked into the marble lobby of the Hotel Seamus. He sat perched like a parrot on a high stool behind the desk, a large, old-fashioned desk made of golden quartersawn oak in interesting contrast to the marble everywhere else. Gave a warmth. The clerk, like the old Irish doorman (the false Whork) was old as the mountains, wrinkled and withered with time. He wore on his head a green celluloid visor of the type used by bookkeepers in the day of Diamond Jim Brady and Lillian Russell. He had an old-maid, wrinkled prune expression on his face. He had none of the silver-haired elegance of a TV critic; he was old Chauncey Gaylord with a green celluloid visor on his head and elastic garters on his shirtsleeves and he had roomed Lil Russell and Diamond Jim Brady—separately, of course, he was an awful prig. The books were his specialty. Otis Dogberry and Horace Smegg at the moment happened to be indisposed, thus Mr. Gaylord was on the job. Most of his time was spent downstairs buried with the books, not far from a certain wall that was not a regular wall by any means. Had Mr. Gaylord not been old and deaf he might have heard quite a bit on the other side of that wall.

Polly wasn't really suspicious of him on second thought, just a snotty old geezer, that was all he was. Not realizing the vital role this white-haired, dignified-looking gentleman would play in her life, she merely glanced at him as she passed by. He, in turn, merely glanced at her, before lowering his gaze discreetly. Ugh, pew, yuck, he thought, what a vulgar girl, headlamps on her like a Bugatti. Mr. Gaylord pursed his lips together in prim disapproval and pulled down the green celluloid visor so he couldn't see her.

But there were other eyes that saw Polly. Black, evil eyes. As she sat innocently in the lobby, knees crossed and her cigarette holder between her teeth, two glowering narrowed eyes peered directly at her. She herself unknowingly looked straight at these pithecoid pits of human terror, the gorilloid orbs of Nicholas Lordgod Sampson, who even then stood crouched and hidden in a partition inside the lobby walls, a secret spy spot long forgotten and known now only to himself.

"What a realistic picture," thought Polly.

Picture?—that was no picture; or not entirely, anyhow. The glowering eyes that stared at her did not belong to Sir Walter Raleigh. They were the eyes of a fiend and they were focused directly on an intended victim. It was unfortunate for Polly that she did not know she was gazing up into the Afric eyes of an unrestrained, rampant monster. It was unfortunate indeed that she didn't know that that monster had already determined that regardless of the cost and irrespective of the possible dangers, she would be *his* to do with and unto as he would. And he was no fainting and failing Archie of the pale and wormlike whork—God no! Too late, the game down the drain? Not quite. Polly had run into a Black Fiend who could master her.

AS DAVENPORT WALKED FROM WASHINGTON SQUARE
over to West Ninth Street, he reflected not only on the dismal
position of the have-nots of art but also on the depressing
change that had occurred in his relationship to his older sister
Patricia since publication of his novel. He had thought it
would be a great satisfaction to get back at her, but it was not.
On the contrary, he felt apologetic and constrained. A deep
anger seemed to possess her. She picked at him with a bitchy
nastiness that was hard to believe. It was painful to be around
her and he saw as little of her as possible.

Among other things she'd developed an odd foible of talking dirty to him. Pat had always been a bit aloof about sex
itself, if not about body secrets and mysteries; she pooh-
poohed sex, denigrated it, said it was of no importance. She
had been reserved, prim, even a trifle priggish. She often had
criticized his own use of "bad" words as childish. Now she
used these words with a gingerly enjoyment and told him the
most intimate things with a cards-on-the-table relish. Dick felt

it had something to do with himself and his book.

He was quite certain of it. The novel had been a horrible shock to her. It literally made her throw up. "A window into Hades," she called it. The mindful brutality of the characters bothered her. Such deliberate schematized cruelty was terrifying, it was like the Nazis; in a way it was worse, because the villainy was more intelligent. And it wasn't really true. "That isn't life," she said. "Life contains beauty and truth and compassion." But the reviews had intimidated her and she pretended to like the book. Nothing could be plainer than that she loathed and despised the very paper upon which it was printed, but she insisted on calling it "a damn good book." Several times Dick had said to her: "Pat, you don't *have* to like the book. I don't like it myself all that much. It has nothing but monsters in it, you don't have to like it." Invariably, she would answer: "Oh, no, I like it. It's a damn good book."

Another peculiar little thing was that she had appropriated the liberal role. Before, she had always taken a conservative and even snobbish position on social issues. Now she was a liberal. A lot of good had come out of the October Revolution, Lenin was a giant and Stalin wasn't all bad, he had industrialized Russia, and the Moscow Trials were horrible but probably necessary. The trouble with Roosevelt was that he hadn't hit the rich hard enough, he'd put a bandage on the mortal wound of capitalism. And recently she'd made a big thing of joining the NAACP.

The most uncomfortable thing to Dick, however, was her new-found liberalism in regard to matters of *sex*. Patricia had always been private about this aspect of human life, but no more. Her talk sometimes made him want to put his hands over his ears; in her way she was almost as bad as Beau St. John. Dick had a name for the kind of conversation in which she indulged; he called it this-is-the-anus-this-is-the-penis talk. Once, he and Naomi had visited liberal friends and watched in consternation as they confronted their small wide-eyed daughter with her newborn naked baby brother. "See, dear? This is the anus and this is the penis."

Horrible, in Davenport's opinion, better to learn about it in the gutter. But worse than Pat's conversation was her insistence on discussing with him the most intimate things about her own love life. Perhaps it was her own situation and time of life that did it, perhaps it had nothing to do with himself. Whatever the cause, it was as if a small psychic dam had burst within her. She told him far more about her lovers and her problems with them than he wanted to know. Probably her new analyst had something to do with it, or maybe she had just taken on the coloration of the Village.

Six months ago Pat had moved from the East Side to a Victorian apartment house on West Ninth Street called the Queen Courts. The place had a wrought-iron gate and a front yard with straggly, sick-looking bushes and skimpy grass blackened with cinders. There were no elevators in the building; it was a four-story walk-up. The wrought-iron gate and spearpoint fence and the balconies with wrought-iron railings gave the residence a New Orleans flavor. The apartments had high ceilings, thick masonry walls, working fireplaces and parquet floors; they were rent controlled and thus cheap and very sought after. Gilded letters on the wrought-iron arch over the gate spelled: "1888."

"Beautiful," said Dick as he sloshed ice cubes in scotch he did not want. "I didn't know people could actually live in this place. How did you get in here, anyhow?"

Patricia smiled without much warmth. "Well, I didn't have to screw the landlord, not quite," she said. "If you'd come to visit me once in a while you'd know all about it. I haven't seen you for months, Dickie."

"Oh, it hasn't been that long."

"It's been quite a while. I haven't seen you since the *Life* party where you insulted Briar by telling him there's nowhere to publish good short stories."

"It wasn't him I insulted, it was Leslie Bougainville I said that to," answered Dick. "And I was just kidding."

"Briar heard it. I don't know why you alienate a man who could do you a lot of good. He has published hundreds of good short stories and he thinks you're talented, or he thought so until you acted like such a smart-ass. It's silly self-destruction. After all, you're not foreign and you're not Jewish. If you want serious prestige as an American writer, *Briar's Weekly* is about the only other way. Of course I guess you like being in a corner all by yourself. The question is, will you like it forever?"

"The stories you guys publish are too hoity-toity," said Dick. "No exclamation points, smile thinly and bear it, the old gang is breaking up but don't even whisper about it—that sort of thing."

"Um-hmm. Well, it's a fact I haven't seen you for months."

Dick smiled in a polite but guarded manner at the older sister who had become something like a stranger to him. A familiar stranger, but a stranger. It was true, Pat wasn't herself anymore. Who was this nervous, pinch-faced woman with the darkening blonde hair and the neck tendons and shrunken breasts in a sexless tweed suit? The change in her was shocking, and in an irrational way he somehow felt responsible for it—hadn't he always disappointed and hurt her, no matter what?

The change in Pat was even more dismaying than the change in St. John, at least in a physical sense. Patricia had been a beautiful young girl with an excellent figure and a calm, fearless gaze, but she was young and unafraid no longer; she was into her frightened thirties and more than looked it. Such was her reward for the selfless effort she had made, such was her compensation for subordinating herself to a prissy hairless monster. What had the years of superfidelity to the insanely remote "genius" Briar gotten her except a downcast mouth and a living room full of books and cheap-expensive antiques? But of course she'd done it to herself; Briar hadn't forced her to keep a hateful cat and feed it canaries. It was an awful thing to say or think, but she had become a neurotic, bitter old maid. She had the drawn look of an unloved and unloving woman whom life threatens to pass by, and that was probably the reason for her recent change of style. The terms of her existence had become intolerable to her, and maybe those flourishing barbarians had the answer: talk dirty and exorcise whatever it was, meet the penis-and-the-anus head on, go to a rally for Henry C. Wallace and live, join the NAACP and turn back the horrible tide. Somehow, Dick felt to blame for it all. He smiled in a polite but guarded manner and said:

"Well, you know Brooklyn. The subway and everything. I don't get into New York all that much and people don't seem to get out there, either. We're having company tonight for a change, a fellow writer is coming out. But how have you been, Pat?"

"Well, you don't care but I'm fine. A little tired if you want to know. How are you yourself?"

"Me? Good, I can't complain."

"How is Naomi?"

"Naomi's great."

"And how's the baby?"

"The baby's great, too."

"You'll all have to come to dinner sometime. Sometime soon, I'd like Naomi to meet Charles."

"Sure, of course." Dick took a sip of his scotch, which had a medicinal iodine flavor that he could not imagine ever enjoying. Pat bought the stuff by the case; every year it seemed she drank more. That was one of her problems, the booze. It showed in her face. Considering the amount she drank, she had to have a chronic hangover. But where was this Charles, anyhow? "Are you going to marry him, do you think?"

"What?"

"I said, are you going to marry Charles, do you think?"

"Well, that's a terribly abrupt question. I don't know. I might."

A raw nerve, thought Dick, something was wrong. "Is he coming for drinks?"

"I'm not sure. I think so. He's been ill."

"Nothing serious, I hope."

"No, it isn't serious. He just isn't feeling very well."

"And you're not sure he's coming?"

"He'll probably come. In fact, I'm sure he will."

"Tell me a little about him. What's his name, what does he do?"

"His name is Charles Prentice and he's a social worker for the city."

"Well, that's interesting. I've been going down to the Lower East Side——"

"Charles and I had a misunderstanding but it isn't serious. Tell me about yourself. Are you writing anything? Have you started a second novel?"

Dick hesitated before answering. He'd fibbed to Beau and he didn't want to fib to Pat, too, but it was a subject he didn't especially want to discuss with her. "Well, more or less," he said. "Brooklyn isn't a very creative place to live, that's my excuse and it isn't very good. Actually I'm getting down to work soon, very soon. But I do wish we were back in Manhattan. Seriously, how did you get this apartment?"

"Cumshaw and a lot of smiles," said Pat. "What do you mean, more or less? Either you're working or you're not, and it sounds like you're not."

Again, Dick smiled in a polite but guarded manner. "Well, I'm sort of working." He put his drink on the glass-topped coffee table and walked across the slightly faded Oriental rug of the living room to the bookshelves on the opposite wall. Pat had thousands of books; she had more books than Dan Hennessey. Dick ran his eye over the many volumes as he walked on to the gilded antique birdcage in the corner by her manuscript-piled desk. A silent canary huddled on a perch in the cage. Pat's cat, an evil-tempered Siamese male, sat on the desk staring intently at the canary. "What's cumshaw, a bribe or something?"

"Yes, it's a bribe. A tip. Only way to get an apartment these days, cumshaw. But it takes smiles, too, and sometimes more. It's almost not a joke about having to screw the landlord. The one here is old and gray and arthritic, but he's very lecherous."

Dick stared at the droopy little silent bird. It was lucky to be alive. The cat obviously had got it; a lot of feathers were missing from its tail. Pat had called several of her canaries "Dickie bird," a thing he didn't much like. "Almost not a joke, huh? What'd he do, ask you to go to the movies with him?"

"No, he pinched my ass," said Pat. "Twice."

Dick put out a hand to pet the big Siamese but, as he expected, got nowhere. The cat bared its teeth, gave a low growl and shrank down on the desk. "I see Devil is as friendly as ever. Does he still eat your canaries? It looks like he got this one."

"Yes, he caught Herbert. It was almost curtains. He had the poor thing right in his mouth."

Herbert, that was a new twist. For years Pat had had a Great Hopeless Affair with a married man whose name just happened to be Herb. It was an on again, off again proposition; she'd had other lovers during the entanglement but none of them had proved durable. Herb was durable despite his dullness, or perhaps because of it; he lasted for a very long time but he had a wife and three sons and would not leave them. It drove Pat nuts. What a torment. Herb also worked for *Briar's Weekly,* but in the business department; he did something like circulation and in Dick's opinion was a petrifyingly boring man. The fellow practically never said a word. It was a mystery what Patricia had ever seen in him; maybe he played the divine instrument of woman like a fiddle or something; but whatever his secret it seemed that now she was naming her canaries for him, and that was a bad omen, to say the least. Her canaries had a brief life expectancy; the mean Siamese had eaten at least three of them through the years. It was gruesome the way the cat kept eating her canaries. They got out of the cage, somehow, and Devil pounced. In Dick's belief she subconsciously left the cage door open on purpose so she could cry about it later. Maybe this wasn't true, maybe it was a slander of Patricia, but he wouldn't have liked to be one of her canaries.

"You still haven't answered me. Are you working? I'd like to know, there's a reason I'm asking."

Dick didn't want to answer her. "In a way, yes, I'm working," he said.

"What do you mean?"

"Well, there's more to writing than sitting at a typewriter and pecking at the keys. There's a lot more to it. You could train a monkey to sit at a typewriter and peck at the keys."

"Yes, I know, and eventually he'd write 'Hamlet.' If there were enough monkeys and enough time. What are you talking about, what do you mean?"

"I just mean there's more to it. People who aren't writers and who've never written anything can't understand it, but most of writing a book isn't writing at all."

"That is the silliest thing I ever heard of. If most of writing a book isn't writing, then what is it?"

"Mmm, I didn't think you'd understand me. Well, now. Let

me put it this way. I hate to use such a cliché, but the actual
writing of a book—that is to say, the pecking of it—is the top
of the iceberg. Ninety per cent of it is below water, invisible.
But if there were no bottom of it you wouldn't see the top of
it."

"And what does the bottom of it consist of?"

Dick moistened his lips, narrowed his eyes and peered off
into space. "Reflection," he said.

Pat stared at him with a little twisted smile. Slowly she
reached for a cigarette, her gaze fixed upon him. A wry philosophical bitterness was in her eyes. It was a thing he'd seen
before and it always shocked him. He'd seen it in Beau, he'd
seen it in Pat, he'd seen it in many former friends and associ-
ates and in plenty of total strangers. *"A child like you,"* she said.
"You don't have even the vaguest idea what you're talking
about. You take it all for granted, you don't worry about it,
it's there. Why should a rich man worry about bills? No muss,
no fuss, just write them a check, there's plenty of money in the
bank. Well, I knew you when you didn't have a dime, and I'm
sorry but there's something *maddening* about such complacency. You say to me that ninety per cent of writing a book
is 'reflection.' You silly little popinjay, do you know how
many people there are who'd give anything to have what
you've got? Aside from the wasteful and downright immoral
use you make of your talent, do you know how rare it is? I'm
sorry but it's infuriating, and I've got to ask you this: in your
smug little success, can you imagine what it's like *not* to have
talent?"

Yes, he'd seen it before and it was always a shock. Davenport felt a tingle in his cheeks, a faint prickly feeling in the skin
of his face. Slowly he took out a cigarette of his own and lit
it. With trembling fingers he took a puff. At moments such as
this he wished he'd never written the damned book in the first
place. The primordial hate was bad enough, but the primor-

dial desire to see him fall on his ass was worse. "Sure," he said. "I can imagine it very easily."

"I don't think so," said Pat. "Oh, certainly, you can recognize it in others, just as a person who can hear can recognize the condition of deafness. But I don't think you can imagine what it's like to be deaf yourself."

It was a thing Dick didn't want to say, but the words came out. "I haven't heard a sound lately, Pat. I wonder if I ever really heard anything. Maybe by accident I did, but right now it's a silent world."

"Well," said Pat, "if that's true it's only temporary and you know it."

"And I'll tell you something else. I don't care, I don't give a damn. What's the point, anyhow? If I have talent, so what? If I don't, then so what? It's Sisyphus, that's all. He's got to push that frigging rock up that hill only to watch it roll down again. If I write another book, then I've got to write another one, and then another."

To his relief and as he had hoped, her face softened. "You make it sound as if it's a fate worse than death," she said with a little smile. "Writing one book and then another, what's so bad about that?"

"Nothing if you like to write," said Dick. "But I don't like it, I hate it. If there's one thing I hate to the core, it's writing."

"They say that's the sign of a real writer," said Pat with another smile. "It's an irony of fate. Those who love it can't do it, those who hate it can. But I doubt seriously if you really hate it and I doubt if there's any ultimate truth in that aphorism."

"Don't worry, I hate it plenty," said Dick. "But you're right, there's no ultimate truth in what you said. Take Beau, for one. It kills him even to write a paragraph. He loathes writing, he detests it, he hates the utter guts out of it and he can't do it at all. He's a talker, not a writer."

"I could have told you that years ago," said Pat. She was much more relaxed now, in a far better mood. "Well, one thing is clear. As I suspected, you're having trouble writing your second novel."

"I'm not having trouble writing it," said Dick truthfully. "I'm having trouble *deciding* to write it."

"That's the same thing. Don't quibble."

"No, it's not the same thing. You can't have trouble doing something that you're not doing."

"It's called a writing block," said Patricia.

"Is that what they call it?" asked Dick. "Well, I can't imagine anything more revolting. It must be kind of like a shank in golf. You know, where you take a swat at the ball and it squirts off at ninety degrees to the right into places where no golf ball ought to go? That's because you have swayed forward like an idiot and hit it with the shaft instead of the face of the club. Bobby Jones said he's never shanked a ball in his life, and I've often wondered if he was lying about that. You'd think he'd shank at least *one* ball, wouldn't you? But I'll tell you the truth, Pat. I don't have a writing block."

"Oh, sure," she said with still another smile. "You just haven't felt like working. But that's real cute about Bobby Jones. You've lost neither your glibness nor your charm, Dickie."

Blood sure wasn't thicker than wine. Or maybe it was thicker, maybe that was the problem. Idly, Dick looked around the apartment. The high ceilings, polished oak floors and marble fireplace reminded him of a flat off Grosvenor Square. A great place, England. He and Naomi had been there for English publication of his book. The novel had sold pretty well, but it had been a little rough for the civilized British. The worst parts had been cut out, and even so the reviews had been not too good. "An appalling American extravagance," one critic had said.

A lot like England, Pat's apartment. Dick liked England very much and often had thought of moving there. He liked the oldness and the coldness of the houses. And he loved to hear the English talk; he could listen to them all day. They could write, too; even when what they wrote was silly, they wrote it elegantly and splendidly. But the problem was to get Pat off of the subject she now was on. Dick put his finger against a yellowish antique globe on a mahogany stand, gave it a spin and said:

"This apartment reminds me of England. I might move there sometime; I feel that I lived in England in other lives. Of course it comes from reading Dickens and Fielding and Trollope and all those guys, but I feel English at heart, I feel English in my *cells*. I might move there soon. Let's face it, America is a terrible place. The houses are too hot and new and people in this country spit out their words vulgarly. But I like this apartment and I like this globe of the world; where did you get it?"

"Briar gave it to me," said Pat. "Stop babbling senselessly. And stop prowling around and come sit here, I want to talk to you."

"I'd like to see the apartment. Is the bedroom down this hall?"

"Yes, but don't go in there, it's a mess. Come sit on the sofa, I have something to say to you."

"Is the kitchen in the other direction?"

"Yes, but it's a mess, too."

Dick left the living room and walked down a dark, high-ceilinged hall to a door with flaking white paint. He opened it and saw an old-fashioned bathroom with blue and white tiles and a big clawfoot tub. Countless bottles of drugs were on the shelves of an open medicine cabinet. Pat was a terrible hypochondriac. Hands on hips, Dick looked around the huge Victorian bathroom. Pretty sloppy for Patricia. Toilet tissue trailed down from the roll, soppy towels hung down the side of the tub and water stood on the tiles. A red rubber douche bag hung down from the shower curtain rod and some kind of pink powder had been spilled all over the side of the tub and the floor. What had gone on in that bathroom?

"Don't snoop around the apartment," said Pat from the hall. "Come on back to the living room."

"What'd you do in here," asked Dick, "make love in the tub?"

Briefly, Pat was silent, then she pursed her mouth and said: "No, I didn't. Come into the living room."

"Well, that's a good tub for it, nice and roomy. Can't I see the bedroom?"

"I'd rather you didn't."

"Why not?"

"Someone is in there."

"Oh," said Dick. His question about making love in the bathtub had been facetious but now he wondered. Somehow he couldn't picture it, Patricia naked in the tub with some man and sloshing water all over everything. Could that have happened? Probably not; Pat couldn't do such things no matter how much she talked with grave solemnity about her "erotic needs." She was his older sister, and older sisters didn't have erotic needs. But the bathroom was certainly a mess, and who was it in the bedroom? The mysterious Charles? If so, why was he lurking in there this time of day? What was going on, anyhow?

In the living room Pat poured herself another large drink and said: "It would be a wonder if you didn't have trouble writing your second novel after such a success with your first one. That's a difficult spot to be in, especially if you're young; but there's a good side to it. It can be a tempering experience. After all, a tool is no good until it's tempered. It won't hold an edge. Of course the tempering process can destroy a tool, too, if the fire gets too hot. But I'm afraid it's necessary. Granted a little talent, anyone can write an adolescent novel, that kind of book practically writes itself; but to go on, something more than instinct is needed. A point of view, an individual style, a broader perception—in short, a cutting edge. And you only get that with tempering. Have you been having a lot of trouble? Anxiety, insomnia, that sort of thing?"

"I don't feel the heat much at all," said Dick.

Pat smiled. "If you didn't have trouble in such a situation as this you'd have the nervous system of an ox. And no writer of any talent has such a nervous system. I've known a lot of them and they are sensitive creatures. That's why I keep towels and aspirin in a drawer of my desk, to give them when they cry and crack up. And I'm afraid it's not a joke. Did you read this morning in the *Times* about James Meaghan's suicide?"

"Yeah, I read about it."

"An awful tragedy. In some ways I think he was the most talented of the young writers since the war. Or potentially talented, anyhow. There was a lot more depth and human feeling in his book than it was given credit for, don't you think?"

Dick clenched his teeth but was careful not to let her know it. She was trying to pick an argument with him about Meaghan. "Well, I enjoyed it a lot," he said. "It was a very funny book."

"It was more than funny, there was real depth in it. He had a rare gift. Of course the reviewers are jealous; a boy like that comes along and writes a wonderful and human book and naturally it makes them sick. What else can they call it but superficial? They like morbidity, the critics. Of course life has that side, but it has a human side, too. Meaghan had a very rare gift and it's sad."

Uh-huh, thought Dick. Meaghan wrote a "human" book. Mystery, mystery, who could she be thinking of who wrote an inhuman book that appealed to the morbidity of the critics? "Yeah, it is," he said. "I'm moving to England before I drown myself in a bathtub with a razor blade for company."

"I really don't think it's anything to make light of, Dickie. That boy is dead. To joke about his death seems to me in very poor taste, to put it mildly."

Again Dick clenched his teeth. She was relentless. Eyes on his cigarette, he said: "Who's joking?"

"Well, you are. You're not going to England to live; you're as American as a hot dog. And you're not going to kill yourself, either; you're far too egocentric. I don't mind that, I expect that, talent is always wrapped up in itself and it's seldom modest. It's a thing I noticed long ago when I first began at Briar's; the better writers are nearly always egomaniacs. Something in the nature of being gifted makes them that way. And it's a leapfrog thing. Who was it who said the slightly talented person assumes great talent, the talented assumes genius, and genius assumes godhood? It's normal; I don't mind the egotism and the vanity, what I object to is your refusal to admit you have it. Now you know perfectly well you think you're a far better writer than James Meaghan. You can put on a nice guy act and praise him because you think his work wasn't even in the same category as your own. And your praise isn't really very generous; what you *don't* say is damning. The truth is that you think his work had no value, it was just popular fluff. Isn't that what you think, that Meaghan's book was just popular fluff that had no value?"

Relentless was the word for Patricia; she seemed absolutely determined to pick a fight with him. Dick blinked at his headache as he tried to think of a reply. What a day it had been! First the frightening suicide of Jim Meaghan, then Herbie and his mother, then Pauline and Natalie, then Beau and his fragment and now Pat in a dither. And looming above it all, a book to write, a book he did not want to write and saw no reason to write. "No, it isn't what I think," he said. "But I'll tell you one thing I do think. I'm rapidly running out of reasons to have a literary career."

"You're doing *what?*" asked Pat.

"There must be easier and better ways to make a living," said Dick.

NICHOLAS LORDGOD SAMPSON HAD BEEN BORN FORTY-
seven years ago in Cretesville, Georgia; or rather, on a farm
not far from the hamlet of that name. He had been the first
of twenty-eight children. His parents were sharecroppers to a
white landowner, Marse Jawn. Since his future attitudes and
psychological motivations were to a large degree shaped and
influenced by his childhood, a word about that childhood
would be appropriate and an aid toward the comprehension
of Nicholas Lordgod himself.

His peculiar middle name was without any direct religious
connotations—he had been named after a southern bird of the
woodpecker family that is called by blacks in the South a
"lordgod." The reason this bird has such a name is not known.
The bird itself is extremely rare, so rare it practically doesn't
exist. But it does live in swamps and elsewhere. It is a big bird
and can make a loud drumming noise, and certain supersti-
tions surround it like an aura. Southern Negroes in olden
times felt that the appearance of a lordgod heralded an event
of baleful significance.

Nicholas had been born at the very moment of the appearance of a lordgod. His head had just emerged upside down from his shrieking, praying mother when suddenly a lordgod bird appeared in the window and drummed madly on the windowsill, its brilliant red plumage gleaming in the hot Georgy sunshine and its l'il diabolical eyes cocked toward the scene on the pallet on the floor, where the mother lay, as Rufus, the father, stared down at the bloody head of the emerging baby and chawed 'backy.

But now Rufus shrank back in superstitious fear, and thus the child was named Lordgod Sampson. And this was slightly amended to Nicholas Lordgod Sampson by the old grandmammy, who understood voodoo and said it was doom (for the entire family) to name the babe Lordgod alone. Later this probably saved Rufus from maddened hogs. Those are the straight facts in this case.

Now, the child was soon known about the district as "bad." It was said of him when he could hardly walk that he was "a bad nigger." The Negroes themselves described Nick in such terms. He was regarded as a satanically mean-hearted and mercilessly cruel child, although very little is on record in any detail about those early years.

However, it is known he was involved in a near-lynching at the age of seventeen and that as a result he murdered quite a few people. The near-lynching came about as the consequence of a conflict between the boy and a white bully in the hamlet of Cretesville. The bully happened to be the nephew of Marse Jawn, who owned the farm on which Nick's parents lived and worked as sharecroppers. Nick had gone into town on the wagon with his father to buy some sorghum, which was the main item of the Sampson family diet along with hoecake and hog jowls. At this time, he stood six feet three and weighed two hundred and ten pounds. He had not begun to get his full growth yet and was a mere gangling boy; neither the strength nor the speed were there. He very likely could have lifted no more than five hundred pounds and if clocked for the hundred-yard dash probably could have done no better than 9.7 or 9.8 seconds—but this debility and sluggishness were only in comparison to what he would be later; in ordinary human terms he was stronger than hell and swift as lightning. However, despite the supergenes energized in part by the lordgod bird, he was of course to the southron mentality just a "niggee bawee" and his large feet trailing off the back of Rufus's wagon must have looked a bit ludicrous, so long and dusty and unshod. In any event, Jaypee, the white boy, ran up and grabbed the feet and pulled young Nicholas off the wagon. It was a little joke. The point was that Jaypee had to take a leak and he wanted something to take it on.

This occurred outside the small country store which was one of the four or five business establishments in Cretesville. Six or seven white youths stood around and they all cackled appreciatively and spat admiring 'backy juice in the dust as the bully Jaypee pulled Nicholas off the wagon, threw him to the red dirt street, and then, since there were no white girls or ladies around, took out his pale unsunburned doogus and pissed on him.

"T'ank you, boss!" said the nigger. "Yaaaahsuh! T'ank you for dis piss. Ah done needed it! Yaaaahsuh!"

Everything seemed normal; but this was "a bad nigger" and the white bully Jaypee had acted most unwisely. To the indignation of the citizenry of Cretesville, he was found later that afternoon lying in a back alley with his head tucked under one arm. Evidently, a single powerful swipe of a razor had decapitated him.

Naturally, a lynching bee was organized to take care of Nicholas, since it was obvious he had done it. Nick, however, was nowhere to be found. The lynching party had to settle on his father Rufus, and they almost had him hanged with barbed wire in a chinaberry tree when they decided to torture him so as to force him to reveal then and there the whereabouts of Nicholas.

"Don't know, sah!" said the man. He was very black, jet black, a real Africky-type nigger like Nicholas himself. The lynchers beat him considerably, jabbed at him quite a bit with a redhot pitchfork and hung him up by his ankles with barbed wire over a bunch of starved wild hogs; but either he didn't know or he stubbornly wouldn't tell, so they never discovered the hiding place of black Nick and thereby many people died.

Carelessly, they left Rufus to the hunger-maddened hogs, assuming that the hogs would finish him off; but Rufus roused up and manfully fought off the hogs, thrusting pegs into their mouths so as to wedge their jaws apart and make them unable to bite, dodging here and there and thrusting a peg, then dodging again and thrusting in another peg, and another, and another, meanwhile confusing the hogs by going "Hoo! Hooo! Hoooo!" at them.

He finally got them all helpless by means of the pegs; then he tied them all up in a line, one hog's haunches tied to a rope, the other end of the rope tied to the next hog's neck, and so on till all the hogs were in an oinking line, each with its jaws propped wide by a peg. Rufus, who was not the father of Nick for nothing, then led the hogs along a country road, cursing all white folks and stumbling a bit from his bruises and injuries. But he got the hogs to a tall cliff and made them all jump over one after the other to their doom on the rocks below. Later he got the carcasses and salted them down for the winter.

During this time, while most of the menfolks were out at the Sampson farm, Nick was laying waste the town of Cretesville. He ignited every barn in it and every house and building as well, with the exception of the Cretesville First Baptist Church of Jesus Loves Me. The reason the church was spared was because Nicholas at this age was afraid of religion. God gave him the willies. It was the sole thing that could cow him.

This fear of religion, however, didn't prevent him from cutting the throat of the minister, Rev'rend Jawn, who also happened to be Marse Jawn, nor did it stop him from assaulting the minister's wife and his three young daughters. Even as his father led the string of captured, baffled hogs to their doom, he was raping the youngest daughter, who was only twelve. He had already raped the wife several times, both normally and abnormally, and now he turned his sex-fiend attention to the daughters, choosing the youngest first because she was hollering the loudest. He raped her twice normally and three times "fancy style" in her tight little behind as the mother looked on and wept, eyes raised to heaven at this sad thing and her lips moving, a thin martyr smile on her face as she prayed: "Strack him daid, Lawd. Strack that niggah's tail with liiightnin', Lawd."

Nick, however, was not struck dead. Razor in hand, he continued the terrible abnormal rape (he was not a normal human being) of the little shrieking towheaded white gal as the sisters, who soon were to get the same disastrous treatment in turn, looked on bug-eyed and wrung their hands and whimpered. They had reason to whimper and look bug-eyed—even in those immature days Nick had a whork on him beyond belief; it was a good eleven inches long and had a head on it like a tangerine. It was an awful scene. Just awful. The whole thing smacked of horror.

Black Nick finally got enough of both normal and abnormal rape and soon thereafter the four white "soda cracker" (as he called them) females lay stacked on top of one another, headless. Their heads were all over the floor; it really was awful. And he wasn't even through, he was a firebug, too. This boy was a maniac already and he was only seventeen. After lopping off their heads Nick rumpled up some newspapers and struck a match to them. Frightened by such an irreligious act, he ran out of the house mumbling: "Don't know it belong to no preachah, dat house. Don't know it for sho." Pure rationalization. He knew it belonged to a preacher.

But this shocking crime did not go unpunished; retribution came. Nick was over in Opelika, Alabama, a few months later —or maybe it was Dothan, some Alabama township—and he happened to insult Sheriff Holt Breech, a proud and sensitive man. What a mistake. Holt Breech would never forget it and later nabbed him for stealing chickens and stuck him on a chang gang. But that was later. What happened first was the insult. Nick was walking down the street past the county courthouse steps when a blob of 'backy juice came whistling from twenty feet away and struck him square in the face. Nick heard comments:

"Hee, hee! Good shawt, Hote! Cotched 'um rott squah, ole buddee! Ain' laws yo' aim yet, Shurf! Tha' niggee bawee do' kno' wha' hit tim! Uh buh-uh-eye, Hote! Lookee nigguh blankee's eyes! Hee hee hee! Haw haw!"

These comments maddened Nick to such an extent that he lost control. He turned, rolling his neck and his eyes toward the laughter and the talk. Then with expressionless dignity he wiped the 'backy juice off his face with the ragged sleeve of his shirt. This act of impudence enraged Sheriff Holt Breech. For a nigger to act in this manner was alien to the southern way of life. Sheriff Breech snatched up his heavy "coon gun" and was on the verge of firing, but then decided to play it *fair* and ask the niggy boy *why* he had *done* that.

"Hey-y, niggah," called the sheriff in a soft singing drawl. "Come back hyah. Rott naow. C'mon back hyah."

"Yaaa-ah sah," sang Nick in turn, and he shuffled slowly around and back up to the courthouse steps, looking at the sheriff who loomed above him. Naturally, a dumb good-natured grin was on Nick's face and his ragged cap was in his hands. He knew his only chance was to "niggerah it up."

"Ah jes' wanna ast you one tha-ang," said the sheriff, "befo' ah shoot off yo' kinky haid. Whut did you wiiipe off that 'backy juice faw? You tryin' to in-*sult* me befo' *mah fr'ens?*"

"Lawsy me, shurf," grinned Nick. "Was dat 'backy juice? Wha', ah ne'h even knowed it, ah thawt a skeetie done sot on me and ah go' strack him off, dat's all, sah. Ah ain' 'bout to wiiipe off no 'backy juice of yourn!"

"Ah doubts yo' black ay-iss," said the sheriff.

"Awww-wrr, naaaw-suh," cackled Nick. "Ah thawt ole skeetie done lit on me, sah. Swah to Gawd dat whut I thawt!"

"You is a' lyin', niggah," said the sheriff, and with that he grabbed his coon gun by the barrel and raised it high. "Ah go' knock out whut e're you got for brains."

"Yaaa-ah-ah, sah," grinned Nick pleasantly. "You de boss, but——" He didn't have time to finish, but of course he was just stalling for time anyhow, hoping that something would distract the sheriff. No such luck. The heavy stock of the rifle came down with a splintering crash on his head. If his skull had not been guided in its construction by supergenes, it would have been cracked like an egg. However, that skull had been energized by the lordgod; it was practically primordial. The result was that although Nick dropped to the sidewalk like a sack of potatoes, the stock of the coon gun was shattered.

"Wha', whut kinda nigguh is that there nigguh, by Gawd?" asked the sheriff, puzzled. Frankly bewildered, Sheriff Breech rubbed at his scalp under his "woolly" hat and tugged at his red galluses as he waddled slowly back up the courthouse steps to his cronies on the bench. "Ah be dawg," he said. "That nigguh sho got some hard haid."

The blow permanently addled the emotional attitude if not the wits of Nicholas Sampson. He always had been bad, even as an infant in his cradle; but now with this terrible and (he felt) unjust blow on the head, he ever after would be bad without limits. And he already was a dubious character; his actions at the time of the near-lynching showed the degree of his moral irresponsibility. But that conk on the head truly rankled him; it turned him *permanently* against the white race. Hitherto, he had been definitely negative toward the whites, but now he *really* had it in for them. However, this does not mean he liked people of other races. Not this fiend. He didn't like people of *any* race, not even blacks. But whites he hated most of all; he hated them primordially.

Furthermore, his hate toward whites was hardly lessened by the third major disaster of his youth in the South, and that was his experience on a Georgia chang gang. What happened was that Sheriff Holt Breech moved over to Ty Ty, Camilla, or maybe it was Cordele, one of those sun-baked south Georgia townships, and nabbed him for his chang gang—a big nigger with a hard head like that would fit in nicely. Besides, he prob'ly stole some chickens.

"Wal, ah be dawg if it ain't that hard-headed nigguh. Our paths have done crost again, son, and this time you ain' go' come out of it livin'."

The Georgia chain gang—or chang gang as it is called locally—is of course a very famous institution in penal circles and even elsewhere. Known for its brutality throughout the civilized world, it deserves some measure of criticism by the idealist. However, there are few things more companionable than an old-fashioned chain gang. The prisoners were, of course, at all times in close physical contact; they did not live with those modern-day barriers that serve to separate men. Also, the chain gang by and large was an entirely democratic organization, in that all members of the gang had the same privileges, the same rights, the same duties and even the same punishments without discrimination.

All the members of the gang slept on the same wooden benches, ate the same hogback and collards and cornmeal mush, relieved themselves in the same tin bunkhouse buckets and had welded about their ankles the same iron rings and chains. All wore identical striped clothing. For the most part, they all had roughly the same numbers of body lice to contend with, though here individual initiative did play a part, since some of the more fussy members spent more time picking off the lice, or cootie bugs as they were called, than did the others and thus had less of them. There was not, however, much time to spend on cooties, except on Sunday, the day of rest. Sheriff Breech believed that work was healthy and the gang was out there from dawn till dusk.

However, the punishments were the same for all. Minor offenses were punished by a blow from the fist of one of the deputies, who were good old bawees picked carefully by the sheriff. These deputies were, of course, rather crude men who prided themselves on their ability to knock down a big nigger unconscious and cold with one blow and not even have skinned knuckles to show for it. A couple of them soaked their "hittin' hands" in brine several hours a day, utilizing a trusty to carry around the bucket and hold it for the hand to rest in. The brine theoretically toughened their knuckles till they were hard as old leather. Their knuckles already were hard, but perhaps this increased the hardness to some degree.

In any event, that was the routine minor punishment for such offenses as leaning on a shovel, looking up at the sky and loafing, spitting and so forth. Or perhaps a prisoner would force a deputy to go off with him to the bushes to relieve himself once too often, and the deputy would retaliate by knocking him down to see if he *really* had to go. If the prisoner did really and truly have a call of nature, then the force of the blow would precipitate a reply to the call and all would be well; the deputy would just snort in acceptance of the genuineness of the request—this was known as "knockin' the shit out of a nigger." But if the force of the blow did not have such a result, then the black son of a bitch had been lying, and more serious measures were called for, possibly the hotbox or the lazy lulu.

The hotbox, of course, is too well known to require any lengthy or detailed description. It consisted merely of a tin structure of sufficient size to admit one (1) prisoner, who would find himself compelled to stand in a semicrouch, unable to sit and also unable to rise to his full height. The structure had no ventilation, except for a tiny hole at the bottom and another tiny hole at the top to prevent the quick suffocation of the occupant.

Under the burning rays of the Georgia sunshine, the hotbox would of course accumulate a certain amount of heat. If the temperature outside were 110 degrees, a common figure on warm days in south Georgia, then the temperature in the hotbox would probably soar to the neighborhood of 145 to 150 degrees—hot as hell, in other words. An hour in this box usually was sufficient to reduce even the most unruly prisoner to a sodden heap unable to move for five or six hours thereafter. Four hours in the box would generally result in prolonged unconsciousness over a period of several days. Weak or sick prisoners sometimes perished in four hours. But five hours often, and six hours almost invariably, meant that when the hotbox was opened a corpse would be inside.

Because of this time factor, prisoners usually were on their very, very best behavior early in the morning and until well past noon. A sentence to the hotbox in midmorning usually meant finis. If Sheriff Breech or a deputy were enraged by the misconduct of a prisoner at 10 A.M. and said, "You got six hours in the box, nigguh!" then this was curtains for the nigger. But, on the other hand, if the sentence occurred at five in the afternoon, the felon would have only an hour or so because the hotbox was in operation only between six in the morning and six at night. He would, of course, have four more hours to serve the next morning, but he would serve two of those hours, or perhaps two and a half of them, before it got really hot. Thus he would survive, in all probability, if he received the sentence at the right time. Otherwise, it was, "Good-bye, Billy."

The lazy lulus were the large bullwhips used by Sheriff Breech and the deputies when direct physical punishment with all its drama seemed advisable. A bullwhip such as the lazy lulu measures approximately four inches in width at the handle, which is roughly the length of a policeman's club and a bit larger in diameter. A lulu tapers in width to approximately two inches and a half at its far end. It is constructed of rough bull hide about a quarter of an inch thick and only moderately flexible, unless in the hands of a master. It is cut off the carcass of the bull from the neck along the flank and up around over the bony rump, up the other flank and on to the neck on the other side; thus it measures approximately nine feet in length.

A well-made lazy lulu will weigh about twenty pounds, no more. It is, of course, used with both hands. Customarily, an erring prisoner has his wrists manacled and is hung by a strong rope attached to his hands and tied overhead to the limb of a convenient chinaberry tree. The deputy who is going to apply the lulu then grasps the large handle in both hands, steps back six or seven paces, swings the lulu back and forth a bit to get the feel, then winds far backward and around, turns gracefully on the ball of his right foot and suddenly, in one powerful, rushing movement, half runs and half jumps forward, so as to bring the lulu around in an apparently lazy but actually quite speedy arc. At the very last moment (*videlicet,* the "late hit" of golf), with an effort that always produces a "Huu-uhhh!" grunt, he *snaps* the huge lulu in such a way that it will arrive at the prisoner with maximum effectiveness and impact.

The effectiveness is considerable. A lulu, really skillfully used, can of course break most of the ribs of a prisoner. Generally, however, prisoners are struck at a spot just below the ribs, so that the lulu will coil around the belly, which is naturally more flexible and better able to give than the rib cage. This type of delivery is most admired, because in actuality it is more painful to the prisoner and does not incapacitate him as do broken bones. A really good stroke can be measured by the effect on the prisoner—if he makes any noise, if he screams or shouts or even groans, that is a bad stroke. A good stroke is known by the utter silence with which it is received; the prisoner merely sags on his rope, out.

Ten blows of the lazy lulu, well administered, can cause death; twenty almost always do. But there are always exceptions to prove a rule. Black Nick, Nicholas Lordgod Sampson, survived on two occasions twenty blows of an expertly applied lazy lulu (in both instances by the hands of Sheriff Holt Breech himself); and on three separate occasions, all in midday during hot spells, he survived even more remarkably six full hours in the hotbox. On each of these five occasions he was adjudged dead. The trusties already had prisoners digging his grave, and each time they had to fill it up again because Black Nick was not dead, he lived on.

Nick had been sentenced to the chain gang for an indeterminate sentence for the theft of poultry and he served nine years. During those nine years he grew to his full height of six feet seven and a half inches and he reached his fighting weight of two hundred and fifty-five pounds. He developed the musculature of a giant swinging his pick and shovel and cutting through the Georgia turpentine forests with his woodsman's axe. His voice deepened to a rumbling bass. He learned to sing in a profound and moving tone (it was the only reason Sheriff Breech didn't kill him outright; it made him cry like a little baby to hear that nigger sing) the old spirituals and sacred songs of the dark Southland.

And he bided his time. Knocked down a hundred times by Sheriff Breech, he was knocked down another hundred times by the deputies, and then another hundred for good measure. His big flat nose became totally flattened. His brows thickened and his ears cauliflowered. His perfect white teeth, one after the other, were knocked out of his mouth by brine-soaked fists or the butts of coon guns.

But he knew someday the opportunity would come and it did. They gave him the woodsman's axe one time too often —and all he needed, with an axe in his hands, was a moment of distraction. The head deputy, a good old boy named Bud Clogg, was standing there coon gun in hand fifteen feet away watching him with narrowed, cautious, porcine eyes when suddenly, of all things, *a lordgod bird* landed on the limb of a nearby pine and began drumming loudly at the trunk. Distracted, Bud Clogg turned his head to look at the lordgod and that was it.

Swwwaa-app! went the axe so fast the eye could not follow it, and the head of Bud Clogg flew thirty feet into a thicket. With the speed of a streaking panther Nick grabbed the coon gun and shot down in rapid succession the other four deputies. Then he shot the praying and blubbering Sheriff Holt Breech himself, first in the balls, then in the gut, then in the head. After that he cut off the head and threw it in a swamp. He had waited nine years to get those soda cracker bastards and it was the happiest moment of his life, due to the lordgod!

Grinning toothlessly, Nick shot off his chains, put on Bud Clogg's clothes, ran five miles in less than twenty minutes through scrub pine to the Macon highway and flagged down a white liberal professor who was foolishly driving through the South on a vacation from up North. Nick cut the professor's throat after a brief discussion of the nigger problem. He then raped normally and abnormally the professor's wife and fourteen-year-old daughter. It wasn't enough rape to suit him, but he had to get going so he cut their throats and threw the family in some bushes. As he sped out of the South in the professor's Packard dressed in the professor's clothes and smoking one of the professor's cigars, he vowed those mammy-jammin' soda crackers would never see the day when they would get him back in a chang gang again, and they didn't.

From a member of a Georgia chain gang to the Unknown King of Harlem is quite a step, and it was not, needless to say, one step but a number of successive steps. Sampson, now a full-grown and hardened man of twenty-seven, was yet to undergo many vital and incredible experiences before finally establishing his setup, as he called it, deep in the unremembered bowels of the Hotel Seamus.

He journeyed first to Baltimore, making his way there on backward country roads to avoid detection. In Baltimore he sold the Packard to a dealer for two hundred dollars no questions asked, then he wisely went to the docks and bribed his way into the stoker's union and signed on board a Norwegian freighter, leaving that same night for Rio de Janeiro, Cape Town, Jo'burg, Madagascar, Suez, Naples and Marseilles— there he skipped ship, having heard from other members of the crew that French girls and women were a rare treat.

The French girls and women were indeed a rare treat, and Black Nick remained in la Belle France for a number of years. His center of operations was Paris but he visited frequently the Riviera and the French Alps and other haunts of the rich. It was in France that he engaged for the first time in white slavery; at his peak he commanded the loyalty of twenty-two French girls. Willingly or unwillingly, they were his slaves. The razor that he carried at all times was famous in France. His sobriquet there was (translated from the French): "the American death of the name, the Razor."

Frenchmen trembled at the very sight of him even though they admired him enormously. How many French he disposed of there is no way of telling. He sliced his way through France, leaving a trail of the headless dead behind him. The slightest false move of an annoying person would be enough to cause the razor to flash and a head to topple to the floor and conk in the sawdust, amidst gasps of horror from the French, whose sensibilities, as is well known, are among the most highly developed in the world. And yet, peculiarly enough, the French adored him.

Why? Possibly because of his animal vigor or perhaps because he was, as they said with Gallic insight, "so typically American." Also, the French were of course sympathetic to him because of moral indignation at the treatment given the Negro in the American South. It was for this reason he usually said to them at the outset: "Je suis l'Américain, mon grenuouille ami. Je suis depuis la Georgia avec de la chang gang, coup de soleil, francamente salchicha, comment, tiens, zut alors, non?"

"Would but that you had been born in France!" his French friends would reply in English, since obviously Nick, for all his charm, spoke challenging French. At times it was hard even to follow his sinister thoughts although the evil gist was there. This language handicap, usually fatal to a foreigner in France, didn't matter in his case. The French would just smile and say: "Extraordinaire!" He was a big hit with the French, but then of course the French like strange and different things.

However, Nick's adventures on the Continent cannot be described in any great detail here. Once he got out of la Belle France, Nick traveled throughout Europe, visiting Holland, Belgium, Denmark, Sweden, Norway, Germany, Switzerland, Italy, Russia and the Balkans. He absorbed a great deal on his travels and left none of it behind him when he sailed on a merchant ship for the Far East via the Middle East. For some time he was in Egypt and later he was in India. India was right up his alley, but he didn't think much of China or Japan. Australia he missed, likewise New Zealand, but he hit the island of Tasmania; he was in Hong Kong and Singapore and he spent several satisfying months in Hawaii before finally coming back to the home shores at San Francisco.

At once he was clapped into San Quentin on charges of aggravated abnormal rape and there he stewed for five years until he was parolled. Those five years took it out of him insofar as any possible lingering pity for the white race was concerned. He came out of San Quentin a truly hardened man and immediately launched himself upon a spree of crime, murdering and robbing and assaulting and raping in all directions as if possessed by Satan himself.

However, Nick had not only become truly hardened, he had also gotten smart. He knew it could not work forever, not out in the open. The FBI sooner or later would nab him. With shrewd insight he saw that he must find somewhere a permanent hiding place so cleverly concealed it would never be found. It must be a foolproof hideout and at the same time readily accessible to a large city. And what city? There was Paris, of course; he could go back there. Paris had its points. But he decided after considerable thought that the city of his operations should be the city that best personifies and embodies the spirit of the twentieth century: New York, New York.

And so to New York went Nicholas Lordgod Sampson, the Black Avenger, Pahlevi, Maharajah, the Unknown King of Harlem and Destroyer of the White Race. He went not merely as an ex-member of a Georgia chain gang and former inmate of San Quentin, he went as a shrewd, cultured and hardened world traveler. He was by all odds the most dangerous fiend to have arrived in New York for many years. And there, in the city to end cities, he established his setup, which beyond all doubt was one of the most amazing arrangements in the history of white slavery.

17

"ALL RIGHT, I KNOW I'M BEING IRRITABLE. I'M BEING IM-possible," said Patricia. "I'm sorry, I've got some troubles. Actually I don't want to be nasty and destructive, that's the last thing I want to do. I want to be helpful, that's the main reason I asked you to come here today. I know you're in trouble! Dick, I know that!"

Dick was listening to her with half his mind. "I wonder why any sensible person would *want* to write books," he said. "You know almost by definition that has got to be a neurotic activity, an escape from reality into a dream world. Why would anyone want to do such a thing?"

"Are you joking?" asked Pat. "There are a hundred reasons, a thousand reasons."

"Sure, and all of them are schizophrenic. What else is schizophrenia but an escape from reality?"

"You remind me of sophomores talking in college," said Pat. "Shall I answer that? Well, all right. The artist creates reality, he doesn't escape from it."

"Yeah," said Dick. "Well, a very successful writer is coming to the apartment for dinner tonight. More successful than myself, both critically and commercially. Nathan Hammerfield, you've heard of him. He's not only successful, he's very bright and a nice guy as well. The thing I am wondering is, what does he think of all of this, what does he make of it, what are his attitudes?"

"I hope healthier than yours because he is talented," said Pat. "But you can't be serious, you know better. What you say would apply to a friend of yours like that towheaded boy; he has no talent. I'm talking about a real artist, not a phony artist, and in the case of the real artist what happens isn't schizophrenia. It might look like it, but it isn't. The real artist can't escape from reality even if he tries. The truth always intrudes like an unwelcome visitor at a banquet."

"What banquet?" asked Dick. "I still say there must be easier and better ways to make a living. I mean, this side of an insane asylum."

"Would you call *The Brothers Karamazov* schizophrenic? Would you call *Madame Bovary* schizophrenic? Would you call *Huckleberry Finn* schizophrenic?"

"Yeah," said Dick, "in a sense."

"Well, I have a new analyst and that is what I wanted to talk to you about. I'm sorry this conversation got off on the wrong foot. If I was nasty and irritable then I apologize, because that is mainly what I wanted to talk to you about, this new man I've been seeing. He's a strictly orthodox Freudian and he's very, very good. I've learned things about myself that I didn't dream of. Some very surprising things, some things that would interest you very much."

Dick didn't believe it. He didn't want to know what an orthodox Freudian would say about Patricia, but it was better than talking about writing. He asked, "Such as, for example?"

"Well, you've always said I'm controlling, that I try to

dominate you and tell you what to do and how to live. I never thought so and I still don't think so in regard to you in particular, but I have come to realize there is some indirect truth in it. Dr. Weisenschaft has made me face some rather unpleasant things about myself."

"Dr. Weisenschaft?"

"Yes, Weisenschaft. Dr. Carl Weisenschaft. Do you know him, have you heard of him?"

"No, but I know somebody by that name. Or at least it was her maiden name. I'm sure she's no relation."

"Who is she?"

"Oh, she's nobody."

"You know a girl named Weisenschaft? Who is she, how do you know her?"

"Pat, she's nobody, just a girl I know casually."

"Well, I was saying, Dr. Weisenschaft has made me face some unpleasant things about myself. I'm not controlling as you say, but unconsciously I resent men. I criticize them, pick at them, try to tear down their self-esteem. I did that to Herb. I thought I was trying to arouse him, to stimulate him mentally and spiritually, make him participate in life, but it was a mistake. I carried it too far. And lately I'm afraid I've been doing the same thing to Charles without intending to. Just like when you come in here and I'm happy to see you and then I say unpleasant things without intending to or wanting to. Do you understand that? It makes me unhappy to behave this way; it makes me miserable. Do you understand that?"

Dick nodded. "Well, yeah," he said. "You're not yourself today, I know that."

"I've had some trouble, a stupid misunderstanding. I don't want to go into it. The point is I do this *thing* to men without even intending to and it's caused me a world of grief. You don't know the grief it has caused me, this thing I do without even realizing it. But Dr. Weisenschaft has made me under-

stand this, face it, admit it. The cause was perfectly plain all
the time but these things have to be brought into conscious-
ness. Of course you've read Freud and you know what it is."

Dick's headache was throbbing in his temple. What was she
talking about? He stared blankly at her. "Well, no," he said,
"I don't, actually."

"It's penis envy," said Pat. "It's a plain, simple, classic case
of penis envy."

A stab of pain hit Davenport between the eyes. "Um, well,"
he said, "that is one Freudian idea I've never wholly understood."

"It's simple. Unconsciously I feel that I'm lacking something, that I'm incomplete. I feel that someone—the doctor at
the hospital or more probably my father—mutilated me when
I was a helpless baby. This causes fear and anxiety. It's very
common among girls and women; in fact, it's universal, but in
some it's worse than in others."

Dick could barely resist saying, "What nonsense." It would
be pointless to argue with her, and rude and cruel as well. He
said, "Well, that's very interesting, Pat, and there's probably
a lot of truth in it symbolically. I know a lot of women resent
men and I don't blame them—it's a man's world, the double
standard and all that. But I'm skeptical of all such theories.
You know the old saying, 'Bullfighting is horseshit.' "

"Bullfighting? What are you talking about?"

"Ah-h, well . . . I mean I don't trust theories. Any kind of
theories. Look at all the theories about bullfighting, just look
at the reams of theories about it. The art, the elegance, the
grace under pressure and so forth. But when you come right
down to it, a man is out there killing a dumb animal and
risking his life for no sensible reason at all. The plain truth is
that bullfighting is horseshit."

"I think you'd get a few arguments in Spain. That's pretty
philistine and ethnocentric, Dickie. Different art exists in dif-

ferent lands. By your reasoning ballet is horseshit, too. What sensible reason is there for girls to run around on a stage on their toes?"

"They look cute," said Dick, "and at least there's no bull chasing them."

Pat stared coolly at him. "I don't like this anti-intellectual tinge that has come into your thinking," she said. "Freud's discovery of penis envy is not a theory. It's a demonstrable scientific fact based on thousands of hours of therapy and research. All girls and women have penis envy in varying degrees."

"Well, that could be," said Dick. "If Freud says so it must be true, but take this little girl I know named Weisenschaft. She might have penis envy, probably she does, but she's also got something else, penis *interest.* And I think penis interest is more important than penis envy. She doesn't want one herself, what would she do with it if she had it? Pee with it? She can do that anyhow, quicker and better than a man. Maybe a Lesbian would want one, that would make sense, it would be reasonable. But let's face it, Pat. Most women don't want to *own* a penis, they just want to *borrow* one. The theory is clever but it doesn't hold up. Bullfighting is horseshit. Women don't have penis envy, not really."

Pat smiled faintly. "Thus glibly he questions one of the great minds of the twentieth century," she said. "Who is this girl, anyhow?"

"She's nobody. I can accept Freud's idea as a metaphor, as an expression of women's resentment at their role, but I have a feeling he meant it literally. And I don't think it's literally true at all."

"You could be wrong, very wrong. Who is this girl? That's the second time you've mentioned her. Who is this girl you know named Weisenschaft?"

Dick hesitated. The conversation was getting a little bit out of control. In a way he was being nastier than Pat herself had been; to deride her faith in this analyst was not only rude and destructive, it was totally pointless. Maybe a straight, simple answer to her question would get the conversation at last into a human frame of reference. He shrugged and said:

"Who is she? I'll tell you who she is. She's a little girl down at the Educational Union on the Lower East Side where I've been teaching writing to kids. She wants to go to bed with me and I hate to admit it but I'm very tempted. Her name is Pauline. She's small-breasted, about five feet two, a brunette and she's married. She has a very sweet smile, but she's a crass little bitch. Her husband is called Nicky. He's an Italian. Her last name actually is Riccobono. Weisenschaft was her maiden name."

"All right, I get the point and that is precisely what I was trying to say to you before," replied Pat in her martyr voice. "I do meddle. It's none of my business the girls you want to play around with and now that you're a successful writer I'm sure there're many of them. But I've got to say I find your sarcasm a little wearing."

"Sarcasm? I wasn't being sarcastic, I swear to God I wasn't."

"And I must say I don't want to hear squalid tales of adultery. It isn't enlightening, it isn't amusing and it isn't fun."

"Well, I'm sorry," said Dick.

"And frankly, I've got to say this, I don't think you should cheat on that nice little Jewish girl. After all, you married her."

The thing to do was get up and leave. Pat was in a totally impossible mood. What was eating on her, anyhow? "Well, at least now she's a *nice* little Jewish girl," said Dick. "That's an improvement over the way you used to talk about her. Then she was just an unmodified little Jewish girl, now she's nice."

"What are you talking about? I like Naomi, I like her very much."

"Sure, some of your best friends."

"Are you accusing me of being anti-Semitic? Good God, Herb was my lover for years, how can you think that? It's not even worth talking about. I like Naomi, I like her very much and you owe her a lot. And frankly I think it would be disgusting for you to go crawl in bed with some married girl. But go ahead and play if you want to, it's none of my business. Have fun."

"Okay, I will," said Dick. "If you're against it there must be something good about it. I have a date with her tomorrow afternoon."

Pat got up and walked to the breakfront and poured more scotch. "The reason I asked you whether or not you're working is because of Dr. Weisenschaft. He's one of the world's foremost authorities on writing block. He's a very brilliant man and he could help you."

"Oh, Christ," said Dick. "You have given me an absolutely splitting headache in no time at all. I have reached the limit, Pat."

"I'm only trying to be helpful. Dr. Weisenschaft is a very, very brilliant man. He wrote a book about writing problems and you should read it even if you don't see him. But you should see him. He's treated some very well known writers and with great success."

"Well, if I need him I'll give him a ring."

"You need him right now. You obviously have a writing block."

"Oh, Christ. I don't even know what that is and I don't expect ever to find out."

"Well, it ties in with rejection of the breast. Completely unconscious, of course. Our culture is ridiculously breast-oriented, Europeans laugh at us."

"Well, they've got them over there, too."

"Yes, but they don't worship them. In America large breasts are worshiped, idolized in the most absurd way."

Dick glanced at his wristwatch. "I've got to go," he said. "I've got to buy some wine, people are coming for dinner."

"Well, all right, go ahead then," she said casually, and then to his numbed surprise she bowed her head, produced a handkerchief from somewhere and began weeping into it. "It's none of my business about you and that girl, I . . . I know that, I didn't mean to pry. I'm sorry, forgive me. I know I haven't behaved very well . . . but I . . . something bad has happened. It's stupid, but it's bad and it's my fault. I've got a problem back in the bedroom, a real problem, and I can't stand it when you're sarcastic with me like that, even though I deserve it. I'm happy for your success, I really am, I don't feel the way you think. . . ."

"Oh, God," said Dick. "Pat, you misunderstood me. I wasn't being sarcastic. Whatever your problem is in the bedroom, I've got a problem, too, a problem with that girl. I wanted to talk to you about her, I wanted to know your opinion. But first things first. What's the trouble back in the bedroom?"

Weeping, Pat replied, "I hurt Charles's sense of manhood. He won't talk to me. Every time I go in there he pulls the covers over his head. It's been four hours since the argument, the misunderstanding. Ever since it happened he won't say a word to me."

"Mmm, I see," said Dick. "He's back there in the bed and every time you go in he pulls the covers over his head?"

"Yes, he does!"

"And it's because you hurt his sense of manhood?"

"Yes!"

"And how did you do that?"

Pat was blushing. It must be something pretty extreme, thought Dick, something pretty awful. "Well, it's a little embarrassing to tell you. I don't know exactly how to put it. I don't want to be clinical. The point is, I hurt his sense of manhood. We were making love and I . . . well, I hurt his sense of manhood."

"I see," said Dick. "You hurt his sense of manhood. Exactly how did you do that?"

"Well, it was the conditions."

"The conditions? What do you mean?"

"Well, the conditions, that's all I can tell you. The conditions weren't good."

Dick blinked and rubbed his jaw. What was she talking about? "You mean the mood you were in, your frame of mind?"

"No, the physical conditions. It wasn't his fault, it was the physical conditions. I couldn't feel him and I told him he was . . . small."

"You told him he was . . . small?"

"Well, yes, in so many words. But I didn't mean a thing by it, I swear I didn't."

"And he's in there now with the covers over his head?"

"Well, he pulls them over whenever I come in. Actually he's staring at the ceiling. Or at least he was last time I peeped through the keyhole. He's just lying there staring up at the ceiling with his jaw gritted."

Again Dick blinked in a grave manner and rubbed his own jaw. As ridiculous as it all was, somehow he had to take it seriously. At least it explained Pat's horrible mood. He asked: "Did you use any insulting, belittling expressions?"

"Oh, no. All I said was that because of the conditions it wasn't working, that I couldn't feel him, he was . . . small."

Conditions? What was this business about conditions? Suddenly Dick remembered the messy bathroom. His facetious question had hit a bull's-eye, she and Charles had made love in the tub. "Umm, well," said Dick, "not the smartest thing to say to a man. No, no, not the smartest. Just hearing about it makes me want to pull the cover over my head, too. In fact this whole thing is a funny little coincidence; I've been having a fantasy lately about a fellow with a problem just like your friend Charles's."

"But Charles has no problem! I mean, he's not abnormal or anything, there's nothing *wrong* with him—and besides, it doesn't make any difference. Not to a woman, it's just male vanity. And I told him so, I told him it didn't matter if he was a little smaller than most men."

"You said *that* to him?" asked Dick. "Good God, Pat. Now I'll admit Charles is being a little extreme in there with the covers over his head, but how would you expect any man in the world to react to such a remark?"

"Oh, I know," said Pat in a feeble voice. "And I did say Herb was bigger. I didn't mean anything by it, but I did tell him that. I said it casually, without thinking."

"Casually, without thinking?"

Pat put a hand on her forehead. "Oh, I know! I know, I know, it was very tactless of me. And it hurt Charles especially because of the myth, the legend. He made some bitter, furious remarks in the bathroom and I don't blame him. And the other day I said something about his bald head and that was against the myth, too. It was very, very tactless of me. I've been reproaching myself all afternoon; that's why I've been in such a horrible mood. I'm afraid I took it out on you and I'm sorry, I know I haven't been very pleasant."

"Well, it's understandable with your boyfriend in there with the covers over his head. He's taking it really hard. Actually, you weren't all that bad, Pat, not to me, a lot that you said was true. I *have* had some trouble getting down to this book and I've got no business playing around with Pauline Riccobono, that is perfectly true."

In deepest gloom, she replied, "I didn't remember about the myth, that was my mistake, I didn't even think about it, the myth. It never even so much as entered my head."

"I don't exactly follow you," said Dick. "What myth?"

"Why, the myth that they're never bald and that they have big ones."

"They're never bald and have big ones? What are you talking about? Who is *they?*"

"Negroes," said Pat. "Didn't I tell you Charles is a Negro?"

"Good God," said Dick, and at once he buttoned his lip. In view of his recent daydreams it was an even funnier little coincidence, but he was not about to mention it. Neither Pat nor Charles would find Nicholas Lordgod Sampson in the least amusing, that was for sure. And it was one myth and legend they were not going to take away from him. He *liked* the myth, there was poetic justice in it. The thing wouldn't work without that particular myth and legend—who could imagine a *white* man hung like that? To hell with Charles and drab reality.

"Oh, Lord," said Pat. "I think I just heard the toilet flush in the bathroom. Charles is up."

"Bring him in and give him a drink," said Dick. "I'm sure he can use one."

"This is serious, I *love* him," said Patricia.

"Well, he'll be all right," said Dick. "Just tell him, 'It's not the size of the weapon that matters, it is the fury of the attack that counts.' That's an old folk saying that goes all the way back to Napoleon. He had one three inches long, you know, and look what he did to Europe."

"I *do* love him," said Pat.

Dick smiled wryly to himself. As you love me, he thought, pick 'em up with one hand and knock 'em down with the other. Freud wasn't wholly wrong of course, "penis envy" was a way to look at it. But the question went deeper than any penis could go, even that of Nicholas Lordgod Sampson himself.

IT WOULD CERTAINLY APPEAR THAT POLLY COULD BE
nothing but putty in the hands of such a fiend as Nicholas
Lordgod Sampson. As has been said, she had run into the one
who could master her, a Dark Demon who possessed not only
criminal inspiration but also the red, white and blue whork of
whorks. Or so it seemed beyond any doubt; her experiences
with such timid flames as Dr. Murger and Another Daddy
(fiend though that one was) and poor little mouse-souled Archie Schnerd could hardly have prepared her to withstand the
elemental blasts of the pit itself, or so it would appear.

"Quite nice," said Nick to himself thoughtfully as he stared
down through the canvas eyes of Sir Walter Raleigh at the
giant-breasted baby doll on the sofa. She would practically
complete the stable. He could pick up an Indian somewhere
to take the place of Running Moose and he'd have the five
basic ponies. "Mm, quite nice indeed. Suitable, I think."

In a completely unguarded mood Polly left the musty old
lobby of the Seamus and bowed with a smile to Chauncey

Gaylord as she exited. He pursed his lips at her disapprovingly, the old fart, but she didn't care. The elderly Irish doorman in the red coat greeted her with a salute and a bow.

Know that man from somewhere, thought Polly. But it didn't matter, on she went, humming a little tune. It was a pleasant day in May; the sun was warm and golden and slanted down cheerfully into the darkened swathe that had once been Broadway.

Polly felt optimistic. True, she had not thus far enjoyed any great triumph—what was six hundred dollars loot a week? But all she needed was time, just a little time to get her sea legs and catch on to the New York scene; then they would dance to her tune. With another pleasant little goatlike switch of the hips that made her behind quiver deliciously, Polly rounded the corner and headed back uptown, her white purse dangling in one hand and the fingers of her other hand extended gracefully out to the side, as if to say: "Ain't I the raspberries?"

Little did the dumb cunt know. As she sashayed along wagging her man-maddening behind, a dark and silent shadow suddenly materialized in the recess formed by the mouldering doorway of an ancient loft building in which Diamond Jim Brady and Lillian Russell once had cavorted. It now was filled with ferns and daisies. So are the mighty fallen and such is the brevity of the day. Once a townhouse, now a wholesale daisy depository. Silent as a haunt in a southern boneyard and twice as menacing, the shadow followed her.

The encounter was outside squat Macy's. Polly was taken entirely by surprise, distracted as she was by the gruesome insanity of the department store. She had stopped for a moment to look into a window and relish all the mad goodies when she felt a presence by her side. A *large* presence. Weirdly, almost as if by a sixth sense or something fourth dimensional that they don't know about, a *chill* ran down her *pink* spine from the downy *nape* of her neck to the plump *cleft* of her gorgeous kissable ass. And huggable, too, that valentine. She turned and for once her blue eyes were not smiling, they were glints of arctic ice cold enough to burn a polar bear.

Shock! Ah-h, ha! Yes-s-s. Yes-yes-yes-yes-yes. Mmm-mm, no menace here but something else again. Mmm, indeed something else, something not only edible but yummy. A tiny knee-knocking gasp came involuntarily from Polly as her sensitive and gifted clit twitched intuitively and poked through the furze and peered upward with cyclopian x-ray vision and perceived overhead through panty and skirt a gigantic, suave-looking, well-clad and divinely handsome maharajah in a silken turban with an enormous jewel glowing in the center of the crisscross folds.

"Pahdon me," he said, sincerely.

"Why . . . why . . . *certainly!*" exclaimed Polly, her blue eyes bugging radiantly as she smiled her best. Yoicks! The *money* he must have if that huge jewel was any indication. Oh, yeah, he had money, he sure as hell did, she had heard about those maharajahs and how their subjects every year gave them their weight in gold. And this was a *big* maharajah, he must weigh two hundred and fifty pounds and all of it bone and muscle —he was at least six feet seven and had a physique that would make Tarzan look puny. And the *whork* he must have on him —holy catfish, what would it be like to have a thing like *that* come at you, rampant? Mmm, thought Polly, as the clit quivered nervously and snuggled down in the hay. But it soon peeked out again, its x-ray vision at work, because before Polly could get too apprehensive about the damage that might be done by such an engine of destruction a warm and humorously tolerant smile of pearly teeth further soothed and coshered her. Again he spoke in that deep rumbling bass:

"I do hope you will pahdon my audacity, fair lady, if I seem a bit forward and presumptuous. But I wonder if you would be so gracious as to render a small assistance to a stranger in your land? Although haply I have maintained here for many years—or rather my subjects have maintained for me—a modest dwelling on your Park Avenue, a small triplex *pied-à-pomme* for my rare visits here, I do not know *les intime* this complex city and I am at the moment *l'avoir de la peine à la perte sèche.* Can you tell me where I am?"

"Why, now, maybe I can," said Polly. She smiled and glanced around at a nearby street sign. "This is . . . Broadway and . . . Thirty-second Street. Manhattan Island, New York, New York!"

"You are most kind," said the turbanned giant. "That orients me."

Polly leaned her head a bit to the side like a chicken studying a storm. The jewel was blood red and big as an orange and it drew her gaze despite her best efforts to show a little aloofness. She couldn't avoid fastening her blue eyes on it, and since the turbanned giant stood quite near this made them cross slightly. "Mmm," she said. "You've got subjects? Where are you from, Persia or someplace?"

"India, fair lady." The incredibly handsome stranger smiled. "I see you are not familiar with the implications of the turban. It is a matter not of mere national dress but of religious moment. But pahdon my audacity for suggesting you are unaware of its meaning, forgive my presumption."

"Don't mention it," said Polly. "What does it mean?"

"My religion and station in life require that I wear this headdress," said the giant in low, cultivated British tones with a trace of French for spice—hardly anything vulgarly American about him at all; this creamboat didn't even need any nutmeg on him, eat him raw with a spoon. "Howevah, that is not strictly true any longer. I fear it is in some measure a matter of sentiment with me, because I have left my native land not wholly by my own choice, alas. As you see I am wearing conventional Western garb except for the headdress and its sacred ruby."

"Well . . . well, this is just fascinating!" exclaimed Polly. "May I ask, what is your name? What . . . what are you called? Do you mind if I inquire that?"

"Certainly not," said the handsome giant. "I am Pahlevi Shagmadragma, Maharajah of Losam-Nehi and the adjoining quaternions of Ramsa-Shakata and Purlong-Shagmadragmanika and Sharvilaka and Mirichakatakika, Guardian of the Great Tiger Ruby Eye of the Idol of Aryaka and Humble Servant of Kali, Knight of the Order of the Slain Badger and Chevalier of la Légion de la Femme Pécheresse Putois."

"Gosh," said Polly. "Maharajah, you don't know what a thrill this is. I'm honored to pieces to meet you, I can't get over it. How did you happen to lose your kingdom over there?"

A shadow passed over the Maharajah's face. "Nehru and the British," he said. "They formed a cabal for the purpose of eating away my power. And they succeeded with the help of Ghandi. My subjects . . . lost faith in my divinity. It broke their hearts and mine. I will always treasure the gold elephant they gave me at the abdication ceremonies."

"Gold elephant? You mean a solid gold elephant?"

"Oh, yes, quite solid."

"A solid gold elephant. You mean a little one?"

"Yes. It stands only nine feet in height."

"Huh? You got a solid gold elephant that stands nine feet high and you call that little? Why, it must be worth millions. Did you melt it down?"

"Melt it down?" asked the Maharajah in horror. "Certainly not, fair lady! It is a work of art!"

"But couldn't you use the money now that you've lost your kingdom?"

The maharajah smiled. "I am hardly impoverished, fair lady. I have on deposit in banks in Geneva, Zurich, New York, London, Amsterdam, Sydney and Buenos Aires well over six hundred million dollars. A fraction of my former wealth, to be sure, but adequate to maintain me. My subjects would not have it otherwise. However, this vulgar talk of money must bore you, Miss . . . Miss . . . ?"

"Claire de Lune," said Polly. "Call me Claire. It doesn't bore me at all. You've got a solid gold elephant nine feet high and more than six hundred million dollars besides—that doesn't bore me. Tell me more."

"You are so charming," said the maharajah. "Would you care to join me for a cooling libation at a nearby watering spot, then come with me to a couturier for a suitable gown and afterward dine and dance with me on the Starlight Roof of the Waldorf-Astoria?"

"Oh boy, would I!" said Polly.

The maharajah made a crook of his arm and whistled piercingly for a taxi through the sexy gap in his pearly choppers. Soon thereafter they were on the Starlight Roof of the Waldorf-Astoria.

"Oh, dear me," said Polly as she danced in the arms of the tall maharajah while dusk spread o'er Manhattan and the moon rose o'er the Bronx, "what was your name again, I didn't quite catch it . . . ?"

"Pahlevi to you, fair lady," said the maharajah with a sexy smile. "How charmingly you dance."

"Oh, Pahlevi, you dance divinely yourself," said Polly. "You have such a sense of rhythm. May I call you Pah?"

"By all means," answered the maharajah, "and may I reciprocate and call you Claire?"

"Huh?"

"Claire, instead of Miss de Lune."

"Oh, yeah, sure. Call me Claire."

"Claire. Ah-h, Claire de Lune . . . that is lovely," said the maharajah. "It's so French, so quintessentially French. Do you like France or do you just tolerate it?"

"Well, I've never been there," replied Polly, "but I love the *idea* of it."

"The idea of France?"

"Yeah, you know, their talking another language and eating snails and everything. The Eiffel Tower, roquefort cheese. And you know, Madame Maintenon, Marie Antoinette, all of that. This teacher I had taught me all about it and I love the idea of it. Have you been there?"

"*Mais oui, mon petite putasserie,*" said the maharajah with a smile of amusement at her naiveté, "I have a small flat in the Palace of Versailles and a more modest *pied-à-pomme* in Notre Dame. Perhaps if you're in France sometime you could call."

"Love to."

"Consider yourself invited, fair lady." The maharajah's huge, powerful arm wound about her waist as he gently but firmly pulled her closer while the orchestra played "Begin the Beguine." Gracefully, they circled the polished floor of the Starlight Roof on top of the Waldorf-Astoria at Forty-ninth Street and Fifth Avenue as other couples looked on in awe. He drew her even closer. Scorching thrills were running through Polly as she felt her breasts mash against his enormous chest. Wow. What did he *have* down there? Made her dizzy to think about it.

"Ah-h, Pah," sighed Polly. "You do dance divinely." Then, to spur him on and inflame mad passion in him, she whispered, "Hold me tighter," and he did; his great arm circled her hourglass waist like an oak band. An even greater dizziness came upon Polly. It had never been like this with Another Daddy or Dr. Murger, that was for sure! She moved her body against him, venturing a small but scrungy little grind the better to inflame him, and a surging male counterpart of her subtle offering flowed back at her on the beat of the music. And what a counterpart. "Oooo-ooo, Pah!" she said. "Do-o-on't!" What was that *thing* down there? . . . was it *possible?* Hmm, leaping lizards.

"My darling of the golden hair," breathed Pahlevi into her

pink ear. "You stir the slumbering manhood in me. I hope you don't mind. Since the death of my precious bride, the maharanee, I have known no woman, fair lady."

"Thought you had a harem," said Polly.

"Well, yes, of course, but the British took it away from me. The British and Nehru. And Ghandi. Dance on, fair lady, dance on."

"Well, that isn't healthy, Pah. You need a girlfriend."

"I think it may be the will of Kali that my period of mourning soon will come to an end. Dance on, fair lady, I am stirred strangely."

"Me too," said Polly.

Rhythmically they circled the dance floor, executing such graceful steps that the other dancers shrank back so as not to interfere. Around and around they circled, sealed together, one.

"You are like the gentle effulgent mist that rises from a lily pond in early morn," whispered Pahlevi. "You are the dawn and the sun, the doe and the tiger, the serpent and the earth." A moist hotness appeared on Polly's neck, a hot tingling wet warmth followed by a noise like that of a mule slowly pulling its hoof out of deep mud.

"Oh, Pah, your kisses are sweet as wine," sighed Polly.

"Not half so sweet as your precious delicate neck, fair lady."

Again there was a sound of a hoof being withdrawn from deep mud, a kind of "Su-u-u-k-k-k-KK!" noise.

"Oh, *Pah!*" said Polly. "What you *do* to me!"

"I burn with the love of you, my pet. The more the tragedy my religion forbids it, the more I visualize you as my new maharanee."

"Oh, do you?" asked Polly. "And to think I only got in from West Virginia last week! Do you really mean it, Pah?"

"Yes, that is my vision and I hope I can square it religious-wise. I mean I hope Kali will look the other way. But come, let us go. I think from the gestures of the varlets we are due at table. No doubt the ostrich tongues have arrived. Shall we?" Head bowed graciously to the side, the maharajah held forth an arm and he and Polly strolled regally across the floor, all eyes upon them. As they sat at the table, Polly said:

"Pah, this dress really *does* become me—you were a woolly lamb to get it for me."

"A whut?" asked Pah in a strange guttural voice. "Whut you say?"

"A lamb. A woolly lamb. I mean, you were awful sweet to get it for me."

The maharajah cleared his throat and replied, "Not at all, my dear. Would but that the gown were better. Actually it is a cheap rag hardly worthy of your sublime beauty."

"Eleven hundred dollars, cheap?" asked Polly. Bug-eyed, she stared down at the pink fluffy evening dress, remembering the great sheaf of bills the maharajah had pulled from his pockets at the sweet moment of purchase. She remembered too the contemptuous manner in which he had spoken to the couturier in the salon:

"This gown is a travesty of feminine attire. *C'est un retentissant saltimbanque de la Rue Rugissement avec non quatorze ragoûtant, vraiment, gaz lacrymogène, zut peut-être pêcherie, voilà! C'est un répoussé marronier,* it is merchandize entirely obscene in conception! Would that we were in Paris! However, your other gowns are quite impossible and we shall try it for the evening! I reserve the right of returning it in the morning should it prove to be as vulgar a creation as my present judgment indicates and I trust in the meanwhile you will have your stitchers and hemmers busy at their tables throughout the night preparing a series of true originals for madame! Eleven hundred pounds—pahdon, dollars—here you are, a receipt, please." What style! What flair! What suavity!

"Ah, I see that the *l'autruche languette entrecôte à la mode de Caen* is ready and lying in aspic," said Pah.

"Yes, isn't it," said Polly.

As they watched the three waiters rush here and there about the table, snipping up bits of *l'autruche languette,* adjusting the wine glasses and sprinkling caviar here and there, Polly and the maharajah chatted on.

"Did you know that some ostriches weigh as much as three hundred pounds?"

"No, I didn't realize that," said Polly.

"And did you know that they can run forty-five miles an hour if they are in the mood?"

"No, I didn't, but I love their tongues. This is just simply delicious. My, the French can cook."

"What they can do to an egg you wouldn't believe," said Pah. "They know more ways to cook an egg than we even begin to know over here. I mean, more than you Ameddicans know, but excuse my presumption."

"Oh, the French can cook up a storm, I know that," said Polly. "I'm afraid the food in West Virginia isn't all *that* good."

"Tell me about yourself, Claire. Where is this place West Virginia? Is it one of your western mountainous states?"

"Well, it's mountainous but it isn't western," said Polly. "Yes, I'll have some ostrich tongue, waiter, but go light on the caviar. Yes, a speck of champagne, thank you. No, Pah. You see, West Virginia is more one of our *southern* states."

"Ah, yes, one of the southern states, I know of them. These are the states of the black slave folk, no?"

"Well, if you mean the niggers, we haven't got a lot of them in West Virginia and the ones we've got are all leaving. We don't care for them down there, they've gotten too uppity. You see, down South we keep them in their place, but up here they can do all *kinds* of things—ride on the subway, walk down the sidewalk and even look straight at white women."

"Um, uh," said Pah. "How distressing."

"Oh, I wouldn't have anything to do with one of them. They're so *black*. And not only are they black, they *stink*. I think they're part pig."

"Whut," asked Pah in a strange muffled voice, "whut you say? Who you call a pig, gal?"

"Why, the niggers," said Polly. "Pah, you shouldn't talk with your mouth full, it's bad manners."

Pahlevi's hand moved slowly across the front of his dinner jacket to the secret pocket wherein rested a folded, bone-handled razor. It was an automatic reflex. He had no intention of using it, at least not at this moment—a blonde head conking on the polished dance floor of the Starlight Roof of the Waldorf-Astoria might cause a certain commotion. "My dear," he said, "your saucy spirit charms me beyond comparison. You are like a fiery dawn in the forest. A word to the wise sufficeth. I shall avoid the Ameddican South with its *black* niggers that *stink* and are *part pig*."

"And part monkey, too," said Polly.

Thus the web was spun. Gradually strand was laid upon strand as the great spider in seeming awkwardness edged back and forth across the area of entrapment, folded with its fore-claws, adjusting, placing, and leaping rapidly back and forth and sailing down temporarily in space, hung on the flowing strand that poured from its horrible innards, great killing fangs shut now but a portent of power and terror. And so the gay buzzing fly proceeded blithely unaware, ignorant in its bliss and smelling nothing of the half-rotted bodies of other flies stung and paralyzed in the spider's lair. It was ever thus. Polly Dawn, Claire de Lune, call her what you will, she could be bested for a while but she could never be won by man born of woman, not even if a lordgod bird presided over the parturition. Sooner or later, the fangs would open and bite.

"You will come with me to my penthouse?"

Polly looked at him in reproach. "Oh, Pah," she said. "You know I can't do that."

"But why not?"

Polly hung her head. "It wouldn't be . . . right," she answered.

"Oh, my dear, certainly it would."

She sighed as if in pain. "You know I'd *like* to, and you know I trust you completely, it isn't that."

"Then what is the problem, fair lady?"

Polly blushed crimson. She smiled sadly and lifted her large blue eyes upon him. A trace of guilty tears could be seen in the soft and glowing indigo orbs. "Maybe . . . maybe it's . . . *myself* I don't trust!" She looked down quickly, overcome with shame at this confession.

"Ah, my dear, you are so delicate," said the maharajah. "I shall cherish you always. Taxi!" With a flashing smile of perfect teeth, he took her arm and helped her into a cab, then said to the driver, "The Park Avenue Towers, please. Rapidly but cautiously. You convey royalty, driver."

"Pah," said Polly. She squeezed the huge forearm under her hand. "Pah, really, you must take me home. I . . . I can't go to your penthouse."

"We will just stop by for a glimpse of the view of Manhattan and a glass of 1814 brandy. New York from up above is a fairyland of wonder."

"Oh, but I can't."

"You are so charming when you protest, so enchanting when you draw away. . . ."

"Now just a sec," said Polly calmly. "If you think I'm that type of girl and that I'm protesting in name only, I mean just on the surface, as a matter of form, then you've got the wrong girl, because I'm sorry, I'm not like that. Now you can just take me home, please."

Pahlevi smiled, his white teeth shining against the honey-golden tan of his skin as the cab sped along Park Avenue. "And if I should balk?" he asked gently. "If I should resist your resistance?"

"I'll yell for the cops," said Polly. "Seriously, Pah, tell the driver to turn around. You know I can't go to your place. Why, it wouldn't be right, and nothing could make it right. No argument could ever make it right for me to go to your apartment *unchaperoned!*"

Pahlevi's smile didn't waver. "I am unfamiliar with your Ameddican customs, my dear. But I had hoped I might surprise you with a small memento of the evening, a souvenir of your night with me. Nothing of any particular importance or value, just a small gift."

"Um-hmm," said Polly. "What gift was that?"

"A triple strand of black pearls, my dear. I had wanted you to have something to remember me by, because alas I fear I have some sad news. I must leave you tonight. I sail at dawn for France on the *Queen Mary*. I had dreamed of you as my maharanee, but we shall never meet again. My aged grandmother lies on her deathbed at Versailles."

"Oh, but Pah!" said Polly. "Take me with you! I've always wanted to see Versailles! Don't leave me, take me with you!"

"Driver," said Pahlevi, "turn the cab. We must——"

"Oh, no!" said Polly. "Keep on, driver. Pah . . . what was that memento you were speaking of? Pearls, you said? Three strands of black pearls? I couldn't accept, but . . . well, I wouldn't want to hurt you. . . ."

"A mere trinket barely worth ten thousand of your dollars——"

"Ten *thousand* dollars?"

"——and since your customs prohibit the exchange of gifts between man and woman. . . ."

"The customs don't," said Polly, "as long as it's understood there are no strings attached to the gift."

"Strings?" asked Pahlevi with a pensive frown. *"C'est à dire, la ficelle, la corde? Le cordon, le chapelet, peut-être? La bride? Le ruban? La fibre? Les filandres? La kyrielle, l'enfilade, la série, la tirade? Reculer pour mieux sauter, le cordage, le licou, un bout de filin? Libre cours, les manoeuvres courants?—qui file, filant, visquex?* Fair lady, begging the pardon of the Hunchback of Notre Dame, pearls black or white must have a string!"

"Look, Pah, stop throwing all that talk at me. What is this supposed to be, French One, Dotesville High? Are you trying to make me feel like a dummy?"

"Not quite, my dear," replied Pahlevi with suave poise. "I simply do not understand this string thing."

"Okay, baby. We're two chickens in the pit and this is it. Suppose I went up to your penthouse and we had some of that 1814 brandy and you called up the *Queen Mary* and booked me a stateroom first class and bought me a few furs and clothes and things for the voyage and said, 'Claire, hold onto your hat, I am taking you to Versailles.' Then would you expect me to feel any . . . *differently* toward you than I do now?"

"Differently, my pet, in what sense?"

"Oh, *you* know."

"But . . . but I don't."

"Sure you do. All you men are the same."

"Fair lady, you confound me! *Hic opus, hic labor est———*"

"Don't play dumb, Pah, you know very well what I mean! You men are all the same! You can only think of one thing! What I mean is . . . well . . . if all I said happened, you know, the ticket and the furs and everything, would you expect me to . . . well . . . *go back in your bedroom with you?*"

Pahlevi gently took her hand. "My dear, you have misunderstood me *grotesquely*. No matter what gifts, tokens or trifles, I would never ask of you such a thing as . . . *that*. What have I done to give you such an apprehension? What, fair lady? What have I done?"

"Well, nothing, and in that case, let's go," said Polly. "Just treat me like a sister and all will be well."

Mm-mmm, thought Pah, as he flung sweat off his forehead from below his turban. She was tougher than he'd thought. But he had a surprise for her, little did she know. And little indeed did Polly know. Even if she had entertained some slight suspicions they would have soon been dispelled by the reception that greeted the tall, turbanned giant at the Park Avenue Towers.

"Good evening, Your Highness!" said the gold-spangled doorman, as he threw back the door of the taxi.

"Good evening, Rupert," said the maharajah.

Grandly, they strolled inside the lobby of the Park Avenue Towers into an atmosphere of maniacal luxury. Marble floors, marble walls and a marble ceiling, and clean modern marble, not dirty old worn-out marble. Tossed on the floor were rich Oriental scatter rugs in the making of which children in Kurdistan mountains and children on the banks of the Kizil Irmak had tied knots for years until their little fingers bled and their souls cried for rest.

NATHAN HAMMERFIELD WAS A CLEAN-CUT, MODEST, quiet young man with a self-deprecating wit that was very disarming. The determined line of his jaw and a calm resolve in his clear gray eyes suggested a certain ambition, but it was ambition well under control. It was a hopeful thing to see. His great success evidently had not affected him in any adverse way at all. "Oh, yes," he said with a laugh. "I thought for a while there I would spend the rest of my life building stands for power tools in Vermont. It was ridiculous."

Dick and Naomi sat in the living room having after-dinner coffee with their guests. It had been a pleasant meal. The conversation had been mostly about politics. Nate and his wife Leah were quite liberal politically; they both felt that revolution in America was possible and even probable in the not-too-distant future. Now, however, the conversation had shifted from politics to the problems of a literary career.

"You built stands for power tools, huh?" asked Dick.

"I built 'em and I built 'em. I thought I would never do

anything else. Every day I would get up and build another stand for a power tool."

"That's true," said Leah. "He built stands for power tools."

"And believe me, nothing is more demoralizing than building stands for power tools. You're not even making anything. You're just getting *ready* to make something."

"Well, it's more constructive than what *I've* been doing," said Dick. "In fact, it's downright healthy compared to what I've been doing."

"What is your escape? How do you avoid the grim jaws?"

"I have fantasies, daydreams," said Dick. "It used to be I had them only at night, now I have them all the time. Wild fantasies, cuckoo daydreams. Complicated, too, with a plot. I can be riding the subway or walking along the street and a whole stretch of it will go through my head. It's maddening."

"Well, it might be maddening, but I don't agree that building stupid stands for power tools is more constructive. I think daydreams are more constructive, at least you're dealing with elements of the mind, the imagination. But stands for power tools? Good God. And that is all I did for weeks and weeks."

"That's true," said Leah. "It's all he did for weeks on end. Every day he would get up and build another stand for a power tool. I thought we both would go out of our minds."

"How did you ever get out of it?" asked Dick.

"Excuse me," said Naomi, "the phone's ringing, I'll be right back. Does anyone want more coffee?"

"I'll pour it," said Leah.

"The pot's empty. I can make some more."

"I'll make it," said Leah.

"Oh, no, that's all right."

"I don't mind. I can do it. I'll find everything."

"Trivia, trivia, trivia," said Nate Hammerfield as the two wives left the living room. "I hate to say it but they're like monkeys. I admire and esteem them but they're like monkeys. What were we talking about?"

"I was asking, how did you get out of it? Building stands for power tools?"

"Well, one day I started to build a stand for a band saw. I already had a stand for it, but it wasn't a *good* stand. So I started to build *another* stand for it. I got the plywood and I was about to cut it and all of a sudden I said to myself, 'Oh, to hell with it. This is the most boring thing in the world, building stands for power tools. I might as well write another book as spend my life building stands for power tools.' So I threw down the saw and went and stared at the typewriter for a couple of hours. You know, sat there and stared at it. A kind of contest, a struggle of wills. Stare at it long enough and hard enough and eventually it'll type something."

"Did it? Did it eventually type something?"

"Not that afternoon. But it did the next morning."

"You just got . . . fed up? Was that it? All of a sudden you got fed up?"

"Well, it wasn't sudden. It took months."

Dick shook his head wearily as Naomi returned. "No one was on the phone," she said. "I mean, someone was there, I could hear breathing, but they hung up."

"A creep, they do that," said Hammerfield. "Call up and breathe and masturbate. There are a lot of castrated men around, one of the consequences, I'm afraid, of our competitive society."

"I don't think it was a man," said Naomi. "Whoever it was cleared their throat a little and it sounded like a girl." She sat on the sofa by Dick, hazel eyes upon him. "Are you expecting someone to call?"

"No," said Davenport. "How could I be expecting someone to call?"

"Well, you could be expecting someone."

"I'm sorry, I can't find the coffee," said Leah from the doorway. She was smiling, a handsome, buxom girl in glasses, a girl of the kind Dick called "sexy Jewish." He rather envied Nathan Hammerfield, but Nate, on the other hand, kept eyeing Naomi. Greener pastures, probably. "It must be in some cupboard I don't know about."

"Oh, I'm sorry, it's my fault, I'll get it," said Naomi.

"It must be in some cupboard."

Again Nate and Dick stared after the two wives as they left the living room. "Monkeys," said Nate. "Are you *expecting* a call. It must be in some other cupboard. I love them and admire them but they're monkeys. They talk just to cause an explosion of breath through their vocal cords. Well, sometimes they do. I don't really mean it. They're not really monkeys."

"Anyhow, that's what happened," said Dick. "You finally got fed up building stands for power tools."

"That's right, about three months ago. I got fed up and started a new novel."

"That's great," said Dick. "How's it going?"

Nathan Hammerfield half-shut his eyes and put a hand on his head of thick curly black hair. "Rough," he said. "Really rough."

"It's hard to get into it?"

"Rough," said Hammerfield.

"How do you like it? Do you like what you've done?"

"*Like* it? Are you joking? I loathe it, I detest it, I abominate it."

"Well, that isn't very encouraging," said Dick. "You see, I haven't even started another one at all."

"Eventually it'll be all right. It's like coming down off a jag. Back into the pit of reality and truth. You have to get the ego down and kick the shit out of it and then you can do whatever you can do. Of course this country doesn't help and success

doesn't help. That's how America destroys its writers, with
success. The bastards pick you up only in order to knock you
down. And baby are they laying for me, the woods are full of
them. There's no way I'm going to get good reviews on my
next book, no way on earth. But who gives a damn? I'll get
them on the book after that, or the book after that."

To judge from the line of his jaw and the resolve in his eyes,
Dick could well believe it. It was, he believed, a very healthy
attitude. "In other words, you've discounted the second book
already, or at least the reviews?"

"Of course," said Hammerfield, "except you can't. It'll hurt
anyhow. Who wants to be called an idiot in public? You can't
discount it. No matter what you say you can't do that. No
writer can do it. The worst bullshit I ever heard was at that
Life party when what's-his-name says he doesn't care about
reviews and doesn't even read them. You know, the tall thin
faggot, not the little fat one."

"Roman Mathe," said Dick.

"Yeah, him, the pretty one that looks like Dorian Gray.
He's as full of shit as a Strasbourg goose when he says he
doesn't read reviews and doesn't care what they say. The only
writers that's true of are *crazy.* They not only read the reviews,
they read them eagerly and slobberingly, they paw at them,
they go and sit on the toilet and read them again. And they
bleed. It's pathetic. Some talentless fool says something unkind
and *blood* comes out, real red *blood.* So you can't discount it.
Even if you know damn well it's going to happen, you can't
discount it. And who wants to face that? Nobody. So I build
stands for power tools and——"

"I'm sorry," said Naomi from the doorway. "There's someone on the phone again. It's for you."

Dick put his hands on his hips in annoyance. Just when
Hammerfield was finally getting going she has to come and
interrupt. "Someone's on the phone? Well, who the hell is it?"

"I don't know. It's some girl. She wants to speak to you."

"Oh, okay," said Dick.

"I build stands for power tools and you put off real work with daydreams, the beauty of which is that they aren't written down and the bastards can't get at them. But you might be lucky, you know; your success was a little different from mine. You didn't have all that commercial thing and not quite as much critical hooraw either, if I may say so. You're not exactly as much an obvious mark and they might let you alone. But me, never; they're sharpening their little hatchets right now. And with all the best will in the world, I say, 'Fuck 'em.' It's the only attitude a writer can have, and I guess I've come all the way to Brooklyn to tell you that, as if you didn't know it already. But your girlfriend is waiting on the phone, don't let me keep you waiting."

"I'll be right back," said Dick. "Naomi will get you some more coffee, sit right there. I've got a couple of questions to ask you."

As he walked down the hall to the bedroom, Davenport's thoughts were not on the telephone call that was waiting for him. Nathan Hammerfield had proved to be something of a surprise. Dick was even more impressed with him than before. Underneath the modest, quiet, self-deprecating manner he was a formidable personality. Most of the writers at the *Life* party had been very clever, especially the two homosexuals and of course the crippled girl from the Deep South—but they were all clever, the bunch at the *Life* party, that was how they'd gotten there. Clever, yes, clever and talented, but how many would survive? Nathan Hammerfield would seem to be a good bet. For some of them, however, the *Life* party would be the zenith of their careers.

The baby was still awake in his crib biting his hands. Dick reached down and took his fingers from his mouth and said, "Don't bite yourself, Sam." His tone was right; the baby radar accepted it, a beautiful smile came on Sam's face. Someone was on the phone; he had to answer it; but for a moment Dick stared down at his very small son. Was it possible for a child so young to feel real love for a parent? If not, where did the smile come from? There seemed to be real love in the baby's eyes. Dick picked up the telephone and said:

"Yes, hello, who is it?"

"It's me," said a faint and distant and muffled voice.

"What? What's that?"

"It's . . . me," said the voice dimly.

"What? I can't hear you. Who is this? I can't hear you, speak up."

"It's *me*, Pauline. I don't want to talk too loud. He's in the bathroom down the hall, Nicky. I don't want him to hear me."

Davenport gritted his teeth in exasperation. "What are you doing calling here at the apartment? Don't you have any sense at all? Was that you before?"

"What?"

"I said . . . did you call before?"

"Oh, well, yeah, I did. I called but your wife answered."

"Why did you hang up, Pauline? Why didn't you speak to me?"

"Well, why do you think, because she answered, your wife."

"Once you called you shouldn't have hung up. Don't you realize——"

"Hey, I just thoughta something funny. Do you know in all of this I never even told you where I live? And it's not the address in the phone book, we moved. What it is is 1313 Pitcairne Avenue, a yellow house."

"I was saying, don't you realize calling back is even more suspicious? For Christ's sake, Pauline, what do you suppose Naomi thinks?"

"Well, I know, that's why I hung up when I called before. Pitcairne."

"Then why did you call *again?*"

"Oh. Yeah, well. I was thinking you could just tell her I'm calling about the class. I'm calling about getting some of the kids' stories mimeographed. That's a good excuse, it's reasonable. Are you keeping the date tomorrow?"

"Damn it, Pauline, I'm *very* outdone with you for calling here."

"Don't be mad at me. Listen. One reason I'm calling is, you know what happened about an hour ago before Nicky blew for Jersey? And his friggin' beer with his friggin' cousin, huh? Well, I was sitting in a chair lookin' at some article in a magazine while Hubby Dear was readin' the paper. And I was thinkin' about our date and your comin' here and everything and I did it."

Dick stared emptily at nothing. What was she talking about? Stupidly, he asked, "You did it? You did what?"

"I did *it.* In my pants. Just from thinkin'. And I mean really, too. All I did was squeeze my legs a little. It's a wonder Nicky didn't notice how I was breathin'. Ha ha, isn't that a laugh, him sittin' right there? What a clown."

Dick put a hand on his forehead, which was slightly damp with sweat. What would it be like to be *married* to a girl like Pauline? Yoicks, perish the thought. "You shouldn't be calling from your apartment like this. Where in the hell is he now, sitting there listening to you? Isn't he in the bathroom?"

"Oh, no, didn't you hear me say he blew for Jersey? Big deal. That cousin who's supposed to be in the rackets. A job he's supposed to get, ha ha. What he'll get is beer, that lazy clown. Oh, sure, he'll stumble in around three, smelling like a brewery. In the rackets, what a laugh."

"Look, there are people here. Don't ever call me here again. I can't tell you how annoyed I am. Good-bye, Pauline."

"I'll see you at two o'clock."

"Good-bye, Pauline."

"Are you coming?"

"Look, there are people here. Good-bye, Pauline."

"Don't hang up. Listen, really, I'm so horny I'm half crazy. I really did it in the chair like I told you. Nicky doesn't satisfy me, he's a lousy lover. And I can't just lie awake all night wondering if you're going to show tomorrow afternoon or not, that's why I called. Are you coming?"

Dick rubbed his sweaty forehead as again he stared emptily at nothing. He heard from the nearby crib a faint, happy gurgling noise. To talk to her in front of the baby was an obscenity. And God knows to say that he would meet her, to confirm and reconfirm the dirty date, would be an even greater obscenity. But it couldn't be helped, it had to happen. There was no way out; he would keep that date and take off Pauline's clothes and get in Nicky's bed with her. It was one of those things that had to happen.

"Yes, I'm coming," said Dick. "I'll be there."

"At two o'clock?"

"Yes, at two o'clock."

"God, I wish you were here *now!* I'm so horny I'm outa my mind—and you know, you *could* come. Nicky won't be in till two, three, four. . . ."

"Good-bye, Pauline!"

Dick replaced the receiver on its cradle with a gingerly haste, then folded his arms as he heard again a faint, happy gurgling noise. Slowly he turned to the nearby crib and put his hand on the baby's shoulder. "Hello, Sam," he said. "Ignorance is bliss. You don't know what kind of father you've got, do you?" Once again the tone was right. Sam smiled in perfect love and trust. Baby radar knew it was a joke.

GRANDLY, THEY STROLLED INSIDE THE LOBBY INTO AN
atmosphere of berserk luxury that smacked of sin and abandon. Marble floors, marble walls. Cast and spread hither and
yon were rich Oriental rugs in the making of which children
in the Kurdistan mountains and on the banks of the Kizil
Irmak had fastened knots for years until their little fingers bled
and their souls screamed for peace. Marble floors, marble
walls and marble ceilings.

"My Ameddican headquarters," said Pah casually. "Suitable for my rare visits to this sprawling, nervous country but
a bit rococo. Please forgive its presumption."

"I like its presumption," said Polly.

In silence they entered the elevator, which was run by a trim
young babe in sky-blue uniform. She smiled, "Good evening,
Your Highness."

"Good evening, child," said Pah. "Come around yet?"

"Not yet, Your Highness."

"Keep jumping off bureaus."

"Yes, Your Highness."

"And try a little castor oil. It can't hurt and you're probably constipated, anyhow."

"Yes, Your Highness."

The constipated girl pressed a button and the elevator surged upward sickeningly. The indicator over the door flashed L for lobby then sped to X and remained there as the car howled and moaned with the speed of ascent. Eighteen seconds later, it dragged vertiginously to a near-halt as the indicator leaped from X to 69 and crawled across 69 to 70. There it almost stopped.

"Get the Duke and the Duchess later," said Pahlevi. "We wish uninterrupted ascent."

"But . . . but their swim, Your Highness?"

"Uninterrupted, child. Let them go back to the Bahamas. They are wet already."

"Yes, Your Highness."

The bloated girl pressed a button and the car again gathered speed. The indicator leaped past 70 and 71 and on to 72, 73, 74—the numbers flashed by almost too rapidly to be counted —75, 76, 77, 78, 79, 80 and then POOL, followed by P–1, P–2, P–3, P–4, P–5, P–6 and finally P–7, the last number on the indicator. With another sudden breathtaking deceleration, it halted, a relay clicked and the gleaming doors of brushed bronze whispered back.

"Here we are, fair Claire," said the maharajah. "Home at last."

"It's cute," said Polly. "Pah, you're a creamboat."

Pahlevi and Polly stood in the elevator foyer, which had but a single door leading to the penthouse foyer itself. They were at the very top of the Park Avenue Towers. With a smile he took forth from his pocket a golden key, inserted it into the lock and with a flick of the wrist opened the door. At once two huge Great Danes came snarling forward, spiked collars about their necks and fangs exposed.

"Down, Khazak! Down, Astrakhan!" commanded Pahlevi, and he turned with an apologetic shrug to Polly. "They are so enthusiastic," he said.

"Aren't they, though," said Polly. She reached out to pet the pony-sized Khazak, but there was a honey-tan flash in the air and she looked down and saw that her wrist had been seized and snatched away.

"Take care," said Pahlevi. "The beast would snap off your delicate little hand at the wrist should you touch him."

"Really?" said Polly. "My goodness. What savagery!"

"I have enemies. The dogs are so trained. Astrakhan! Khazak! To your stations!" Sullenly, the donkey-sized dogs lumbered off and disappeared somewhere. "And now, my dear, let us enter."

The apartment was a typical Park Avenue penthouse, though perhaps a bit more elaborate than most. It was, as Pahlevi said, a triplex; the main staircase was at the front and a smaller servants' stairway was in the rear. Technically, the penthouse was only a duplex, since the maharajah's observation study could hardly be counted as a floor. The study was at the very top of the building; it was a single large room entirely enclosed in plate glass tinted a mild light green as protection against the rays of the sun. Numerous orchids in small pots were there, plus many ferns, begonias, elephant ear plants and other jungle foliage. A telescope was built into the study in such a way that it could be swung in any direction.

As the maharajah explained to Polly: "The celestial artifacts lure me on a winter's eve." He also was enabled by this powerful telescope with its tremendous focal possibilities to view practically all of Greater New York. Ninety-nine per cent of it lay *naked* before him. By means of this telescope he obtained an eagle's eye view of the city that privately he liked to think of as someday *belonging* to him. And it wasn't just an idle thought. If and when he could discover a scientific principle that would allow him to gain *telepathic hypnotic control* over the human brain, then he could enslave Greater New York in its entirety. Such were his mad dreams.

The lower floor of the penthouse contained the gallery, the dining hall, the library, the music room with its hi-fi and the vast living room with its great stone fireplace and massive Oriental furniture. Incense burned thither and hither. A great jade statue of Buddha squatted in one corner with pendulous belly and cryptic sneer, squint-eyed and silent in a hollowed dim-lit niche amidst curls of smoke from brass incense pots that dangled on chains. In some far distant area were the great pantries, kitchens and wine cellars, and behind that the honey-comb servant quarters.

Outside the living room was the tiled terrace with its wrought-iron balcony stretched along its curving length of two hundred feet. The terrace overlooked the west and south and north of the city. The floor above, which was smaller, contained the royal sleeping quarters, the royal bath and three guest apartments. The royal sleeping quarters consisted of a large bedroom, a huge dressing room with much interesting equipment, a comfortable sitting room and the royal bath with dry and wet sauna. The bedroom and sitting room opened on a smaller terrace that overlooked the east, affording a view of Brooklyn, Queens and Long Island.

"Somewhat primitive and cramped," said Pahlevi. "Of course I am seldom here. It's a mere *pied-à-pomme.*"

"I like it," said Polly.

They strolled into the great living room past the blond mahogany bar that rounded the corner from the grand foyer. The room was fifty feet wide and eighty feet long with a thirty-foot ceiling. It contained near the great stone fireplace a five-foot-deep sunken area approximately twenty feet square —the "intimate pit," Pah called it.

"Gives me claustrophobia, this room," said Pahlevi with a sigh. "I do miss the palace, but such is exile."

"What is that place down there?" asked Polly.

"That is the intimate pit. We will take brandy there. Come, my pet."

No apprehension was in Polly as she sat on a large velvet hassock in the sunken and low-lighted area by the great rock fireplace in which nine-foot logs burned. She watched with a keen birdlike interest as Pahlevi suddenly clapped his hands three times. Seconds later three turbanned Arab servants rushed forth from nowhere and flung themselves at his feet, kissing the air in the general area of his gleaming black shoes.

"Rise," he said.

The servants bowed low, half erect, salaaming in a worshipful manner.

"Mahtoud!" said Pahlevi. "The 1814 Napoleon! Ahmed! My slippers and *le smoking.* Jahadra! Scented spring water for the lady."

The servants again salaamed then backed away rapidly. In no time they were back, one with a golden bowl of scented water floating with rose petals, another with ermine slippers and a silk *le smoking* embroidered with gold and silver threads, and the last with a platinum tray upon which rested two thin-stemmed brandy snifters and an old, cobweb-covered, dust-splashed bottle of brandy, its lettering long since faded by the mists of time.

"This is a rather pleasing cognac," said Pahlevi. "It's quite rare, but fortunately I still have a few dozen cases of it. Say when."

"When," said Polly. "It looks adorable."

"Here you are, my radiant goat," said Pahlevi with a gentle smile, his hazel-gold eyes warm and soft in the flickering flames of the logs in the great fireplace. That was practically the only illumination now; in some subtle way the lights had dimmed. Meanwhile, Mahtoud, Jahadra and Ahmed stood bowed, waiting for orders.

"*Thank* you, Pah," said Polly. "You're so considerate."

Pahlevi clapped his hands once, sharply. "Retire," he whispered. The servants leaped as if flicked by a bit of glass at the end of a lash and rushed from the intimate pit like scatted cats. Pahlevi turned with a smile to Polly and held aloft his brandy snifter. She held up hers in turn, smiling birdlike. "To this night," said Pahlevi, "may it be a dream of spouting stardust . . . and to you, my dewy rose at dawn, my furry Andean pet, my moist Himalayan gazelle . . . to you . . . stardust. . . ."

"Thank you, Pah. You really know how to make a girl feel wanted." Polly took a sip of the brandy. "Mmm, my, isn't this good. Is it really from the year 1814?"

"Yes," said Pah.

Polly took another sip. "Was it Napoleon's own brand?"

"Of course. It came from his cellar."

"That's fascinating," said Polly as she took another sip. "I wonder what he was *like,* Napoleon. He was very short, wasn't he? Is it true that his . . . ahem, natural endowment was no great shakes? Excuse me for asking, but was it only . . . ahem, half that of a normal man?"

"That is the prevailing opinion of history, my pet."

"Well, ha ha ha, it didn't seem to slow him down," said Polly. "Look at what he did to Europe. You know that old saying, 'It is not the size of the weapon that matters, but the fury of the attack.' Ha, ha, ha."

"True, my dear," said Pah politely with a thin smile. "However, a popgun hurls a furious cork four and a half feet, whereas Big Bertha throws a two-ton shell nineteen miles."

"Oh, go on," said Polly with an amused wave of her hand. "Big Bertha, ha ha ha ha! Pah, you're a card."

"Enough talk of Napoleon and artillery!" Suddenly Pahlevi jumped up from the purple velour sofa on which he was sitting, his handsome face contorted as if in pain. "Come," he said, "come with me to the royal boudoir, I must possess your loveliness!"

"Pah, you said you wouldn't," answered Polly. "Really, this is a bit thick, you're not keeping your word."

"Love knows no word," said Pah. "Come, I must possess your beauty!"

Polly coolly took another sip of the brandy. "No," she said. "No, no, no. No. No, no, no, no, no-no-no. I'm sorry, the answer is no. No-no. No, no, no, no. We must remains *friends.* Maybe . . . just maybe-maybe-maybe . . . later. A lot later, when I know you better, when we have a relationship."

The maharajah stared long and hard at her and there was something new, something different in his eyes. "I want your loveliness *now,*" he said.

"Well, you can't have it and that's that. Let's change the subject, I'm not that type of girl. Besides, we have other things to think about. Where is that memento you were going to give me? The triple strand of pearls. I'm dying to see them, where are they?"

Again Pahlevi stared long and hard at her. Softly he asked, "Are your eyelids drooping?"

"My . . . eyelids?" asked Polly. Hmm. As a matter of fact, her eyelids *were* drooping. Polly looked down at the empty brandy snifter in her hand.

"You are ready, my pet," said Pahlevi.

"Puh-puh-puh-puh-Pah!" stammered Polly. "What have you duh-duh-*done* to me?" To her horror she couldn't move. Her blue eyes stared ahead emptily as she felt herself picked up by strong hands and laid down on her stomach across the large hassock. She felt the evening gown pulled over her head and off. She felt her slip come down and then her panties and shoes and stockings. Naked as nature made her, Polly lay draped over the hassock with her round pink behind up in the air. Her blue eyes stared dazedly at the pattern of the Persian rug. She couldn't move, she was helpless. Naked and drugged by a fiend!

"That's right, kiddo," said Pahlevi. "More than a slight

dash of scopolamine." As he spoke he was carefully filling a large hypodermic from a frosty vial. Skillfully, he inserted the big needle into the rubber cap, thrust it in and slowly withdrew the plunger as the glass body gradually filled with an amber fluid. "This is stronger medicine, my pet. I thresh it myself in the dressing room la-borra-try. Lovely stuff. You're going to relish it, the effect is delightful. Heats up the pip beautifully and loads it with static electricity. You'll spark all over yourself shortly—and if you squeeze your legs together, watch out, you'll go through the roof."

"Mmmmuuu-uuh!" said Polly.

Pahlevi leaned over and squeezed with his fingers the plump right cheek of Polly's uplifted behind. "Pahdon me, pet. This will stick a bit." He jabbed in the big needle. Polly quivered in reflex but otherwise lay quiescent. "A mild sting now," he said basso. Expertly, he pushed in the plunger and the amber fluid slowly descended to a callibrated point in the glass shaft. Deftly he withdrew the needle. "Not too much in one side," he said pleasantly. "The goodness must spread through the entire area. It is *total* ass we want, my pet, not *half* ass."

"Mmmffuuh!" said Polly. Already she could feel a maddening heat in the medicated right side of her behind and a gathering static electricity in the clit. "Mmffuuh!" she said again, as she felt another stinging stick in her other buttock. Now the maddening heat began to spread on that side as well, and she felt a sharp tingle and another and another as the clit sparked. The heat was spreading everywhere. A hellish electromagnetic biochemical glow was rapidly enfiltering throughout the area called by the French, *le bassin!* The man was an unscrupulous monster!

"Yes, my pet, as you are doubtless aware by now, a *very* potent love juice. It would make the most desiccated and withered old maid on earth ravenous with lust. A dose of it

would make the most virtuous virgin saint in all of history tear
off her clothes and spraddle before a hyena. It's cute stuff, I
devised it myself and in comparison cantharides don't even
tickle. A business necessity, my pet. I do a strictly volume
business and I keep the ponies loaded with it at all times,
makes them happy in their work. You will find that now you
can speak. It doesn't restore free will, but it neutralizes
scopolamine. You can also move, at my order of course. Sit
up, pet, and face me."

"Yes, Pah," said Polly. Zombielike, she sat on the hassock
as told, her blue eyes intently upon him as the area called by
the French *le bassin* glowed. "Please, Pah, sprinkle me with
stardust, stardust me——"

"Quiet!" said Pah. "I don't care for that type of obscene
language and I don't like begging ponies. Is that clear?"

"Yes, Pah."

"Henceforth, you are to address me as *master.*"

"Yes, master."

"Now, I realize the injected love juice is tormenting you
and I am not wholly without mercy. Be patient. You will be
tested as all the ponies are."

"Tested?" asked Polly. "You mean you'll m-m-mount me,
master, you'll stardust me?"

"I said I don't like that kind of language. Are you trying to
annoy me?"

"Forgive me, master."

"The proper, dignified word is *test.* And yes, you'll be
tested. All the ponies are tested and tested thoroughly. Now
what is your real name? Claire won't do."

"P-p-polly," said Polly. "Test me, master. Don't hesitate,
test me *soon.*"

"Hmmm, Polly. Yes, a bit more class to it, the homespun
effect. That's better, it'll do. Suzette, Wan Lo, Vasentesenka
and Polly. A proper little stable."

"Test me, master. Test me right now. Test me, test me—"

"Quiet!" said the handsome turbanned giant. Without further ado, he picked her up and threw her naked body over his shoulder and the next thing Polly knew she was lying on a huge bed beneath a gigantic silken canopy. Arms folded, Pahlevi gazed down at the reclining white body now softly but indirectly illuminated by his special lighting, which seemed to come from everywhere and nowhere. "Yes," he said, "spread-eagles nicely. Natural talent but needs some training, I suspect." Thoughtfully, he glanced up above and pulled a drawstring to the right of the bed.

Suddenly, to Polly's horror, a large red and white and black, hairy-legged, hissing giant spider came falling down and landed on her belly, its legs wriggling rapidly and its huge fangs set to bite. It was half as big as a cat. With a buzzing hiss, it ran up Polly's belly over her taut diaphragm until it was perched on her breasts, its hairy face and long fangs raised over her eyes as it prepared to bite her on the nose, its feelers working and waving. At this, Polly's blue eyes opened wide, glazed over and rolled back in her head.

"Bully!" said Pahlevi, as he snatched up the spider and inserted a key in it and wound it up again for the next time. He'd have to be getting an Indian to take the place of Running Moose and of course she'd have to be checked out, too. "Good horror reaction. Nothing jaded about this pony."

Pleased by this test of Polly's sensitivity, Pahlevi pulled on the drawstring and the now silent and motionless spider was slowly lifted back up to its tiny trapdoor in the canopy. The pony had seemed a trifle remote and he'd been concerned about it, but she was sensitive. "Yes, quite sensitive," he murmured. "A lot of women wouldn't have batted an eye at that."

When Polly revived she was sitting in a silk-upholstered chair, still naked. Slowly, she blinked her eyes. As she sat there on the chair in the royal bedroom of the royal sleeping quarters, she witnessed a thing she would not have believed possible, a horrible and dreadful transmogrification of the flesh, the hideous and horrendous metamorphosis of a maharjah into a . . .

"My true self demands liberation," said Pahlevi.

Polly sat slumped in the silk-covered chair, head back limply against the large carved thronelike back of ebony. Her hands hung palm outward and her feet rested on their sides, her knees askew, collapsed. Her giant breasts, though still a staggering sight to behold, were schlumpfed a trifle as though in momentary gloom and the cherry eyes upon them stared in opposite directions. Her jaw hung open and the look on her face was one of vacant, attentive concentration. There was plenty for her to concentrate on.

First, off came the turban. It unwound around and around and suddenly collapsed into a pile of white silk and was thrown into a corner. Above the hairline of the golden tan forehead grew nappy black hair unmistakably of Africa not India. It stood up as though charged with vital electricity. The Unknown King liked to wear it long and potent.

Polly's blue eyes bugged as she saw the erstwhile maharajah remove his well-tailored evening clothes, first the dinner jacket and then the trousers. Then the shirt, and the undershirt, and the shorts, and the silk hosiery, and the English shoes. He still wore an enormous strange codpiece, a great gold lamé jockstrap, but otherwise a naked giant stood before her and he was *jet black!*

In the prime of his prime Nick Sampson weighed two hundred and seventy pounds and the very sight of him would have sent any heavyweight champion reeling back in terror. The tremendous biceps and triceps were like carved and glistening ebony and hard as iron—not a trace of fat was on him, muscle, muscle, muscle, muscle was there, great bands and coils of muscle

244 / Calder Willingham

rippling with sinews. A black powerhouse stood before her and if Polly had possessed the power of speech she would have whimpered and begged for mercy. And this was only the *surface* impression made by Nicholas Lordgod Sampson, the worst (or the best) was yet to come. . . .

Even in her fear Polly was bewildered and puzzled and intrigued. The body was jet black but the face and neck remained a light golden tan. How could this be? The features were handsomely aquiline, the eyes a soft hazel-gold. He was still the maharajah, but the maharajah with a great ebony body. How could that be, Polly wondered. And then she saw the answer as the giant delicately tilted back his head and with the fingernails of his right thumb and forefinger dislocated and then removed the tinted contact lenses from his eyeballs, first the right and then the left.

Paralyzed and drugged as she was, Polly shrank in horror on the silk-covered chair. Two puddly-black bloodshot eyes glared at her with all the primordial rage of the jungle. The eyes bulged forth with hyperthyroid fury, showing a great deal of the whites; but the whites were not white, they were a jaundiced yellow and patterned like a road map with red veins. They were not soft and gentle hazel-gold eyes any longer; they were the puddly-black eyes of an insane psychopath, and the motto of those eyes might well have been: "Let him who looks into these orbs tremble for his life." And so Polly would have trembled had she had possession of her body. She could only stare in helplessness wondering what would come next.

And that she soon discovered. No sooner had the jet giant removed the tinted contact lenses than carefully the fingers reached up to the scalp line, dug in cautiously and wedged forward and down as slowly the maharajah's golden tan face peeled off. Down it came, leaving behind it a gleaming, perspiration-covered, ebony forehead. On down peeled the tan lifelike plastic over huge brows and on over a sunken nose bridge and down over a great flat nose—carefully here, as aquiline putty slipped loose. Polly's bulging blue eyes flickered shut and flickered open again.

The black fingers had stopped working on the face to peel tan plastic from the hands themselves, a matter no doubt of sensitivity in the fingertips since the maharajah face was adjusted and fitted very delicately around the nose and mouth area. Now the black fingers were over the face again, working and moving and hiding from her sight the features. Then suddenly the plastic peeled down over the chin and out plopped a set of even pearly false teeth, and the Maharajah of Losam-Nehi was gone. Nicholas Lordgod Sampson, Black Avenger and Destroyer of the White Race, held in his hands a mass of thin artful plastic and putty and whalebone clips and pearly teeth—Pahelvi Shagmadragma.

"Uhhh-hh-hh," said Polly.

It must be admitted that Polly had her fair share of racial prejudice and the sight of him was a cruel shock to her sensibilities. A nigger, horrors! And not only was this man black, he was blackly black, he was black as black as black as black, he was blacker than black, he was black to the point of blacked out blackness. What was worse to Polly than even his black blackness was his—she would have called it, if she had been able to talk—*niggerishness.* The man was a southern dream of niggerhood lifted to an art form. His nose was large and his nostrils were great spread caverns each the size of a quarter. His nose, of course, was very flat; it had hardly any altitude at all. His lips naturally were great thick lips that protruded outward like liverwurst. And his brows were gorillaish, his eyes sunken like caves. He was the most blood-clabberingly ugly man Polly had ever seen, so ugly there was a supreme greatness about his very ugliness. She felt it even in her terror. Such inspired ugliness as this was beyond ugliness and beyond handsomeness—the white male movie stars faded into pale insignificance compared to such truly magnificent ugliness. Whatever the white standard of beauty is, he did not have it.

Furthermore, aside from Nick Sampson's truly great ugliness, his face was rendered even more indescribably hideous as a consequence of the scars and blows it had received in the past. The fists and coon-gun butts of southern white men had crushed most of the bones of his face at one time or another. As a result his face was corrugated with depressions and pits and scars and welts and ridges and pocks and wartlike traumatic growths. He also had an especially grotesque expression about the mouth in consequence of the loss of all his teeth years before. They had been knocked out, of course, by Holt Breech and his good old boys.

"Nick Thampthon at your thervith," he said lispily. "Thet there, gal."

Polly watched bug-eyed as he strode rapidly across the room to a large bureau, ebony muscles rippling in his giant's body. The man really made Tarzan look like a sickly shrimp. He could have knocked Charles Atlas thirty feet with the back of his hand. In awe Polly watched him reach into a small drawer and pull forth a gleaming silver-like object which he crammed into his mouth. It was a set of highly polished and gleaming stainless steel teeth, extra-large-sized and filed all around to sharp triangular points. With these teeth in mouth, he strode up before Polly, his puddly-dark eyes absent of all feeling as the teeth smiled, lips spread back to show the twin rows of sharklike fangs. Now he could talk without lisping. Polly cringed inwardly as she heard him say:

"The bettah to bite yo' ass with, white gal."

"Uhhh-uhh-hh," said Polly weakly, her head still back limp on the chair.

"Go' whup you now," said Nick. "Dat's de second part of de test, to see if you'll holler good. I don' want no crackah workin' for me dat won't holler. Dey's dangerous, dem quiet ones."

Suiting action to words, Nick again strode rapidly across the room, opened a drawer of the bureau and took out a cat-o'-nine-tails. He walked slowly back to Polly, cat in his hand. "Stand up, white gal," he said.

"Yes, master," said Polly.

A moment later, Polly shrieked as the cat-o'-nine wrapped around her body. "Ohhh-hh-HHH!" she screamed. "Mercy, master! Mercy!" Ten blows and ten shrieks later, Nick said:

"Ah reckon you c'n holler good enough. Now for de last test. Set in de chair, white gal, so's you don't swoon yo'self."

"Y-y-yes, master!" wept Polly. Tears streamed down as she sat on the silk-covered chair; then suddenly she froze into paralyzed fright, she didn't even breathe. The Black Fiend was taking off the great gold lamé codpiece.

"You done passed de *easy* parts of de test," said Nick softly. "But all de same, you gonna *like* dis last part, baby. Git up on dat bed and spread yo' crackah legs, honey, you gonna git what ever l'il milky face gal in dis country want and you gonna git it till de cows come home."

For a moment, willing and eager as she was to comply, Polly couldn't move. She was petrified and amazed by what she saw. Weirdly and strangely, not all of Black Nick Sampson was black. In open-mouthed wonder Polly gazed at the awesome sight before her. The most astonishing thing about it was not the enormity, although its dimensions were wondrous indeed —it had, first, a mighty girth of seven and five-eighths inches circumference and a full three and one-eighths inches diameter, and it extended from stem to stern precisely and exactly fifteen and seven-eighths inches. But the most awesome thing was its coloration: although it was basically black, the great doorknob head had a definite ruby undertone, the outer extremity of the powerful shaft seemed to have lost pigment and was pale, and the vein-engorged lower shaft and root were a dark blue. From somewhere she thought she heard the strain of "Stars and Stripes Forever." Well might she have done so! It was, of course, the all-American red, white and blue whork of whorks.

DAVENPORT'S SLIGHTLY INSANE AND RATHER RUDE DE-
parture from the Samussons' took Dick himself by surprise. In
the midst of boredom listening to Victor and Nate yack about
the rabbit of prestige versus the rabbit of work, the deliciously
diabolical thought occurred to him that he could excuse himself to go to the bathroom, walk outside to the street, hop in
a taxi and in fifteen minutes be at Pauline's—and five minutes
after that, naked in bed with her. He could then rush back in
a cab to the soiree and tell them he'd gone for a walk and some
air. The very idea made him dizzy and weak at the knees. Why
wait until two o'clock the next afternoon?

"A man, any man, must decide what path he wants to follow," said Samusson. "And so must the artist. The artist is no
different, he is a man, too. This business of success and failure
is a test of the artist *as a man,* that is all. He must decide what
he will make of it, what path he will follow, what road he will
take. It's a test, success."

"So is failure," said Nate. "If you're lying in a gutter in the

Bowery in your own vomit, that ain't good."

"Success is a harder test. Much harder; there's no comparison. That's the real fork in the road, Mr. Hammerfield, the fork of forks, so to speak, the choice that makes a lifetime of difference. I like the famed lines of the Yankee poet. 'Two roads diverged in a yellow wood,/And sorry I could not travel both/And be one traveler, long I stood/And looked down one as far as I could. . . .' "

"Well, frankly," said Nate, "I could never stand that folksy old bastard."

It was not impossible. A little crazy, but not impossible. The soiree would go on for another three hours at least. Fifteen minutes to get to Pauline's, fifteen minutes back, an hour there —back in an hour and a half, an hour and forty-five minutes at the most. No one would miss him. They were all talking, Nate was having a good time, Samusson was holding forth . . . it could be done. He was out "for a walk," that was all. It was plausible. Everyone knew he was in a moody mood. In twenty minutes he could be in bed banging away with Pauline and it was a terrifically sexy idea. The only thing needed was just the *nerve* to do it.

"Every five-year-old child is a genius," declared Samusson, "until society kicks the shit out of him or her. Aside from interest or absorption in some particular art or scientific problem, and a childlike absorption at that, the main difference between an ordinary person and a genius is one thing. The genius has a tough ass. He can take kicks that other people can't."

"Well, I like that," said Nate. "I think it's true."

In actuality, as Dick well knew, the bald and wise and wrinkled Samusson had proved to be a bit of a bore to the Hammerfields. He and Naomi had found the open-house soirees on Adlerian psychology interesting and they thought Nate and his wife Leah might like it, but probably they would have done better to stay home and hang fellow writers or find some other amusement. About a dozen people were there and one woman kept talking all the time in a nasal whine. She prefaced every remark with the phrase "in our society" and after a while even Samusson's eyes glazed over. Nate himself looked acutely bored. And yet what could they do if he got up and went out for a walk? Nothing.

"Oh, yes, it's true, the genius has a tough behind, and mostly because of his or her total childlike absorption in the particular art or science of his or her concern." Such as, thought Davenport, the particular art or science of getting a piece of ass with the swiftness of striking lightning, in the midst of an innocuous situation where no one would *expect* such a thing. The very idea gave him a gluey taste in his mouth. He could fuck her little tail off while they were all jabbering. It was a delicious idea. "The genius is too busy at work-play for vanity to ruin him or her. And too busy to need the solace of conformity."

"What is this him-and-her and he-and-she stuff?" asked Nate with a grin. "Women belong in the kitchen or in a bed."

"In our so-ci-ety," began the whining woman, "what we have got——"

"And what is this business about the solace of conformity? Do you think conformity was a solace to Babbitt or was it a curse?"

"Oh, not a curse. Conformity was a great solace to Babbitt, as it is to us all. What Babbitt couldn't bear was separateness. Very few of us can bear that; the thing that makes cowards of us all is to stand alone. That is what genius can do. You see, it is fear that destroys creativity, fear of disapproval, fear of rejection, fear of isolation from the comforting herd."

It would be too rude. There was a limit. To abandon Nate to all of this for an hour and a half would be very bad manners. But on the other hand, why shouldn't he get a little education from Samusson? It couldn't hurt him. An hour and a half. Maybe an hour and twenty minutes. That time would fly. The nasal woman would talk a lot.

"All right," said Nate. "That's all very well and good, but let's get to the nub of it. Sure, most people have self-doubt at times, they wouldn't be human if they didn't. And sure, success rouses doubt, or often it does, anyhow. But you talk about fear of rejection, fear of isolation from the comforting herd— okay, that exists, it's there, but what do you *do* about it, how do you overcome that fear?"

"By childlike absorption in work-play and by a fellow-feeling that outweighs vanity and ambition," said Samusson. "By escape from the self, by mastery of what Freud calls the ego. Adler of course would have approached it teleologically, he would have looked at underlying purpose in terms of a developing humanity and fellow-feeling."

"Excuse me a moment," said Dick. "Victor, where is the bathroom, down the hall?"

"You know where it is," said Samusson. "By developing humanity and fellow-feeling, that is the answer, mastery of the so-called ego."

"Mastery of the ego throws me," said Nate. "What's wrong with a good healthy ego? Show me one artist, much less a genius, who doesn't have one."

"Well, let me try to make myself a little clearer. You see, Adler believes that the *purpose of* neurotic behavior is more important than the *cause behind* it. That is why he adopts a teleological approach——"

Yes, slightly insane and rather rude, there was no doubt about it. Had Naomi given him a funny look as he left? Not really, she'd glanced up, that was all. Trembly-kneed, as he sat in a yellow taxi on his way to a yellow house, Dick justified his behavior on two grounds: first, he'd heard all of that boring stuff from Samusson before; second, he wouldn't *really* do anything at Pauline's, he would just scout the scene, check it out, look things over as a preliminary to the real tryst on the following afternoon. Definitely, he would *not* do anything, just a cup of coffee, that was all.

On several occasions in the past, Dick had noticed that sudden spontaneous "wickedness" had a rare power of titillation. True, he'd never been unfaithful to Naomi after he'd married her, but there had been an incident before they married that could have been called a crass betrayal. He was living with Naomi, actually living on her while writing his book, and an old girl who had been with the Red Cross in the South Pacific returned to the States and telephoned one afternoon. He invited her up for a drink, then called Naomi and asked her to come home early from work to meet this old friend, this nice girl who'd been off with the soldiers in New Guinea. Betty, come meet Betty. Naomi said she would, she'd be there at five, when Betty herself was due. But Betty arrived early at four thirty, and that was how it happened—quick, like that, in the wink of an eye, before he even knew it; in five minutes, no more, her panties were off, her skirt was up almost to her neck, her legs were locked around him and there they were, heaving and snorting on the bed as if she'd left town yesterday. And fantastically sexy, too. The wickedness of it was delicious. They were having orgasms five minutes before Naomi arrived and she never suspected a thing.

As the yellow taxi roared across dark Brooklyn streets toward a yellow house, Dick Davenport nervously checked his watch. Eighteen minutes, twenty, twenty-two. It was too much. This was crazy. He would have to just stay in the cab and go right back. Suppose he couldn't get another taxi to return? Suppose he lost track of time and stayed longer at Pauline's than he had allowed? It was impossible; he would have to go back; it was a crazy idea in the first place and Naomi *had* suspected something, she'd given him a puzzled, questioning look when he slipped out of the Samusson living room.

"This is it," said the cab driver. "The address you asked for, 1313 Pitcairne Avenue."

Davenport moistened his lips and swallowed. *Dingy*. The house was dingy, the street was dingy, the entire neighborhood was dingy. And it wasn't a house, it was one of those half-house things, an apartment really. Two doors on the gray porch, one 1313–A, the other 1313–B. He would have to go back. "Yeah, okay," said Dick.

Five minutes. A cup of coffee, then back through the dark Brooklyn streets in another taxi. There was an avenue with stores not far away, cabs were there; he'd stay no more than six or seven minutes. And hands off of her, no fiddling with her or putting of fingers in her or any of that type of madness. Especially no putting of fingers in her, that could lead to grief. Slowly, he walked up the wooden stairs to the front porch.

Filled with the bittersweet sadness of the knowledge that there still was time to correct his insane folly, still time to turn and flee down the wooden steps to the avenue and another taxi, Dick paused to survey the neighborhood, giving the noisy asphalt and the surrounding houses a slow thoughtful pan. It was grimy. Not a nice area of Brooklyn, not nice at all. Cheapo. Dismally unaesthetic. How could people live in such an ugly place? Probably they had no choice, but Borneo really would be better. Dick moistened his lips, swallowed with difficulty and peered at the cards beneath the bells on the yellow doors of the gray dingy porch. Under the numerals 1313–B the name Riccobono was written in pen and ink. What a thing, what a crudity, at least they could have typed it. Riccobono. God, what madness, but maybe she wasn't home; maybe she'd gone out—and in any case wherever she was no putting of fingers in her, that above all else. But probably she wasn't home, very likely not, she was probably at a movie or playing bingo in church. A watery weakness came in Dick's knees as he put his finger on the bell. He rang it and for ten seconds nothing, not a sound. He had escaped; fate had saved him. Then a rattle at the door and it opened and Pauline stood before him in pink plastic hair curlers and a man's ratty bathrobe. Pauline herself, otherwise and better known as Polly of the night hours, there she was in the flesh—yes, in the living flesh, Pauline herself at last. For a moment she stared with a blank emptiness at him, then a slow smile spread on her face, a sweet smile that was girlish and innocent, and with the sweet smile came a little glitter in her eyes that was neither girlish nor innocent but lewd, unmistakably and irrevocably and inevitably lewd. She was a dirty girl, that was all there was to it; Pauline was a dirty girl and he himself was a dirty boy and the whole thing was more fun than Coney Island, which in actual fact was not far away. A slow, sweet smile and then she said:

"Well, well, well. Look what the cat dragged in."

"Yeah," said Dick. "I can only stay a minute."

"If I'd known you were coming I wouldn't be like this. I just had a bath and washed my hair. I didn't expect you tonight."

"Your husband isn't here?"

"No, I told you he's in Jersey."

"Um, well. I can only stay a minute."

"Come in. Come on in."

"Is that Nicky's bathrobe?"

The Riccobono apartment was even more depressing than Dick had expected. The smell of garlic from Italian cooking was not unpleasant, but visually the living room was grim and so was the tiny hallway leading to the front door. The first thing he saw was a large, mustard-brown, gleaming sofa bracketed by unattractive "modern" floor lamps with aluminum-colored shades that still had protective plastic on them. It was a cruel thing to say or think, but the tastelessness of everything in the room was complete. The phony overstuffed sofa, the phony Persian rug, the phony silk draperies, all were horrible. Not a single real thing was in the room, except Pauline herself —cheapness, imitation, pretense ruled the minute, and sadly enough some of it had cost money; not a lot of money, but money, money that would have bought plain honest things that were real. With an unfaltering precision, the Riccobonos had chosen the meretricious and the untrue. But Pauline herself, God knows, was real enough; as she sat on the shiny brown velour sofa, she let her half-tied bathrobe hang casually open and Dick caught a glimpse of dark pubic hair.

"Do you want a drink?" she asked, with a calm politeness that struck him as inappropriate to the scene. "How long can you stay?"

"Long enough to go to bed, I guess," said Dick, "if we can be quick about it."

"Well, let's go back to the bedroom," said Pauline.

"Maybe we better not. What's wrong with this sofa?"

"Nothing, just that it isn't very comfortable."

Dick moved over closer to her on the sofa and put his hand on her leg under the bathrobe. "Yeah, but your husband might come home. I mean, it would be awkward if he came in and we were there in his damn bed."

"He won't be home till late."

"Yeah, but he might."

"There's no danger, baby, not a bit, believe me."

The word *baby* was revolting somehow. Nevertheless, the girl herself was extremely sexy. Dick moved his hand up the warm flesh of her leg, pulled the bathrobe aside and there it was, the little ingenuous notch, dim behind curling black hair. "Let's get this open a little more," said Dick, as he untied the bathrobe and pulled it farther apart, exposing her breasts, which were small but had large nipples that tilted upward. They were darling little titties, just as he had known they would be. The only thing he didn't much like was that the areolae were unusually small, somewhere between a nickel and a quarter, and each of them had three or four skinny black hairs growing at the rim—dumb girl ought to shave them off. But they were darling titties. Cautiously, he pinched the acornlike nipple on her left breast and felt it tighten under his fingers.

"Whew-w," said Pauline. "I feel that all the way in my toes. This is the best thing that's happened all day. Let's go in the bedroom."

"Nicky might come in."

"No, he won't. He's drinking beer with his cousin."

"Maybe his cousin is sick."

"No, his cousin never gets sick."

Dick pinched the nipple on her other breast. "You have a sexy body," he said. "I love these little titties, they're great. Just like little volcanoes."

"The volcano is down a little lower."

"Um-m, yeah. No. No, Pauline. You can't call that a volcano, not even with extreme poetic license. But you do have a sexy body, very sexy."

"Listen, really and truly, Nicky won't come home. Let's go in the bedroom and take all our clothes off, that'll be even sexier. Believe me, it'll be sexier. Come on, let's go."

"Wait a minute. I'd rather not, it's too dangerous."

"But it isn't, really it isn't. He'll stay drinking beer till two in the morning, he always does."

A sick feverishness had long ago stricken Davenport; he felt dazed, drunk as if on ether. The whole thing was crazy. He had gotten up in the middle of a social occasion and walked out, leaving his wife and his guests with strangers. Insanity was what it was. The weeks of struggling to get to work on that damned book had been too much for him; he had cracked up; he had taken leave of his mentality. And yet insane as it was, how could he resist such a thing as this, how could any man?

The plain bald horrible truth was that he wanted to fuck her; he had wanted to fuck her for days and weeks and now finally he would do it, finally at long last the moment had come; he would lie the little nasty bitch on her ass and fuck her ears off. It was fate, that was what it was, it was a thing that had had to happen from the very beginning. Gently but firmly, Dick put his hands on her shoulders beneath the bathrobe and pushed. "Lie back, honey," he said.

"Well, all right," said Pauline, in a voice suddenly small. Dick moved on the mustard-brown sofa to accommodate her and she lifted her feet upon it, raised her behind, pulled the bathrobe up under her and opened her legs wide with a teleological candor. Despite himself, a slight shock ran through Davenport. The little ingenuous notch was no longer either little or ingenuous, and it was not dim either, behind the growth of curly hair; he could plainly see all that was there to see, and it was darling, just as he had thought it would be—except there was something kind of *raw* about it, something very *naked* and *exposed*. Was it absolutely necessary, he wondered, for those little pink inner lips to show and that little pip of a clit to peek through? Well, she certainly hadn't seemed all that surprised when he suddenly arrived at her house.

"You have a pretty pussy," said Dick, "as pussies go."

Pauline smiled unperturbed as she lay there with her legs opened wide. "I don't know whether that's a compliment or not," she said. "But whatever it is, it's all yours."

True, thought Dick, true enough, and one thing at least could certainly be said for little Pauline Riccobono—she was a girl of her word, she had said she would do this with him and she meant it. Dreamily, Dick stared at her tilted knees and the wet hairy area between her thighs—it was a moment of such delicious, wicked fulfillment he hated for it to end; it ought artistically to be prolonged. But he could go through it again on the following afternoon; beyond a doubt he'd be back the next day and then they'd have all afternoon. There was no point in dillydallying now; he who dillydallies is sometimes lost. . . . Slowly, Dick unbuckled his belt, but then the thought occurred to him that he really knew almost *nothing* about Pauline Riccobono as *a human being* and therefore he paused to ask her a couple of questions about herself. That was a good idea, to *talk to her* a little bit *humanly.* In the meanwhile, he could play with her and stir her up and then the sex not only would be sexier but would have a deeper human dimension, too. What was the rush? Precipitous screwing was unaesthetic. Ten minutes later she sat on the edge of the sofa with the bathrobe half around her and Dick smoked a teleological cigarette and listened as she said:

"Why, the stupid clown don't make hardly enough money for us to live, I have to work, too! Who could blame me for screwing around a little? Not that I do this much, only a coupla times since we been married and then only when I get so goddamn horny I just can't stand it. I've got to get laid sometimes, I've just got to, it's nature, I can't help it. But the worst thing is no money. You don't know what a financial strain it is to be married to a guy like him. If you want money you can just sit down and write a book, but he can't do anything like that; he's stupid and ignorant. Why, we can't afford anything, nothing, his family gave us all this furniture; I insisted we have furniture or I wouldn't marry him. And we can't even have a baby; we can't afford it. I don't want any baby right now and I sure don't want one with him, but I couldn't have one if I wanted to, that's the point. And I ask, is that fair? How can a person respect a guy like that, huh? He just don't care, Nicky. He's a *slob;* I'm wasting my life with that guy, and that's the truth. And on top of everything else he's the lousiest lay you ever heard of; he's such a stinking loss in bed it's beyond belief; that guy can't fuck for sour owl shit."

"You poor little thing," said Dick. "What you need is sympathy, sympathy where you are most bereft, down here in your poor little unfucked pussy. . . ."

"Well, it doesn't get fucked *much,* I can tell you that."

"Poor little baby, husband doesn't fuck her, most criminal thing I ever heard of . . . this poor neglected thing needs attention. . . ." As he spoke, Dick put his hand between her legs, searched for the silky notch and found it. She was wet and warm; his finger slid into her easily as she began again to talk. Dick wasn't listening, or at least was trying not to listen. That had been a poor idea, the thought of getting to know her humanly. He knew her humanly already. But it was a good idea on the whole; this would make the sex better. As she angrily chattered on about Nicky's deplorable defects, he pushed his finger deep into her trying to feel her cervix but he couldn't, all he felt was the warm rubbery folds of her vagina. In her whining anger at her husband she seemed oblivious of his attentions but sure wasn't, she was getting very wet down there, slipperiness was all over his hand and running down his wrist. Dimly, it occurred to him that he was doing the very thing he'd said he wouldn't—but what did that matter, it had to happen anyhow, and besides he couldn't resist. Putting his finger in her somehow or other had a fascination; there was something elemental about it.

"Terrible, criminal," said Dick. "Is he really as . . . inept a lover as you say? Is he *that* bad, honey?"

"Do you think I'm kidding? He's *worse!* I really don't get much attention down there and that's the God's truth, and what I get nobody would want. Bang, bang, thank you, ma'am, that type of thing, except he don't even say thanks. And he wouldn't warm that thing up like you're doing, God no; he wouldn't put his finger in me, just his prick that's all, for about a minute. Why, that slob never heard of love play. Watch out, that hurts a little. Hey, you're hurting me."

"Sorry," said Dick. He put the palm of his left hand on her

lower abdomen and pressed down. "It's funny. I can feel your uterus like this, but I can't feel your cervix inside you. Have you got one?"

"Sure I do. What do you think, I don't?"

"Well, where is it? I can't feel it."

"Up higher, more to the front, like. It's the angle. You have to turn your hand and push your finger up."

"Toward your navel?"

"Yeah, like that. Hey, you know, this is getting me sexy."

"It's getting me sexy, too," said Dick.

"Mmm, it's getting me definitely sexy, and to tell you the truth I'd rather have something else than your hand down there. Let's go back to the bedroom, huh?"

"I think I feel it a little now," said Dick, as the tip of his finger touched a smooth cherrylike object. "Yeah, this is the cervix, it has an indentation in it. Hmm. Imagine babies coming out of this. Nature is wonderful."

"You keep that up much longer and you'll make me come. Let's go back to the bedroom. This is getting me too excited. I'll do it in a minute if you keep on."

It was true, she was extremely wet now and was breathing hard; he could feel her chest rise and fall against his shoulder. As he pushed his finger here and there in the velvetlike sheath of her vagina, she made little involuntary grinds of her pelvis against his hand. The girl obviously was at the point of orgasm and a trip to the bedroom was overdue—or prompt action on the sofa, anyhow—but the moment was too wickedly delicious to end quite yet. Dick asked:

"Pauline, were you very unhappy as a small girl?"

On rare occasions Pauline could be funny. Wearily, she said, "I'm unhappy right now as a *big* girl."

"No, really. Were you very unhappy?"

"Unhappy? Christ, I don't know. Let's go to the bedroom."

"Okay, but tell me this. When you play with it, how do you

do it, do you attack the clit or do you go for the whole damn thing? I know it's a ridiculous question, but I'm curious about it. How do you do it?"

Pauline laughed and groaned at the same time. "I put a mop handle in it," she said. "If you're trying to get me really aroused, you sure are succeeding. I can't stand much more of this. Please, let's go to the bedroom, huh?"

Dick gave a little sigh. "Well, all right," he said. It had to be. Further dillydallying was both impossible and inhuman; he would have to fuck her. However, he who dillydallies is sometimes lost, or at least lost for the time being. As Dick made up his mind to stop teasing both Pauline and himself, deliverance in the form of Nicolo Riccobono was walking up the sidewalk of Pitcairne Avenue on his way home.

"I'll get glasses and some whisky," said Pauline happily. "I like to screw and drink, don't you?"

"Well, no, but you go ahead."

"Not much, just a little. It makes it more orgyish. God, you've got no idea how horny I am! I hope you're in the mood, baby, because you're going to have a wild woman under you, and I mean *wild.* . . ."

"You can get on top if you want to."

"I *love* it on top," said Pauline. "I love it every way there is to do it, sideways, backwards, every way there is. . . ."

At that moment of tender promise and anticipation, tragically there came the sound of footsteps on the front porch and the ominous rattle of a key in the front door.

"Who is that?" asked Dick.

"*Shit!*" whispered Pauline, with a look of mingled despair and rage. "It must be Nicky. *Shit!* Oh, *shit!*"

"And you wanted me to go to that bedroom," whispered Dick.

"I swear to God I wasn't expecting him," said Pauline angrily, as she wrapped the bathrobe around her and tied it. "Something must have gone wrong."

"Yeah, sure," said Dick. With trembling fingers he lit a
cigarette. From the sublime to the ridiculous. Now an embarrassing confrontation with a husband. Good God, he might
even get beaten up. In as innocent and friendly a manner as
possible, he smiled as a heavyset and rather amiable-looking
Italian boy of about twenty-three appeared in the tiny hallway
and in the door of the living room, a slightly puzzled frown
on his face. It was Nicky.

"Hi, there," said Dick.

"Hi," said Nicky.

"What are you doing home so early?" asked Pauline.

"Well, Sal didn't feel so good," said Nicky.

"Did you go to Jersey?"

"Yeah, sure."

In plain disbelief, Pauline frowned at him. Finally, with a
sour glance at Dick, she said, "Nicky, I'd like you to meet
Dick Davenport. He's here about some stuff about the kids at
the Union."

Dick clenched his teeth. What a lame explanation! And
showing her vexation so obviously; a stupid girl, Pauline. But
it didn't seem to matter. A slow, pleased smile spread on
Nicky's face as he walked forward and held out his hand. "Oh,
yeah, yeah, sure," he said. "I heard a lot about you. I'm real
pleased to meet you." Two minutes later, sitting on the yellow
sofa with a beer in his hand, Nicky said:

"It's a real thrill to meet you, Dick. Tell me something.
Where do you get your ideas?"

"My what?" asked Dick.

"Your ideas when you write something. Where do you get
them?"

"Oh . . . well, I don't know, here and there."

"I was reading your book. Part of it anyhow, I'm not much
of a reader. Course Pauline first thing had to run out and buy
it, that was the first thing she did when you started down at
the settlement house. She had met an author, it was a thrill for

her, you know? And I was reading it. It was kind of interesting. I was wondering if any of that happened or did you just
dream it up?"

Incredible. As Dick puffed nervously at his cigarette he
could smell Pauline's pussy juice on his fingers. Didn't the
poor fellow even remotely suspect it? Evidently not. "Ah-h,
well, a little of this, a little of that," said Dick.

"Um-m. I guess partly you dreamed it up, partly you didn't.
Tell me this. Do you work when you're in the mood, or do
you just sit down every day and write whether you feel like
it or not?"

On the porch Pauline whispered, "I swear to God I was sure
he'd be out till two at least. You heard him, his cousin's sick
like you said, that's why he came in so early. It was an accident,
Dick, he won't be here tomorrow."

"Good night," said Dick.

"Are you mad?"

"Of course not, why should I be? But I'm sure glad I didn't
go back in that bedroom with you."

"It'll be safe tomorrow, he has to work. I'll see you then,
okay?"

Dick sighed. "Okay," he said.

"You'll really come? At two?"

Again Dick sighed. "Yes," he said. "I'll be here."

In the taxi going back to the Samussons', Davenport tried
to convince himself that Nicky's unexpected appearance was
a true deliverance and a sign that he should not keep the date
on the following day. But he couldn't. The early return home
of Pauline's husband was no sign, it was merely an accident,
just as she said. The dumb mistake he'd made was in not going
ahead when he had her legs opened wide on the sofa. It was
all there and like a damn fool he'd stopped to try to get to
know her as a human being, when he already knew the
damned little bitch as a human being. What an idiot idea,

trying to get to know her humanly. On the other hand, it had indeed been sexy putting his finger in her; it had been sexy as hell. If Nicky hadn't walked in, they'd have had a fantastic time in that bedroom. Well, it had been delayed until the next afternoon, that was all; and it would be sexier than ever as a result. That was what would happen, unless in the meanwhile he had some kind of an attack of childish morality and he saw no way such a thing was possible. It was inevitable, it had to happen, sooner or later, for better or for worse; he would go to bed with Pauline Riccobono and it would be great, fantastic, the sexiest experience of his life. In some strange and paradoxical way, it would help him solve the basic problem and get to work.

". . . that is why success is so deadly and dangerous," said Samusson. "Kipling wrote of it in his jungle stories: 'And then fear came.' The child has no such fear. The child is innocent, the child has nothing to lose. But the adult who has tasted of success has this fear and he must make a choice between prestige and work. He must decide which rabbit he will chase."

"In our society," said the whining woman, "what we have got is an *awful* competition. I don't see how you can call it a real civilization when everybody is trying to get ahead of everybody else like in a jungle——"

"Just a second," said Nate. "Let him finish about the rabbits. That's interesting."

"Well, Dick—who I see now has returned—asked us earlier this evening about success and its problems, which I gather you were discussing before, and I don't wonder, you have both had quite a taste of it. And in early youth, too, which is of course a kind of double whammy. . . ."

"I was interested in the rabbits. Dick mentioned that at the apartment, that you had some rabbits. I would like to find out more about these rabbits."

"Well, there is the rabbit of prestige or status, on the one hand, and the rabbit of work and achievement, on the other. A man has got to decide which rabbit he will chase."

"Why not chase them both?" asked Nate.

"That doesn't work. If you chase them both, they will both get away. It has got to be one or the other."

"Um-hmm, well, that sounds drearily Calvinistic to me, a tired and sleazy Puritan work ethic, to say nothing of a holier-than-thou attitude. May I ask what is wrong with prestige and status if they are earned?"

"Nothing," said Samusson. "But it has got to be coinciden-tal. A man can't divide himself in half and he can't divide his life effort in half. He has got to chase one rabbit or the other, not both of them. If you want prestige and status, then go after it hook, line and sinker and don't let anything distract you from it, least of all honest work and real achievement."

"I agree with that," said Dick. "Success is a lying whore bitch everybody wants and nobody really can get."

"What do you mean, nobody *really* can get?" asked Nate. "She can be had."

"Not really," said Dick. "Success is opinion."

"Opinion?"

"What Dick means, I think, is that success is a measure of the opinion of the world, and the opinion of the world can't be controlled by any man, least of all an artist. A clever person can attempt to influence and win the approval of the opinion makers, but that has nothing to do with being either an artist or a man."

"Amen," said Dick. "She's a no-good, lying whore bitch that everybody wants and nobody can get. She'll ruin you if you try, she'll put a hatpin in your brain. It's what Frost meant in his poem. You have to turn your back on that bitch and go another way. Now God knows I don't have any right to quote that poem, I don't know what road I'm taking or if I'm taking any road at all, but the key is what he says at the end. Let me quote that, Nate, and you'll have to admit that old man was great. . . ."

"I'm sorry, but I disagree completely with you both," replied Nate. "It's the most pious, holier-than-thou idea I ever heard of. Don't you think Dick wants to be a better writer than me and I want to be a better writer than him? Sure success is a bitch, but the bitch can be had if you've got the nerve and the guts to go after her. And I say if you can get the lying whore, why not fuck her?"

"A splendid statement," replied Samusson, "admirable in its ballsiness, and 'twould be simple 'twere it so. But I am afraid there are two rabbits out there, not one, and they are totally different animals. If you chase them both, they will both get away. I've been telling Dick this for weeks, while he sits paralyzed looking at both those creatures wondering which one he wants. Or to use his own perhaps more vivid metaphor, while he sits dreaming idly of the idiot whore bitch that he knows in his bones he can never get. One real woman is worth a thousand of her, but he still sits looking at the lying whore, hypnotized."

"So true, so true," said Dick. "I never did have much sense. She's no good, that bitch, but I can't resist her, I just don't have the character."

AND FROM WHERE HAD IT ALL COME? OF COURSE WHEN
a man's born with a lordgod bird sitting on the windowsill, he
is bound to be a bit apart from other men, which of itself is
a maddening and infuriating proposition: "To be great is to
be lonely." That was from where it came, the damned lordgod
bird. But what was the locus and focus of it? How and where
did the genius of Black Nick fulfill itself? Beyond a doubt, in
that nest egg of old New York: the Seamus, erstwhile haunt
of Diamond Jim Brady and Lillian Russell.

Hotel Seamus had changed hands many times since its hey-
day; that is, various banks had owned it, first one bank and
then another. The banks traded it back and forth as banks will.
The Seamus would go broke under the ownership of one
bank, then that bank would give it to another bank, which in
turn would pass it on. It was one of those undesirable bank-
type properties of the white elephant category, and thus was
the plaything of finance capital in a small way.

Why it didn't occur to some bank to tear the thing down is

a mystery. Of course it was eventually torn down and thus the hidden empire of Black Nick Sampson was discovered, but the Seamus for quite a while was the ostensible plaything of banks even as it served a darker purpose. Nevertheless, despite its being tossed from one bank to another, the management of the hotel did not change. Mr. Gaylord, Mr. Dogberry and Mr. Smegg remained, ruled over by the manager Mr. Cleet. They aged and faded and grew senile, particularly Mr. Cleet, who developed twitches. But they stayed on. They were settled in the Seamus like oxen in a bog. In a sense they *were* the Seamus. Dust had gotten in their very veins and whirled gradually about their circulatory systems in place of blood. All except old Chauncey Gaylord. Chauncey still (incredibly) retained in his withered frame a few juices stewed into a sluggish concentrate by the years, as we will see.

One day Mr. Cleet hired a new janitor. The old janitor, an ancient black man known as "the Parson," had been found in a Harlem alley with his head neatly severed and tucked under his arm. The single stroke of a razor had done it. There was no known motive for the crime. The janitor had been a quiet, respectable old dad, rather conservative and God-minded— his only flaw was a tendency every few days to get skonk drunk. He had been at the Seamus longer than Mr. Gaylord, longer, even, than Messrs. Dogberry, Smegg and Cleet. For countless years the Parson had fired the furnaces and taught algebra to the boilers.

And then a stroke of a razor removed him from the picture. Gone. Off to potter's field. And in his place a new janitor. A tall, gigantic fellow, but very softspoken and polite, an old-timey colored boy.

"Yaaaaasuh," said the new janitor. "Ohh, yaaaasuh, Mistah Cleet, Ah *sho* would lak dis hyah job, sah, iffen yo' wants to gie it to me. Mah name is Nick 'Sambo' Sampson, yaaaah-suh. . . ."

Splendid janitor.

And a week later a scene in Mr. Cleet's office he would never forget, a razor at his throat and the eyes of a fiend six inches from his own. No wonder he twitched. First, however, a bit of background on the peculiar situation that existed at the Hotel Seamus, the situation that lured the genius of Black Nick in the first place.

Years ago the Seamus had contained deep in its bowels a large though disconnected area of cell-like, windowless rooms for the maids, chauffeurs and valets of the guests. Also, extensive areas, likewise disconnected, were set aside for the storage of the innumerable trunks of the guests and for various items of furniture belonging to them, since many of the residents in those days preferred to furnish their own suites.

Through the years this space had lost its purpose. The guests no longer had maids, chauffeurs and valets. One small and readily accessible room served to store the luggage. The old bowel area gradually became infested with giant rats as the result of a break in an ancient sewer no longer used by the city. Rats the size of fox terriers poured in from this sewer and nested in the lower walls, from which they climbed up into walls of the hotel itself. Guests could hear them gnashing and squeaking in there, and sometimes the rats would break through and chase the old ladies up on top of toilets.

The rat problem became so severe as to be intolerable. Exterminators could accomplish little. The lower rooms in the bowel had rotted in the dampness and thousands upon thousands of giant brown rats *(Rattus norvegicus)* nested in the walls, a fierce breed. The only solution was to close off these lower rooms entirely, and that was done. The rooms were bricked up, sealed and plastered over. The exterminator crews then hollowed out the exterior main walls of the building at lobby level in order to fumigate them thoroughly. These walls, being old-fashioned, were about three feet thick or more, and the resourceful exterminators chiseled them out all the way around the building. Of course this weakened the structure of the Seamus, but it was weak anyhow. The point is that this hollowed passage in the outer walls and in the main lobby walls made it a practical matter to trap the rats down below. They were, in effect, sealed off from above and sealed off from below, too.

All of this was years and years in the past. *Rattus norvegicus* is an extraordinarily intelligent animal. Unlike other rats *(Rattus rattus)* it has a certain reasoning power. Product of a harsh, hard land, it could be regarded as a Viking among rats, and to a certain degree as an Einstein among rats, since under normal conditions it used only about three per cent of its rat brainpower. It would be too much to say that these thousands of trapped rats got together and had a conference and discussed the whole thing and came up with a solution. That would be going too far.

But is it not true that sometimes animals have strange reasoning powers? Is it not a scientific fact that some animals can count? Animal life is weird, no doubt about it. All is not as it seems. Rats do think. They think *in their way,* and who can be sure what sort of conferences and whisker wigglings and tail waggings went on down there in those dark days?

In any event, a cornered rat is a desperate rat. Long before, the original entryway into the Seamus via the ancient forgotten sewer had been accidentally sealed up by a Consolidated Edison crew. They came across the old sewer a couple of blocks from the Seamus, stared at it in puzzlement since it was not on the charts, and then dug on through it looking for a gas pipe. Later, the gas pipe was found elsewhere. The Con Ed crew, in departing, filled up the erroneous hole entirely with piles of old brick and stone, thus sealing the old sewer permanently.

True, there were other exits from it, antique conduits leading to various semiforgotten gutters and mostly-paved-over manholes that led through narrow and winding tributary tunnels and sometimes steep, angular descending drainage weepholes to old lead and tile pipe which reached in one way or another the modern sewer system of the city—or rather, approached and fed indirectly and *subtly* into the modern sewer system, since the modern system is bricked in to render it rat proof . . . and, one might add, in view of all the caviling and mewling about it, crocodile proof, too. There are no crocodiles in the New York sewer system, or pet alligators either, contrary to the persistent legend. No crocodile or alligator or cayman could survive for two minutes the millions of tons of corruption that float and circulate in the very foundation of Gotham, the city of cities, the city to end cities.

But a rat can. The sewers had in them rats aplenty, and these particular rats were hopelessly trapped. Starvation was inevitable. Starvation or death through lack of oxygen, and even a rat needs oxygen. There was enough oxygen in the arena of entrapment to last the rats approximately three weeks. Those who had not starved in that time would die of oxygen deficiency.

Now, in such a situation as this, one might expect that anarchy would prevail, that each selfish rat would strike out for himself egocentrically and try to kill and devour as many fellow rats as possible so as to cut down on the drain of precious oxygen and at the same time feed himself. One might expect that type of (realistic) fear and hostility; but those rats stuck together with real rat feeling. Possibly they were mutated rats. They might have been *Rattus norvegicus* mutated into a new species of almost human intelligence such as *Rattus manhattanus sapiens*. But one thing is clear: before they began to eat each other, they tried to figure out some method of escape. In fact, evidence indicates a considerable cooperative effort before all hope was lost.

What happened was that the rats began to gnaw in the

general direction of Broadway. They knew solid masonry was above them, dense, old-fashioned, Diamond Jim Brady–type construction they could never pierce. Their only hope, they knew, was to gnaw upward at a slanting rise in a long diagonal toward Broadway. That was their chance, to reach the gutters of Broadway. And so, madly, insanely, ferociously they gnawed and gnawed and gnawed, and they dug and dug and dug. On and on they tunneled, hundreds of them, in shifts, as the oxygen ran low.

It was terrible. Tragically, they went the wrong way—they would easily have made it several times over, but no doubt confused in the depths they lost their direction and instead of digging toward Broadway they dug toward Thirty-fourth Street. It was the rumble of crosstown buses on Thirty-fourth, apparently, that revealed to them their error, because the rat tunnel at Thirty-fourth veers sharply—but not to the west . . . *east!* Again, the rats were confused. Undoubtedly they thought Thirty-fourth was Twenty-third Street. So, instead of heading toward Broadway they doubled back toward Fifth Avenue. And they did reach it, they got to Fifth Avenue. Here the tunnel began to narrow a bit as the rats were getting exhausted.

The disappointment that waited at Fifth Avenue undoubtedly was bitter, because numerous flaky rat bones are there. A mutiny against the rat leaders. But new leaders evidently sprang forward, for here the tunnel veers away from the shallow and useless molded-iron gutters of Fifth Avenue toward the deeper gutters of Broadway. On and on the tunnel goes, narrowing a bit along the way as the rats become further exhausted. And they almost made it. The tunnel ends nine feet short of the deep and serviceable gutters of Broadway itself. The end of that tunnel is tragically choked, piled high to its very ceiling with a mass of whitened, pathetic rat skeletons, many gnawed and half eaten.

Thus the perishing of the rats despite a magnificent struggle.

Trapped in madness looking for Broadway and winding up in a pile of bones. And yet the thing was admirable and even phenomenal in its way. Those thousands of trapped rats had cut a tunnel almost a mile long, four feet high and three feet wide! Incredible creatures! Who can say animals are . . . merely animals? Perhaps there is a *purpose* behind their existence . . . mmm. In any event, sheer rat heroism of this ilk might well make a man hesitate the next time he thinks about rats.

Such, then, was the empire in its physical aspect that Nick Sampson took over when he cut the throat of the old black Parson who foolishly and tipsily told him of the brave rats trapped thirty years before in the hidden bowels of the Seamus.

THE WORDS HAUNTED HIM STILL. IN SOME DARK RECESS
of the mind and spirit he could hear the song: "Oh, if I had
the wings of an angel, over these prison walls I would fly. . . ."
Something very alien to himself, he felt, must have provoked
such an egotistical display; he couldn't have done it all on his
own. Death did it, or helped, anyhow. No doubt part of it was
the grim thought of what he had to face at eight o'clock in the
morning. However, if the stark reality of death can cause all
of human endeavor to be regarded with a perspective
removed from petty striving, it can also spur a man to say
things that he means and does not mean at the same time.
Surely, he was not such an egotistical ass as he sounded!

A distressing event occurred about half past eleven not long
after Dick and Naomi got back from walking the Hammerfields to the subway. A very distressing event, a very frightening event. For the first time in his life, leaving aside the funeral
of his grandmother in the course of which he beheld the
painted and powdered remains, Richard Davenport saw not

only a dead person, he saw a person die. He was there, he heard the final choked rattle of breath and felt with his own hands the dying spasms in thin, gray, naked legs. It was the last blow really, the perfect end to a horrible day.

Ironically, only minutes before it happened, he and Naomi were sitting talking in the kitchen about the unlikelihood of sudden death. It was spooky. There was a Yiddish word for it, a concept that maybe was a product of an uncertain life in years of persecution: just as you say a thing won't happen, it happens—*kinehora,* that overweening complacency which invites the wrath of fate and the laughter of the gods.

Hot chocolate seemed to help the insomnia, hot chocolate with a little whipped cream on top with a few jimmies to make it pretty. Dick was in no hurry to get to bed. Naomi had said, as she sat there in her rather flimsy nightgown, "Frankly, I feel sexy tonight." Unfortunately, his own thoughts in that area were elsewhere. No hurry about bed; let her sit there and get sleepy and maybe she would forget about it. And so, thanks to Mrs. Riccobono, they talked over cocoa perhaps a little longer than they would have done ordinarily. The conversation ranged from Nate Hammerfield to Beau St. John to little fat Natalie, but it began on Pat's new black boyfriend Charles and his wife, who had suddenly died of a heart attack at thirty-seven.

"Can you imagine that?" asked Dick. "An apparently healthy woman with no history of heart disease suddenly keels over with a heart attack in a movie theater lobby at *thirty-seven?*"

"There must have been something wrong with her heart. She must have had rheumatic fever as a child or something like that, or maybe a congenital defect of some type."

"No, the autopsy showed *nothing* wrong with her heart, it just stopped. Suddenly, like that. For no reason that they know of. It sometimes happens. But actually, thank God, it's very rare. Sudden death of any kind is rare. The truth is it seldom happens. Even people with severe heart attacks don't usually die like that, they linger awhile—it isn't you're here one minute, and blip you're gone the next. It's scary, though. Can you imagine innocently coming out of that movie and seeing a woman keel over in the lobby dead, can you picture it?"

"Well, I don't like to," said Naomi. "What do you think of your sister's new boyfriend?"

Dick shrugged. "He seems okay, kind of shy and quiet. I only saw him for about five minutes. They'd had a ridiculous argument and he wouldn't come out of the bedroom. We didn't talk much. He's a social worker and kind of pedantic in his manner, like a teacher or something, not much sense of humor there. Wears glasses, balding, very neat. He works with Puerto Ricans in East Harlem; a lot of them are coming up from the island and he says what this town does to them is unbelievable. They're exploited right and left with utter mercilessness. I didn't know there were that many Puerto Ricans. I've added them to the fantasy. The Chinese were never wholly convincing; there isn't that much won ton soup around. That thing is hideously racist, you know. I was wondering what Pat and Charles would make of Nick Sampson; he'd probably drive them out of their minds."

"Probably would," said Naomi. "That would be like asking a Jew to think anti-Semitism is funny."

"Well, I guess I'm a racist swine, then, because I think Nick is funny. I think he's funnier than ketchup with his filed-down teeth and especially with his Tarzan suit. But maybe I have a distressed sense of humor. I didn't mention him to Patricia and Charles."

"Does it bother you that he's black?"

Dick rubbed pensively at his jaw. "Well, I don't think so. It bothers me that she's so self-righteously liberal about it. I can't help but think it's an act. And I'll tell you one thing that bothers me; I don't think he has the balls to cope with her. She'll eat this Charles for breakfast just like she did Herb."

"I'm sorry for her," said Naomi. "She's very unhappy."

"Don't waste your tears. Pat has *always* been unhappy. It's an awful thing to say and God forbid, but ever since I can remember she's been afraid of getting cancer and secretly I think she'd love to have it. I can picture her screaming silently with masochistic triumph as they shoot her with those last needles in some ward. God forbid, deep inside she's a selfless soul; I don't mean all that about her, but she *is* a godawful pain in the ass. But I'll tell you someone who is a *worse* pain in the ass, and that is Beau."

"I meant to ask you about him. Did he write a story, did you read it?"

"Oh, Christ. I don't want to think about it. Don't remind me."

"Bad, real bad?"

"Bad isn't the word for it. You can't describe a thing like that as either bad or good. It's off in a dimension by itself, huddled humidly. Actually a thing like that has crawled up its own asshole out of sight. There is no other way to put it."

Naomi smiled faintly. "It must have been a pretty horrible story."

"It wasn't a story at all. Beau is out of his masturbating mind. Failure has gone to his head. But there was one encouraging thing today, practically the only encouraging thing except a safe didn't fall on me. Natalie. You remember I mentioned little fat Natalie at the settlement house?"

"You've mentioned her many times, the little girl with talent."

"Yeah, the little girl with talent. She's a thousand times better writer than Beau. She wrote another story and it was good. It has a great title, 'Once a Tree, Now a Paper.' It's about this tree up in the North Woods that's kind to animals and lumberjacks come along and cut it down and it gets chopped up and made into newsprint and it accepts its fate nobly. A great story. That Natalie is something else. The only sad thing . . . well, I don't want to depress you, this has been a bad enough day already, but it really was pathetic. . . ."

"We had better go to bed," said Naomi. "But I'm curious, what was the sad thing about Natalie and her story?"

"Well, she asked me if she could get it *published* somewhere. This girl, this woman who works there was walking me to the subway and Natalie tagged along and asked me that. She's jealous of this girl and that made it worse. I didn't know how to handle it or what to say. I really didn't, I didn't know what to tell her . . . I'm afraid I hurt her. . . ."

"What girl is this?" asked Naomi softly. "The one she's jealous of?"

"Not a *girl,* this woman who's a teacher there. She's nobody. The point is, Natalie is jealous of her. You see, I have a kind of hate-love thing with Natalie; she pretends to despise me but she doesn't. And she asked me could her story get *published* somewhere. That little girl, I tell you if I didn't have a heart of flint . . . it would bother me. She was serious, very serious. Where can her story be published? I've committed a kind of sin there; I've given her hope; I've made her see something in herself . . . there is hope for her, something beautiful is in her. And what could I say, how could I answer her? Tell her to keep writing and go to college and in ten years *Briar's Weekly* will publish one of her stories?"

"I don't think you've committed a sin at all. How do you know what she might do someday or what effect it might have on her life because of what you've given her?"

"I haven't given her anything at all," said Dick, "except illusions."

"I don't believe that. It's late, unless you want more cocoa we'd better go to bed."

"It's only eleven thirty."

"Yes, but if you're going to get up at seven, that's late."

Dick struck a match for another cigarette. Half smiling, he stared into Naomi's eyes. Quietly, he said, "You don't think I'm going to start that book tomorrow, do you? Well, no one thinks so. Beau, Pat, Samusson, they all think I'm in a neurotic quandary, and maybe I have been. But I'm going to fool them, Naomi, and you, too. I've been bracing myself for it all day, taking one last look around before I jump into that icy water. Tomorrow morning at eight is H hour, and I ain't kiddin'."

"Then you better get some rest," said Naomi with a smile.

"Okay, but before we go, what did you think of Nate Hammerfield?"

Naomi hesitated. "What did *you* think of him?"

"Well, I liked him very much. I was very impressed with him. He's a talker like Beau but he can write, too. He's nervy, he's daring, even reckless; he has balls hanging all over him. And he has terrific energy, there's a lot of life in him. As an artist there's something meretricious; maybe he leans a little too much on ideology. But that was only his first book and the book had real narrative power. That's his gift, I think, he's a terrific storyteller. Of course that isn't fashionable now, writing up a storm is fashionable. And he can do that; he has great verbal facility and inventiveness. He's very ambitious, maybe too much so. I was impressed; he's very clever and talented."

"I couldn't stand how he talked about women; it made me want to vomit."

"He was kind of joking, I don't think he completely means that."

"The hell he doesn't. Maybe he likes women, but he likes them in their place. But I agree with you, he's very talented and clever. In fact I think he is cleverer than he acted tonight; he was on guard competing with you."

"*Me?* I'm no threat, not in his mind; he was just being nice including me in that paddock. His book was a giant success, much bigger than mine."

"Not all that much bigger except maybe commercially," said Naomi, "and it certainly wasn't a better novel, if it was as good. You're a threat to him all right; any other writer who is taken half-seriously is a threat to him. He's very competitive, even moreso than that little pretty boy who was out here and told me he liked girls as much as boys and kept staring at me as if I was a snake and might bite him."

"*Zut alors,*" said Dick, "poor Roman. If he could hear you say that he'd piss all over himself. But you're crazy, honey. Nate is nowhere *near* that competitive. He was joking a lot of the time, you don't understand him."

"Well, I will admit he's very shrewd and smart, and I'm sure he's very talented, too. Of course he is, it's obvious. And as for his opinion about women, well, maybe he's joking, maybe he isn't, but I don't like it. . . . ."

Thus they talked over cocoa about the people and events of the day for fifteen or twenty minutes and then it was bedtime. But the day was not quite over; its worst event was soon to occur, its worst event by far. Dick went into the bathroom to brush his teeth and get ready to go to bed and he noticed water dripping from the ceiling. There was quite a bit of it; a stream ran down the wall over the small window. Something was wrong in the apartment above.

"There's water all over the bathroom," he said to Naomi. "The Steiner girl's husband left her, didn't he? She's up there alone with a baby or something?"

"It's a small child, a little girl I think," answered Naomi. "Her mother lives there now, too."

"Something's wrong up there. Maybe the child left the water running in the tub. I'd better go get the super."

Dick and Naomi's apartment was on the second floor and the apartment of the building superintendent was directly beneath them. The super was a little squint-eyed man with a nasty disposition. His wife was twice his size, a huge fat woman with popped blue eyes—Dick and Naomi often heard her through the floor whooping loudly at Gorgeous George on television, the wrestler who put on a fag act and sprayed perfume out of a flit can all over the ring. "He is kind of *effeminate,*" she explained.

In Davenport's opinion, Gorgeous George was a spiritual abomination of the first order and television itself was not much better, but the shrimpy super and his wife were enthusiastic devotees of the spanking new medium; they had a fancy set with a water-filled lens in front of the six-inch tube to enlarge the ghostly and ghastly images on it, and the one thing they did not like was to be interrupted while watching the damnable thing. But this was an emergency, and Dick put a bathrobe over his pajamas and walked down the stairs to the ground floor and rang the super's bell. After a long time, angry eyes squinted at him through a crack in the door.

"We're watching the television. It has to wait till the morning. This is a show my wife don't want me to miss."

"Now, look. Water is all over my bathroom. It's coming down from the ceiling in a flood. I'm sorry to take you away from Gorgeous George, but something's wrong in that bathroom upstairs——"

"He ain't on. What kind of hour do you think this is? But oh hell, all right, I'll get my kit. The little girl probably let the tub run over and she's too small to open the door. It happens all the time; they shouldn't let 'em take baths alone——"

The tub in the apartment on the third floor had indeed run over; but it wasn't the child. For a reason he later described as dumb curiosity, Dick tagged along with the super. The divorcée, Mrs. Steiner, a thin girl of about twenty-six, opened the front door of the apartment and stood there for a moment in a man's bathrobe looking puzzled; but she turned an instant ashy white when the super told her that water was coming through the floor of her bathroom. "My mother is in there," she said.

Dick knew it wouldn't be good. Something was very wrong in that bathroom. But he couldn't leave now, help very likely might be needed. A trifle weak at the knees, Dick waited in the hall a few feet away as the superintendent picked with some kind of tool at the bathroom lock. There had been not a sound in reply to his irritated banging on the door. The thin Mrs. Steiner kept asking: "Why doesn't she answer? Why doesn't she answer?" And then the super forced the door open and water gushed into the hall and Dick flinched as he heard a sudden piercing scream. An echoing cry that seemed almost instantaneous came from a small child in a nearby bedroom, but it was a sympathetic cry of fright; the child could not have seen anything. Paralyzed, briefly unable to move a muscle, Dick stared in shock through the opened bathroom door at the superintendent crouched by the side of the tub.

"Come in here and help me with this woman!" cried the super.

"Oh! Oh, God! Oh, God!" cried young Mrs. Steiner.

A gray-haired woman who looked to be in her sixties lay in the tub. The bathtub faucets were not running, but the shower was; it sprinkled down among macerated carrots that she had vomited. Bright red blood was on the side of the tub and on her face and head, which evidently she had struck as she fell. The woman was breathing in a horrible rattling manner and foam was on her lips. Her face was a milklike blue. One hand hung helplessly over the side of the tub, palm uplifted.

"She's vomited, she's had a stroke," said the super. "We've got to get her in the bedroom. Grab her by the legs, I'll get her under the arms."

"Call the police, quick!" yelled the super. "Tell 'em to send an ambulance and do it right now if you want your mother to live!"

With great reluctance, Dick walked into the inch of water

on the bathroom floor and reached down into the tub and took the woman by the legs just above her ankles. The legs were thin but she was fat. He could not help but see her big sagging breasts and her melonlike belly and the gray, tub-soaked pubic hair which seemed pathetically thin and scanty. It didn't matter, she could not be embarrassed, but it bothered him to look at her.

"Turn her over, damn it!"

"But can't we carry her like this?"

"Turn her over like I said! It'll hurt her, her head hanging down backward! Turn her over, damn it!"

Naomi knew her slightly, and Dick later learned that the lady's name was Mrs. Silverman. She often took care of the child out front. She was a widow seventy-three years old but looked younger than that. Death came to her as they carried her down the hall, her big breasts hanging almost to the floor and her fat waffled behind in the air. Of course it didn't matter, nothing in the world mattered to the woman, and such a painful visual invasion could hardly embarrass her; but it bothered Dick very much and he tried to look elsewhere.

"I called the police, they're coming!" cried Mrs. Steiner, whose man's bathrobe had come undone in her distress. Her modesty was ravaged too. Dick could see her nipples and a shadow between her thighs through the thin nightgown and again he tried to look elsewhere as the screaming of the child in the bedroom rang in his ears. It was a waking nightmare; all hell had broken loose in the apartment on the third floor. "They're sending an ambulance, they promised it will be here right away!"

"I'm afraid it's too late, she's going," said the super.

"Oh, God, no! No! No!"

Dick didn't want to believe it either; he'd never really seen a dead person, much less a person die; but it was true. The horrendous rattling noise of the woman's breathing had stopped, and he could feel strong spasms in the muscles of her legs as if she were trying to get away from him. A kind of tremble was running through her, too. The lady was in her death throes. She was dying as strangers carried her stark naked down a dark hall. Dick still couldn't quite believe it; maybe it wasn't true, maybe she would revive in the bedroom, maybe she would have a final moment with her daughter, one human moment at least.

"Granma! Granma!" cried a little girl standing on a cot, as Dick and the super laid the naked gray-haired woman on a bed. There was no sign of life in her; her glazed eyes were now open. She was dead. A few minutes later, the police emergency squad gave her artificial respiration and oxygen for a while because the daughter was screaming at them to do something; but it was absolutely to no avail. The lady was dead and gone.

At one in the morning Dick sat in the kitchen having whisky, not cocoa, with Naomi. It was a distressing and frightening experience, to say the least, and a strange wild mood had come upon him.

"It must have been awful," said Naomi. "I don't wonder that you're shaking, I'd be shaking myself."

"She died right there in the hall while we were carrying her. She was breathing before in this horrible way, but then it stopped and she began trembling. I could feel her legs contract like a frog or something! Jesus Christ! I'm telling you, Naomi, I'm telling you, you wouldn't have wanted to be up there. . . ."

"Oh, God, I would have fainted. Try not to think about it. Really, try to put it out of your mind; it doesn't do any good to think about it. . . ."

"How can I *not* think about it?" asked Dick. In an effort to get a grip on himself, he took another swallow of whisky and made a face. "I hate this goddamn stuff, I hate it; I don't see how people drink it. Filthy fucking stuff. Jesus, I hate it!"

"Dick, please calm down," said Naomi in a worried tone. "I know it was horrible and you're hypersensitive, anyhow, but——"

"I am *not* hypersensitive!" said Dick angrily. "This would bother *any*body! I don't care how much of a phlegmatic slug you are! But all right. All right, I'll calm down. I really am all right. After all, it's nothing but death. It comes to us all sooner or later and thank God for that. Who would want to live in this filthy world forever? Not me! God, no! I can't imagine anything more horrible. I don't even want to live beyond a normal life span, and that's the truth! Once I get senile, if I ever do, I hope Nazis or something put me in a gas chamber. I'll welcome it. I'll say, 'Hi, fellas! Gas chamber all ready?' I'm not kidding, Naomi, I'm serious."

"It's after one o'clock and we have to get up tomorrow morning. Please, finish the drink and let's go to bed and get some sleep."

"You don't have to remind me, damn it. I know what I have to do and I'm going to do it—start a filthy book. But I might puke, I reserve that right."

"I wasn't trying to remind you of anything, it's just that it's late."

"Well, I'll tell you this," said Dick. "A thing like that upstairs cuts through all the nonsense; it gets you right down to the goddamn fundamentals. Speaking of puking, do you know what I feel when I think about that conversation I had tonight with Nate Hammerfield? *Nausea.* That is exactly what I feel. *Nausea.* Let me tell you something I've known for months but never would admit to myself, much less say out loud. This whole writing thing is *horseshit!* That's what it is, there isn't an ounce of truth or value in it anywhere, not even a particle! It's vanity, that's all it is, vanity pure and simple! Vanity in me, vanity in Hammerfield, vanity in them all."

"Well, now you're upset," said Naomi. "Let's go right now back to the bedroom, we can talk back *there. . . .*"

"Vanity, Naomi. That's all, vanity, vanity, vanity. And Nate Hammerfield is more honest than I am, at least he admits it. He's an ambitious son of a bitch and he makes no bones about it. And me? Jesus Christ, I really might vomit. There I am apologizing to him for quoting Frost when I know goddamn well I'm right and he's wrong. You're damn right I'm going on one road and you're damn right he's going on another, and we'll see which road leads where. He can have his goddamn thing, let him win his fucking horse race. I'm no damn horse and I'm not even at the race track! Now why did I apologize to him for quoting Frost, huh? Tell me, why did I do it? You just tell me what kind of chickenshit is that, for me to eat humble pie before this superficial ambitious clown! Tell me that, huh?"

"Well, I don't think . . . you ate any humble pie. You . . . you were nice to him, that's all. A couple of times I thought . . . *he* was rude, and you just passed it off."

"Fuck him!" cried Dick in an unreasoning fury. "The nerve he's got. He says he wants to be a 'better writer' than me and I want to be a 'better writer' than him. 'Better' in the eyes of *who?* The pile of idiots who call themselves *the literary world?* I'd rather wipe a polar bear's ass than to suck up to those death-head bastards. He can do that if he wants to win a horse race, I'll never do it myself. They can go to hell and so can he. Fuck him!"

Naomi was beginning to look worried. Gently, and rather haltingly, as always when she was upset or frightened, she said, "It doesn't matter who's a 'better' writer. You can do what you do . . . and he can do what he does. Of course he's talented, but . . . you don't have to compete with him, you have . . . things that you can do, too, that maybe he can't . . . frankly, I think you write a lot better. . . ."

"Are you out of your mother-loving *mind?* Do you dream for one moment that I have inferior feelings toward that ambitious fool? I can write rings around him, and then I can write rings around the rings I've written around him. There's no comparison between my gifts as a writer and his, none at all; that jackass is not fit to change my typewriter ribbon. That's my opinion and that's exactly what I'm getting at. It's vanity. The whole thing is vanity, vanity, vanity. The only difference between my vanity and his is that mine has been hidden and concealed. Pat accused me of it this afternoon and she was right."

"Well, I . . . I don't think you ought to get into one of these moods about writing if you're going to start the new book tomorrow," said Naomi. "You know what it always does to you later."

"No, I don't know. I don't know what you're talking about."

"I was thinking . . . about when you wrote the first book. Whenever you would get euphoric and . . . and think it was good, well . . ."

"Finish the sentence. *Please* finish the sentence."

"Well, you would have an awful day the next day . . . maybe even for the next week, especially when you would criticize other writers. I don't think it's going to help you tomorrow to talk like this tonight. It . . . it isn't even you talking, Dick. That awful business upstairs has got you upset."

"It *is* me talking. For the first time in months it is me talking and thank God for that. Do you know the *shit* I took off of Beau and Pat this afternoon? Good God, what they put me through! Both of them hate my goddamn guts because I happen to have a talent for writing and they don't! And I've been going around *apologizing* for it, saying *excuse me,* I'm so *sorry,* terribly crude of me, forgive me, *piss* on me, I deserve it— that's exactly what has been wrong with me! I've been trying to play a 'nicey' role, a 'nicey' part, but finally at last it is *me* talking! And let me tell you this. I've learned something from this miserable day and I've learned something from our company tonight——"

Pityingly, in a sorrowful little voice, Naomi interrupted. "Don't say it, Dick. Please don't."

"——and I have a confession to make. Since it's all vanity, anyhow, why not live with it? And my confession . . ."

"Dick, please. You'll be sorry."

". . . and my confession is this. Those guys aren't that good."

"Oh, Dick, please!"

"Let me finish, don't interrupt," said Davenport with an icy calm, as Nick flicked the cat-o'-nine on Archie's scrawny back. "They aren't that good. Not only can I write rings around Nathan Hammerfield, I can write rings around them all and I will. Naomi, they are a bunch of bums. I have opened their heads and inspected the contents carefully and I can certify there is not one writer of my generation who has the capacity for greatness, and I have got that capacity. Now I don't give a damn how egotistical that sounds, it is the truth. Half my problem is that I've been avoiding the responsibility for what I can do, hating it, shrinking from it. And it is a curse and a burden, Naomi, a fucking curse and a burden. All jokes to one side, truly, to be great is to be lonely."

"Oh, God," said Naomi.

So began the prisoner's song and Richard Davenport still was singing it. In the midst of his unfortunate affliction, which of course was brought about as much by the thought of eight o'clock in the morning as it was by the stark shock of death, he could hear somewhere deep in his bedeviled mind and spirit the sad, haunting words:

"If I had the wings of an angel, over these prison walls I would fly . . ."

NICK PRESSED A STUD ON THE DASHBOARD OF THE CADIL-
lac car and an ultrasonic inaudible wail rent the atmosphere as
dogs in apartments for blocks around howled suddenly and
put their paws over their ears. Men and women in nearby
streets, though they heard nothing, felt an inner unease, a
disquiet that could not be defined. From somewhere inside the
ancient employees' parlor basement, now redesigned as a
shambles of a garage, there came a faint responding buzz and
heavy paint-flaked iron doors rose silently on oiled bearings,
efficient despite the unprepossessing exterior. A garage was
revealed therein and Sampson slowly guided the Cadillac car
inside. In greased silence the garage doors rolled down and
snapped shut. The monster had reached his lair at last!

Like a great cat Nick quickly slid from the front seat and
down to the floor, his chauffeur's boots clicking on the concrete as he whirled all in one motion and headed for the rear
of the Cadillac car. He opened the trunk, seized a suspiciously
plump gunnysack with one hand, lifted it out, slung it over his

shoulder and walked toward the bare concrete wall. *"Mal-laka!"* he called in a basso voice, and on greased precision bearings the wall itself swung open, revealing a long dark descending flight of steps lit by dim catvus bulbs and bored straight through clayey walls of earth. It was a dank vista dripping moisture and fetidly lacking in oxygen and suggested a total absence of the appurtenances of civilized life. And guess who was in the gunny sack!?

Nick had, of course, long ago totally intimidated old Mr. Cleet, the apple-cheeked manager of the Seamus, not any problem there. And Gaylord, Dogberry, Smegg and the old Hibernian doorman out front knew nothing and he hadn't bothered with them, except slightly with Whork, who kept sniffing around. And not even much with him; he had merely placed his razor beneath the ancient doorman's chin and said, "One blink of yo' l'il pig eyes and yo' haid will fall." Then he'd tied the old gent up and tormented him awhile, cuffing him about the head and giving him a taste of the cat-o'-nine-tails that he found useful in the tombs for the girls and to drive the Chinese and Puerto Ricans . . . and then he let him go. Overconfidence there, but actually the old doorman knew (he was sniffing blindly) only a hundredth part of the sho' nuff truth. The error lay elsewhere; but how could Nick have anticipated that *Chauncey Gaylord,* of all people, would lose his hat down that sewer while absorbed in the *New York Times Book Review?*

As a result of that unpredictable accident, Polly made the acquaintance of Mr. Gaylord and subsequently she encountered again Roger Whork, otherwise known as the false Whork. That, however, was toward the end of her terrible ordeal with the Chinese and the Puerto Ricans and a few small Greeks.

Her ordeal in Nick's setup, however, boring eternity though it seemed to her, can be described rather briefly. The tombs were merely a rather elaborate house of prostitution; that was the setup and this was the source of Nick's income. He had exploited the population upsurge of Chinese and Puerto Ricans, that was all. He had in the tombs four girls: a black girl, Suzette; a yellow girl, Wan Lo; and a brown girl, Vasentesenka; and now he had a white girl, Polly.

The physical arrangements he'd worked out long before. He had taken over and considerably enlarged the rat tunnel system so as to allow egress at a number of various points. The tombs were in part furnished luxuriously, especially in the private quarters of Sampson himself. Most of it was business-like. Each pony had her own room with a foam rubber bed and little more—just a bed and on either wall a round hole approximately fourteen inches in diameter. All of the girls were too large to get out of these holes.

The rooms naturally contained a water closet and a trapdoor in each ceiling that allowed food to descend periodically. None boasted a washbasin or any such luxury, and the ponies had no clothes except for fancy hats.

"A hat suggests e'rething, baby," said Nick when he gave Polly the big straw with the fancy cherries on it. "Ah is so sho' of you, gal, you can even have a hatpin to hold it on yo' haid. And what is mo', ah even gie you all the chocklit candy you want, hee hee hee!" Vanity, vanity, giving her that hatpin, a good way to get lobotomized.

The candy was of course loaded with love juice, and it must be added that escape from the tombs was *a theoretical impossibility.* Nick was not totally inhuman, though. He had fixed it up so the girls could communicate with each other through speaking tubes. This was in order that they might have some social life when they so desired during off hours. And not only that, once a week he hosed them down. That was because they liked it and also because after a while they got a little gamey, even the delicate Wan Lo, whose name meant "lotus blossom."

The main entrance (that is, the public entrance) into the lair of this Monster Fiend was located in an unpretentious grocery store over on Eighth Avenue. The tunnel for this was quite long and about two feet high. Each day at four o'clock in the afternoon the grocery store entrance was opened by Smart Juan, the crafty and thinly moustached boy who served as Nick's assistant in charge of traffic control and fee collection.

Soon after Smart Juan opened up, the Chinese and Puerto Ricans would begin to come. Singly they would wander into the grocery store and gaze about idly as if on no special business; then suddenly they would step back into the rear room and Smart Juan would pop them head foremost into the slanting tunnel. They would crawl rapidly down the tunnel one after the other. The return tunnel, also about two feet high, was located across the rear room in an opening between crates of canned goods. As the satiated, "had" Chinese and Puerto Ricans emerged from the return tunnel, Smart Juan would collect ten dollars and send them on their way. It was this very reasonable charge that made "Juan's Place" such a roaring success.

"Ah does a volume business," said Nick. In his obtuse opinion, the Chinese and Puerto Ricans come quick. One thing he'd never allow in the tunnels was a john with even the merest smidgin of the potent blood of Africa in his veins. "Dem niggers wear out de ponies," he said. Such was his obtusity. Nick also disliked intensely uptown white folks getting in there; it slowed down the flow. "Dem crackahs is lazy risers," he said. Drove him berserk. When it happened the cat-o'-nine would whistle and if the sluiceways still remained clogged the razor would flash and soft parts would fall. One thing that cured a lazy-rising cracker was to cut him like a hawg. "Dem mothahs don't nevah come back," declared Nick. And it was true, they never did; cutting cured them permanently.

Thus Sampson flourished and waxed mighty in the prime of his prime. However, although Black Nick did not dream of it, his doom was already sealed. He had bitten off more than he could chew even with pointed stainless-steel teeth. It was Matteawan for him, a mindless vegetable. Polly was just biding her time, waiting for a chance to lobotomize him. And the opportunity came sooner than she had expected. Chauncey Gaylord brought it about, with a vital assist from . . . *the false Whork,* who beneath his clever and brilliant disguise was no one else than Arnold "Archie" Schnerd, master of "The Flight of the Bumblebee" and one of her earliest and best customers! How true it was, the whore bitch could be bested for a while but she could never be won.

Chauncey Princecoat Gaylord had reached that age of life marked by peace from the tumults and passions of youth. Though he doddered and faltered, though his hearing deteriorated and his eyesight went bad, though he hardly could taste any but the most highly seasoned foods and hardly could digest those, though he was lame and halt and rheumatic and his fingers trembled and his false teeth didn't fit and his corns and bunions plagued him, he nevertheless cherished what was left of himself and in dreams now and then thought that perhaps there was life left in the old goat. Occasionally Mr. Gaylord peered thoughtfully over his spectacles at the old ladies who resided at the Seamus. A few of them still had a little snap in their tits and at times something resembling a glint came into his bleared old eyes; but then he would sigh, shake his head in a wobbly manner from side to side, adjust his green eyeshade and shuffle off about his business. It never occurred to Mr. Gaylord even in his wildest dreams that such a creature as Polly Dawn could ever come into his life. The very idea would have made him jerk back in dignified surprise.

But the most unlikely things logically enough happen to the most unlikely people. One afternoon Mr. Gaylord left the hotel about five o'clock and was walking up the street absorbed in the race track column of *Briar's Weekly* when a gust of wind blew off his hat. "Oh, dear me," said Mr. Gaylord. "Drat it." With the awkwardness of old age, he chased after the hat as it bobbled along. The street was deserted and rather dark, with a hint of rain in the lowering sky above. "Curse it," said Mr. Gaylord. The hat had skittered along the sidewalk and off into the gutter and down a drainpipe.

"Dear, dear!" He could see the hat nestling in the drainpipe about three feet below the curb. "My stars, what can I do?" muttered Mr. Gaylord, talking aloud to himself as the aged are wont to do. It was a new hat. A large gray Stetson. He could ill afford to lose it. With a sigh, he stared downward. What a pity. A new hat resting just there, just a bit below reach. Once again Mr. Gaylord sighed in irritation and annoyance and then he made up his mind. He would not allow a chance gust of wind to deprive him of his hat. He could easily rescue the hat at a slight cost to his dignity.

Seizing an old broom that chanced to be lying against the side of a nearby building, Mr. Gaylord scurried across the sidewalk and with awkward movements he rapidly swept away dust and dirt from the large drainpipe, clearing and cleaning the environs. Quickly, with a furtive glance around to see if he was being observed, he unfolded his copy of the *World Telegraph* and laid it about the narrow opening of the hole. Then, cautiously and carefully, he got down on his hands and knees, held his breath as protection against dank sewer gas, and stuck his head into the hole. The drainpipe was about sixteen inches in diameter. It was designed and intended to be contained by a cast-iron grating, but this had either never been put in place or had been dislodged. The drainpipe descended at an angle of forty-five degrees, widening as it went.

All was dark down there, but Mr. Gaylord could see the gray hat wedged to one side against slimy bricks and mortar.

He could almost reach the hat. His fingertips were just at the edge of it. But he couldn't quite get it. "Drat it!" exclaimed Mr. Gaylord.

He realized now that he was in an extremely embarrassing posture. His bony old legs and behind stuck up into the street as if he had been cut off at the waist. So with a sudden wriggling upside-down lurch, he heaved himself down and forward and, as he grasped the hat, went into the drainpipe as though sucked into it as a great fish would suck in a smaller fish.

Mr. Gaylord slid forward for perhaps thirty feet over slimy brick before he stopped. The gray hat was mashed up against his face. He was caught head downward just above a huge sewer main. Another foot and he would have toppled on into a swirling, frothy river. Dim gloomy light from somewhere half-illuminated the scene. Malodorous sewer gas filled Mr. Gaylord's lungs.

"Help, help," he called weakly.

But no one could possibly hear. He could feel himself slipping. Soon he would descend head foremost into that rushing torrent and be swept on away to the Atlantic Ocean or perhaps to a sewage disposal plant. "Oooooooh," he groaned. Desperately, he clutched at the slimy bricks, trying to halt his slow, remorseless downward slipping.

"Ooooooh," cried Mr. Gaylord again. Then he was through, falling. Splash. He sank like a stone, then was caught by a powerful current and dragged along head over heels, banged around a corner, whirled up to the arched ceiling. Gasping for breath, he bumped along the ceiling. No catwalk or ledge could be seen anywhere. Half swimming and half treading water, he was swept around a corner and now he saw hanging from the ceiling on an iron chain a catvus bulb. "Thanks heavens!" cried Mr. Gaylord. Feebly, he swam in the direction of the bulb; beyond it he saw an ancient stone platform. "Oh, oh!" cried Mr. Gaylord. He barely made it. Weakly, he clung to the stones, unable for the moment to drag himself out of the water. But he was safe for the moment. Exactly where he was, was a question, but at least he wouldn't drown or wind up in a sewage disposal plant.

At last he stood on the stone platform. There seemed to be no exit and no entrance, but unbeknownst to him he was standing at that very moment on a hidden trapdoor. When his entire weight was on it, it gave way and he found himself suddenly catapulted down a long greased slide, faster and faster, till all at once he shot headfirst into an earth tunnel down from above, across several small crawling bodies.

"Eh?" asked Mr. Gaylord. Hands pushed him angrily from behind. He heard words in a language or languages he could not understand. Hands now were pushing him from underneath. Turned almost upside down, he protested, "Help! Murder!" But it did no good. The hands still pushed. To escape he crawled forward, first slowly and then faster. It was pitch dark. Mr. Gaylord had an impression that someone was crawling ahead of him and that someone was crawling behind him. He could hear whispered voices and now and then his head bumped into some person as he himself was sometimes bumped from behind.

The tunnel straightened out again and rose at a slight grade, leveled off, turned another curve in the opposite direction, straightened out, ran along for some distance; then all of a sudden a large trapdoor slammed shut before his face. He couldn't see it but he could hear it and feel it. As it shut, a similar door to the right opened. Now he could see a dim indirect glow overhead. He crawled forward unwillingly into a much larger area with a huge high ceiling.

Wham, a boot kicked him in the side and he heard a guttural voice: "Whut dis lazy-risin' crackah doin' in here?" A thousand needles seemed to pierce his side. Mr. Gaylord was too stunned even to cry out. He looked up in fright and saw over his shoulder a giant looming figure in a leopard skin. It was a Black Fiend seven feet tall! The fiend carried a whip and as Mr. Gaylord stared up at him in horror the whip whistled. "Yeee-owww!" cried Mr. Gaylord as the whip lashed down upon his bony rear. "Hold up de flow and you go' git *cut,* crackah," said the fiend. "Git!" Mr. Gaylord hurriedly crawled forward in the direction of a tiny hole in one wall. It was there, evidently, that the fiend wanted him to go. Panting, sodden with sweat and astink with the sewerage wastes of the city to end cities, scared out of his wits, Mr. Gaylord crawled to the hole and wiggled through it.

There a strange sight greeted his eyes. This room was brightly lighted in comparison to the other area. He could see across it a similar hole in the opposite wall and there he caught a glimpse of the rear of a man as the man wriggled out through the hole. In the center of the room, on her back on a large bed and munching candy from a box of chocolates, was a woman with blonde hair. She was naked as a sunset and propped back on a pillow. Another pillow was under her ample behind, which hardly needed a pillow in the first place. The woman had a magnificent physique with a wondrous belly and great Persian-melon breasts with maraschino cherry eyes. That which the French in their wisdom call *le bassin* was lifted upward by the pillow, and clouds of gnats and wasps and fruitflies droned around it. As Mr. Gaylord crawled into the cell-like room panting with exhaustion and fear, he asked himself: what is all of this?

"Hello, there," said the woman. "It's so nice to see you. Come here."

Mr. Gaylord crept forward. He felt himself seized by the hair, dragged up upon the bed, pulled down upon the woman, even as another hand tugged at his sodden clothes. And then a small miracle happened. Perhaps it was the romance of it all, perhaps it was the lash of the whip, perhaps it was the fruitflies, but whatever it was, it was a small miracle—life stirred in the ninety-four-year-old frame of Chauncey Gaylord, and soon thereafter to his own astonished disbelief he found himself bouncing in a dream of humidiferous bliss. Eee-gad! Could it be true after all those years hunched over the books? From somewhere up above he heard a basso voice:

"Whut goin' on? Dere been a clog in de flow, gal. Is dat crackah a lazy risah?"

"No, for an old coot he's not bad," said Polly. "Do it, Daddy. Go, you cute old thing."

"Yeee-ow, wow!" cried Mr. Gaylord. "Whoopee! Wow!"

As has been said, the most unlikely things logically enough happen to the most unlikely people. Who would have thought that a worn-out hulk like ninety-four-year-old Chauncey Gaylord would succeed and a young and healthy fellow like Arnold "Archie" Schnerd would fail? That very idea soon would inflame and madden the false Whork.

Ninety seconds later Mr. Gaylord scrambled happily out of the opposite hole, a moist and exultant look of "had" in his rheumy old eyes. Out he crawled into another narrow winding tunnel. On and on it went, much farther than the previous tunnel. He had begun to despair of ever reaching the end when finally he saw light ahead. With a desperate effort he crawled on and suddenly popped out into what seemed to be the back room of a grocery store. A thinly moustached, shrewd-looking young Puerto Rican stuck his palm out and said, "Ten bucks."

"Of course," said Mr. Gaylord. With dignity, he reached into his hip pocket, pulled forth his wallet and took out two damp five-dollar bills. "Thank you," he said.

"That way out."

"Certainly," said Mr. Gaylord.

With dignity he strolled out of the room, bowing to the

Puerto Rican youth. The room, as he had thought, was located behind an ordinary small grocery store. He strolled out past tomato soup cans onto Eighth Avenue.

Sadly, the wits of old Mr. Gaylord were addled by this experience. Obviously his wits were addled; otherwise he never would have "palled it up" with the likes of Roger Whork, who was far beneath him on the social scale.

"Roge," said Mr. Gaylord with a leer, "I promise you, I give you my word it was the most amazing experience of my life. You ought to try it yourself, boy."

"Hmmm," said the false Whork. He stared thoughtfully at the old bookkeeper. Was it true? Was that where she'd vanished? Down into the sewers? It was a pretty wild story. "Descrrribe the goy-ild ag'in, Chauncey," he said. "A big blonde, ye say, with blue oyes and joy-int titsies?"

"That's her," said Mr. Gaylord with a huge wink. "Want to come with me, old boy?"

"Mmm, well, now, begooorah, I think I've encountered her before, Chauncey, yis I think so. And didn't have much luck with her, nooo-oo. Did ye have any luck yeself, Chauncey?"

"Oh boy, oh boy, oh boy!" said Mr. Gaylord. "Heh heh heh heh, hee hee hee hee!"

"Mmm, yis. Wal, now, I been eatin' hearty, in trainin' ye know to build up me stren'th. Begooorah, look at the belly on me and the arse, too! Chauncey, I am with ye! I'd like another crack at 'er!"

"Heh heh heh heh," said old addled Gaylord. "Let's be off, lad!"

Restraining their grins of enthusiasm and newborn excitement, Mr. Gaylord and the false Whork tiptoed out of the former's office and strolled casually across the lobby of the Seamus, avoiding the quizzical glances of Smegg and Dogberry at the desk. Out the door they went and down the street.

"Psssst!" said Mr. Gaylord. "Here it is." Quickly, he lowered himself feet first into the drainpipe. "Take my hands so I don't slip all the way down."

"Righto."

Slowly, gradually, Mr. Gaylord slid down until only his head and shoulders remained visible. "Now," he said, "I'm going on down, Roge."

"Hmm," said the false Whork. He jumped into the hole and slid down the greased chute and fell with a thump on Mr. Gaylord himself, who had landed on a smaller figure. Hands pushed now in all directions as the flow again was interrupted as it had been the previous week when Mr. Gaylord had come on the trip alone. But as before it soon righted itself and Mr. Gaylord and Roger crawled on one after the other.

"Why, hello there!" said Polly. "It's so nice to see you! And how have you been, well I hope?"

"He hee hee hee!" said Mr. Gaylord, who was overcome with the spirit of regaining his youth.

"Chauncey! Pull me through, I'm stuck, me arse won't go through this hole."

But Mr. Gaylord was busy. He clutched at Polly as a man drowning in the North Sea in January would clutch at a life belt, feebly and yet enthusiastically at the same time. Polly smiled dreamily, her hand idly flopping over upon a box of chocolates.

"Chauncey, pull me through!"

"Wheeeee!" yelled Gaylord. He had been transformed into a veritable old goat. His thin, withered, slablike body strung out across the soft phosphorescent whiteness was so agitated by the power of youth regained that he looked like a live toad roasting on a griddle; it seemed that only the glowing phosphor legs wrapped around him prevented him from bouncing all the way up to the iron catwalk high above the crib. It was Nick's perch and even at this moment Nick was staring down, whip in hand.

"Wow! Yow!" yelled Gaylord.

"Hey! Hey! Damn ye, can't ye see I'm stuck in this bloomin' hole? Me arse won't go through, Chauncey! Damn ye, get off tha' whoor and pull me through!"

Up above, Nick's eyes narrowed. "Whut dis?" he said. He was in a foul mood already. Wan Lo had crossed him and only the thought of the bother of getting another pony had saved her head. Nick put the whip between his teeth and handwalked along the ceiling on the grating in the manner of Tarzan. Like a great cat he dropped down into tunnel four. "Dat's jes' what ah thought, a crackah done got in," said Nick. Coiling the cat in his hand and stroking off bits of dried flesh, he drew it back and let it fall.

"Oi, begorrah! Bees are bitin' me arse! Chauncey!"

"Git through theah!" yelled Nick. Again he applied the cat-o'-nine.

"Wheeee," said Mr. Gaylord, a bit more weakly. The old fellow was about pooped.

"Gaylord! Millions o' bees are feastin' on me arse!"

"Dis heah won't do," said Nick. The customers were piling up. It was a clog situation and it was getting worse all the time. His own security might even be threatened. The Chinese were peaceful, but the Puerto Ricans could be extremely dangerous when aroused. Nick leaped for the ceiling grating and handwalked back to his perch, then once more stared down from the catwalk into the crib below. Rage ran through him. "Dat mothah ain't movin' and dat mothah is stuck," he said. "Dem two crackahs has got to go." Nick swung out onto the grating and dropped down into the crib. In a fury he grabbed the arms of the fat-assed one stuck in the entry and hauled him through, then he turned and said to Polly:

"Shove dat crackah here."

"Yes, master," said Polly in her usual submissive tone, but a funny look was in her eyes. She shoved off the pooped

Chauncey, who was semiconscious and wouldn't have lived long anyhow—Nick grabbed him, the razor flashed, and the mortal head of Chauncey Gaylord hit the dust. Calmly, Nick wiped the razor, an eye on Polly. It was unwise to get too close to the ponies in their cribs. Nick kicked away the head and smiled at the second cracker.

"Killin' too good for you," he said. "Ah is gwine *cut* you."

"Hello, again! It's me, Archie Schnerd! Huh? *Cut* me?"

"Dat is right, you lazy-risin' crackah. Lak a hawg."

"Excuse-*meh*. Let me introduce myself. I am Arnold 'Archie' Schnerd and I can play 'The Flight of the Bumblebee' on the alto saxophone in practically *one* breath! That's something you ought to go for—you people like *jass,* don't you?"

"Man," said Nick, "oh-h, man, ah is gonna cut you *good.*"

Polly saw her chance. As Nick grabbed the the little fellow on the floor she drew out her hatpin and sneaked up behind him.

"Garrrr-ghhh-uuhhhh!" screamed Archie.

"Nothin' much to cut," said Nick. "You ain' even go' miss it."

"Ahhhhhhhrrr-ghhhh!" gurgled Archie.

"Yug," said Nick as a hatpin entered his brain.

THE DAY WAS FRIDAY, MAY 13, AND IT DID NOT BEGIN
auspiciously. Later that day, much later on that very bad and
very good day, Richard Davenport amused himself with a
question-and-answer dialogue that went as follows:

Q: Pauline Weisenschaft Spraypussy Riccobono, where are
you?

A: *Somewhere lost in the city streets in the howl of the asphalt with
a mop handle up it.*

Q: Now, now, none of that. Where are you and your secret
recesses, Pauline, pray tell where?

A: *In the arms of a sequined harlequin at fling doing it on top and
every which-a-way in the reek and the roar.*

Q: What is your address, dear, teleologically speaking? Be
precise, please, don't try to piss standing up or you'll splash
your ankles.

A: *Doubt it not, doubt it never, it is a repulsive piece of merchandize
with warm folds and you can't find the cervix and what's more the
harlequin is rancid and hairs on volcanoes are cute and you know it.*

Q: Tell me specifically, dear, where you and your sweet

cooze live and how I'll find you and get into it deeply and satisfyingly at last with a vengeance on top and every which-a-way till the cows come home.

A: *Oh boy, now you're finally talking, 1313 Pitcairne Avenue, B, that's the place, baby, and you'll find me refreshed from a shower in Nicky's reechoing charlatan buffoon bathrobe with fourteen tasty pleasing tear gas fishery, a foul breath and no fair flower but a hell of a piece of ass that will do you good and help you too and imbue you with life force and solve all your problems strangely and paradoxically, and what's more never forget that although a cat can look at a king only a king can fuck a cat and that is how the soil sears, baby, that is how it sears and parches and flakes away.*

An amusement. Such things often ran through his head and more often than not they had little or no meaning. First things first. The first thing Dick did that morning, or practically the first thing, was to call Pauline and tell her no. When Naomi went downstairs to get the mail, he telephoned Mrs. Riccobono and informed her he could not come to her apartment at two that afternoon. In view of the mad titillation they both had endured the night before, she was very calm and philosophical about it.

"Well," she said, "I know you have other things on your mind, such as a book to write. I had a feeling after last night you wouldn't come and maybe it's just as well you don't. After all, I have a husband. I did marry Nicky and I should try to love him. I should have a child, that's what he wants. I've been afraid but it's what I ought to do, be a mother, really become Mrs. Riccobono, ha ha ha. Can you hold my hand and talk me into that? Guess not. Well, anyhow, thanks for calling, I'm sorry I won't see you."

Hmmph, surprising, thought Dick. Was it some kind of game she was playing or did she mean it? Were there depths in her he had not guessed? Yet her speech didn't add up; the "ha ha ha, be a mother" stuff was all wrong. There were no depths in her he had not seen, he knew her humanly only too well. Quietly, he said, "This whole thing has been my fault, Pauline. I should never have flirted with you the way I did and I should never have gone to your house last night. I don't know what got into me. The devil, I guess. I'm sorry. I really am and I hope things straighten out with you and Nicky and that you have a good life. A baby would be a very good idea, I think. There's no telling what effect it would have on you. Motherhood is a very powerful thing. I've got to tell you, by the way, Nicky seems like a very nice guy. I liked him. Anyhow, I do wish you luck."

"It sounds as if you're telling me good-bye. Won't I see you at the Educational Union?"

"No, Pauline, I'm quitting there. I'm sending them a letter today. I won't have the time for it and it's impossible anyhow. You can't teach children that age how to write, you can't teach people of any age how to write. I myself sure can't do such a thing, and in any event I don't have the time."

There was such a long silence Dick began to worry about Naomi coming back, but he waited. Finally, she said, "Well, Natalie will miss you. And so will I."

"Natalie is one reason I'm giving it up," said Dick. "Maybe I'll see her again sometime, maybe there is something I can do for Natalie, but as far as the class is concerned I'm just arousing false hopes in her, that's all."

"Um-hmm, the way you did me. And last night especially."

Dick winced. "Well, yeah," he said. "That was pretty awful. But in all truth I don't think it's quite the same thing, Pauline. And as I said, I'm sorry about that. I really am. I hope sometime you can forgive me."

Another silence. Then with a calm dignity that surprised him again, she said, "Well, I guess I won't be seeing you anymore. Good-bye, Dick. I want to wish you a lot of luck with your future career."

Davenport was nonplussed more than a trifle. From where had she gotten such poise? "That's very generous of you,

Pauline. I'll need it. Good luck to you, too, honey."

Still another silence. Dick thought she would hang up, but then in a different voice she said, "Do you know something funny? Nicky fucked me last night. Something turned him on, I don't know what, maybe it was your being there. And he was great. It was never like that before! I came six times, twice on top of him. It was just great. You wouldn't believe it. He went down on me, I went down on him, it was a real orgy. The best sex we ever had, how about that? We were fucking for about two hours. And do you know the funniest thing of all? This morning I'm *hornier than ever.* Come out this afternoon, I'll fuck you. I'll fuck you all afternoon."

Somehow, Dick said, "There's no point, Pauline. It'd just be an escape for me and an escape for you, too. I'd like to come, you know I would, but . . . well, sooner or later I've got to face reality and so do you. I'm sorry, but it wouldn't do either one of us a bit of good."

"Well, it might not do us any good but it sure would be a lot of fun. I'm feeling very, very sexy and I'll be here . . . if you change your mind."

Dick moistened his lips and swallowed. "I won't," he said.

"I know you probably won't. What could I say that would tempt you? Hmm, let's see. I'll be here naked in Nicky's bathrobe and it can be taken off very easily. Very, very easily. I'll shower at one thirty just in case. . . ."

Dick flinched slightly as he heard the front door of the apartment open. Naomi was back with the mail and there was no point in prolonging this. "Good-bye, Pauline," he said.

"Good-bye," she replied.

To hell with her, thought Dick, as he hung up the telephone and left the bedroom. So she'd never been worried; she thought he would keep the date and that was the reason for her calm and poise. He'd be there no matter what he said. Behind that certainty the crass little amoral bitch was smiling and laughing at him. Naked under Nicky's bathrobe! Well, she would wait in that bathrobe a long time before he would show up at that grimy apartment, hell would freeze over before he would take that bathrobe off of her and crawl with her into Nicky's bed.

Davenport genuinely believed it. The damned little bitch was predatory as a man and crass beyond reckoning. What a nerve she had, telling him she'd take a shower and be waiting naked in her husband's bathrobe! Well, he'd seen another woman in a man's bathrobe only hours before under very different conditions, Mrs. Steiner in the apartment upstairs— and that was life, that was reality, to hell with amoral little Pauline. "What could I say that would tempt you?" she asked. To hell with her and good riddance!

Emancipation, that was what it was. He genuinely believed it. The thing was done and finished, thought Dick, as he sat back down at his desk and rolled a sheet of paper into his typewriter. He was finally free of the succubus of Pauline-Polly, the doppleganger female demon who for days and weeks had tormented his sleeping and his waking dreams. Enough of her, enough of her and begone! Good-bye, Pauline, a lot of luck and go to hell.

Sadly, as he sat at his desk, Dick turned the pages of a rather worn copy of *War and Peace*. It was mildly ironic that Naomi would use it in their little first-sentence-of-famous-novels game. He himself earlier that morning had been thinking of the reported fact that the great Count's first drafts read as if written by a fifteen-year-old imbecile. Of course Tolstoy had come up the night before in the conversation at Samusson's, that was what had put it in Naomi's head.

In gloom, Dick turned the dog-eared pages of the worn volume as well-remembered scenes and characters more real than life itself flashed through his mind. Natásha singing, beautiful Natásha, the most wonderful girl in all of fiction. Denísov proposing to her. The old Prince at his lathe. Dólokhov winning the forty-three thousand rubles from Nicholas.

Prince Andrew and his blue sky. The beautiful heart and soul of Princess Mary. "Uncle" and the wolf. Pierre and the French officer who looks into his eyes and cannot have him shot. Pierre and Platón Karatáev. "Lay me down like a stone, O God, and raise me up like a loaf." Napoleon, Kutúzov, the beautiful Hélène, Pétya dead on the ground, endless wealth on and on.

In a deepening gloom, Dick turned the worn pages. How could any man conceive much less write such a book? A hundred novels were in it and each of them could be called brilliant. Well, he had described *War and Peace* pretty accurately to Naomi during their little game. She of course had predicted he would be sorry for his remarks the night before, but as insane as his boasts were, measured against such a masterpiece, there was truth in what he'd said. It takes all kinds, infinite riches were in a little room, a man could be great within the limits of his own gifts and strength, a cat could look at a king. Dick shut the book, put it on his desk and stared at the piece of paper in his typewriter.

Strictly speaking, the good-luck-and-go-to-hell telephone call to Pauline was not the first thing Dick did that morning. The mail didn't arrive until about nine thirty. At two minutes of eight he had gone into the living room, sat down at his desk and put a sheet of paper into his typewriter. At twenty after eight he typed a sentence upon the sheet of paper. At a quarter of nine he typed another sentence. Seven minutes went by and in a sudden burst of creation he typed three sentences in succession. He had what is called a paragraph and he paused to read it over.

Unfortunately, the paragraph was not one of the greatest paragraphs he had ever written. Quickly, before anyone could come into the living room and look over his shoulder and see it, he tore the sheet out of the typewriter and crumpled it into a ball and threw it on the floor. Calmly—it was nothing to get excited about, nothing to shriek and pull one's hair about—

he put another sheet of paper into the typewriter and without hesitation typed a sentence upon it. This time, in order not to compound the error, he paused to read the sentence before writing another and this proved to be a wise procedure. Quickly, he tore the sheet of paper out of the typewriter and crumpled it into a ball and threw it on the floor. Then he went into the kitchen and had a cup of coffee.

The fact was, he needed to think. It was a good idea before starting a new book to do a bit of cogitation. How could a man blindly plunge into an intricate story without reflecting on it first? Who were the characters? What was it about? Where was the narrative located, in what era of time? What was the point of it, what did it say of the human condition that might be worth reading? Where did it begin and where did it end, where did it start and where did it go? Of course he'd already thought about the book he intended to write; he'd devoted many hours of thought to it; but obviously he needed to think about it some more.

"I heard you in there for a little," said Naomi, as she put Sam into his playpen on the kitchen floor. "Then it got quiet."

"Umm," said Dick.

"I guess it's a little hard to break the ice."

"Yeah, it is," said Dick. "It's an apocryphal truth, there's nothing to it really, but you know that old saying that the hardest part of any book is the first sentence."

"How about, 'Call me Ishmael.' "

"That's been done."

"Well, let's see. How about, 'Stately, plump Buck Mulligan came from the stairhead, bearing a bowl of lather on which a mirror and a razor lay crossed.' "

"That has been done, too."

"All right, here's an idea. 'Well, Prince, so Genoa and Lucca are now just family estates of the Buonapartes.' How about that?"

"I'd settle for a hell of a lot less, believe me I would. You

were right about my having that fit last night. I can hardly
write a line this morning, it's pitiful. I spend weeks and months
getting my damn head down and then it balloons all up on me
at the worst possible moment. Now I've got to shrink the
damn thing down again, and that's painful. It's nine thirty, the
postman has probably come. I don't want to cut short our
game, but you wouldn't feel like getting the mail, would
you?"

"Well, of course *Moby Dick* is easy. 'Call me Ishmael,' everyone knows that. And I guess most people know Buck Mulligan
and his bowl of lather. But did you really recognize the third
one?"

"Of course I recognized it, it's easier than *Ulysses.* Genoa
and Lucca and the *Buon*apartes? That's the first sentence of the
greatest novel ever written, Naomi, probably the greatest
novel that ever will be written in all of time by mortal man.
Anna Schérer is speaking and she is talking to Prince Vasíli
Kurágin, a man of high rank and importance with a scented
and shining bald head. The lady has *la grippe,* a new word in
Petersburgh used only by the elite. Soon Pierre will come in
with a policeman tied to a bear, figuratively if not literally."

Naomi of course knew that he knew. She had seen the look
of death on his face and was trying to cheer him up. A beautiful soul, Naomi. Quite a woman, the "little Jewish girl" he
had casually married one day. There was not a trace of malice
in her, only loyalty and love were in her heart. How could he
ever repay her for the weeks and months of her devotion to
him in this painful time? "Yes, that's right, that's very good.
War and Peace. But I know one you'll never get. Never."

Dick shook his head and said with a wry smile, "Honey, I
ain't kiddin' you. I'd settle for a hell of a lot less than any of
them. Why don't you be a real sweet girl and go get the mail?
I'd go myself but I'm all tired out from my creative exertions
at the typewriter. It's pretty hard on us, you know. To be great
is to be lonely. Besides, this coffee would get cold."

A trace of tears came into Naomi's eyes as she stared at him. "All right," she said, "but I'm thinking of the first sentence of a very great novel and I'll bet money you won't recognize it. It's a very famous first sentence and it's very simple. 'For a long time I used to go to bed early.' Do you know that?"

"That isn't the first sentence of *any*thing," said Dick. "You just made that up."

"Oh, no. It's the first sentence of a great and famous novel."

"Well, you never know what some idiot will consider great. There are people who think *Little Women* is great. There are people who think *War and Peace* is a big fat bore. To a certain extent, greatness is in the eye of the beholder."

"Oh, I know, I know. But it's nothing like *Little Women;* it's nothing like that. 'For a long time I used to go to bed early.' That's the first sentence of a book many people regard as great. You must have read the novel, I'm sure you have, and I'll give you this much of a hint. It isn't the sort of book you'd really like. I mean, you'd respect it but I don't think it's on your wavelength."

"Neither is *Moby Dick.* I could never understand why that man carried on so about that whale just because it bit off his leg. What did he expect, anyhow, for it to kiss him? Wasn't he sticking a harpoon in it, or trying to? Whalefighting is bullshit, Naomi. And as for that thing about going to bed early, there is no such first sentence in all of world literature."

"Yes, there is," said Naomi. "See if you can think of it while I get the mail."

"Before you go let me tell you something funny. After all that godawful mess yesterday, do you know what I dreamed last night? I dreamed that Polly was dead. I really did, I dreamed that she was dead and they had a big gangster-type funeral for her. I was watching the procession down there on Twenty-eighth Street near Henry's frame shop in the whole-sale florist district. And that isn't all. I was broke, stone broke. I was in kind of rags; I didn't even have a nickel for a cup of coffee and I couldn't figure out what had happened. Then I realized what it was. I had written the book and it was the biggest failure you ever saw."

Naomi turned away her head. "That doesn't matter," she said. "That doesn't matter at all. I'll get the mail."

Before she got out of the kitchen Dick called after her, "Naomi, wait a minute." Slowly, with some hesitation and with some embarrassment, he got up from the table and walked over to her in the doorway and put his hands on her shoulders. Her head was bowed; she was staring down at the floor. Dick put his hand under her chin to make her look up at him, then said:

"I'll tell you what. I don't want to wear myself out on this book all at once; no book is worth it. That isn't the most important thing I'll ever do in my life. It's another beautiful day outside. Why don't I work until around three, then you and I and Sam will take a walk in Flatbush. Would you like that?"

Naomi was blinking at tears but they were under very good control. "Yes, I would," she said. "I'd like a walk this afternoon and so would the baby. That's a good idea and now I'll get the mail."

"Naomi, you're something else," said Dick. "Love you a lot, you're a thundering explosion."

When she was gone Dick put his hand for a moment on the near-blond head of the baby in the playpen. Sam paid no attention to him; he was breathing hard and literally sweating with intent absorption in a toy. The work-play instinct, no doubt. Well, there had better be such a thing and it had better come to his rescue, because God knows how else he would ever write that book. "Sit tight, Sam," he said. "I've got to make a phone call. I'll be back in a flash with some more hash." Not a smile. Sam didn't even look up.

At exactly and precisely three o'clock that afternoon, Naomi came into the living room. She took a look at the many crumpled balls of typewriter paper on the floor and said, "It's three o'clock. How are you doing?"

"Oh, God," sighed Dick. "Just as I expected, a bad, bad day."

"Do you still want to go for a walk with me and Sam?"

"Sure, I'd love to."

Wearily, Dick stared down at the three pages of his new book that somehow he had written. It was pretty sad stuff. But sad as it was and bad as the day had been, at least it was a beginning. At three o'clock in the morning he'd thought there would be no day at all, that his last hour on earth had come. He had never experienced acute anxiety until then, and when it came it hit him full force.

It had been quite a little scene, and the strangest, eeriest moment of all was when the baby suddenly began to cry. In the dark of the night with the stealth of a thief he had crept out of bed and gone down the hall barefoot in pajamas. The heat was off in the building and a chill was in the air. He lighted the gas oven and sat at the kitchen table smoking a cigarette. Then for want of something better to do he filled a bucket with warm water and began to mop the kitchen floor. The first sight or sound he had of the living world was Naomi, in a bathrobe in the kitchen doorway. In a small frightened voice, she asked:

"What are you doing?"

"As you see, I'm mopping the kitchen floor."

Frightened as she was, Naomi was half awake. "It's clean. Why are you doing that?" Dick couldn't answer her. At this moment, strangely and eerily, the baby began to cry in the living room. In a daze he heard Naomi say: "Sit down. It'll be all right, I'll help you. Sit here at the table."

Why? Why did the baby awaken at that moment and begin to cry? Was it a weird spiritual telepathy beyond the knowledge of science, an inexplicable awareness that his father was in danger? Was it mere coincidence, unexpected noises in the kitchen at an unusual hour? Whatever the cause, the baby began to cry as his mother walked in bare feet across the wet linoleum and put her hand on his father's shoulder. Dick did as she told him. He sat down, put his elbows on the kitchen table and said:

"It's too much for me. I'm licked, Naomi, I can't do it. I don't have the courage. I'm licked and beaten and there's nothing left of me. I had it but it's all gone now like that Bechet record. It's gone, Naomi."

"No, it isn't gone. You just think it is. It isn't really gone."

"Naomi, I can't do it. I knew it all along inside. That silly talk of mine tonight is final and conclusive proof. A man who has got it doesn't have to talk about it. I'm licked, my dreams of glory are dead and gone. Old ladies are sprinkling water on the violets that grow on the grave."

"You'll be all right," said Naomi with a little smile. "Come on to bed. I'll get the baby, he's scared. We'll take him in with us for a little while."

Dick and Naomi often took the baby into bed with them and they had no compunctions about making love in front of him. He liked for them to do this; he thought they were playing some kind of funny game. It annoyed him a little because he had trouble getting their attention; he would pull their hair, put his fat little hand between them, lean over and make solemn talking noises at them and then laugh. The heavy breathing and whispered endearments of the moment of truth struck him as especially hilarious.

"Ve-ry funny," said Dick, as he lay on Naomi's shoulder and as the laughing baby successfully got space for his own head between her ample breasts. "Very, very funny. Who do you think you are, boy? Oedipus Rex?"

Sam laughed aloud and snuggled his face deeper into the valley between, amused baby eyes on his father. Beyond any question it was a joke, and a funny one, too, baby radar told him so.

"Ha ha ha," said Dick. "Okay, Sam, you can laugh now but the day will come when you won't think this is all that funny. You'll be pretty damn serious about it."

Dick felt lips against his cheek and heard a soft voice: "Are you feeling better? Do you see that . . . it isn't important? I mean, of course it's very important, but . . ."

"Love you a lot," said Dick. "You are beautiful, Naomi."

"Oh, God. It has been bad, what a life! I can't tell you how much better I feel myself, I just can't tell you. . . ."

"Well, it's better to have two babies laughing on your shoulder than to have them crying there."

That was certainly true, thought Davenport on the following morning. It was better to have two babies laughing on your shoulder than to have them crying there. And another thing was true as well. One smile from a living and breathing human being was worth more than all the works of civilization. It was in the service of that smile that those works existed. This was the realization that had come to him at four o'clock in the morning in the gray early dawn. What gave the beast such a terrible and paralyzing might?—fear. What greater power could conquer her and lie her low?—a baby's smile.

Wearily, Dick stared down at the three pages of his new book that somehow he had written. It was pretty sad stuff. But sad as it was and bad as the day had been, at least it was a beginning and not an end.

"I'll get Sam and put him in the stroller."

"Okay, honey, whenever you're ready."

"Oh, yes, I almost forgot," said Naomi. "The first sentence of that famous book. It was *Remembrance of Things Past.*"

"Of course," said Dick with a little smile. "What else?"

Richard Davenport was a prisoner no longer, he had flown the walls. He was free. The whore bitch was dead and the big nickel was spent and gone.